Anonymous

Instruction for Heavy Artillery

SALZWASSER
VERLAG

Anonymous

Instruction for Heavy Artillery

Reprint of the original, first published in 1863.

1st Edition 2022 | ISBN: 978-3-37500-091-2

Verlag (Publisher): Salzwasser Verlag GmbH, Zeilweg 44, 60439 Frankfurt, Deutschland
Vertretungsberechtigt (Authorized to represent): E. Roepke, Zeilweg 44, 60439 Frankfurt, Deutschland
Druck (Print): Books on Demand GmbH, In de Tarpen 42, 22848 Norderstedt, Deutschland

INSTRUCTION

FOR

HEAVY ARTILLERY;

PREPARED BY A

BOARD OF OFFICERS,

FOR THE USE OF THE

ARMY OF THE UNITED STATES.

WASHINGTON:

1863.

WAR DEPARTMENT,

Washington, D. C., October 20, 1862.

This system of Heavy Artillery Tactics, prepared under direction of the War Department, having been approved by the President, is adopted for the instruction of troops when acting as heavy artillery.

EDWIN M. STANTON,

Secretary of War.

CONTENTS.

PART I.

SERVING HEAVY ARTILLERY.

ARTICLE I.

ARTICLE II.

ARTICLE III.

PART II.

MECHANICAL MANŒUVRES.

ARTICLE I.

ARTICLE II.

LESSON 18.

Lesson 19.

Lesson 20.

Lesson 21.

Lesson 22.

Lesson 23.

Lesson 24.

ARTICLE III.

LESSON 25.

LESSON 26.

LESSON 27.

LESSON 28.

LESSON 29.

LESSON 30.

LESSON 31.

Lesson 32.

Lesson 33.

Lesson 34.

ARTICLE IV.

Lesson 35.

Lesson 36.

Lesson 37.

Lesson 38.

Lesson 39.

Lesson 40.

Lesson 41.

Lesson 42.

Lesson 43.

Lesson 44.

Lesson 45.

PART III.

MISCELLANEOUS.

ARTICLE I.

ARTICLE II.

LIST OF PLATES.

INSTRUCTION

FOR

HEAVY ARTILLERY.

PART I.

SERVING HEAVY ARTILLERY.

ARTICLE I.

SERVICE OF THE PIECE.

1. The cannoneer, previous to receiving instruction in HEAVY ARTILLERY, should be thoroughly instructed in the *School of the Piece*, Field Artillery.

2. The manner of serving heavy artillery varies with the kind of piece, and the carriage upon which it is mounted.

3. There are four kinds of heavy pieces in the land service, viz: the GUN, the HOWITZER, the MORTAR, and the COLUMBIAD.

They are distinguished, according to their use, as *Siege*, *Garrison*, and *Sea-coast Artillery*.

For their service six distinct kinds of carriages are necessary, viz: the *Siege*, the *Barbette*, the *Casemate*, the *Flank-Casemate*, the *Columbiad*, and the carriage upon which the Mortar is mounted, which is technically called its bed.

Siege Artillery is used in the attack of places, and, as it follows armies in their operations, is mounted upon carriages which serve for its transportation.

Garrison Artillery is employed in the defence of forts, more especially those of the interior; and *Sea-coast Artillery*, consisting of the heaviest calibres, is used for the defence of the sea-coast. Their carriages do not subserve the purpose of transportation; the barbette carriage may, however, be used for moving its piece for short distances, as from one front of a work to another.

The following are the kinds and calibres of Heavy Artillery used in the land service of the United States:

Kind of ordnance.		Calibre.	Material.
GUNS	Siege and garrison	12-pdr.	Iron.
		18-pdr.	
		24-pdr.	
	Sea-coast	32-pdr.	
		42-pdr.	
HOWITZERS	Siege and garrison	8-inch.	
		24-pdr.	
	Sea-coast	8-inch.	
		10-inch.	
COLUMBIADS		8-inch.	
		10-inch.	
MORTARS	Siege	8-inch.	
		10-inch.	
	Sea-coast	10-inch.	
		13-inch.	
	Stone	16-inch.	Bronze.
	Cohorn	24-pdr.	

4. The detachment for serving a piece is formed into two ranks, and numbered from right to left. The odd numbers form the rear rank, and serve on the right of the piece; the even numbers and the gunner form the front rank, and serve on its left. The right file is numbered 1 and 2; the next file 3 and 4; the gunner is uncovered, and generally on the left of No. 4; and on his left are as many files as are deemed necessary, numbered 5 and 6, 7 and 8, &c.

5. A piece is in battery when it is in the proper position to be fired.

The right of a piece, when in battery, is the right of the cannoneer when facing to the object to be fired at; the front is the direction towards which the muzzle points.

The term *battery* is applied to one or more pieces, or the places where the pieces are fired.

A *platform* is the support upon which a piece is manœuvred when in battery.

6. The detachment is marched to the battery by a flank. It is halted, and faced to the front, when its centre is opposite to the middle of the platform, and (if there be room) four yards from it.

7. To cause the cannoneers to take their posts, the instructor commands:

1. *Detachment, to your posts.*
2. MARCH.

At the first command, the detachment is faced to the right by the chief of piece.

At the second command, it files to the left, and the two ranks separate; the rear rank marching to the right of the piece, and the front rank to the left, in lines parallel to its axis. As each man arrives at his post, he halts and faces to the piece; Nos. 1 and 2 one yard from the epaulment, parapet, or scarp, their breasts eighteen inches outside of the wheels of the carriage or cheeks of the mortar bed, as the case may be; and the other numbers and the gunner, dressing on Nos. 1 and 2 respectively, at intervals of one yard, except that between Nos. 3 and 5 there is an interval of two yards. With the mortar, Nos. 1 and 2 are opposite to the front manœuvring bolts, and Nos. 3 and 4 opposite to those in the rear.

Under the fire of the enemy, the men will be directed to cover themselves by the parapet as much as may be consistent with the execution of their duties.

8. *The chief of piece* (a non-commissioned officer) assists the instructor in effecting a correct execution of the movements.

While at the battery, he will generally be one yard outside of the cannoneers of the left, facing the piece, and two yards in rear of the platform or rearmost part of the carriage. He communicates, and attends to the execution of, all orders he may receive in relation to the service of his piece; as, for instance, the kind of ammunition to be used, the weight of charge, the kind and length of fuze, &c.

9. The movements of the cannoneers at the battery are in *double-quick time.*

10. Posts are changed at the discretion of the instructor.

11. To allow the detachment to rest, the instructor commands:

In place—REST; or, REST.

The cannoneers lay down their handspikes.

In the first case, the men remain at their posts; in the second case, they may leave their posts, but will remain near the piece.

To resume the exercise, the instructor commands:

Attention—DETACHMENT.

At which command, all resume their posts and handspikes.

12. Until the cannoneer becomes well versed in his duties at the piece, the instructor will himself, by way of example, occasionally execute the movements which he orders. In the intervals of rest he will minutely instruct the men in the names and uses of the implements, and in the nomenclatures of the piece, its carriage or bed, and of the parts of the fortification near the battery. In the course of the instruction he will require every man to point out and designate by name all the parts enumerated in these nomenclatures, and to answer questions relative to the service of the piece; such as the weight of charge, the manner of making cartridges and wads, of heating shot and throwing hot shot, of laying plat-

forms, pointing, &c. And although he is to consider precision of movement as highly essential, yet he is to inculcate that something more is necessary than a merely mechanical performance of duty. He will, therefore, endeavor to impress upon the cannoneer not only the habit of a soldier-like manner of working his gun, but an accurate understanding of all the elements necessary to the efficiency of its fire.

13. To leave the battery, the instructor commands:

1. *Detachment, rear.*
2. MARCH.

At the first command, the detachment is faced from the epaulment by the chief of piece.

At the second command, it marches to the rear—the cannoneers of the left closing upon those of the right—files to the right, and is halted and faced to the front by the chief of piece, so as to bring its centre opposite to the middle of the platform, and four yards from it. The chief of piece places himself upon the right.

The detachment is marched from the battery by a flank.

LESSON I.

SERVICE OF A GUN MOUNTED ON A SIEGE CARRIAGE.

(PLATES I, II, III, IV, V, AND VI.)

Seven men are necessary—one gunner and six other cannoneers.

14. The piece is in battery upon its platform.
The implements, &c., are arranged as follows:

HANDSPIKES	Three on each side of the carriage, leaning against the epaulment, in line with the cannoneers.
SPONGE RAMMER	One yard behind and parallel to the line of cannoneers of the right, the sponge uppermost, the sponge and rammer-heads turned from the epaulment, and supported upon a prop.
PASS-BOX	Against the epaulment, outside of the pile of balls.
TUBE-POUCH	Containing friction tubes, and the lanyard, which is habitually wound in the form of St. Andrew's cross upon its handle. Suspended from the knob of the cascable.
GUNNER'S POUCH	Containing the gunner's level, breech-sight, fingerstall, priming wire, gimlet, vent-pouch, and chalk. Suspended from the knob of the cascable.

CHOCKS .... One on each side of the piece, near the ends of the hurter.

VENT-COVER.........Covering the vent.

TOMPION ....In the muzzle.

BROOM.............. Leaning against the epaulment, outside of the pile of balls.

When several guns are served together, there will be only one gunner's level and two vent-punches to each battery, not exceeding six pieces. To the same battery there will be one *worm*, one *ladle*, and one *wrench*.

The balls are regularly piled on the left of the piece, near the epaulment, and close to the edge of the platform.

The wads are placed between the epaulment and the balls, partly resting on them.

15. The cannoneers having been marched to their posts, the instructor directs them to place their muskets against the epaulment, and then explains to them the names and uses of the implements, and the nomenclatures of the gun, its carriage, and the battery.

16. To cause the implements to be distributed, the instructor commands:

TAKE IMPLEMENTS.

The gunner steps to the knob of the cascable; takes off the vent-cover, handing it to No. 2 to place against the epaulment, outside of the pass-box; gives the tube-pouch to No. 3; equips himself with his own pouch and the fingerstall, wearing the latter on the second finger of the left hand; levels the piece by the elevating screw; applies his level to ascertain the highest points of the base-ring and swell of the muzzle, which he marks with chalk and resumes his post.

No. 3 equips himself with the tube-pouch.

Nos. 1 and 2, after passing two handspikes each to Nos. 3 and 4, take each one for himself. Nos. 5 and 6 receive theirs from Nos. 3 and 4.

17. The handspike is held in both hands; the hand nearest to the epaulment grasping it near the small end and at the height of the shoulder, back of the hand down, elbow touching the body; the other hand back up, the arm extended naturally; the butt of the handspike upon the platform on the side furthest from the epaulment, and six inches in advance of the alignment.

18. When the cannoneer lays down his handspike, he places it directly before him, about six inches in advance of, and parrallel to, the alignment, the small end towards the epaulment; and whenever he thus lays it down for the discharge of any particular duty, he will resume it on returning to his post after the completion of that duty.

19. The instructor causes the service of the piece to be executed by the following commands:

1. FROM BATTERY.

The gunner moves two paces to his right.

Nos. 1, 2, 3, 4, 5, and 6, facing from the epaulment, embar; Nos. 1 and 2 under the front of the wheels; Nos. 3 and 4 through the rear spokes of the wheels, near the felly, under and perpendicularly to the cheeks; and Nos. 5 and 6 under the manœuvring bolts.

All being ready, the gunner gives the command HEAVE, which will be repeated as often as may be necessary. He sees that Nos. 5 and 6 guide the trail in prolongation of the directrix of the embrasure, and, as soon as the face of the piece is about one yard from the epaulment, commands HALT. All unbar and resume their posts. Nos. 1 and 2 chock the wheels.

2. *Load by detail*—LOAD.

20. Nos. 1, 2, and 4 lay down their handspikes.

No. 2 takes out the tompion, and places it near the vent-cover.

No. 1 faces once and a half to his left; steps over the sponge and rammer; faces to the piece; takes the sponge with both hands, the backs down, the right hand three feet from the sponge-head, the left hand eighteen inches nearer to it; returns to the piece, entering the staff in the embrasure; places the left foot in line with the face of the piece, half way between it and the wheels; breaks to the right with the right foot, the heels on line parallel to the direction of the piece, the left leg straightened, the right knee bent, the body erect upon the haunches; and rests the end of the sponge in the muzzle, the staff in prolongation of the bore, supported by the right hand, the right arm extended, the left hand flat against the side of the thigh.

No. 2 steps to the muzzle, and occupies a position on the left of the piece corresponding to that of No. 1 on his right. He seizes the staff with the left hand, back down, near to and outside the hand of No. 1.

No. 3 facing towards the epaulment, embars under the breech, and maintains the piece in a convenient position for inserting the sponge, until he receives a signal from the gunner to unbar. He then lays down his handspike; steps over the rammer and seizes the staff with both hands, as prescribed for the sponge; and stands ready to exchange with No. 1.

No. 4 takes the pass-box and goes to the rear for a cartridge; returns with it, and places himself, facing the piece, about eighteen inches to the rear and right of No. 2.

The gunner places himself near the stock, the left foot advanced; closes the vent with the second finger of the left hand, bending well forward to cover himself by the breech; turns the elevating screw with the right hand, so as to adjust the piece conveniently for loading and makes a signal for No. 3 to unbar.

21. In the mean time, Nos. 1 and 2 insert the sponge by the following motions: at the words ONE—TWO—THREE—FOUR—FIVE.

1st motion. They insert the sponge as far as the hand of No. 1, bodies erect, shoulders square.

2d motion. They slide the hands along the staff and seize it at arms length.

3d motion. They force the sponge down as prescribed in the first motion.

4th motion. They repeat the second motion.

5th motion. They push the sponge to the bottom of the bore. No. 1 replaces the left hand on the staff, back up, six inches nearer to the muzzle than the right. No. 2 places the right hand, back up, between the hands of No. 1.

If in executing these motions, or the corresponding ones with the rammer, it be found that the sponge or rammer is at home at the third or fourth motion, then what is prescribed for the fifth motion will be performed at the third or fourth. The knee on the side towards which the body is to be inclined is always bent, the other straightened; and the weight of the body added, as much as possible, to the effort exerted by the arms.

3. Sponge.

22. Nos. 1 and 2, pressing the sponge firmly against the bottom of the bore, turn it three times from right to left, and three times from left to right; replace the hands on the thighs; and withdraw the sponge by motions contrary to those prescribed for inserting it.

Remark.—To handle the sponge when it is new and fits tight, it may become necessary for Nos. 1 and 2 to use both hands. In this case it will be inserted and withdrawn by short and quick motions.

No. 2 quits the staff, and turning towards No. 4 receives from him the cartridge, which he takes in both hands, backs down, and introduces into the bore bottom foremost, seams to the sides; he then grasps the rammer in the way prescribed for the sponge.

No. 1, rising upon the right leg and turning towards his left, passes the sponge above the rammer with the left hand to No. 3, and receiving the rammer with the right, presents it as prescribed for the sponge, except that he rests the rammer-head against the right side of the face of the piece.

No. 3, as soon as the sponge is withdrawn, passing the rammer under the sponge into the embrasure with the right hand, receives the sponge from No. 1 with the left, replaces it upon the prop, and resumes his post.

No. 4, setting down the pass-box, takes out the cartridge and presents it in both hands to No. 2, the choke to the front; returns the pass-box to its place; and picks up a ball, and afterwards a wad, should one be required.

Nos. 1 and 2 force down the cartridge by the motions prescribed for forcing down the sponge.

4. Ram.

23. Nos. 1 and 2, drawing the rammer out to the full extent of their arms, ram with a single stroke. No. 2 quits the staff, and turning towards No. 4, receives from him the ball and wad, whilst No. 1 throws out the rammer, and holds the head against the right side of the face of the piece. No. 2, receiving successively the ball and wad, introduces them into the bore, the ball first, and seizes the staff with the left hand. No. 4 then resumes his post.

Nos. 1 and 2 force down the ball and wad together by the same motions, and ram in the same manner as prescribed for the cartridge. No. 2 quits the rammer; sweeps, if necessary, the platform on his own side; passes the broom to No. 1; and resumes his post. No. 1 throws out the rammer, and places it upon the prop below the sponge; finishes the sweeping; and resumes his post.

The gunner pricks, leaving the priming wire in the vent; resumes his post; and, if firing beyond point-blank range, adjusts the breech-sight to the distance.

5. In battery.

24. Nos. 1 and 2 unchock the wheels, and with Nos. 3, 4, 5, and 6, all facing towards the epaulment, embar: Nos. 1 and 2 through the front spokes of the wheels near the felly, under and perpendicularly to the cheeks; Nos. 3 and 4 under the rear of the wheels; and Nos. 5 and 6 under the manœuvring bolts perpendicularly to the stock.

All being ready, the gunner commands HEAVE, and the piece is run into battery; Nos. 5 and 6 being careful to guide the chase into the middle of the embrasure. As soon as the wheels touch the hurter, he commands HALT. All unbar, and Nos. 1, 2, 3, and 4 resume their posts.

6. POINT.

25. No 3 lays down his handspike; passes the hook of the lanyard through the eye of a tube from front to rear; and holds the handle of the lanyard with the right hand, the hook between the thumb and forefinger.

Nos. 5 and 6 embar under and perpendicularly to the trail, near the manœuvring bolts.

The gunner, placing himself at the stock, as at the command LOAD, withdraws the priming wire, and, aided by Nos. 5 and 6, gives the direction; causing the trail to be moved by commanding LEFT, or RIGHT, tapping, at the same time, on the right side of the breech for No. 5 to move the trail to the left, or on the left side for No. 6 to move it to the right.

He then places the centre point of the breech-sight accurately upon the chalk mark on the base-ring, and by the elevating screw gives the proper elevation, rectifying the direction, if necessary.

The moment the piece is correctly pointed, he rises on the left leg, and gives the word READY, making a signal with both hands, at which Nos. 5 and 6 unbar, and resume their posts; takes the breech-sight with the left hand; and goes to the windward to observe the effect of the shot.

No. 3 inserts the tube in the vent; drops the handle, allowing the lanyard to uncoil as he steps back to his post, holding it slightly stretched with the right hand, the cord passing between the fingers, back of the hand up; and breaks to the rear a full face with the left foot, the left hand against the thigh.

At the word READY, Nos. 1 and 2 take the chocks, and breaking off with the feet furthest from the epaulment, stand ready to chock the wheels.

26. In directing the piece to be fired, the instructor will designate it by its number, as, for example:

7. *Number one*—FIRE.

No. 3 gives a smart pull upon the lanyard.

Immediately after the discharge of the piece, Nos. 1 and 2 chock the wheels, and resume the erect position. No. 3 resumes the erect position, and rewinds the lanyard in St. Andrew's cross upon its handle, returning it, if dry, to the tube-pouch. The gunner, having observed the effect of the shot, returns to his post.

27. Whenever the piece is to be fired by a *lock*, *portfire*, or *slow-match*, it will be done by No. 3, as prescribed for No. 4, in the instruction for field artillery.

28. To continue the exercise, the instructor resumes the series of commands beginning with FROM BATTERY.

TO CHANGE POSTS.

29. To change posts, the instructor commands:

1. *Change posts.*
2. MARCH.
3. CALL-OFF.

At the first command, the cannoneers lay down their handspikes; place their equipments on the parts of the carriage nearest to them; and face to their left.

At the second command, they step off, each advancing one post; No. 2 taking that of No. 1. Nos. 2 and 5 pass to the rear of the trail; No. 2 on the outside of all the cannoneers. On arriving at their posts, they face to the piece, and equip themselves.

At the third command, they call-off, according to the posts they are to occupy.

TO LOAD FOR ACTION.

30. The cannoneers having been sufficiently instructed in the details of the movements, the instructor commands:

Load for action—LOAD.

The piece is run from battery, loaded, run into battery pointed, and prepared for firing, by the following commands from the gunner: FROM BATTERY—LOAD—IN BATTEY—POINT—READY.

At the command, or signal, from the instructor to commence firing, the gunner gives the command FIRE, and continues the action until the instructor directs the firing to cease.

TO CEASE FIRING.

31. To cause the firing to cease, the instructor commands:

CEASE FIRING.

Whether the cannoneers are *loading by detail* or *for action*, the piece is sponged out, and all resume their posts. If the cartridge has been inserted the loading will be completed, unless the instructor should otherwise direct.

TO SECURE PIECE, AND REPLACE IMPLEMENTS.

32. To discontinue the exercise, the instructor having ordered the firing to cease, and caused the piece to be run into battery, gives the following commands:

1. SECURE PIECE.

No. 2 returns the tompion to the muzzle. The gunner puts on the vent-cover, which he receives from No. 2, and depresses the piece.

2. REPLACE IMPLEMENTS.

Nos. 1 and 2 replace the handspikes against the epaulment, those of Nos. 3, 4, 5, and 6 being passed to them by Nos. 3 and 4 for that purpose. The gunner hangs the pouches upon the knob of the cascable.

TO LEAVE THE BATTERY.

33. The instructor causes the muskets to be taken; forms the detachment in rear of the piece; and marches it from the battery as prescribed in No. 13.

Remarks.

34. The service of a 24-pdr. siege gun, as it respects running from and to battery, and pointing, is performed by five men, as prescribed for the siege Howitzer in LESSON II. Five men suffice for the service of the 18 and 12-pdrs. To perform, however, all the duties incident to a battery of heavy artillery on a war establishment, including transportation and the mechanical manœuvres, the details for its daily service, at three reliefs, should allow, at least, twenty privates to each piece.

TO SERVE THE PIECE WITH REDUCED NUMBERS.

35. The smallest number of men with which heavy pieces can be served with facility has been given as five. It may be necessary, however, from the men being disabled, or from other circumstances, to serve a gun with a less number.

With four men. They will be told off as gunner, and Nos. 1, 2 and 3. In this case, No. 2 will, in addition to his own duties, perform those of No. 4.

With three men. They will be told off as gunner, and Nos. 1 and 2. No. 1 performs the duties prescribed for No. 3, as well as his own. No. 2 performs those of No. 4, as in the preceding case.

When No. 2 serves ammunition, he goes for the cartridge, and places the pass-box behind his post, before assisting No. 1 to sponge.

TRANSPORTATION.

36. The transportation of a 24-pdr. gun requires ten horses and five drivers; an 18-pdr. eight horses and four drivers; a battery wagon six horses and three drivers; and spare carriages—at the rate of one for every five pieces—require, each, six horses and three drivers.

CHARGES, &c.

37. The ordinary service charge of powder for heavy guns is *one-fourth* the weight of the shot. For firing double shot it is *one-sixth* that weight. The breaching charge is *one-third* the weight of the shot.

Range of a 24-pounder, at an angle of 1° 30′, (*point blank,*) charge 6 lbs	950 yards.
Range of a 24-pounder, at an angle of 5°, charge 6 lbs	1900 "
Range of an 18-pounder, at an angle of 1° 30′, charge 4½ lbs.	800 "
Range of an 18-pounder, at an angle of 5°, charge 4½ lbs.	1600 "
Proof range of powder	300 "

The range of a 12-pounder is about the same as that of an 18-pounder.

Greatest elevation that a 24-pounder carriage admits	12°
Greatest elevation that an 18-pounder carriage admits	12°
Greatest elevation that a 12-pounder carriage admits	13°
Greatest depression that a 24-pounder carriage admits	4°
Greatest depression that an 18-pounder carriage admits	4°
Greatest depression that a 12-pounder carriage admits	4°

See Tables in PART III.

WADS.

38. *Wads* are not generally necessary, except when firing at angles of depression; and then only one is used, and that on the ball. When, however, the piece has been fired so often that the ball has caused a *lodgment* in the bore, it is well to use wads differing in length, according to the position and extent of the lodgment, between the shot and the cartridge.

Hay wads may be made by twisting hay into a rope of about one inch in diameter, folding it together of any desired length, and then winding the folds from one end to the other, leaving the wad a little larger than the bore.

BREACHING BATTERIES.

39. *Breaching batteries* established against walls are—*First.* To make a horizontal section the length of the desired breach along the scarp, at one-third its height from the bottom of the ditch, and to a depth equal to the thickness of the wall.

Secondly. To make vertical cuts through the wall, not further than ten yards apart, and not exceeding one to each piece; beginning at the horizontal section, and ascending gradually to the top of the wall.

Thirdly. To fire at the most prominent points of the masonry left standing; beginning always at the bottom, and gradually approaching the top.

Fourthly. To fire into the broken mass with howitzers until the breach is practicable.

Breaches of more than twenty yards in length have been opened by way of experiment, and rendered practicable, in less than ten hours, by about two hundred and thirty 24-pdr. balls and forty shells in one case, and by three hundred 18-pdr. balls and forty shells in another.

RAPIDITY OF FIRING.

40. Iron guns sustain long-continued and rapid firing better than brass guns. An iron gun should sustain twelve hundred discharges, at the rate of twelve an hour; but whatever may be the rate of fire, it is deemed unsafe after that number of discharges. As many as twenty an hour have been made for sixteen consecutive hours.

PENETRATION OF SHOT.

41. The penetration of balls increases to a certain extent with their calibre. The mean result from several experiments gives the penetration of a 24-pdr. ball, with the charge of one-third of its weight, at the distance of one hundred yards, as follows:

	Feet.	Inches.
In earth of old parapets	8	6
In earth recently thrown up	15	0
In oak wood, sound and hard	4	6
In rubble stone masonry	1	10
In brick	3	0

LESSON II.

SERVICE OF AN 8-INCH SIEGE HOWITZER, MOUNTED ON A 24-POUNDER SIEGE CARRIAGE.

(PLATE VII.)

Five men are necessary—one gunner and four other cannoneers.

42. The piece is in battery upon its platform.
The implements, &c., are arranged as follows:

HANDSPIKES	Three on the left of the carriage, and two on the right, leaning against the epaulment, in line with the cannoneers.
SPONGE AND RAMMER	On props, eighteen inches behind and parallel to the cannoneers of the right, the sponge-head turned towards the epaulment.
HAVERSACK	Containing fuzes, a pair of sleeves, and a priming-wire, bent at right angles at the point, for withdrawing the cartridge used in instruction. Suspended from the knob of the cascable.
TUBE-POUCH	Containing friction tubes, and the lanyard, wound in St. Andrew's cross upon its handle. Suspended from the knob of the cascable.

GUNNER'S POUCH....	Containing the gunner's level, breech-sight, finger-stall, priming wire, gimlet, vent-punch, and chalk. Suspended from the knob of the cascable.
LOADING-TONGS .... QUADRANT.......... PLUMMET .... SCRAPER .... WIPER .... SPLINTS	In a basket, or on a shelf, against the epaulment, outside of and near the handspikes of the left.
GRUMMET-WAD	On the end of the hurter, near No. 2.
CHOCKS	One on each side of the piece, near the ends of the hurter.
VENT-COVER	Covering the vent.
TOMPION	In the muzzle.
QUOIN	Under the breech.
BROOM	Leaning against the epaulment, outside of the basket or shelf.

When several howitzers are served together there will be only one gunner's level and two vent-punches to each battery, not exceeding six pieces. To the same battery there will be one *wrench*.

One shell and one bombazine cartridge bag for instruction—the bag filled with saw dust, and having loops of thread at the choke end—are at the magazine, or other safe place in rear of the piece.

43. The cannoneers having been marched to their posts, the instructor directs them to place their muskets against the epaulment, and then explains to them the names and uses of the implements, and the nomenclatures of the howitzer, its carriage, and the battery.

44. To cause the implements to be distributed, the instructor commands:

TAKE IMPLEMENTS.

The gunner steps to the knob of the cascable; takes off the vent-cover, handing it to No. 2 to place against the epaulment, outside of the basket; gives the tube-pouch to No. 3, and the haversack to No. 4; and equips himself with his own pouch and the finger-stall, wearing the latter on the second finger of the left hand.

No. 2 puts on the sleeves.

No. 3 equips himself with the tube-pouch.

No. 4 equips himself with the haversack, which he wears from the right shoulder to the left side; takes out the sleeves, and assists No. 2 to put them on.

Nos. 1 and 2, after passing handspikes to Nos. 3 and 4 and the gunner, take each one for himself. The gunner, receiving his from No. 4, lays it in the alignment, the small end towards the epaulment, and two yards to his right. The other handspikes are held, laid down, and resumed, as prescribed in Nos. 17 and 18.

The gunner directs No. 3 to raise the breech to enable him to level the piece; applies his level to ascertain the highest points of the base-ring and muzzle-band, which he marks with chalk; and resumes his post.

45. The instructor causes the service of the piece to be executed by the following commands:

1. FROM BATTERY.

The gunner moves two paces to his right.

Nos. 1, 2, 3 and 4, facing from the epaulment, embar: Nos. 1 and 2 through the rear spokes of the wheels, near the felly, under and perpendicularly to the cheeks; and Nos. 3 and 4 under the manœuvring bolts.

All being ready, the gunner gives the command HEAVE, which will be repeated as often as may be necessary. He sees that Nos. 3 and 4 guide the trail in prolongation of the directrix of the embrasure, and as soon as the wheels are about one yard from the epaulment, commands HALT. All unbar, and resume their posts. Nos. 1 and 2 chock the wheels.

2. *Load by detail*—LOAD.

46. Nos. 1, 2, and 4 lay down their handspikes.

No. 2 takes out the tompion, and places it near the vent-cover; sweeps, if necessary, his side of the platform; passes the broom to the right side of the piece, and resumes his post.

No. 1 faces to his right, and seizes the sponge-staff at its middle with the right hand, back up; places himself at the muzzle; forces the sponge to the bottom of the chamber; and grasps the staff with both hands; all nearly as in field artillery.

No. 3, facing towards the epaulment, embars under the breech or knob of the cascable, until he receives a signal from the gunner to unbar, when he resumes his post.

No. 4 goes to the rear for a cartridge and shell; puts the cartridge in his haversack; takes the shell in both hands; returns and places it on the grummet-wad; and stands, facing the piece, about eighteen inches to the rear and left of No. 2.

The gunner places himself near the stock, as in No. 20, and closes the vent with the second finger of the left hand; adjusts the piece with the quoin just about one degree's elevation; and makes a signal for No. 3 to unbar.

3. SPONGE.

47. No. 1, pressing the sponge firmly against the bottom of the chamber, turns it three times from the right to left, and three times from left to right; draws it out to the front of the chamber; wipes out the bore; reinserts the sponge along the upper side of the bore as far as the chamber; draws it entirely out, pressing it upon the upper side of the bore; turns the sponge over towards the embrasure; and presents the rammer-head against the right side of the face of the piece, holding the staff in both hands, backs down.

No. 2, as soon as the sponging is completed, takes the

tongs and occupies a position at the muzzle corresponding to that prescribed for No. 1 on the right; turns to his left on the right heel, advancing the left foot, and presents the tongs in both hands, the left hand nearest him, the tongs opened, their legs in the same vertical plane.

No. 4 takes out the cartridge and inserts it as far as its middle in the tongs, choke foremost, the seam downwards; removes the stopper from, and inserts the fuze into, the fuze plug; scrapes its end; and takes the wiper.

No. 2 having received the cartridge in the tongs, makes a face and a half to his right on the right heel, and breaks off with the left foot; places the right hand against the head of the left cheek of the carriage, and with the left hand introduces the cartridge into the chamber, keeping the legs of the tongs in a vertical plane; then slightly withdrawing and closing the tongs, he presses them in the direction of the axis of the piece against the end of the cartridge, and shoves it home. Withdrawing the tongs, he makes a face and a half to his left on the right heel, and puts the hooks of the tongs into the ears of the shell, which he lifts and holds about two feet from the ground, whilst No. 4 wipes it.

No. 1, as soon as the tongs are withdrawn, inserts the rammer, and holds it with the head against the cartridge, the staff in the axis of the piece.

4. Ram.

48. No. 1 presses firmly upon the cartridge; throws out the rammer, and places it upon the props; sweeps, if necessary, his side of the platform; passes the broom to the left side of the piece, and resumes his post.

No. 2 introduces the shell, and shoves it home in a manner similar to that prescribed for the cartridge; withdraws the hooks, and looks to see that the fuse is in the axis of the piece.

If the piece is to be fired horizontally, or at an angle of depression, No. 4, having replaced the wiper, hands a splint to No. 2, and resumes his post.

No. 2 presses the splint under the shell with the left hand; replaces the tongs and broom, and resumes his post.

The gunner pricks, leaving the priming-wire in the vent, and resumes his post.

5. In battery.

49. Nos. 1 and 2 unchock the wheels, and with Nos. 3 and 4, all facing towards the epaulment, embar; Nos. 1 and 2 through the front spokes of the wheels, near the felly, under and perpendicularly to the cheeks; and Nos. 3 and 4 under the rear of the wheels.

The gunner, seizing his handspike, embars under one of the manœuvring bolts; gives the command HEAVE; and guides the piece to the middle of the embrasure. As soon as the wheels touch the hurter, he commands HALT. All unbar, and resume their posts.

6. Point.

50. Nos. 1 and 4 embar under and perpendicularly to the trail, near the manœuvring bolts.

No. 2, facing towards the epaulment, embars under the breech or knob of the cascable.

No. 3 lays down his handspike; passes the hook of the lanyard through the eye of a tube from front to rear; and holds the handle of the lanyard with the right hand, the hook between the thumb and forefinger.

The gunner, placing himself at the stock, as at the command LOAD, withdraws the priming wire, and, aided by Nos. 1 and 4, gives the direction; causing the trail to be moved by commanding LEFT, or RIGHT, tapping, at the same time, on the right side of the breech for No. 1 to move the trail to the left, or on the left side for No. 4 to move it to the right.

He then places the centre point of the breech-sight accurately upon the chalk mark on the base-ring, and commands LOWER, or RAISE, tapping, at the same time, on the upper side of the knob of the cascable with the left hand, and drawing out the quoin with the right, in order to elevate, or tapping upwards on the lower side, and shoving in the quoin, in order to depress the piece; rectifying the direction, if necessary.

If the piece is to be fired point blank, horizontally, or at an angle of depression, he does not apply the breech-sight.

If the piece is masked from the object fired at, he places himself astride the stock, or in rear of the trail, and gives the direction by the plummet.

To give the elevation when the piece is masked, or when the desired range is greater than the breech-sight ranges, he applies the quadrant to the upper surface of the lock-piece, making the allowance due to its inclination with the axis of the piece, which ought to be previously determined.

The moment the piece is correctly pointed, he rises on the left leg, and gives the word READY, making a signal with both hands, at which Nos. 1, 2, and 4 unbar, and resume their posts; takes the breech-sight with the left hand; and goes to the windward to observe the effect of the shot.

No. 3 inserts the tube in the vent; drops the handle, allowing the lanyard to uncoil as he steps back to his post, holding it slightly stretched with the right hand, the cord passing between the fingers, back of the hand up; and breaks to the rear a full pace with the left foot, the left hand against the thigh.

Nos. 1 and 2, on resuming their posts, take the chocks, and break off with the feet furthest from the epaulment, inclining well to that side in order to avoid the blast.

7. *Number one* (or the like)—FIRE.

51. Executed as in No. 26.

What is prescribed in No. 27 will apply to this piece.

52. To continue the exercise, the instructor resumes the series of commands beginning with FROM BATTERY.

TO UNLOAD.

53. The piece having been run from battery, the instructor directs No. 2 to take out the shell and cartridge; No. 4 carrying them to their place in rear of the piece. No. 3 assists No. 2, by raising the breech until the shell rolls to the muzzle.

TO SCRAPE THE PIECE.

54. In the course of firing it may become necessary to scrape the piece. To cause this to be done, the instructor directs the piece to be moved from battery, and then commands:

SCRAPE THE PIECE.

Nos. 1 and 2 lay down their handspikes.

No. 2 takes the scraper and wiper, giving the latter to No. 1; thoroughly scrapes the chamber and bore; draws out the scrapings with the spoon; returns the scraper to its place, and resumes his post.

No. 1, enveloping the sponge-head in the wiper, wipes out the bore, and returns the wiper to No. 2, who replaces it; puts the sponge upon the props, and resumes his post.

TO CHANGE POSTS.
TO LOAD FOR ACTION.
TO CEASE FIRING.
TO SECURE PIECE, AND REPLACE IMPLEMENTS.
TO LEAVE THE BATTERY.

Executed as in Nos. 29, 30, 31, 32, and 33; No. 4 assisting No. 2 to take off the sleeves.

TO SERVE THE PIECE WITH REDUCED NUMBERS.

Executed as in No. 35.

TRANSPORTATION.

55. The transportation of an 8-inch siege howitzer requires eight horses and four drivers.

CHARGES, &c.

56. Greatest charge of powder	4 lbs.
Greatest charge, shell filled with bullets	3 lbs.
Charge of the shell filled with powder	2 lbs. 9 oz.
Bursting charge of the shell	1 lb.
Charge to blow out the fuze	4 oz.
Greatest elevation the carriage admits	15°
Greatest depression the carriage admits	10°
Range at an angle of 1°, charge 4 lbs	430 yds.

Range at an angle of 5°, charge 4 lbs	1,150 yards.
Range at an angle of 15°, charge 4 lbs	2,300 "
Proof range of powder	300 "
Weight of shell	45 lbs.
Weight of the shell filled with bullets	65 lbs.
The *black* fuze burns to the inch	2″
The *red* fuze burns to the inch	3″
The *green* fuze burns to the inch	4″
The *yellow* fuze burns to the inch	5″
At 2° elevation, black fuze, full charge, the shell bursts at	500 to 600 yards.
At 3°.25 elevation, red fuze, full charge, the shell bursts at	800 to 900 "
At 4°.25 elevation, green fuze, full charge, the shell bursts at	900 to 1,000 "
At 5°.25 elevation, yellow fuze, full charge, the shell bursts at	1,000 to 1,100 "

A proper charge for enfilading, at the distance of 600 yards, on a horizontal plane, relief of the epaulment seven feet, elevation 2°.75, red fuze, is three pounds.

See Tables in PART III.

TO PREPARE AMMUNITION.

57. If the ammunition for howitzers is to be prepared and issued by the artillery, two men, numbered 5 and 6, are added to each detachment for that purpose. They are sent to the magazine, where they are provided with the following implements and stores:

ONE SET OF POWDER MEASURES.
ONE FUNNEL.
ONE FUZE-MALLET.
ONE FUZE-SETTER.
ONE FUZE-PLUG REAMER.
ONE RASP.
ONE BASKET. Containing fuze-plugs.
TWO GRUMMET-WADS, OR } On which to place the shells
TWO HOLLOW BLOCKS. } while putting in the charge.
ONE WIPER.
ONE BUDGE-BARREL.
ONE DARK LANTERN.
TOW. For stoppers.

CARTRIDGE BAGS. Of bombazine.
TWINE.
POWDER.
MUSKET BULLETS.
INCENDIARY COMPOSITION.

They first fill and tie a number of cartridges, according to the directions received from the battery, and then prepare a corresponding number of shells.

To fill the cartridges.—One holds the bag, while the other (by means of the funnel) pours in the powder. The cartridges thus filled are placed upright in a box until tied, when they are transported to the budge-barrel.

Cartridges of reduced charges for ricochet firing may be made thus:

The charge having been poured into the bag, a wad of hay about six inches in length is placed upon it. This wad is made by laying wisps of hay evenly together so as to form a cylinder nearly of the diameter of the cartridge bag. The wad is tied about an inch from each end, and the ends are cut squarely off, so as to present an even surface to the powder. In handling these cartridges the powder end of the bag should always be kept downwards.

To prepare the shells.—No. 5 places one upon a grummet-wad; cleans it, if necessary, with a rasp; drives in a fuze-plug until it does not project more than the tenth of an inch; and reams it out with the reamer. No. 6, transferring it to the other grummet-wad, charges it with powder; puts in a stopper of tow; marks it with chalk, and places it conveniently for No. 4.

If the shell is to be loaded with bullets or incendiary composition, it is charged before the fuze-plug is driven. It should contain about three hundred and twenty bullets, and one pound and a quarter of powder.

If filled only with powder, No. 6 marks the shell with a cross; if with incendiary composition, he makes a circle around the fuze-plug; and if with bullets, he makes two circles on one side. The shells thus differently charged are kept separate.

LESSON III.

SERVICE OF A TEN-INCH SIEGE MORTAR.

(PLATES VIII AND IX.)

Five men are necessary; one gunner and four other cannoneers.

58. The mortar is upon its platform.

The implements, &c., are arranged as follows:

HANDSPIKES	Two on each side of the bed, against the cheeks, leaning upon the four manœuvring bolts, the small ends towards the epaulment, those of the front handspikes even with the front of the cheeks.
HAVERSACK	Containing fuzes, and a pair of sleeves. Attached to the tompion, and lying upon the mortar.
TUBE-POUCH	Containing the priming-wire, friction tubes, and the lanyard, wound in St. Andrew's cross upon its handle. Attached to the tompion, and lying upon the mortar.
GUNNER'S-POUCH	Containing the gunner's level, gimlet, vent-punch, and chalk. Attached to the tompion, and lying upon the mortar.
QUADRANT PLUMMET POINTING-CORD SCRAPER WIPER SHELL-HOOKS	In a basket, between the cheeks of the mortar bed.

TOMPION	In the muzzle.
QUOIN	Under the mortar upon the bolster, its handle to the left.
POINTING-STAKES	With the basket.
MAUL	
BROOM	

When several mortars are served together there will be only one gunner's level and two vent-pouches to each battery, not exceeding six pieces. To the same battery there will be one *hammer-wrench.*

One shell and one paper cartridge bag for instruction are at the magazine or other safe place in rear of the piece.

59. The cannoneers having been marched to their posts, the instructor directs them to place their muskets against the epaulment, and then explains to them the names and uses of the implements, and the nomenclatures of the mortar, its bed, and the battery.

60. To cause the pointing-stakes to be established in position, the instructor commands:

PLANT THE POINTING-STAKES.

The gunner, assisted by Nos. 1 and 2, plant the stakes as prescribed in pointing mortars, No. 193.

No. 1, having driven the pointing-stakes, drives another stake one yard behind his post for holding the wiper, and replaces the maul near the basket.

The gunner lays the slack of the pointing-cord at the foot of the epaulment, leaving the plummet at the stake in rear of the piece.

All resume their posts.

61. To cause the implements to be distributed, the instructor commands:

TAKE IMPLEMENTS.

The gunner steps to the front of the piece; gives to No. 1 the sleeves and the wiper; to No. 2 the basket and maul; to

No. 3 the tube-pouch and broom; and to No. 4 the haversack; equips himself with the gunner's pouch; applies his level to ascertain the line of metal, which he marks with chalk, and resumes his post.

No. 1 places the wiper upon the stake behind him, and, assisted by No. 3, puts on the sleeves.

No. 2 removes the tompion, which he places, with the basket and maul, one yard behind him, and lays the shell-hooks on the ground between himself and the basket.

No. 3 lays the broom on the ground behind him, and equips himself with the tube-pouch.

No. 4 equips himself with the haversack, which he wears from the right shoulder to the left side.

All take their handspikes.

62. The handspikes are held as in No. 17. When laid down they are returned, except in one case, to their places on the manœuvring bolts.

63. The instructor causes the service of the piece to be executed by the following commands:

1. IN BATTERY.

The gunner, making a half face to his right, steps off, left foot first, and places himself two paces in rear of the platform, facing the piece.

Nos. 1, 2, 3, and 4, facing towards the epaulment, embar: Nos. 1 and 2 under the front manœuvring bolts, and Nos. 3 and 4 under those in the rear, engaging the butts of their handspikes about three inches.

All being ready, the gunner gives the command HEAVE, which will be repeated as often as may be necessary. As soon as the piece is on the middle of the platform, he commands HALT. All unbar, and resume their posts.

2. *Load by detail*—LOAD.

64. Nos. 1, 3 and 4 lay down their handspikes.

The gunner, taking the scraper, places himself in front of the muzzle, and scrapes the bore and chamber; draws out the scrapings with the spoon; returns the scraper to the basket; and again places himself at the muzzle, one yard in its front.

No. 1, turning to his right, takes the wiper with the right, faces to his left, and places the left foot near the manœuvring bolt, the right in front of the muzzle, the left hand upon the face of the piece; thoroughly wipes out the chamber and bore, and resumes his post.

No. 3, as soon as the piece is wiped, clears the vent with the priming-wire; sweeps the platform, if necessary; and resumes his post and handspike.

Nos. 2 and 4, facing to their right—No. 2 holding his handspike at the middle under the left arm, butt end foremost, and taking the shell-hooks in the right—go to the rear for a cartridge and shell. While No. 4 is getting the cartridge, No. 2 inserts the shell-hooks in the ears of the shell, and passes the small end of the handspike through the ring. In carrying the shell they hold the handspike with their right hands, No. 4 at the small end and in advance of No. 2. Passing by the left of the piece, between the gunner and the muzzle, they rest the shell upon the platform against the middle of the transom.

No. 1, placing the wiper upon the handspikes, receives the small end of the handspike from No. 4, who gives the cartridge to the gunner.

The gunner advances the left foot, and places the left hand upon the face of the piece; introduces the cartridge into the mouth of the chamber with the right hand, and carefully pours in the powder; returns the cartridge bag to No. 4; and distributes the powder evenly over the bottom of the chamber. In firing with paper fuzes, he receives one from No. 4, and inserts it in the fuze-plug.

No. 4, returning the cartridge bag to the haversack, takes the wiper.

Nos. 1 and 2 raise the shell and hold it about a foot from the ground, while No. 4 wipes it; they then lift it into the muzzle.

The gunner steps forward, and with the left hand over the handspike, the right hand under and nearer to it, seizes the shell-hooks and assists to lower the shell gently into its place. No. 2 then withdraws his handspike from the ring, and resumes his post. No. 1 takes his handspike. The gunner adjusts the shell so that the fuze is in the axis of the piece;

throws the shell-hooks to their place behind No. 2; and, if firing with wooden fuzes, uncaps the fuze.

No. 4, as soon as he wipes the shell, returns the wiper to its place; takes the slack of the pointing-cord, which he lays over the left manœuvring bolts, leaving its end at the rear pointing stake; and resumes his post and handspike.

3. Point.

65. Nos. 1 and 2, facing towards the epaulment, embar upon the bolster, under and perpendicularly to the piece.

The gunner, taking the quadrant from the basket, applies it to the left side of the face of the piece with the left hand, and inserts or draws out the quoin with the right, giving the command RAISE or LOWER, until the piece is at the elevation required—usually 45°. Returning the quadrant to the basket—Nos. 1 and 2 at the same time unbarring and resuming their posts—he places himself in rear of the rear pointing-stake, and holding the pointing-cord in the left hand and the plummet in the right gives the direction; commanding MORTAR LEFT—MORTAR RIGHT—MUZZLE LEFT—MUZZLE RIGHT—TRAIL LEFT—TRAIL RIGHT, as may be required.

To throw the mortar to the left. Nos. 2 and 4 facing each other, embar under the manœuvring bolts. Nos. 1 and 3 facing towards the epaulment, embar under the notches near them. When all are ready, the gunner gives the commands HEAVE—STEADY. The cannoneers remain embarred until he gives some other command, or makes the signal to unbar.

To throw the mortar to the right. Nos. 1 and 3 embar under the manœuvring bolts. Nos. 2 and 4 embar under the notches.

To throw the muzzle to the left. Nos. 1 and 3, facing towards the epaulment, embar under the front notches; No. 1 under the inside of the left notch.

To throw the trail to the left. Nos. 1 and 3, facing towards the epaulment, embar under the rear notches; No. 3 under the inside of the left notch.

The muzzle or trail is thrown to the right, in a similar manner to the preceding, by Nos. 2 and 4.

The direction having been given, the gunner gives the

word READY, and makes a signal with both hands; leaves the plummet at the stake; returns the pointing-cord to the foot of the epaulment, and goes to the windward to observe the effect of the shot.

Nos. 1, 2, and 4, taking their handspikes with them, go four yards in rear of the platform, and face to the front; No. 4 between Nos. 1 and 2, their handsikes held erect by the right side, the right arm extended naturally.

No. 3 lays down his handspike six inches in his front, parallel to the edge of the platform, and makes ready a friction tube, as in No. 25; advancing the right foot, he puts the tube in the vent; rises on the left leg, and moves three paces to the rear in prolongation of the right cheek; faces to the front; holds the handle of the lanyard with the right hand, the lanyard slightly stretched, the cord passing between the fingers, back of the hand up; and breaks to the rear a full pace with the left foot, the left hand against the thigh.

Remark.—To discharge the mortars now in use by means of a friction tube, the lanyard should be passed under a rope attached to and tightly drawn between the rear manœuvring bolts, or through a loop of rope attached to the rear right manœuvring bolt.

4. *Number one* (or the like)—FIRE.

66. Executed as in No. 26.

On the discharge of the piece, all resume their posts except the gunner, who waits to observe the effect of the shot. As soon as the shot strikes, he resumes his post.

What is prescribed in No. 27 will apply to this piece, omitting the word "*lock.*"

67. To continue the exercise, the instructor causes the piece to be moved towards the rear of the platform, directs Nos. 2 and 4 to take out the shell and carry it to the rear, and then resumes the series of commands beginning with IN BATTERY.

TO CHANGE POSTS.
TO LOAD FOR ACTION.
TO CEASE FIRING.

Executed as in Nos. 29, 30, and 31, except that in changing posts, No. 2 passes by the front of the piece.

TO SECURE PIECE AND REPLACE IMPLEMENTS.

68. To discontinue the exercise, the instructor, having ordered the firing to case, and caused the piece to be placed as at the command IN BATTERY, gives the command:

REPLACE IMPLEMENTS.

All lay down their handspikes. No. 2 puts in the tompion and assists No. 1 to pull up the pointing stakes. The gunner receives the implements from the cannoneers, and replaces them between the cheeks.

TO LEAVE THE BATTERY.

Executed as in No. 33.

TRANSPORTATION.

69. One mortar wagon is allowed to each 10-inch siege mortar and bed, to transport which requires eight horses and four drivers.

CHARGES, &c.

70. Greatest charge of powder	4 lbs.
Ordinary service charge	3 "
Charge of the shell filled with powder	5 "
Bursting charge of the shell	2 "
Charge to blow out the fuze	5 oz.
Range, charge 4 lbs., time of flight 21″	2,100 yds.
Range, charge 3 lbs., time of flight 19′	1,700 "
Range, charge 2 lbs., time of flight 14″	1,000 "
Proof range of powder	300 "
Weight of the shell	90 lbs.

Fire balls, according to their size, are fired from mortars of corresponding calibres. With a charge of *one twenty-fifth* of its weight the ball is thrown from six hundred to seven hundred yards.

See tables in PART III.

TO PREPARE AMMUNITION.

71. If the ammunition for mortars is to be prepared and issued by the artillery, two men, numbered 5 and 6, are added to each detachment for that purpose. Their duties at the magazine are similar to those prescribed in No. 57.

Should wooden fuzes be used, in addition to the implements therein mentioned, a *fuze-saw* will be required for reducing the fuzes to the proper lengths. The shell being first charged, the fuze, cut at the right length, is then driven.

The paper fuze is marked with the number of seconds which it burns per inch. It may be cut with a knife to any desired length.

TIME OF FLIGHT.

72. The time of flight for siege mortars, at an elevation of 45°, with ordinary charges, is nearly equal to the square root of the range in feet divided by four. The experimental length of the fuze may be given according to this rule.

TO ASCERTAIN THE DISTANCE BY THE REPORT OF FIRE-ARMS.

73. Multiply the number of seconds which elapse between seeing the flash and hearing the report by 1100; the product will be nearly the distance in feet.

RAPIDITY OF FIRING.

74. Siege mortars can be fired conveniently at the rate of twelve rounds an hour continuously, but they may, in case of need, be fired with greater rapidity.

LESSON IV.

SERVICE OF AN 8-INCH SIEGE MORTAR.

(PLATES VIII AND IX.)

Three men are necessary—one gunner and two other cannoneers.

75. The mortar is upon its platform.

The implements, &c., omitting two handspikes, and adding one grummet-wad, are the same as prescribed for the 10-inch siege mortar in No. 58. They are arranged as prescribed in that number. The wad is in the basket.

76. The instruction for this piece is the same as that prescribed in LESSON III, with the following modifications:

At the command TAKE IMPLEMENTS, No. 1 performs the duties enjoined on No. 3, and No. 2 those of No. 4, each in addition to his own. No. 2 assists No. 1 to put on the sleeves, and places the wad on the platform in front of the transom.

77. At the command IN BATTERY, No. 1 embars under the right front manœuvring bolt. No. 2 embars under the left rear manœuvring bolt.

78. At the command LOAD, No. 1, having wiped out the mortar, places the wiper upon the stake; pricks; and, if necessary, sweeps the platform.

No. 2, laying down his handspike, goes for a cartridge and shell; carries the shell in the right arm; passes between the gunner and the muzzle, and places it on the wad; gives to the gunner the cartridge, and, if firing with paper fuzes, a fuze; and takes the wiper from the stake.

The gunner, on returning the scraper to the basket, takes the shell-hooks and lays them on the ground between himself and the muzzle. Having carefully poured in the powder, he returns the cartridge bag to No. 2, and distributes the powder evenly over the bottom of the chamber; puts the fuze in the fuze-plug; inserts the hooks in the ears of the shell; raises it about a foot from the ground and holds it, while No. 2 wipes it; and then places it in the bore.

No. 2 replaces the wiper upon the stake; lays the slack of the pointing-cord over the left manœuvring bolts, and resumes his post.

79. At the command POINT, Nos. 1 and 2 embar under either of the front or rear notches as required. At the signal from the gunner, No. 1 prepares to fire the piece, as prescribed for No. 3 in No. 65.

TRANSPORTATION.

80. One mortar wagon will carry three 8-inch siege mortars, with their beds; to transport which requires eight horses and four drivers.

CHARGES, &c.

81. Greatest charge of powder	2 lbs.
Ordinary service charge	1 lb. 12 oz.
Charge of the shell filled with powder	2 lbs. 9 oz.
Bursting charge of the shell	1 lb.
Charge to blow out the fuze	4 oz.
Range, charge 2 lbs., time of flight 20″	1,837 yds.
Range, charge 1½ lb., time of flight 14″	943 "
Proof range of powder	300 "
Weight of shell	45 lbs.

See tables in PART III.

LESSON V.

SERVICE OF A COEHORN MORTAR.

(PLATE IX.)

Three men are necessary—one gunner and two other cannoneers.

82. The mortar is upon its platform.

The implements, &c., and their arrangement, are the same as prescribed for the 8-inch siege mortar in No. 75. A 24-pdr. shell is used.

83. The instruction for this piece is the same as that prescribed in LESSON IV.

To prepare its ammunition, and to transport it by hand with ease, two additional men are required. The gunner carries the basket and implements.

84. It is fired either from behind intrenchments, like other mortars, or it may accompany troops in effecting lodgements in towns and fortified places.

85. As the shell is without ears, it should be strapped with tin, having loops attached, through which a cord is passed for the purpose of lowering it into the bore. The chamber being cylindrical, a sponge is used, which is handled by No. 1.

CHARGES, &c.

86. Greatest charge of powder	8 oz.
Charge of the shell filled with powder	1 lb.
Bursting charge of the shell	8 oz.
Charge to blow out the fuze	2 oz.
Range, charge 8 oz.	1,200 yds.
Range, charge 6 oz.	900 "
Range, charge 4 oz.	430 "
Proof range of powder	300 "
Weight of shell	17 lbs.

See tables in PART III.

LESSON VI.

SERVICE OF A 10-INCH SEA-COAST MORTAR.

(PLATE IX.)

Five men are necessary—one gunner and four other cannoneers.

87. The mortar is upon its platform.

The implements, &c., with the addition of one sponge, are the same as prescribed for the 10-inch siege mortar in No. 58. They are arranged as prescribed in that number, except that the sponge is placed upon props one yard behind No. 1, the sponge-head turned towards the epaulment.

88. The instruction for this piece is the same as that prescribed in LESSON III, with the following modifications:

No. 1, after wiping the bore, sponges out the chamber; for this purpose mounting upon the right cheek and bolster.

To scrape the bore, and to put in the cartridge and shell, the gunner mounts upon a block in front of the muzzle.

The cartridge—its bag being of bombazine or flannel—is put directly into the chamber by the gunner, and rammed by No. 1.

To lift the shell into the muzzle, Nos. 2 and 3 mount the cheeks, and are assisted, respectively, by the gunner and No. 1.

In giving the elevation, Nos. 1 and 2 are assisted by Nos. 3 and 4.

Before priming, No. 3 pricks a second time.

CHARGES, &c.

89. Greatest charge of powder..........................	10 lbs.
Charge of shell filled with powder..........................	5 "
Bursting charge of the shell..........................	2 "
Charge to blow out the fuze..........................	5 oz.
Range, charge 10 lbs., time of flight 36″..................	4,250 yds.
Proof range of powder..........................	300 "
Weight of shell..........................	90 lbs.

See tables in PART III.

LESSON VII.

SERVICE OF A 13-INCH SEA-COAST MORTAR.

(PLATE IX.)

Five men are necessary—one gunner and four other cannoneers.

90. The mortar is upon its platform.

The implements, &c., and their arrangement, are the same as prescribed for the 10-inch sea-coast mortar in No. 87.

91. The instruction for this piece differs in no respect from that prescribed in LESSON VI.

CHARGES, &c.

92. Greatest charge of powder	20 lbs.
Charge of the shell filled with powder	11 "
Bursting charge of the shell	6 "
Charge to blow out the fuze	6 oz.
Range, charge 20 lbs., time of flight (about) 40″	4,325 yds.
Proof range of powder	300 "
Weight of the shell	200 lbs.

See tables in PART III.

LESSON VIII.

SERVICE OF A STONE MORTAR.

(PLATE IX.)

Five men are necessary—one gunner and four other cannoneers.

93. The mortar is upon its platform.

The implements, &c., and their arrangement, are the same as prescribed for the 10-inch sea-coast mortar in No. 87.

94. The instruction for this piece differs in no respect from that prescribed in LESSON VI.

A wooden bottom is placed over the mouth of the chamber to receive the basket which contains the charge of stones.

CHARGES, &c.

95. With a charge of a pound and a half of powder, and one hundred and twenty pounds of stones, at an elevation of 60°, the stones are thrown from one hundred and fifty to two hundred and fifty yards.

With fifteen 6-pounder shells, fuze fifteen seconds, charge of powder one pound, elevation 33°, the shells may be thrown from fifty to one hundred and fifty yards.

96. As the shells are liable to burst on leaving the bore, the piece is fired by a slow match applied to a train of quick-match, giving the men time to place themselves under cover.

LESSON IX.

SERVICE OF A GUN MOUNTED ON A BARBETTE CARRIAGE.

(PLATES X, XI, AND XII.)

Remark.—The instruction for a barbette gun, although in many respects precisely the same as that for a siege gun, is given in full, because the siege gun is seldom found in the forts on the seaboard.

Five men are necessary—one gunner and four other cannoneers.

97. The piece is in battery.
The implements, &c., are arranged as follows:

HANDSPIKES	Two on each side of the carriage, leaning against the parapet, in line with the cannoneers.
SPONGE .... RAMMER............	One yard behind the cannoneers of the right, the sponge uppermost, the sponge and rammer-heads turned from the parapet, inclined slightly from the piece, and supported upon a prop; or, when this cannot be done conveniently, placed against the wall, the sponge and rammer-heads nearest the piece.
PASS-BOX	Against the parapet outside the pile of balls.
TUBE-POUCH	Containing friction tubes, and the lanyard, wound in St. Andrew's cross upon its handle. Suspended from the knob of the cascable.

GUNNER'S POUCH....	Containing the gunner's level, breech-sight, finger-stall, priming-wire, gimlet, vent-punch, chalk-line, and chalk. Suspended from the knob of the cascable.
CHOCKS............	One on each side of the piece, at the foot of the parapet, inside the handspikes.
VENT-COVER..........	Covering the vent.
TOMPION............	In the muzzle.
BROOM..............	Leaning against the parapet, outside of the pile of balls.
BUDGE-BARREL.....	Containing cartridges, at the safest and most convenient place in rear of the piece.

When several guns are served together, there will be only one gunner's level and two vent-punches to each battery, not exceeding six pieces. To the same battery there will be one *worm*, one *ladle*, and one *wrench*.

The balls are regularly piled on the banquette, on the left of the piece.

The wads are placed between the parapet and the balls, partly resting on them.

98. The cannoneers having been marched to their posts, the instructor explains to them the names and uses of the implements, and the nomenclatures of the gun, its carriage, and the battery.

99. To cause the implements to be distributed, the instructor commands:

TAKE IMPLEMENTS.

The gunner mounts upon the tongue; takes off the vent-cover, handing it to No. 2 to place against the parapet, outside of the pass-box; gives the tube-pouch to No. 3; equips himself with his own pouch and the finger-stall, wearing the latter on the second finger of the left hand; levels the piece by the elevating screw; applies his level to ascertain the line of metal, which, with the assistance of No. 2, he marks with the chalk-line; and resumes his post.

No. 3 equips himself with the tube-pouch.

Nos. 1 and 2, after passing handspikes to Nos. 3 and 4, take each one for himself.

100. The handspike is held in both hands; the hand nearest to the parapet grasping it near the small end and at the height of the shoulder, back of the hand down, elbow touching the body; the other hand back up, the arm extended naturally; the butt of the handspike upon the ground on the side furthest from the parapet, and six inches in advance of the alignment.

101. When the cannoneer lays down his handspike, he places it directly before him, about six inches in advance of and parallel to the alignment, the small end towards the parapet; and whenever he thus lays it down for the performance of any particular duty, he will resume it on returning to his post after the completion of that duty.

102. The instructor causes the service of the piece to be executed by the following commands:

1. FROM BATTERY.

The gunner moves two paces to his right.

Nos. 1, 2, 3, and 4, facing from the parapet, embar near the tire; Nos. 1 and 2—first placing the chocks on the rails in front of the rollers—through the front spokes of the wheels, over the front manœuvring bolts; and Nos. 3 and 4 through the rear spokes, under the rear manœuvring bolts.

Should there be no rear manœuvring bolt, Nos. 3 and 4 embar under the braces, near the manœuvring staples.

All being ready, the gunner gives the command HEAVE, which will be repeated as often as may be necessary. As soon as the face of the piece is about one yard from the parapet, he commands HALT. All unbar, and resume their posts. Nos. 1 and 2 chock the rollers.

2. *Load by detail*—LOAD.

103. Nos. 1, 2, 3, and 4 lay down their handspikes.

No. 2 takes out the tompion and places it near the vent-cover.

No. 1 faces once and a half to his left; steps over the sponge and rammer; faces to the piece; takes the sponge with both hands, the backs down, the right hand three feet from the sponge-head, the left hand eighteen inches nearer to it; returns to the piece, placing the left foot on the rail of the chassis in line with the face of the piece, the right in the most convenient position; and rests the end of the sponge in the muzzle, the staff in the prolongation of the bore, supported by the right hand, the right arm extended, the left hand flat against the side of the thigh.

Remark. In order that Nos. 1 and 2 may load with facility without standing on the chassis, a banquette should be placed between the head of the chassis and the wall, or a platform attached to the head of the chassis.

No. 2 steps upon the rail on his side, and occupies a position on the left of the piece corresponding to that of No. 1 on its right. He seizes the staff with the left hand, back down, near to and outside of the hand of No. 1.

No. 3, as soon as the sponge is inserted in the bore, steps over the rammer and seizes the staff with both hands, as prescribed for the sponge; returns to his post; and stands ready to exchange with No. 1.

No. 4 takes the pass-box and goes to the rear for a cartridge; returns with it, and places himself, facing the piece, about eighteen inches to the rear and right of No. 2.

The gunner mounts upon the tongue of the chassis, placing the left foot about six inches from the rear transom of the gun carriage, and breaks well to the rear with the right foot, the toe to the right; closes the vent with the second finger of the left hand, bending well forward to cover himself by the breech; and turns the elevating screw with the right hand, so as to adjust the piece conveniently for loading.

104. In the mean time, Nos. 1 and 2 insert the sponge by the following motions, at the words ONE—TWO—THREE—FOUR—FIVE:

1st motion. They insert the sponge as far as the hand of No. 1, bodies erect, shoulders square.

2d motion. They slide the hands along the staff and seize it at arm's length.

3d motion. They force the sponge down as prescribed in the first motion.

4th motion. They repeat the second motion.

5th motion. They push the sponge to the bottom of the bore. No. 1 replaces the left hand on the staff, back up, six inches nearer to the muzzle than the right. No. 2 places the right hand, back up, between the hands of No. 1.

If in executing these motions, or the corresponding ones with the rammer, it be found that the sponge or rammer is at home at the third or fourth motion, then what is prescribed for the fifth motion will be performed at the third or fourth. The knee on the side towards which the body is to be inclined is always bent, the other straightened; and the weight of the body added, as much as possible, to the effort exerted by the arms.

3. SPONGE.

105. Nos. 1 and 2, pressing the sponge firmly against the bottom of the bore, turn it three times from right to left, and three times from left to right; replace the hands on the thighs, and withdraw the sponge by motions contrary to those prescribed for inserting it.

Remark. To handle the sponge when it is new and fits tight, it may become necessary for Nos. 1 and 2 to use both hands. In this case it will be inserted and withdrawn by short and quick motions.

No. 2 quits the staff, and turning towards No. 4, receives from him the cartridge, which he takes in both hands, backs down, and introduces into the bore bottom foremost, seams to the sides; he then grasps the rammer in the way prescribed for the sponge.

No. 1, rising upon the right leg and turning towards his left, passes the sponge above the rammer with the left hand to No. 3, and receiving the rammer with the right, presents it as prescribed for the sponge, except that he rests the rammer-head against the right side of the face of the piece.

No. 3, as soon as the sponge is withdrawn, passing the rammer under the sponge with the right hand, receives the sponge from No. 1 with the left, replaces it upon the prop, and resumes his post.

No. 4, setting down the pass-box, takes out the cartridge and presents it in both hands to No. 2, the choke to the front; returns the pass-box to its place; and picks up a ball, and afterwards a wad, should one be required.

Nos. 1 and 2 force down the cartridge by the motions prescribed for forcing down the sponge.

4. RAM.

106. Nos. 1 and 2, drawing the rammer out to the full extent of their arms, ram with a single stroke. No. 2 quits the staff, and turning towards No. 4, receives from him the ball and wad, while No. 1 throws out the rammer, and holds the head against the right side of the face of the piece. No. 2, receiving successively the ball and wad, introduces them into the bore, the ball first, and seizes the staff with the left hand. No. 4 then resumes his post.

Nos. 1 and 2 force down the ball and wad together by the same motions, and ram in the same manner as prescribed for the cartridge. No. 2 quits the rammer; sweeps, if necessary, the platform on his own side; passes the broom to No. 1, and resumes his post. No. 1 throws out the rammer, and places it upon the prop below the sponge; finishes the sweeping, and resumes his post.

The gunner pricks, leaving the priming-wire in the vent, and, if firing beyond point-blank range, adjusts the breech-sight to the distance.

5. BATTERY.

107. Nos. 1 and 2 unchock the rollers, and with Nos. 3 and 4, all facing towards the parapet, embar: Nos. 1 and 2

through the front spokes of the wheels, near the tire, under the manœuvring bolts; and Nos. 3 and 4 under the braces, near the manœuvring staples.

All being ready, the gunner commands HEAVE, and the piece is run into battery; the gunner following up the movement. As soon as the rollers touch the hurters, he commands HALT. All unbar, and Nos. 1, 2, 3, and 4 resume their post.

6. POINT.

108. No. 3 lays down his handspike; passes the hook of the lanyard through the eye of a tube from front to rear; and holds the handle of the lanyard with the right hand, the hook between the thumb and forefinger.

Nos. 1 and 4 go to the traverse wheels, and, facing towards the parapet, embar under the fork-bolts or under the wheels. No. 1, in passing from and to his post, moves on the outside of No. 3.

The gunner withdraws the priming-wire, and, aided by Nos. 1 and 4, gives the direction; causing the trail to be moved by commanding LEFT or RIGHT, tapping, at the same time, on the right side of the breech for No. 1 to move the chassis to the left, or on the left side for No. 4 to move it to the right.

He then places the centre point of the breech-sight accurately upon the chalk-mark on the base-ring, and by the elevating screw gives the proper elevation, rectifying the direction, if necessary.

The moment the piece is correctly pointed, he rises on the left leg, and gives the word READY, making a signal with both hands, at which Nos. 1 and 4 unbar, and resume their posts; takes the breech-sight with the left hand, and receiving the tube from No. 3, inserts it in the vent; dismounts from the tongue, and goes to the windward to observe the effect of the shot.

No. 3 drops the handle, allowing the lanyard to uncoil as he steps back to his post, holding it slightly stretched with the right hand, the cord passing between the fingers, back of the hand up, and breaks to the rear a full pace with the left foot, the left hand against the thigh.

At the word READY, Nos. 1 and 2 take the chocks, and, breaking off with the feet furthest from the parapet, stand ready to chock the rollers.

109. In directing the piece to be fired, the instructor will designate it by its number, as, for example:

7. *Number one*—FIRE.

No 3 gives a smart pull upon the lanyard.

Immediately after the discharge of the piece, Nos. 1 and 2 chock the rollers, and resume the erect position. No. 3 resumes the erect position, and rewinds the lanyard in St. Andrew's cross upon its handle, returning it, if dry, to the tube-pouch. The gunner, having observed the effect of the shot, returns to his post.

110. Whenever the piece is to be fired by a *lock*, *portfire*, or *slowmatch*, it will be done by No. 3, as prescribed for No. 4 in the instruction for field artillery.

111. To continue the exercise, the instructor resumes the series of commands, beginning with FROM BATTERY.

TO CHANGE POSTS.

112. To change posts, the instructor commands:

1. *Change posts.*
2. MARCH.
3. CALL OFF.

At the first command, the cannoneers lay down their handspikes; place their equipments on the parts of the carriage nearest to them, and face to their left.

At the second command, they step off, each advancing one post; No. 2 taking that of No. 1. Nos. 2 and 3 pass to the rear of the chassis; No. 2 on the outside of all the cannoneers. On arriving at their posts, they face to the piece, and equip themselves.

At the third command, they call off, according to the posts they are to occupy.

TO LOAD FOR ACTION.

113. The cannoneers having been sufficiently instructed in the details of the movements, the instructor commands:

Load for action—LOAD.

The piece is run from battery, loaded, run into battery, pointed, and prepared for firing, by the following commands from the gunner: FROM BATTERY—LOAD—IN BATTERY—POINT—READY.

At the command, or signal, from the instructor to commence firing, the gunner gives the command FIRE, and continues the action until the instructor directs the firing to cease.

TO CEASE FIRING.

114. To cause the firing to cease, the instructor commands:

CEASE FIRING.

Whether the cannoneers are loading *by detail* or *for action*, the piece is sponged out, and all resume their posts. If the cartridge has been inserted the loading will be completed, unless the instructor should otherwise direct.

TO SECURE PIECE AND REPLACE IMPLEMENTS.

115. To discontinue the exercise, the instructor having ordered the firing to cease, and caused the piece to be run into battery, gives the following commands:

1. SECURE PIECE.

No. 2 returns the tompion to the muzzle. The gunner puts on the vent-cover, which he receives from No. 2, and depresses the piece.

2. REPLACE IMPLEMENTS.

Nos. 1 and 2 replace the handspikes against the parapet, Nos. 3 and 4 passing theirs to them for that purpose. The gunner hangs the pouches upon the knob of the cascable.

TO LEAVE THE BATTERY.

116. The instructor forms the detachment in rear of the piece, and marches it from the battery as prescribed in No. 13.

TO SERVE THE PIECE WITH REDUCED NUMBERS.

Executed as in No. 35.

CHARGES, &c.

See tables in PART III.

WADS.
RAPIDITY OF FIRING.
PENETRATION OF SHOT.

See Nos. 38, 40, and 41.

LESSON X.

SERVICE OF AN 8-INCH SEA-COAST HOWITZER MOUNTED ON A BARBETTE CARRIAGE.

(PLATES X, XI, XII, AND XIII.)

Five men are necessary—one gunner and four other cannoneers.

117. The piece is in battery.

The implements, &c., and their arrangement, are the same as prescribed for the barbette gun in No. 97, substituting *haversack*—worn by No. 4 from the right shoulder to the left side—for *pass-box*.

The shells are at the magazine, or other safe position, and are brought, as required, to the place prescribed for the budge-barrel.

118. The instruction for this piece does not differ materially from that prescribed in LESSON IX.

It is loaded with a shell, which is attached to a sabot. The shell is brought up by No. 4, together with the cartridge, and is set home in the same manner as the ball, except that it is not rammed.

CHARGES, &c.

See tables in PART III

LESSON XI.

SERVICE OF A 10-INCH SEA-COAST HOWITZER MOUNTED ON A BARBETTE CARRIAGE.

(PLATES X, XI, XII, AND XIII.)

Seven men are necessary—one gunner and six other cannoneers.

119. The piece is in battery.

The implements, &c., with the addition of one handspike, and their arrangement, are the same as prescribed for the 8-inch sea-coast howitzer in No. 117.

120. The instruction for this piece varies but slightly from that prescribed in LESSON X.

The shell is brought up in the following manner:

No. 6 takes the handspike and goes for the shell, followed by No. 5. He passes the small end of the handspike through the ring of the shell-hooks, if the shell has ears, or through the loop of the rope handle; No. 5 holds the small end of the handspike with the right hand, No. 6 the butt end, No. 5 in front. They bring it up on the left of the piece, and place themselves parallel to the parapet, No. 5 behind No. 2. No. 5, stepping between the parapet and the face of the piece, gives his end of the handspike to No. 1, and places himself on the tongue or on the platform, opposite to the muzzle; No. 6 gives his end of the handspike to No. 2. Nos. 1 and 2 raise the shell until it is opposite to the muzzle, when No. 5, applying his hands under it, raises the sabot and inserts it in the muzzle. No. 2 withdraws the handspike and passes it to No. 6, who replaces it. No. 5 pushes the shell into the muzzle and returns to his post.

CHARGES, &c.

See tables in PART III.

LESSON XII.

SERVICE OF A GUN MOUNTED ON A CASEMATE CARRIAGE.

(PLATE XIV.)

Five men are necessary—one gunner and four other cannoneers.

121. The piece is in battery.

The implements, &c., are arranged as follows:

TRUCK HANDSPIKES.	One on each side of the carriage, leaning against the wall, in line with the cannoneers.
ELEVATING HANDSPIKES	One on each side of the carriage, leaning against the wall, behind Nos. 3 and 4.*
TRAVERSING HANDSPIKES	One on each side of the carriage, leaning against the wall, opposite to the end of the tongue.*
ROLLER HANDSPIKE.	Leaning against the wall, behind the gunner, or laid down in the alignment on his right.
SPONGE .... RAMMER...........	About one yard behind the cannoneers of the right, the sponge uppermost, the sponge and rammer-heads turned from the embrasure, inclined slightly from the piece, and supported upon a prop or block.

---

* These are *manœuvring* handspikes. With two pieces in one casemate, or where the pieces are not separated by piers, they may pe placed against the nearest wall, or laid down in the most convenient position.

PASS-BOX	Behind No. 4.
TUBE-POUCH	Containing friction tubes, and the lanyard wound in St. Andrew's cross upon its handle. Suspended from the knob of the cascable.
GUNNER'S POUCH	Containing the gunner's level, breech-sight, finger-stall, priming-wire, gimlet, vent-punch, chalk-line, and chalk. Suspended from the knob of the cascable.
CHOCKS	One on each side of the carriage, on the front transom of the chassis, handles outwards.
VENT-COVER	Covering the vent.
TOMPION	In the muzzle.
BROOM	Leaning against the scarp wall, on the left of the piece.
BUDGE-BARREL	Containing cartridges, at the safest and most convenient place in rear of the piece.

When several guns are served together, there will be only one gunner's level and two vent-punches to each battery, not exceeding six pieces. To the same battery there will be one *worm*, one *ladle*, and one *wrench*.

The balls are regularly piled against the wall, behind No. 2.

The wads are placed between the wall and the balls, partly resting on them.

122 The cannoneers having been marched to their posts, the instructor explains to them the names and uses of the implements, and the nomenclatures of the gun, its carriage, and the battery.

123. To cause the implements to be distributed, the instructor commands:

TAKE IMPLEMENTS.

The gunner mounts upon the tongue; takes off the vent-cover, handing it to No. 2 to place against the scarp; gives the tube-pouch to No. 3; and equips himself with his own pouch and the finger-stall, wearing the latter on the second finger of the left hand. With the assistance of No. 3 he levels the piece, and applies his level to ascertain the line of metal, which, with the assistance of No. 2, he marks with the chalk-line. (If the gun has permanent sights, this is only necessary for instruction, or for verifying the sight.) He then takes the roller handspike, and resumes his post. This handspike is held vertically with the right hand, the lower end upon the ground in line with the toes, the arm extended naturally.

No. 3 equips himself with the tube-pouch.

Nos. 1 and 2 take the truck handspikes with the hand furthest from the wall, and carry them to that side, holding them vertically, the lower end upon the ground in line with the toes, the arm extended naturally.

124. The instructor causes the service of the piece to be executed by the following commands:

1. FROM BATTERY.

The gunner embars in the left mortise of the roller.

Nos. 1 and 2, facing from the scarp wall, embar in the most convenient front mortises of the truck-wheels, the hand furthest from the carriage at the top of the handspike, the other hand eight inches lower.

Nos. 3 and 4 go to the assistance of Nos. 1 and 2, and, facing towards them, seize the handspikes with both hands between those of Nos. 1 and 2.

Nos. 1, 2, 3, and 4, in applying themselves to the carriage, either to run it from or to the battery, break to the rear with the foot nearest to the carriage.

All being ready, the gunner presses the roller under the rear transom of the gun carriage, by bearing down upon his handspike, and gives the command HEAVE.

Nos. 1, 2, 3, and 4 act together, and bear upon the handspikes until they are nearly down to the rails. The gunner then disengages the roller from under the transom by raising his handspike, and commands UNBAR. Nos. 1 and 2 let go the handspikes with the hand nearest to the carriage, and chock the wheels. Nos. 3 and 4 withdraw the handspikes and pass them to Nos. 1 and 2, who reinsert them in the front mortises.

The gunner again bearing down upon his handspike, gives the command HEAVE, and so on, until the face of the piece is about one yard from the wall, when, raising his handspike, he commands HALT, and shifts it into the right mortise of the roller; Nos. 1 and 2 chock the wheels, and replace their handspikes against the wall. All resume their posts.

2. *Load by detail*—LOAD.

125. Executed as in Nos. 103 and 104, with the following modification: No. 3 facing towards the scarp, embars under the breech, and maintains the piece in a convenient position for inserting the sponge, until he receives a signal from the gunner to unbar.

3. SPONGE.

126. Executed as in No. 105.

4. RAM.

127. Executed as in No. 106.

5. IN BATTERY.

128. Nos. 1 and 2 unchock the wheels, and, facing from the scarp wall, apply their hands to the front of the cheeks.

Nos. 3 and 4, facing towards the scarp wall, lay hold of the handles.

The gunner bears down carefully upon the roller handspike, and the piece is run into battery. As soon as the wheels touch the hurters, he commands HALT. Nos. 1, 2, 3, and 4 resume their posts.

6. POINT.

129. Nos. 1 and 4 take the traversing handspikes, and, facing towards the scarp wall, embar under the ends of the rear transom of the chassis. No. 1, in passing from and to his post, moves on the outside of No. 3.

When the elevation is given by the quoin, No. 2 takes an elevating handspike and embars upon the left cheek under the reinforce.

The gunner withdraws the priming-wire, and, aided by Nos. 1 and 4, gives the direction, as in No. 108.

He then applies the breech-sight if necessary, and points the piece; commanding LOWER, or RAISE, tapping, at the same time, on the upper side of the knob of the cascable with the left hand and drawing out the quoin with the right, in order to elevate, or tapping upwards on the lower side and shoving in the quoin, in order to depress the piece.

The moment the piece is correctly pointed, he rises on the left leg, and gives the word READY, making a signal with both hands, at which Nos. 1, 2, and 4 unbar, replace their handspikes, and resume their posts; takes the breech-sight with the left hand, the roller handspike with the right, and disposes himself to observe the effect of the shot.

If the elevation is given by a screw, No. 3 turns its handle by direction of the gunner.

No. 3, having passed the hook of the lanyard through the eye of a tube from front to rear, inserts it in the vent, and stretches the lanyard as in No. 108.

At the word READY, Nos. 1 and 2 take the chocks, and, breaking off with the feet furthest from the wall, stand ready to chock the wheels.

7. *Number one* (or the like)—FIRE.

130. Executed as in No. 109.

What is prescribed in No. 110 will apply to this piece.

131. To continue the exercise, the instructor resumes the series of commands, beginning with FROM BATTERY.

TO CHANGE POSTS.
TO LOAD FOR ACTION.
TO CEASE FIRING.
TO SECURE PIECE AND REPLACE IMPLEMENTS.

Executed as in Nos. 112, 113, 114, and 115.

TO LEAVE THE BATTERY.

132. The instructor forms the detachment in rear of the piece, and marches it from the battery as prescribed in No. 13.

133. *Remark.* The service of a gun mounted on a casemate carriage of the old pattern (which is without the eccentric roller) will require the following modification: The roller handspike is dispensed with, and the gunner, at the command FROM BATTERY, moves two paces to his right.

TO SERVE THE PIECE WITH REDUCED NUMBERS.

Executed as in No. 35.

CHARGES, &c.

134. The ordinary service charge of powder for heavy guns is *one-fourth* the weight of the shot. For firing double shot it is *one-sixth* that weight.

Range of a 42-pdr., at an elevation of 1° 30′, charge 10½ lbs.	860 yds.
Range of a 42-pdr., at an elevation of 5°, charge 10½ lbs...	1,955 "
Range of a 32-pdr., at an elevation of 1° 30′, charge 8 lbs..	800 "
Range of a 32-pdr., at an elevation of 5°, charge 8 lbs.....	1,922 "
Proof range of powder..................................	300 "
Greatest elevation the carriage admits....................	8°
Greatest depression the carriage admits...................	4°

See tables in PART III.

WADS.
RAPIDITY OF FIRING.
PENETRATION OF SHOT.

See Nos. 38, 40, and 41.

LESSON XIII.

SERVICE OF AN 8-INCH COLUMBIAD MOUNTED ON A CASEMATE CARRIAGE.

(PLATE XIV.)

Five men are necessary—one gunner and four other cannoneers.

135. The piece is in battery.

The implements, &c., and their arrangement, are the same as prescribed for the casemate gun in No. 121, substituting *haversack*—worn by No. 4 from the right shoulder to the left side—for *pass-box*.

The shells are at the magazine, or other safe position, and are brought, as required, to the place prescribed for the budge-barrel.

136. The instruction for this piece differs in no material respect from that prescribed in LESSON XII.

It is loaded with a shell, which is attached to a sabot. The shell is brought up by No. 4, together with the cartridge, and is set home in the same manner as the ball, except that it is not rammed.

CHARGES, &c.

137. Greatest charge of powder		10 lbs.
Charge of the shell filled with powder		2 lbs. 9 oz.
Bursting charge of the shell		1 lb.
Charge to blow out the fuze		4 oz.
Range at an angle of 1°, charge 10 lbs.,	axis of the piece 16 feet above the water.	919 yards.
Range at an angle of 5°, charge 10 lbs.,		1,813 "
Proof range of powder		300 "
Weight of the shell		50 lbs.

See tables in PART III.

LESSON XIV.

SERVICE OF A 24-PDR. HOWITZER MOUNTED ON A FLANK CASEMATE CARRIAGE.

(PLATES XV AND XVI.)

Three men are necessary—one gunner and two other cannoneers.

138. The piece is in battery.
The implements, &c., are arranged as follows:

ROLLER HANDSPIKE..	Leaning against the scarp wall, behind No. 2.
SPONGE AND RAMMER	Leaning against the scarp wall, behind No. 1, the rammer-head upon the ground.
HAVERSACK........	Suspended from the knob of the cascable.
TUBE-POUCH.......	Containing the finger-stall, priming-wire, friction tubes, and the lanyard wound in St. Andrew's cross upon its handle. Suspended from the knob of the cascable.
VENT-COVER.......	Covering the vent.
TOMPION..........	In the muzzle.
BROOM............	On the left of the piece.
BUDGE-BARREL.....	Containing cartridges, at the safest and most convenient place in rear of the piece.

The rounds of canister are arranged against the scarp wall, behind No. 2. The shells, if used, are at the magazine, or other safe position, and are brought, as required, to the place prescribed for the budge-barrel.

139. The cannoneers having been marched to their posts, the instructor explains to them the names and uses of the implements, and the nomenclatures of the howitzer, its carriage, and the battery.

140. To cause the implements to be distributed, the instructor commands:

TAKE IMPLEMENTS.

The gunner takes the priming-wire and finger-stall, wearing the latter on the second finger of the right hand; gives the tube-pouch to No. 1, and the haversack to No. 2; takes off the vent-cover and places it against the scarp wall outside of the canisters; seizes the roller handspike with the right hand, and resumes his post: holding the handspike vertically on the right side, its lower end in line with the toes, the arm extended naturally.

No. 1 equips himself with the tube-pouch.

No. 2 equips himself with the haversack, which he wears from the right shoulder to the left side.

141. The instructor causes the service of the piece to be executed by the following commands:

1. FROM BATTERY.

The gunner, embarring in the left mortise, presses the roller under the rear transom, and seizes the left handle with the left hand.

Nos. 1 and 2 lay hold of the manœuvring rings and handles.

All being ready, the gunner gives the command HEAVE, and the carriage is run to the rear until the face of the piece is about one yard from the wall, when, disengaging the roller, he commands HALT. All resume their posts.

2. *Load by detail*—LOAD.

142. The gunner places himself at the breech; breaks to the rear with the right foot; closes the vent with the second finger of the right hand, and manages the elevating screw with the left.

No. 1, seizing the sponge-staff at its middle, brings it across his body; plants the left foot opposite to the muzzle, close to the carriage, and breaks off with the right foot; at the same time throwing the sponge-staff into the left hand, back down, and extending both hands towards the ends of the staff so as to enter the rammer-head into the embrasure and bring the sponge opposite to the muzzle. He then inserts it, and presses it to the bottom of the chamber with three motions.

No. 2 goes for a cartridge, and returns to his post. If shells are used, he brings a shell at the same time.

3. SPONGE.

143. No. 1, using both hands, sponges the chamber carefully; withdraws the sponge, pressing it against the bottom of the bore; turns it over, stepping to his left for this purpose, and rests the rammer-head against the right side of the face of the piece.

No. 2 introduces the cartridge, bottom foremost, seams downwards No. 1 sets it home by three motions with the right hand.

4. RAM.

144. No. 1, drawing out the rammer to the full extent of his arm, rams once, and throws out the rammer, holding it as before, the rammer-head against the right side of the face of the piece.

No. 2 introduces the canister or shell, and resumes his post.

No. 1 sets the canister or shell home with care; throws out the rammer; replaces it, and resumes his post.

The gunner, rising upon the left leg, pricks, leaving the priming-wire in the vent, and resumes his post.

5. In battery.

145. All apply themselves to the carriage, as prescribed in No. 141, and ease the piece into battery. As soon as it touches the hurters, the gunner commands Halt. All resume their posts.

6. Point.

146. No. 1 makes ready a tube, as prescribed for No. 3 in No. 25.

No. 2 goes to the rear of the chassis, and, facing to the front, applies himself to it by hand, in order to traverse it.

The gunner withdraws the priming-wire, and, having pointed the piece, gives the word Ready, making a signal with both hands, at which No. 2 resumes his post; takes out the roller handspike, and resumes his post.

No. 1 steps to the vent and inserts the tube, holding the lanyard slightly stretched with the right hand, the cord passing between the fingers, back of the hand up, and breaks to his rear a full pace with the left foot, the left hand against the thigh.

7. *Number one* (or the like)—Fire.

147. No. 1 fires as prescribed for No. 3 in No. 26.

What is prescribed in No. 27 will apply to this piece, substituting No. 1 for No. 3.

148. To continue the exercise, the instructor resumes the series of commands, beginning with From battery.

TO CHANGE POSTS.
TO LOAD FOR ACTION.
TO CEASE FIRING.
TO SECURE PIECE AND REPLACE IMPLEMENTS.
TO LEAVE THE BATTERY.

Executed as in Nos. 112, 113, 114, 115, and 116.

CHARGES, &c.

149. Charge of powder	2 lbs.
Range at an angle of 0°, charge 2 lbs., shell	295 yds.
Range at an angle of 1°, charge 2 lbs., shell	516 "
Range at an angle of 5°, charge 2 lbs., shell	1,322 "
Range at an angle of 2°, charge 1¼ lb., spherical case, time 2″	600 "
Range at an angle of 5° 30′, charge 1½ lb., spherical case, time 4″	1,050 "
Range at an angle of 3° 30′, charge 2 lbs., spherical case, time 3″	880 "
Proof range of powder	300 "
Weight of the 24-pounder shell	17 lbs.
Weight of the round of canister	21 lbs.
Number of bullets in a round of canister	48

See tables in PART III.

LESSON XV.

SERVICE OF AN 8-INCH COLUMBIAD MOUNTED ON A COLUMBIAD CARRIAGE.

(PLATES XVII, XVIII, AND XIX.)

Five men are necessary—one gunner and four other cannoneers.

150. The piece is in battery.

The implements, &c., are arranged as follows:

TRUCK HANDSPIKES..	Two on each side of the carriage, laid on the rails, one in rear of each front truck-wheel, and one in rear of each rear truck-wheel.
MANŒUVRING HANDSPIKES.	One on each side of the carriage, laid on the ground in a line with the cannoneers, opposite to the traverse wheels, the small ends towards the parapet.
ELEVATING BAR	Laid across the ties at the junction of the braces, handle to the left.
SPONGE .... RAMMER	One yard behind the cannoneers of the right, the sponge uppermost, the sponge and rammer-heads turned from the parapet, inclined slightly from the piece, and supported upon a prop.
HAVERSACK	Suspended from the knob of the cascable.

TUBE-POUCH	Containing friction tubes, and the lanyard wound in St. Andrew's cross upon its handle. Suspended from the knob of the cascable.
GUNNER'S POUCH....	Containing the gunner's level, breech-sight, finger-stall, priming-wire, gunner's gimlet, vent-punch, chalk-line, and chalk. Suspended from the knob of the cascable.
CHOCKS	One on each side of the piece, laid on the front of the rails.
VENT-COVER	Covering the vent.
TOMPION	In the muzzle.
BROOM	Leaning against the parapet, to the left of the piece.
BUDGE-BARREL	Containing cartridges, at the safest and most convenient place in rear of the piece.

When several columbiads are served together, there will be only one gunner's level and two vent-punches to each battery, not exceeding six pieces. To the same battery there will be one *worm* and one *wrench*.

The shells are at the magazine, or other safe position, and are brought, as required, to the place prescribed for the budge-barrel.

151. The cannoneers having been marched to their posts, the instructor explains to them the names and uses of the implements, and the nomenclatures of the columbiad, its carriage, and the battery.

152. To cause the implements to be distributed, the instructor commands:

TAKE IMPLEMENTS.

The gunner steps to the knob of the cascable; takes off the vent-cover, handing it to No. 2 to place against the parapet, in rear of his post; gives the tube-pouch to No. 3, and the haversack to No. 4; equips himself with his own pouch and the finger-stall, wearing the latter on the second finger of the left hand; takes the elevating bar, and, stepping between the rails, levels the piece conveniently for loading; applies his level to verify the line of sight which is marked on the piece, marking it, if necessary, with the chalk-line, assisted by No. 2; and resumes his post, holding the elevating bar with the right hand.

No. 3 equips himself with the tube-pouch.

No. 4 equips himself with the haversack, which he wears from the right shoulder to the left side.

Nos. 1, 2, 3, and 4 take the truck handspikes with the hand furthest from the parapet, and carry them to that side, holding them vertically, the arm extended naturally.

153. The instructor causes the service of the piece to be executed by the following commands:

1. FROM BATTERY.

The gunner moves two paces to the right of his post.

Nos. 1, 2, 3, and 4, facing from the parapet, place the wrenches on the ends of the axletrees, the handspikes elevated about 30° to the rear, and at the word HEAVE by the gunner, bear down and throw the wheels into gear; Nos. 3 and 4 immediately after laying their handspikes on the platform in front of their posts.

Nos. 1 and 2, facing from the parapet, embar in the most convenient front mortises of the truck-wheels, the hand furthest from the carriage at the top of the handspike, the other hand eight inches lower.

Nos. 3 and 4 go to the assistance of Nos. 1 and 2, and,

facing towards them, seize the handspikes with both hands between those of Nos. 1 and 2.

Nos. 1, 2, 3, and 4, in applying themselves to the carriage, to run it from or to battery, break to the rear with the foot nearest to the carriage.

All being ready, the gunner gives the command HEAVE.

Nos. 1, 2, 3, and 4 act together, and bear upon the handspikes until they are nearly down to the rails, when the gunner commands UNBAR. Nos. 1 and 2 let go the handspikes with the hand nearest to the carriage, and chock the wheels. Nos. 3 and 4 withdraw the handspikes and pass them to Nos. 1 and 2, who reinsert them in the front mortises.

The gunner again gives the command HEAVE, and so on, until the face of the piece is about one yard from the parapet, when he commands HALT. Nos. 3 and 4 take their posts. Nos. 1 and 2 chock the wheels as before, unbar, and place the wrench of their handspikes on the ends of the axletree of the front wheels. At the command OUT OF GEAR by the gunner, they throw the wheels out of gear; lay their handspikes on the rails between the wheels, and take their posts.

2. *Load by detail*—LOAD.

154. Executed as in Nos. 103 and 104. The gunner, if necessary, adjusts the piece conveniently for loading before closing the vent. No. 4 brings up a shell together with the cartridge.

3. SPONGE.

155. Executed as in No. 105.

4. RAM.

156. Executed as in No. 106, except that the shell is set carefully home without being rammed.

5. IN BATTERY.

157. Nos. 1 and 2 unchock the wheels, and place the chocks on the ties.

Nos. 1, 2, 3, and 4, facing towards the parapet, apply the wrenches of their handspikes to the ends of the axletrees; Nos. 1 and 2 so as to throw the front wheels into gear, and Nos. 3 and 4 so as to throw the rear wheels out of gear.

The gunner commands HEAVE, when the front wheels are thrown into gear.

Should the carriage run too easily after it is in motion, the gunner will command REAR WHEELS OUT OF GEAR, when the rear wheels are thrown out of gear. Nos. 3 and 4 each take a chock and hold it in front of the rear wheels, ready to apply it under them if necessary.

When the head of the cheeks is about one foot from the end of the rails, the gunner commands CHOCK, when Nos. 3 and 4 chock the rear wheels. The wheels are unchocked, and the piece run gently into battery, by Nos. 3 and 4 throwing the rear wheels alternately out of and into gear. As soon as the head of the carriage touches the hurters, the gunner commands OUT OF GEAR, when the front wheels are thrown out of gear; also the rear wheels should they be in gear. Nos. 1, 2, 3, and 4 take their posts, and lay their handspikes on the platform just in front of them.

6. POINT.

158. No. 3 passes the hook of the lanyard through the eye of a tube from front to rear; holds the handle of the lanyard with the right hand, the hook between the thumb and forefinger, and stands ready to hand it to the gunner.

Nos. 1 and 2, passing outside of the other cannoneers, move to the rear of the chassis, and, each taking one of the manœuvring handspikes, embar with the bevelled end under the traverse wheels. For traversing large angles, Nos. 1, 2, 3, and 4 apply themselves by hand at the end of the chassis.

The gunner withdraws the priming-wire; inserts the pawl of the elevating machine in the proper notch by means of the elevating bar, and with the breech-sight gives the required elevation; No. 4 turning the handle of the screw according to his direction.

The moment the piece is correctly pointed he rises on the left leg, and gives the word READY, making a signal with both hands, at which Nos. 1 and 2 unbar, lay down the handspikes, and resume their posts; receives the tube from No. 3, which he inserts in the vent; dismounts from the chassis, and goes to the windward to observe the effect of the shot.

No. 3 stretches the lanyard as in No. 108.

7. *Number one* (or the like)—FIRE.

159. Executed as in No. 109.

What is prescribed in No. 110 will apply to this piece.

160. *Remark.* If the piece is to be fired at high angles, it is elevated in the following manner:

Nos. 1 and 2—the former carrying his traversing handspike with him—move to the muzzle; place the handspike in the bore; pass the bight of a trace-rope over it, and bear down slightly on the handspike to enable the gunner to free the pawl from the notch. The gunner draws the pawl back by its handle, and commands EASE AWAY. Nos. 1 and 2 holding the ends of the rope, ease down the breech steadily, until the gunner commands STEADY, when he inserts the pawl in the proper notch.

161. To continue the exercise, the instructor resumes the series of commands, beginning with FROM BATTERY.

TO CHANGE POSTS.
TO LOAD FOR ACTION.
TO CEASE FIRING.
TO SECURE PIECE AND REPLACE IMPLEMENTS.
TO LEAVE THE BATTERY.

Executed as in Nos. 112, 113, 114, 115, and 116.

CHARGES, &c.

See tables in PART III.

LESSON XVI.

SERVICE OF A 10-INCH COLUMBIAD MOUNTED ON A COLUMBIAD CARRIAGE.

(PLATES XVII, XVIII, AND XIX.)

Seven men are necessary—one gunner and six other cannoneers.

162. The piece is in battery.

The implements, &c., with the addition of one manœuvring handspike, and substituting *pass-box*—placed against the parapet, behind No. 2—for *haversack*, and their arrangement, are the same as prescribed for the 8-inch columbiad in No. 150.

163. The instruction for this piece differs but slightly from that prescribed in LESSON XV.

The shell is brought up and inserted as prescribed in No. 120.

CHARGES, &c.

See tables in PART III.

LESSON XVII.

SERVICE OF A GUN OR COLUMBIAD MOUNTED ON AN IRON CARRIAGE.

Five or seven men are necessary—one gunner and four or six cannoneers.

164. The piece is in battery.

The implements are arranged as follows:

TRUCK HANDSPIKES, *(Iron.)*	One on each side of the carriage, placed on their hooks.
MANŒUVRING HANDSPIKES, *(Wood.)*	One on each side of the carriage, laid on the ground to the rear, in a line with the cannoneers, the small ends toward the parapet.
SPONGE, RAMMER...	One yard behind the cannoneers of the right, the sponge uppermost; the sponge and rammer-heads turned from the parapet, inclined slightly from the piece, and supported upon a prop.
PASS-BOX..............	Against the parapet, outside of No. 2.
TUBE-POUCH.........	Containing friction tubes, and the lanyard wound in St. Andrew's cross upon its handle. Suspended from the knob of the cascable.
GUNNER'S POUCH....	Containing breech-sight, finger-stall, priming-wire, gunner's gimlet, and vent-punch. When the breech-sight has no fixed seat, there will be added a gunner's level, chalk-line, and chalk.

CHOCKS.............One on each hurter.

VENT-COVER..........Covering the vent.

TOMPION............In the muzzle.

BROOM............Leaning against the parapet, to the left of the piece.

BUDGE-BARREL.....Containing cartridges; at the safest and most convenient place in rear of the piece.

When several pieces are served together, there will be one gunner's level, one worm, one wrench, and two vent-punches to each battery of not exceeding six pieces.

The shells are at the magazine, or other safe position, and are brought as required to the place prescribed for the budge-barrel.

165. The cannoneers having been marched to their posts, the instructor explains to them the names and uses of the implements, and the nomenclatures of the piece, its carriage, and the battery.

166. To cause the implements to be distributed, the instructor commands:

TAKE IMPLEMENTS.

The gunner steps to the knob of the cascable, takes off the vent-cover, hands it to No. 2, to place against the parapet in rear of his post; gives the tube-pouch to No. 3; equips himself with his own pouch and finger-stall, wearing the latter on the second finger of the left hand; levels the piece conveniently for loading, and resumes his post.

No. 3. equips himself with the tube-pouch.

Nos. 3 and 4 take the truck handspikes with the hand furthest from the parapet, and carry them to that side, holding them vertically, wrench down, arm extended naturally.

167. The instructor causes the service of the piece to be executed by the following commands:

1. FROM BATTERY.

The gunner moves two paces to the right of his post; Nos. 3 and 4, facing towards the parapet, place the wrenches on the ends of the axletree, the small ends of the handspikes well to the rear, and, assisted by Nos. 1 and 2, facing to the rear, throw the wheels into gear at the command HEAVE, given by the gunner. The wheels are shown to be in or out of gear by the points on the ends of the axletree. Nos. 3 and 4 remove the wrenches from the axletree, and embar in the most convenient front mortises of the truck wheels, the hand nearest the carriage at the top of the handspike, the other hand eight inches lower. Nos. 1 and 2 go to the assistance of Nos. 3 and 4, and, facing towards them, seize the handspikes with both hands between those of Nos. 3 and 4.

Nos. 1, 2, 3, and 4, in executing the command FROM and IN BATTERY, break to the rear with the foot nearest the carriage.

All being ready, the gunner gives the command HEAVE.

Nos. 1, 2, 3, and 4 act together, and bear on the handspikes until they are nearly down to the rails, when the gunner commands UNBAR. Nos. 1 and 2 let go the handspikes, and chock the wheels. Nos. 3 and 4 then withdraw the handspikes, and reinsert them in the front mortises.

If the carriage is moved with great difficulty, the handspikes should be embarred in the rear mortises.

The gunner again gives the command HEAVE, which will be executed as before, and repeated until the face of the piece is about one yard from the parapet, when he commands HALT. Nos. 1 and 2 chock the wheels. Nos. 3 and 4 unbar, and place the wrenches of their handspikes on the axletree, the handspikes at right angles with the rail; and, assisted by Nos. 1 and 2, at the command OUT OF GEAR, given by the gunner, throw the wheels out of gear, by turning the handspikes to the rear. Nos. 3 and 4 then remove their handspikes, place them on their hooks, and all take their posts.

2. *Load by detail*—LOAD.

168. Executed as in Nos. 103 and 104. No. 4 brings the cartridge and shell. If Nos. 5 and 6 are at the piece, they bring up the shell.

3. SPONGE.

169. Executed as in No. 105.

4. RAM.

170. Executed as in No. 106, except that the shell is set carefully home without being rammed. With large rifle shells, No. 5 holding the fuze end and No. 6 the butt, pass to the left of the piece, and, stopping between the parapet and the face, No. 2 receives the butt of the projectile from No. 6, and, assisted by Nos. 1 and 5, insert it in the muzzle. Nos. 5 and 6 resume their posts. Large round shells are loaded as in No. 120.

Before running the piece into battery, it should be elevated at least 2° above the horizontal, to prevent the displacement of the projectile.

5. IN BATTERY.

171. Nos. 1 and 2 unchock the wheels, and place the chocks on the hurters. Nos. 3 and 4 apply the wrenches of their handspikes to the ends of the axletree, the small ends to the rear, and stand ready to throw the wheels into gear by turning the handspikes to the front. The gunner commands HEAVE, when the wheels are thrown into gear sufficient to run the carriage into battery without shock, the gunner, if necessary, giving the command OUT OF GEAR. Nos. 3 and 4 throw the wheels out of gear. Should the carriage not move when in gear, the gunner will direct No. 3 to remove his handspike, insert the small end in the mortise, and heave the carriage forward. As soon as the piece is in battery, Nos. 3 and 4 remove their handspikes, place them on their hooks, and resume their posts.

6. POINT.

172. No. 3 passes the hook of the lanyard through the eye of the tube, holds the handle of the lanyard with the right hand, the hook between the thumb and forefinger, and stands ready to hand it to the gunner.

Nos. 1 and 2, passing outside the other cannoneers, move to the rear of the chassis, and, each taking a manœuvring handspike, embar with the bevelled end under the traverse wheels. The gunner withdraws the priming-wire, gives the direction as in No. 108, and with the breech-sight gives the required elevation, No. 4 turning the handle of the screw according to his direction.

The moment the piece is correctly pointed, he rises on his left leg and gives the word READY, making at the same time a signal with both hands, at which Nos. 1 and 2 unbar, lay down the handspikes, and resume their posts. With six cannoneers, Nos. 5 and 6 take the handspikes, and, assisted by Nos. 1 and 2, give the direction. The piece being pointed, the gunner receives the tube from No. 3, which he inserts in the vent, dismounts from the chassis, and goes to the windward to observe the effect of the shot.

At the word READY, Nos. 1 and 2 take the chocks, and breaking off with the feet furthest from the parapet, stand ready to chock the rollers.

No. 3 stretches the lanyard as in No. 108.

7. FIRE.

173. Executed as in No. 109. Nos. 3 and 4 resume their handspikes.

174. The centre-pintle carriage requires six cannoneers and four manœuvring handspikes; and in pointing, Nos. 1 and 2, facing to the rear, embar with their handspikes under the front traverse wheels. The handspikes of Nos. 1 and 2, when not in use, are placed against the parapet near them. If there are mortises in the front traverse wheels, Nos. 1 and 2 will insert the truck handspikes in them to give the direction.

175. To continue the exercise, the instructor resumes the series of commands, beginning with FROM BATTERY.

TO CHANGE POSTS.
TO LOAD FOR ACTION.
TO CEASE FIRING.
TO SECURE PIECE AND REPLACE IMPLEMENTS.
TO LEAVE THE BATTERY.

Executed as in Nos. 112, 113, 114, 115, and 116.

CHARGES, &c.

See tables in PART III.

ARTICLE II.

FORMATION OF A COMPANY INTO DETACHMENTS FOR THE SERVICE OF A BATTERY OF SEVERAL PIECES.—SERVICE OF A BATTERY OF SEVERAL PIECES.

FORMATION OF A COMPANY INTO DETACHMENTS FOR THE SERVICE OF A BATTERY OF SEVERAL PIECES.

176. The company should be instructed in the school of the soldier and company as infantry, and all movements not herein prescribed will be executed as required by the Field Artillery Tactics.

When formed for artillery drill, the flank movements will be executed without doubling files.

177. The company, equipped with muskets, accoutrements, &c., unless the commanding officer otherwise directs, being formed in two ranks faced to the front, the non-commissioned officers in the rank of file-closers, is divided into the number of platoons corresponding to the number of pieces to be served. A platoon may comprise one or more detachments, and if more than one, is divided into as many complete detachments (see No. 4) as it will form; the remaining files, if any, are added to the left detachment of the platoon. The senior non-commissioned officers are posted as chiefs of pieces, and the junior ones as gunners.

178. The chief of piece is posted on the right of his platoon. The gunner one pace behind the right file of his detachment.

Two or more platoons form a section, commanded by a subaltern, and, if circumstances will permit, the company will have as many sections as there are subalterns to command them. The commanders of sections will be posted in line and in column of sections, two yards in the front and centre of their sections, and in column of platoons, two yards from the wheeling flanks of the leading platoons of their section. When the company is faced by a flank, the commander of the leading section will be by the side of the leading guide, the other section commanders remaining opposite the centre of their section.

In column of platoons the chiefs of pieces act as guides and commanders, and are on the right or left of their platoons, according as the guide may be right or left.

In column of sections, the right guide is the chief of piece of the right platoon, and the left guide is the gunner of the left detachment of the section. The gunner of the left detachment of the company is the left guide of the company, and will be posted on the left of the front rank.

179. To march the platoons to their pieces the commander wheels them into column or faces them by a flank to the right if he is to approach the battery on the left, and to the left if he is to approach the battery on the right.

180. When the company arrives at the left or right of the battery the commander orders:

PLATOONS, OPPOSITE YOUR PIECES.

As each platoon arrives in rear of its piece it is halted by its chief of piece, and wheeled into line or faced to the front, the centre of the first detachment on the line of the axis of the piece. The chiefs of sections place themselves one pace in front of the centre of their sections, the chiefs of pieces on the right of their platoons, and the gunners take their places in the front rank, as prescribed in No. 4.

The commander then orders:

CALL OFF.

Each chief of piece steps promptly to the front to see that the cannoneers call off properly, and then returns to his post.

181. The first detachment of platoons are then marched to their posts, as prescribed in No. 7. At the command TAKE IMPLEMENTS, the muskets are placed against the epaulment outside of the line of cannoneers or in some secure place, and resumed after the command REPLACE IMPLEMENTS. At the conclusion of the exercise, or to change the detachments, the detachments are formed in rear of their pieces, as prescribed in No. 13.

182. To reform the company the commander orders:

1. *Platoons, right (or left) face.*
2. *Close order,* MARCH.

At the first command the platoons face to the right, (or left,) the gunners taking their places in the rank of file-closers, and at the command MARCH, repeated by all the chiefs of pieces, excepting the leading one, who faces his platoon to the *front,* and dresses it to the right; each platoon closes on the one in front of it, is halted, faced to the front, and dressed towards the leading platoon by its chief.

SERVICE OF A BATTERY OF SEVERAL PIECES.

183. The pieces are numbered from right to left. In directing them to be fired, they are always designated by their numbers, as, *Number one*—FIRE; *Number two*—FIRE; &c.

When the wind comes from the right, the firing should commence on the left, and reciprocally.

184. In mortar batteries (which should not exceed three or four pieces) the cannoneers remain at their posts until the signal, or command, COMMENCE FIRING; all then move to the rear of the platform, except No. 3 of the mortar, which is to commence firing.

After having fired, each No. 3 joins his detachment, which remains in its position until all the pieces having been discharged, the signal, or command, TO YOUR POSTS, is given.

A similar precaution may be necessary to avoid the blast in a battery composed entirely of howitzers.

ARTICLE III.

POINTING GUNS AND HOWITZERS.
POINTING MORTARS.
TABLE OF TANGENT AND TANGENT SCALES.
RICOCHET FIRING.
FIRING HOT SHOT.
NIGHT FIRING.
PLATFORMS.

POINTING GUNS AND HOWITZERS.

(PLATE V.)

185. The *dispart* of a piece is the difference between the semi-diameters of the base-ring and swell of the muzzle; or, it is the tangent of the angle which the line of metal makes with the axis, the radius being the distance between the rear of the base-ring and the highest point of the swell of the muzzle.

186. The *line of metal,* called also the *natural line of sight,* is the right line passing through the highest points of the base-ring and swell of the muzzle.

187. In ordinary practice there is but one case where the object is struck by directing the line of metal upon it. The firing in this case is called *point-blank firing,* and the range the *point-blank range.*

A knowledge of this range, which must be ascertained by experiment, is essential to accuracy in pointing; it increases with the calibre, charge, and dispart.

For all ranges less than the point-blank range, the line of metal must be aimed under the object; and for all distances greater than the point-blank range, it must be aimed over it.

188. To point the gun when the line of metal passes over the object, the gunner's quadrant, or a breech-sight, (tangent-scale,) becomes necessary. The use of these instruments supposes that the distance of the object, and the degree of elevation necessary to reach it, are both known.

189. *To point with the quadrant.* The gun is aimed at the object by the line of metal; the quadrant is then applied either by its longer branch to the face of the piece, or this branch is run into the bore parallel with the axis, and the elevating screw turned, or the quoin adjusted, until the required degree is indicated.

190. *To point with the breech-sight.* The sight is set to correspond with the distance; it is then applied to the highest point of metal on the base-ring, and by the elevating screw, or quoin, the notch of the breech-sight, the highest point on the swell of the muzzle, and the object, are brought in the same line.

191. In the absence of a breech-sight, or quadrant, the gunner may point his gun by placing one or more fingers of the left hand upon the base-ring perpendicularly to the axis, and using them as a breech-sight.

192. The theory of pointing is based upon the supposition that the trajectory of the ball lies in the vertical plane passed through the line of metal, and that this plane includes the centre of the object; but as in practice there are circumstances (as, for instance, a strong wind blowing across the field of fire) which will cause the ball to deviate from this plane, it follows that to strike the object in such a case, the line of metal must be directed to its right or left; the gunner judging of this distance by observing the striking of the shot.

193. The line of metal can be correctly ascertained only by the use of instruments. The instrument generally used for this purpose is the gunner's level. Being properly applied to the base-ring and to the swell of the muzzle or muzzle-band, their highest points are indicated by the style; these points are marked with chalk.

194. In batteries for garrison and sea-coast defence, where the platforms are fixed, the line of metal may be considered as nearly permanent; but with siege guns which are mounted on travelling carriages, the wheels of which are liable to vary in position from unevenness of ground, or unequal settling in newly constructed platforms, this line is constantly changing. It approximates the higher wheel in proportion to the difference of level between the wheels; and hence, to secure the greatest accuracy of fire, it must be frequently verified; the old marks, if not found correct, should be erased and new ones substituted.

195. To point a gun, then, is to give it such a direction and elevation, or depression, that the shot may strike the object; and the general rule is: First give the direction, and then the elevation or depression.

196. The direction is given by directing the line of metal upon the object. The elevation, or depression, which depends upon the charge, the distance, and the position of the object above or below the battery, must be ascertained from tables or by experiment, and the proper degree given by means of instruments.

197. When the elevation or depression has once been ascertained for any given distance, the firing at that distance may be facilitated by noting some point on the elevating screw, or quoin, adjusting some fixed measurement from a point on the stock to another point on the under side of the breech, or by a chalk mark drawn across the face of a trunnion and its corresponding cheek.

198. When, from the nearness of the object, the line of metal must be so depressed as to fall below it, an attentive observance of the striking of the shot, and of the remarkable points of the intervening ground, may furnish the gunner an object to aim at; and even when firing beyond point-blank range, some fixed object may often present itself which will serve as a point upon which to direct the line of metal. Indeed, in every case the gunner must be governed to a very considerable extent by the striking of his shot; but he should

neglect no means that may tend to secure accuracy of aim; for the shot that is thrown away by carelessness in pointing had better not be thrown at all.

199. *Remark.* The 42-pdr. and 32-pdr. sea-coast guns have no natural line of sight, as the swell of the muzzle is not visible when the eye is on a level with the base-ring. The inclination of the reinforce varies with different pieces in service; and as in some guns it is as great as 3°, the gun aimed by the line of metal would give a range of thirteen hundred yards before striking on a horizontal plane. In practice the shot would probably pass over an object at a less distance, as it would be difficult to get the men to depress sufficiently. These pieces should have a sight attached to the muzzle or neck, and the line of sight thus made parallel to the axis. The necessary elevation may be given with a breech-sight, (tangent-scale,) or the elevating screw, or the quoin, should be marked to indicate the elevation of the bore.

POINTING MORTARS.

(PLATE V.)

200. In pointing mortars the elevation is first given and then the direction.

201. The elevation, which is usually that of the greatest range of projectiles in *vacuo,* viz: 45°, is determined by applying the quadrant to the face of the piece, and adjusting the quoin until that number of degrees is indicated.

202. The charge of powder is varied to suit the required range.

To give the shell for the same range a greater velocity in the descending branch of its trajectory, the mortar is sometimes fired at an angle of 60°; in which case the charge of powder must be increased accordingly.

203. As mortars are usually masked from the object to be bombarded by an epaulment or parapet, different means from those which are used with guns and howitzers become necessary for giving them their direction.

There are several means proposed, all of which, however, are reduced to determining practically two fixed points which shall be in line with the piece and the object, and sufficiently near to be readily distinguished by the eye. These points being covered by the plummet, determine a vertical plane, which, when including the line of metal, becomes the plane of fire.

Premising that the platform is so laid that its axis will be nearly in the plane of fire, and that the line of metal is ascertained by the gunner's level and marked with chalk, the simplest manner of directing the mortar is by means of *pointing-wires.*

204. The two fixed points required are determined by planting two wires upon the epaulment, one upon its crest, and the other about a yard in advance of it, both as nearly as possible in the vertical plane passing through the axis of the platform and the object.

The points being thus established, the direction is given to the mortar by causing a plummet held in rear of it to cover the wires and the line of metal. This method is, however, defective, not only in accuracy of aim, but because of the liability of the wires to be deranged by the shots of the enemy, or by other causes.

205. A better method is by means of *pointing-stakes,* to establish one of the fixed points upon the crest of the parapet, and another in rear of the piece. Then by a cord, called the *pointing-cord,* stretched between these two points, with the plummet suspended from it, a vertical plane is determined with which the line of metal is made to coincide.

To fix the points, a stake, a foot or more in length, is driven firmly into the crest of the epaulment as nearly as practicable in the vertical plane passing through the axis of the platform; sighting by this stake, another long one is planted three or four feet in front of it in line with the object. To this stake the cord is temporarily attached, and stretched by the first stake, just grazing it, to a point on the ground one yard in rear of the platform. At this point a third stake is driven. The *pointing-board** is laid on the ground at the foot of the stake. The cord is removed from the second stake, which may now be taken away, and permanently attached to the first.

To direct the mortar, the cord is stretched to the top of the stake by the left hand, while the plummet is suspended against it by the right, or, the plummet may be attached to the cord just in rear of the mortar.

It is evident that when the cord, the plummet, and the line of metal are in the same plane, the mortar is properly directed.

In case the shell should, nevertheless, strike constantly to the right or left of the object, the pointing-cord is shifted to some notch on the pointing-board to the right or left, until the shell falls at the desired point.

206. Another mode of planting the stakes is as follows: The mortar being placed upon the middle of the platform, the gunner mounts upon it and suspends the plummet in front of the muzzle, covering the object. Where the plummet, thus suspended, cuts the crest of the epaulment, the first stake is driven. A second stake is then driven in the same line between the mortar and the epaulment. The pointing-cord being attached to the first stake, and stretched to the rear over the point where the plummet touches the top of the mortar, determines the point on the ground at which the rear stake is driven.

---

*This is a piece of wood one foot long, two or three inches wide, and one inch thick, having a notch cut in the middle of one side to fit on the stake, and which is graduated into equal divisions from its middle. It serves to wind the pointing-cord on when not in use.

207. *Table of tangents and tangent-scales.*

TANGENTS—RADIUS UNITY.			TANGENT-SCALES FOR THE 24-PDR. GUN AND 8-IN. SIEGE HOWITZER.	
			Tangents.	
Degrees.	Minutes.	Tangents.	24-pounder.	8-inch howitzer.
1	00	.01745	....	Natural angle of sight.
	30	.02618	Natural angle of sight.	0.45 inches.
2	00	.03492	0.97 inches.	0.90 "
	30	.04366	1.94 "	1.35 "
3	00	.05240	2.91 "	1.80 "
	30	.06116	3.88 "	2.25 "
4	00	.06992	4.85 "	2.70 "
	30	.07870	5.82 "	3.15 "
5	00	.08748	6.79 "	3.60 "
	30	.09628	7.76 "	4.05 "
6	00	.10510	8.76 "	4.50 "
	30	.11393	....	4.96 "
7	00	.12278	....	5.42 "
	30	.13165	....	5.88 "
8	00	.14054	....	6.34 "
	30	.14945	....	6.80 "
9	00	.15838	....	7.26 "
	30	.16734	....	7.72 "
10	00	.17632	....	8.18 "

RICOCHET FIRING.

208. The theory of projectiles in *vacuo* proves that the angle of fall is equal to the angle of elevation; but in air the angle of fall is somewhat the larger.

209. It is known by experiment that the projectile which falls upon the ground of ordinary firmness, at an angle not greater than ten degrees, or upon water at four or five degrees, will generally make one or more bounds. In this case the projectile is said to *ricochet*.

210. The object of ricochet firing is generally to enfilade a face of the enemy's work; which is effected by causing a projectile to bound along the terreplein of the face with the view of annoying his cannoneers and dismounting his pieces.

The object to be fired at in this case is usually some point of the interior crest of the parapet which covers a flank of the terreplein to be reached.

211. The point of the terreplein which is first struck by the projectile, after having grazed the interior crest, is called the *point of fall*.

212. The *angle of fall* is the angle made at the point of fall by the tangent to the trajectory with a horizontal line in the plane of fire.

213. The charge and elevation depend upon the distance of the object from the battery; upon the difference of level between these points; the distance of the desired point of fall from the parapet; the height of the parapet, &c. These having been determined, if the embrasure through which the piece is fired is so constructed as to allow the line of metal to be directed upon the object, the piece is pointed in the manner already prescribed.

But if the embrasure is such that the object is masked, the direction must be given, as with the mortar, by the plummet. This is held by the person who points in such a manner as to cover both the line of metal and the object. The elevation is then given by the quadrant.

214. In ricochet firing against troops, the angle of elevation ought seldom to exceed three degrees above the surface of the ground occupied by the troops. Against fortresses, forts, and fortified lines, this angle will be found to vary from three to six and nine degrees above the horizontal.

215. A ricochet battery will not probably be very effective if established at a greater distance from the object than six hundred yards. The projectile should be made to graze the parapet while in the descending branch of the trajectory; and this must be effected by regulating the charges and elevating or depressing the piece until the shot is seen to fall just over the interior crest of the parapet. Light charges are generally used, varying from *two-thirds* to *one-eighth* of the ordinary charge.

216. Rules for enfilade firing must, however, be deduced from experiments. As our service is deficient in this respect, a few data are here given from that of the French. In their application to our artillery they can only be relied upon as approximative; serving merely as guides to facilitate our obtaining more accurate results.

CHARGES.

217. Charges for a *flattened ricochet* for siege guns at an angle of about 3°.

Distance.	Elevation.	Charge.	Remarks.
660 yards	2° 45′	$\frac{1}{12}$ weight of ball..	
550 yards	3°	$\frac{1}{15}$......do.......	
440 yards	3° 15′	$\frac{1}{20}$......do.......	
330 yards	3° 35′	$\frac{1}{30}$......do.......	
220 yards	3° 35′	$\frac{1}{40}$......do.......	

218. Charges for a *flattened ricochet* for siege howitzers at an angle of about 3°.

Distance.	Elevation.	Charge.	Remarks.
550 yards	1° 45′	3 lbs	
440 yards	2° 15′	2 lbs. 3 oz........	
330 yards	2° 15′	1 lb. 12 oz........	
220 yards	2° 45′	1 lb. 2 oz..........	

219. Charges for a *curvated ricochet* for a siege howitzer at an angle of about 10°.

Distance.	Elevation.	Charge.	Remarks.
550 yards	7° 30′	1 lb. 4 oz..........	The height of the object above the level of the battery being supposed to be 20 ft.
440 yards	7° 30′	1 lb. 1 oz..........	
330 yards	7° 30′	14 oz	
220 yards	7° 30′	10 oz	

FIRING HOT SHOT.

(PLATE VI.)

220. The use of hot shot for setting fire to ships, buildings, &c., renders some modifications in the service of the piece necessary. For the heavier calibres the detachment consists of seven men.

221. The additional implements required are placed as follows:

2 POKERS	For stirring the fire.	At the furnace.
2 IRON FORKS	For taking out the shot.	
1 RASP	For cleaning over-heated shot.	
1 STAND	For cleaning shot on.	
1 PAIR OF TONGS	For handling shot.	
1 IRON RAKE	For removing cinders from the ash pit.	
1 TROUGH............	For cooling the tongs, &c.	
1 LADLE	For carrying hot shot.	
1 TUB	For soaking wads. Behind No. 2.	
1 BUCKET............	Near and outside of the rammer-head.	
1 LADLE	For carrying hot shot. Leaning against the epaulment near the pass-box.	
1 WORM	With the sponge and rammer.	

When clay wads are used, the rammer has a circular iron plate upon its head to remove clay from the sides of the bore.

222. The cartridge bags are made of woollen stuff, and the cartridge is inserted, choke foremost, in a cartridge bag of the next higher calibre, and the end folded under. The bags should be examined carefully; and too great care cannot be taken to prevent the powder from spilling or sifting in the bore.

223. The wads are made of clay or hay. Clay wads should consist of pure clay, or fuller's earth, free from sand or gravel, well kneaded with just enough moisture to work well. They are cylindrical and one calibre in length.

Hay wads should remain in the tub to soak at least ten or fifteen minutes. Before being used the water is pressed out of them.

When hay wads are used vapor may be seen escaping from the vent on the insertion of the ball; but as this is only the effect of the heat of the ball on the water contained in the wad, no danger need be apprehended from it.

224. With proper precautions in loading, the ball may be permitted to cool in the gun without igniting the charge. The

piece, however, should be fired with as little delay as possible, as the vapor would diminish the strength of the powder.

TO LOAD WITH HOT SHOT.

225. The piece should be sponged with great care, and the worm frequently passed into the bore. As a precaution it is well to insert a wet sponge just before putting in the ball.

The muzzle being sufficiently elevated to allow the ball to roll down the bore, the cartridge is inserted, the mouth of the outer bag foremost, the fold down, and carefully pushed home without breaking it; a dry hay wad is placed upon it and rammed once; then a clay or wet hay wad and rammed twice; and finally, if firing at angles of depression, a wad of clay a half calibre in length, or a wet hay wad, is put on the ball.

226. At the command LOAD, No. 6, accompanied by No. 5, takes the ladle and goes to the furnace for a shot. In carrying the shot No. 5 is in advance, holding his handle of the ladle with the right hand. On approaching the piece, they halt, if necessary, near the post of the gunner, until the wads are set home; they then advance and place themselves behind No. 2, on a line parallel to the epaulment.

No. 1 throws out the rammer and allows it to rest upon the epaulment, or on the sole of the embrasure.

No. 5, stepping between the epaulment and the face of the piece, gives his handle of the ladle to No. 1, and No. 6 gives his handle to No. 2.

Nos. 1 and 2 put the shot in the bore; Nos. 5 and 6 take the ladle and go to the furnace for another shot; No. 1 seizes the rammer; and the service of the piece is continued as heretofore prescribed.

227. In the exercise for instruction, a sawdust cartridge enveloped in another as above described, with the wads and hot shot, should always be put into the gun.

228. When the instructor directs the piece to be unloaded, Nos. 1 and 2 stand ready with the ladle to receive the shot; the gunner depresses the muzzle until the shot rolls out. Nos. 5 and 6 return it to the furnace; and No. 1 draws out the wads and cartridge with the worm.

CHARGES, &c.

229. Small charges should be used in hot shot firing, varying from *one-fourth* to *one-sixth* of the weight of the ball. Balls fired with small velocities split the wood in a manner which is favorable to its burning; with a great velocity the hole closes, the ball sinks deep, and, deprived of air, it chars without setting fire to the surrounding wood.

Hot shot should not penetrate deeper than ten or twelve inches. They do not set fire to the wood until some time after their penetration. They retain sufficient heat to ignite wood after having made several ricochets upon water, though a total immersion of four or five seconds will deprive them of this property.

FURNACES FOR HEATING SHOT.

230. Furnaces for heating shot are erected at the forts on the sea-coast. These furnaces hold sixty or more shot. The shot being placed, and the furnace cold, it requires one hour and fifteen minutes to heat them to a red heat; but after the furnace is once heated, a 24-pounder shot is brought to a red heat in twenty-five minutes; the 32-pounder and 42-pounder shot require a few minutes longer. Three men are required to attend the furnace; one takes out the hot shot and places them on the stand to be scraped; another scrapes them and puts them in the ladle; and the third supplies cold shot and fuel.

GRATES FOR HEATING SHOT.

231. In siege or other batteries, where there are no furnaces, a grate is used for heating shot. This grate consists of four bars 1.75 inch square, three feet long, placed four inches apart on three iron stands one foot in height. It is placed in an excavation one foot in depth, of the width of the grate, perpendicular at the back and side, open in front, the legs resting on bricks or stones rising about four or five inches from the bottom. A roof is made over it with hoops of flat iron covered with sods and eighteen inches of earth, having in the back part a chimney six inches square.

The shot are placed on the back part of the grate, leaving one-fourth of its front part free, and under and on the front part the wood is put, cut in pieces about fourteen inches long and two inches thick. A thick sod is used as a register to regulate the draught of the chimney, so that no flame can issue from the front. This grate, which will contain about fifteen 24-pounder balls, heats them to a red heat in an hour, and will supply three guns. It requires the attendance of one man.

232. Expansion of shot heated to a white heat:

Calibre.	8-inch.	42-pdr.	32-pdr.	24-pdr.	18-pdr.	12-pdr.
Expansion	*In.* .149	*In.* .11	*In.* .10	*In.* .08	*In.* .06	*In.* .04

Heated shot do not return to their original dimensions on cooling, but retain a permanent enlargement.

233. For calibres below the 24-pounder a ladle with a single handle is used, and only one additional man is required to serve shot.

NIGHT FIRING.

234. When a fixed object is to be fired at by night the piece should be directed during the day, and two narrow and well-dressed strips of wood laid on the inside of the wheels, and two others outside of the trail, of a siege carriage, and nailed or screwed to the platform.

The traverse wheels of a barbette carriage are chocked in the proper position.

235. To preserve the elevation, measure the height of the elevating screw above its box, or take the measure between

two points, one on the gun, the other on the stock; cut a stick to this length and adjust the gun on it at each fire.

236. Night firing with *guns* should be limited to a small number of rounds, as it consumes ammunition to little advantage.

237. For mortars, the direction is preserved by nailing or screwing two boards to the platform outside of the cheeks. The elevation is marked on the quoin, or the quoin may be nailed in the proper position.

PLATFORMS.

238. To insure accuracy of fire with heavy guns and mortars, it is absolutely necessary to have solid and substantial platforms.

239. For casemate and barbette batteries in fortifications, fixed platforms are constructed with the works.

240. Platforms for siege pieces are constructed at the arsenals, and should accompany every piece. As these move with the army it is desirable to have them as light as is compatible with sufficient strength to endure the shock of firing.

The platforms for guns, howitzers, and mortars, hereafter described, combine, in a high degree, the essential qualities of strength and portability. All the pieces composing them are of the same dimensions; and as the weight of each piece is only fifty pounds, an infantry soldier can carry one from the depot to the batteries, or any moderate distance, in addition to his arms and equipments.

Another platform for mortars is described, which is very simple, strong, and well suited to positions where trees or timber can be easily procured. This is designated the *rail-platform*.

PLATFORM FOR A SIEGE GUN OR HOWITZER.

(PLATE XX.)

241. To lay this platform, establish the centre line of the embrasure, and stretch a cord on this line from the middle of the embrasure to the rear. This is the *directrix* of the platform.

Lay the two outside sleepers parallel to this directrix, their outside edges being fifty-four inches distant from it. The four other sleepers are laid parallel to these, the edge of each fifteen and a half inches from the edge of the next. The upper service of the front ends of these sleepers to be fifty inches, on a vertical line, below the sole of the embrasure.

They are laid with an elevation to the rear of one and a half inches to the yard, or four and a half inches in their whole length. This elevation may be determined by placing a block four and a half inches high on the front end of the sleeper, and laying a straight edge, with a gunner's level on it, from this block to the rear end, then so arrange the earth as to bring the level true in this position.

The next set of sleepers are laid against and inside of the first, overlapping them three feet, having the rear ends inclined outwards, so that the outer edges of the exterior ones shall each be fifty-four inches from the directrix, and the spaces between the rear edges of the others the same as in the first set, viz: fifteen and a half inches from the edge of one to the edge of the next, all having the elevation to the rear of one and a half inches to the yard, and perfectly level across. The earth is then rammed firmly around these sleepers, and made even with their upper surface. The first deck plank, with a hole through each end for the eye-bolts, is laid in place, perpendicular to the directrix, its holes corresponding with those in the sleepers. The hurter is placed on it, and the bolts driven through the corresponding holes in these pieces.

The hurter should be so placed as to prevent the wheels from striking against the epaulment when the piece is in battery. If the interior slope has a base of two-sevenths of its height the inner edge of the hurter should be two and a half inches from the foot of the slope. The other planks are then laid, each one forced against the preceding, the last plank having holes for the rear eye-bolts. By drawing out or driving in the outside sleepers the holes through their rear ends are made to correspond with those in the last deck plank, and the bolts are put in.

Drive stakes in rear of each sleeper, leaving their tops level with the upper surface of the platform. Raise, ram, and level the earth in rear of the platform, so as to have a plain hard surface to support the trail when the recoil is great.

The earth should be raised nearly as high as the platform at the sides, and well rammed, giving it a slight inclination outwards to allow the water to run off.

PLATFORM FOR A MORTAR.

(PLATE XXI.)

242. The mortar platform is composed of only half the number of sleepers and deck planks required for the gun or howitzer platform. It is laid level, and the front and rear deck planks are connected by eye-bolts to every sleeper.

THE RAIL-PLATFORM.

(PLATE XXI.)

243. The rail-platform for siege mortars, composed of three sleepers and two rails for the cheeks of the mortar bed to slide on instead of the deck planks, is very strong, and easily constructed and laid.

The pieces being notched to fit are driven together at the battery, the rails being twenty-five and a half inches apart from centre to centre for the 10-inch mortar, and twelve and three-fourths inches for the 8-inch mortar.

The earth is excavated eight and a half inches, the depth of the sleepers, and the bottom made perfectly level. The directrix being exactly marked by stakes, the platform is placed in position, its centre line coinciding with a cord stretched between the stakes marking the line of fire. The earth is filled in as high as the upper surface of the sleepers and firmly rammed, and stakes are driven in the rear angles formed by the sleepers and rails, and one at the rear end of each rail.

THE RICOCHET PLATFORM.

244. To lay this platform, place the hurter perpendicular to the line of fire, and secure it by four stakes, one at each end and two in front, thirty-one and a half inches from the middle towards each end; lay the three sleepers parallel to the hurter, the first sixteen inches from the rear edge of the hurter, the second forty-three and a half inches from the rear edge of the first, and the third forty-three and a half inches from the rear edge of the second. Lay the plank thirty-one and a half inches from the directrix of the platform to the centre of the plank. Place the piece of plank sixty inches from the rear edge of the last sleeper, and bed it in the ground. Place on the last sleeper and this piece of plank *the* plank, (eighty-four inches long,) its front end one hundred and six inches from the rear edge of the hurter.

This platform will bear firing with charges as high as three pounds.

Platforms of this kind of larger dimensions may be used for guns and howitzers in firing at a fixed object with full charges.

245. Dimensions, &c., of siege platforms.

NAMES OF PIECES.	GUNS & HOWITZERS.					MORTARS.					Kind of timber used.
	No. of pieces.	Length.	Width.	Thickness.	Weight.	No. of pieces.	Length.	Width.	Thickness.	Weight.	
		In.	*In.*	*In.*	*lbs.*		*In.*	*In.*	*In.*	*lbs.*	
Hurter...............	1	108	5	3.5	51	..	....	....	....	....	Yellow pine.
Sleepers	12	108	5	3.5	608	6	96	5	3.5	230	Yellow pine.
Deck planks	36	108	5	3.5	1854	18	108	5	3.5	927	Yellow pine.
Stakes, (securing).....	6	48	3.5	2	70	6	48	3.5	2	70	Yellow pine.
Stakes, (implements) .	4	32	2	1	10	..	....	....	....	....	Yellow pine.
Stakes, (pointing).....	..	....	....	....	....	4	48	1	1	....	Yellow pine.
Eye-bolts, (iron)......	4	14	.75	r'nd	....	12	11	.75	r'nd	....	....

246. Dimensions, &c., of the rail-platform.

NAMES OF PIECES.	SIEGE MORTARS.					Kind of timber used.
	No. of pieces.	Length.	Width.	Thickness.	Weight.	
		In.	*In.*	*In.*	*lbs.*	
Sleepers....................	3	60	11.5	3.5	......	Yellow pine.
Rails	2	84	10	10	......	Yellow pine.
Stakes, (securing)..........	14	48	3.5	3	......	Yellow pine.
Platform complete..........	......	......	......	......	816	Yellow pine.

247. Dimensions, &c., of the ricochet platform.

NAMES OF PIECES.	No. of pieces.	Length.	Width.	Thickness.	Weight.	Kind of timber used.
		In.	*In.*	*In.*	*lbs.*	
Hurter	1	96	8	8	174	Yellow pine.
Sleepers	3	108	5.5	5.5	147	Yellow pine.
Planks	2	128	13	2.25	166	Beech, yellow pine, or oak.
Plank	1	84	13	2.25	60	Beech, yellow pine, or oak.
Pieces of plank	1	30	13	2.25	21	Beech, yellow pine, or oak.
Stakes	18	48	1.25	1.25	32	Hickory or oak.
Total weight	..	....	....	....	600	

PART II.

MECHANICAL MANŒUVRES.

ARTICLE I.

GENERAL DIRECTIONS.

(PLATES XXII AND XXIII.)

248. The MECHANICAL MANŒUVRES are the simplest application of the mechanical powers for mounting, dismounting, moving, and transporting heavy artillery.

249. The implements generally used for the execution of the manœuvres with siege pieces are:

SIX HANDSPIKES.
TWO LONG ROLLERS.
THREE SHORT ROLLERS.
TWO HALF ROLLERS.
SIXTEEN BLOCKS.
SIX HALF BLOCKS.
TWO QUARTER BLOCKS.
SIX GUN CHOCKS.
SIX WHEEL CHOCKS.
SIX ROLLER CHOCKS.
TWO SKIDS.
ONE SHIFTING-PLANK.
ONE TRACE-ROPE.
TWO TRUNNION-LOOPS.
ONE HAMMER-WRENCH.

250. The detachment for mechanical manœuvres consists of a non-commissioned officer and eleven men. It is formed by

adding four men—numbered 7, 8, 9, and 10—to the ordinary detachment for serving a siege piece.

The non-commissioned officer is designated *chief of detachment.*

The gunner is always uncovered.

The men are marched to and from their posts, and their posts are changed, as in Nos. 6, 7, 13, and 29. They are posted two yards from the axis of the piece; Nos. 1 and 2 opposite to the muzzle; the other numbers and the gunner, dressing on Nos. 1 and 2 respectively, at intervals of one yard, except between Nos. 3 and 5, where there is an interval of two yards.

The chief of detachment is posted two yards in rear of the breech or trail, or on the left of the pole, two yards from and opposite to its end, according as the piece is dismounted, unlimbered, or limbered. During the execution of the manœuvres he will go wherever his presence may be necessary; but will habitually place himself opposite to the gunner, in the interval between Nos. 3 and 5.

251. The men having been marched to their posts, the instructor goes with them for the implements, if they are not already in position, and explains their names, dimensions, uses, and who are to have charge of them. He then commands:

PREPARE TO MANŒUVRE.

The men take the implements, repair to their posts, and place them upon the ground in their rear; the handspikes behind Nos. 1, 2, 3, 4, 5, and 6, perpendicularly to the axis of the piece, their small ends on a line with the right toe; the skids parallel to the piece, their middle behind Nos. 3 and 4; the blocks, half blocks, quarter blocks, and chocks equally divided, behind and perpendicular to the skids; the long rollers and half rollers near and parallel to the blocks, behind No. 4; and the short rollers, shifting-plank, trace-rope, trunnion-loops, and hammer-wrench in rear of the gunner.

252. Whenever, in the course of a manœuvre, an implement is not in immediate use, it is returned to its designated place.

253. The instructor gives the commands, and has a general supervision of the manœuvres. He sees that each man performs the duties assigned him; that everything is in a proper state of readiness before giving the command of execution; and that particular care is taken to avoid all shocks and sudden movements.

254. The chief of detachment attends directly to the execution of the movements, and particularly assists and directs the gunner in all his duties.

255. The gunner places the shifting-plank; attaches and takes off the trace-rope; removes and replaces the elevating screw; places and removes, and chocks and unchocks the short rollers; superintends the righting of the piece; directs the pole of the limber, &c.

Nos. 1, 2, 3, 4, 5, and 6 have charge of the handspikes.

Nos. 1 and 2 rig and work the windlass; raise and lower the chase, &c.

Nos. 3 and 4 chock and unchock the wheels, the gun, and the long rollers; take off and replace the cap-squares; place and remove the skids, blocks, half blocks, quarter blocks, long rollers, and half rollers; assist Nos. 1 and 2 in lowering and raising the chase, &c.

Nos. 5 and 6 embar on the cheeks, and under the manœuvring bolts; steady and right the piece; assist Nos. 3 and 4 in placing the skids and half blocks; haul on the rope, &c.

Nos. 7, 8, 9, and 10 assist the others. Nos. 7 and 8 generally assist Nos. 1 and 2 or 3 and 4; Nos. 9 and 10 assist Nos. 3 and 4 or 5 and 6. They help to place the implements in preparing to manœuvre; haul upon the rope; and apply themselves by hand to move the carriage.

256. When men on the opposite sides of a piece apply themselves to a handspike, the handspike used is that of one of the even numbers; the man to whom it belongs is at the small end, the corresponding odd number at the butt end. Those who come to their assistance place themselves inside.

257. When two or more men work at the same end of a handspike, the man to whom it belongs is at the small end.

258. When several handspikes are to be crossed at the muzzle in order to raise or lower it, they are applied in the order of the numbers of the men to whom they belong, those of the highest numbers nearest to the trunnions.

259. The handspikes used in the mechanical manœuvres are beveled on one side, as these will enter into places or under bodies where square handspikes could not be used.

260. When a handspike rests on a fulcrum, and the weight on one end is to be raised by bearing down on the other, the weight should never rest on the beveled side, as the handspike would not then give a good hold, and would be liable to split. In this case the beveled side should be down. But if used for lifting, as when two handspikes are crossed under the breech or chase of a gun to heave it upwards, their ends resting on the ground or platform, the beveled side should be up.

261. At the completion of each movement of a manœuvre, the men retain the places they are in at its conclusion, ready to proceed to the next movement; resuming their posts only at the command TO YOUR POSTS, which is given at the end of each manœuvre.

262. The front, when a piece is unlimbered or dismounted, is the direction in which its muzzle points; when limbered, it is the direction in which the poll points. In the execution of the following manœuvres, when a piece is put in motion upon rollers, the terms back and forward are applied to the direction of the breech and muzzle.

263. A body moving upon a roller gains twice the distance passed over by the roller.

264. The ground should be level and firm, and the implements in good order.

265. The number and kind of implements vary with the manœuvre; but as Nos. 1, 2, 3, 4, 5, and 6 always have handspikes, these are omitted from the list of implements given at the head of each manœuvre.

266. Dimensions and weights of the implements used in the mechanical manœuvres. (Siege.)

Dimensions and weights of implements.

Names.	Number.	Length.	Width.	Thickness.	Weight.		Total weight.		Remarks.
		in.	*in.*	*in.*	*lbs.*	*oz.*	*lbs.*	*oz.*	
Handspikes	6	84	......	......	12	0	72	0	
Long rollers	2	42	6	Round.	25	0	50	0	Grooved ¼ in. deep in the middle.
Short rollers	3	12	7	Round.	12	0	36	0	
Half rollers	2	46	6	6	31	0	62	0	Top rounded 3 inches.
Blocks	16	20	8	8	26	0	416	0	
Half blocks	6	20	8	4	13	0	78	0	
Quarter blocks	2	20	8	2	6	8	13	0	Pieces of 2-inch plank, or broken handspikes will answer.
Gun chocks	6	3.6	2.75	2.5	0	6	2	4	Wedge shape.
Wheel chocks	6	7	6	3	2	4	13	8	Section of a triangle. Top rounded ¼ of an inch.
Roller chocks	6	7	5	2	1	0	6	0	
Skids	2	72	8	8	97	0	194	0	
Shifting-plank	1	67	12	2.25	48	0	48	0	Ends beveled on opposite sides.
Trace-rope	1	360	2.25	Round.	7	8	7	8	
Trunnion-loops	2	18	1.5	Round.	......		......		Ends spliced together.
Hammer-wrench	1	......	......	......	2	4	2	4	

ARTICLE II.

PRELIMINARY MANŒUVRES.

LESSON XVIII.

A GUN LYING UPON THE GROUND, TO PLACE BLOCKS UNDER THE CHASE AND REINFORCE.
TO REMOVE THE BLOCKS.
TO SLEW THE GUN.
TO MOVE THE GUN SHORT DISTANCES TO THE FRONT OR REAR.
TO MOVE THE GUN SHORT DISTANCES BY ROLLING IT.
TO ROLL THE GUN UP AN INCLINED PLANE.

---

267. The implements necessary are:

TWO BLOCKS.
SIX GUN CHOCKS.
TWO SKIDS.
TWO TRUNNION-LOOPS.

A GUN LYING UPON THE GROUND, TO PLACE BLOCKS UNDER THE CHASE AND REINFORCE.

268. The instructor commands:

RAISE THE CHASE.

The gunner takes the handspike of No. 4, runs its small end into the bore, the other end projecting eighteen inches, beveled side up, and chocks it above. Nos. 1, 2, 5, and 6 cross their handspikes under and perpendicular to the handspike in the bore, eighteen inches from the butt ends, beveled sides up, assisted by Nos. 7, 8, 9, and 10, respectively; Nos. 1, 2, 5 and 6 facing the axis of the piece, and Nos. 7 and 9 and 8 and 10 facing each other. No. 4 stands ready with a block, and is assisted to place it by No. 3.

HEAVE.

269. The men at the handspikes act together and raise the chase. Nos. 3 and 4 place a block under and perpendicular to the direction of the piece, as far in rear of the chase-ring as it will go.

EASE AWAY.

270 The piece is allowed to rest on the block, and the men at the handspikes take another purchase under the swell of the muzzle.

HEAVE.

271. Nos. 3 and 4 run the block back until its middle is under the junction of the chase with the reinforce.

EASE AWAY.

272. The piece is allowed to rest upon the block. Nos. 3 and 4 chock it.

RAISE THE BREECH.

273. Nos. 1 and 2 lay their handspikes evenly across the handspike in the bore, and are assisted in bearing down by Nos. 7 and 8. Nos. 5 and 6, assisted by Nos. 9 and 10, embar under the knob of the cascabel. No. 3 stands ready with a block.

HEAVE.

274. Nos. 3 and 4 place the block under and perpendicular to the direction of the piece, at the middle of the reinforce.

EASE AWAY.

275. The piece is allowed to rest upon the block. Nos. 3 and 4 immediately chock it.

TO YOUR POSTS.

276. The implements are replaced, and all resume their posts.

TO REMOVE THE BLOCKS.

277. The instructor commands:

RAISE THE BREECH—HEAVE—EASE AWAY.

The gunner puts the handspike of No. 4 in the bore, as in No. 268. Nos. 1 and 2, assisted by Nos. 7 and 8, cross their handspikes over it and bear down. Nos. 5 and 6, assisted by Nos. 9 and 10, embar under the knob of the cascabel. No. 4 takes out the block, and the breech is allowed to rest on the ground.

RAISE THE CHASE—HEAVE—EASE AWAY.

278. The men at the handspikes embar under the swell of the muzzle. Nos. 3 and 4 run the blocks forward just in rear of the chase-ring. The men at the handspikes take another purchase under the handspikes in the bore.

HEAVE—EASE AWAY.

279. No. 3 takes out the block, and the piece is allowed to rest upon the ground.

TO YOUR POSTS.

280. The implements are replaced, and all resume their posts.

Remarks.—281. This manœuvre can be performed by using the limber of a siege carriage as a lever.

A trunnion-ring, or a chain with a hook at one end, is required.

Run the small end of a handspike into the bore, its butt projecting eighteen inches; back the limber to the muzzle; raise the pole; put the trunnion-ring, or the chain, around the handspike in the bore, and fasten it on the pintle; raise the chase, by bearing down the pole, and place a block under it.

The breech can be raised in a similar manner by placing the trunnion-ring, or chain, around the cascabel.

282. The limber makes a powerful lever, and may be used as such in many cases. If the weight to be raised is too high to apply the trunnion-ring from the pintle, the pole should be turned over so as to bring the pintle below, (first reversing the linch-pins,) and apply the rear end of the fork under the weight to be raised.

TO SLEW THE GUN.

283. If the vent is not uppermost, the instructor commands:

SLEW THE PIECE TO THE LEFT (OR RIGHT)—HEAVE.

The gunner passes a trunnion-loop over one of the trunnions, and inserts the handspike of No. 3 or 4, according to the side on which he acts.

If the piece is to be slewed to the left, he is assisted in heaving by Nos. 1 and 5. Nos. 2 and 6 chock the piece on the left by placing their handspikes horizontally upon the blocks, and perpendicularly to the axis, the butt ends against the piece, beveled sides up. Nos. 3 and 4 attend to taking out and replacing the chocks.

If the piece is to be slewed to the right, Nos. 2 and 6 assist the gunner, and Nos. 1 and 5 chock with their handspikes.

Heaving the piece upon these handspikes causes it to turn upon its axis in its place.

TO MOVE THE GUN SHORT DISTANCES TO THE FRONT OR REAR.

284. Place the blocks under the middle of the chase and reinforce and lay two skids under the trunnions, parallel to

the axis of the piece. Nos. 5 and 6 embar under the rear or front of the trunnions, and move the piece to the front or rear.

TO MOVE THE GUN SHORT DISTANCES BY ROLLING IT.

285. Place a skid under the middle of the reinforce, and another under the middle of the chase, and roll the gun over on its axis. By inclining the skids as required, and slewing the muzzle to suit, it may be moved in different directions.

TO ROLL THE GUN UP AN INCLINED PLANE.

286. Additional implements required:

FOUR SKIDS.
TWO SINGLE PROLONGES.

The gun is on two blocks at the foot of the ramp, its axis perpendicular to the direction of the ramp, and the muzzle turned to the side on which there is most room.

287. Nos. 3 and 4 and 5 and 6 lay two skids parallel to each other, and perpendicular to the axis of the piece, at the middle of the chase and reinforce; they then lay the other skids in the prolongation of the first. Nos. 1 and 2 embar under the piece with their handspikes;* chock the piece when necessary, and throw forward the chase when required. Nos. 3 and 4 lay the ropes on each side of the lower trunnion, and assist the chief of detachment and gunner to overhaul one end of each. These ends are passed over the piece, one a few inches in front and the other the same distance in rear of its trunnions, and three turns taken around the piece, the turns gaining towards the trunnions; just enough of the ropes being overhauled for the men to take hold of their ends.

All the men, except Nos. 1 and 2 and the gunner, haul upon the ropes.

The odd numbers haul upon the right rope—*i. e.* the rope on the right of one who, hauling either rope, faces towards the piece—the even numbers upon the left. The gunner holds in his hand the slack of both ropes.

---

* Crowbars curved at the butt ends, and beveled, are better for this operation.

HEAVE AND HAUL.

288. All act together and roll the piece up the skids until it becomes necessary to rectify the diagonal direction it will assume.

289. As the breech gains on the muzzle the instructor commands:

HALT—SLEW FORWARD THE CHASE.

The numbers who act on the rope towards the reinforce cease hauling. Nos. 1 and 2 with their handspikes (or crowbars) assist the other numbers to throw forward the chase.

HALT—SHIFT THE SKIDS.

290. Nos. 1 and 2 chock the piece with the butts of their handspikes. Nos. 3, 4, 5, and 6 shift the skids, passing them over the piece.

291. When the slack of the rope has been drawn out, the instructor directs Nos. 1 and 2 to chock the piece, and commands:

OVERHAUL THE ROPES.

The men nearest to the piece slack the turns, while the gunner and chief of detachment haul all the slack, except enough for the men to hold on by, to the lower side of the piece.

LESSON XIX.

A HOWITZER LYING UPON THE GROUND, TO PLACE BLOCKS UNDER THE CHASE AND REINFORCE.
TO REMOVE THE BLOCKS.
TO RAISE THE HOWITZER UPON ITS MUZZLE.
TO SLEW THE HOWITZER WHILE STANDING UPON ITS MUZZLE.

---

292. The implements necessary are:

FIVE BLOCKS.
ONE HALF BLOCK.
SIX GUN CHOCKS.
TWO WHEEL CHOCKS.
ONE TRACE-ROPE.
TWO TRUNNION-LOOPS.

A HOWITZER LYING UPON THE GROUND, TO PLACE BLOCKS UNDER THE CHASE AND REINFORCE.

293. The instructor commands:

RAISE THE CHASE—HEAVE—EASE AWAY.

Nos. 1 and 2 insert their handspikes eighteen inches in the bore, which the gunner chocks above with a wheel chock. Nos. 7 and 8 assist Nos. 1 and 2. No. 4, assisted by No. 3, places a block under the chase, as near the trunnions as it will go, and chocks.

LOWER THE CHASE—HEAVE—EASE AWAY.

294. Nos. 1 and 2 shift the wheel chock below their handspikes, and bear down the muzzle. Nos. 4 and 3 place a block under the breech, and chock. The gunner lifts at the knob of the cascable and steadies the breech.

TO REMOVE THE BLOCKS.

295. The blocks are removed in the inverse way to the foregoing, by the same commands.

TO RAISE THE HOWITZER UPON ITS MUZZLE.

296. The howitzer is lying upon two blocks, one under the front of the trunnions, the other under the breech.

297. The instructor commands:

RAISE THE CHASE—HEAVE—EASE AWAY.

The chase is raised as in No. 293. A half block is placed upon the front block, and the piece is chocked.

LOWER THE CHASE—HEAVE—EASE AWAY.

298. The chase is lowered as in No. 282. A block is placed upon the rear block.

RAISE THE CHASE—HEAVE—EASE AWAY.

299. A block is added to the front scaffold, the half block topmost.

LOWER THE CHASE—HEAVE—EASE AWAY.

300. A block is placed upon the rear scaffold.

Nos. 3 and 4 alternate in placing the blocks—No. 4 placing the first—and carefully attend to the chocks. Nos. 5 and 6 steady the scaffolds with their handspikes.

LOWER THE MUZZLE—HEAVE—EASE AWAY.

301. No. 1 takes out the wheel chock. Nos. 5 and 6 embar under the front of the trunnions, to steady the rear scaffold. Nos. 3 and 4 take the two blocks of the front scaffold and

place them side by side, parallel with the axis of the piece, their rear ends about two inches in rear of the muzzle. Nos. 1, 2, 7, and 8 carefully allow the muzzle to rest upon the blocks.

RAISE THE BREECH.

302. The gunner attaches the rope by the middle with a double hitch to the knob of the cascabel; crosses the ends on the highest point of the base-ring, and passes them to Nos. 7, 8, 9, and 10. No. 2 places the middle of his handspike under the knob of the cascabel, and is assisted to lift by the gunner and Nos. 1, 3, and 4. Nos. 5 and 6 embar under the breech.

HEAVE AND HAUL.

303. They act steadily and carefully together and raise the piece on its muzzle upon the blocks.

TO SLEW THE HOWITZER WHILE STANDING UPON ITS MUZZLE.

304. The instructor commands:

SLEW THE PIECE.

The gunner passes the trunnion-loops over the trunnions, into which Nos. 1 and 2 insert their handspikes horizontally, and pull at the small ends. Nos. 5 and 6 keep the blocks in their places, chocking them with their handspikes.

305. When it is desired to lay the howitzer on the ground, it is pushed over on planks, laid to receive it.

LESSON XX.

A MORTAR LYING UPON THE GROUND, TO RAISE IT UPON ITS MUZZLE.
TO SLEW THE MORTAR.
TO SLEW THE MORTAR-BED.

---

306. The implement necessary is:

ONE TRACE ROPE.

A MORTAR LYING UPON THE GROUND, TO RAISE IT UPON ITS MUZZLE.

307. The instructor commands:

RAISE THE MORTAR UPON ITS MUZZLE.

The gunner, taking the two ends of the rope, passes them under and up over the trunnions to the front, and hands them to Nos. 5, 6, 7, 8, 9, and 10, who haul upon them, keeping them parallel with the axis of the piece. Nos. 1 and 2, facing to the front, embar under the trunnions. Nos. 3 and 4, passing to the rear of Nos. 1 and 2, stand ready to embar under the mortar as soon as its elevation will permit.

HEAVE AND HAUL.

308. They act steadily together and raise the mortar upon its muzzle.

TO SLEW THE MORTAR.

309. The instructor commands:

SLEW THE PIECE TO THE RIGHT, (OR LEFT.)

Nos. 1 and 2 lay the butt ends of their handspikes upon the trunnions, overlapping them by about an inch, beveled sides up. The gunner lashes them to the trunnions with the rope. Nos. 1 and 3 and 2 and 4 apply themselves to the small ends of the handspikes to haul in opposite directions.

HEAVE.

310. The mortar is turned round upon its axis. By alternately bearing down upon one handspike and hauling upon the other, it is moved in any direction that the instructor may direct.

TO SLEW THE MORTAR BED.

311. The bed is either with or without its mortar

312. The instructor commands:

SLEW THE BED TO THE RIGHT, (OR LEFT.)

Nos. 1 and 3, facing to the front, embar under the rear notches; No. 3 under the inside of the left notch. Nos. 2 and 4, facing to the front, embar under the front notches; No. 2 under the inside of the right notch.

HEAVE.

313. They act together, and by repeated efforts the bed is turned round in its place.

314. To slew the bed to the left, Nos. 1 and 3 embar under the front notches, and Nos. 2 and 4 under the rear notches.

LESSON XXI.

TO PLACE A LONG ROLLER UNDER A MORTAR-BED. TO REMOVE THE LONG ROLLER.

---

315. The implements necessary are:

ONE LONG ROLLER.
ONE BLOCK.
TWO HALF BLOCKS.
TWO QUARTER BLOCKS.
TWO WHEEL CHOCKS.
TWO ROLLER CHOCKS.

TO PLACE A LONG ROLLER UNDER A MORTAR-BED.

316. The mortar is on its bed, and the bed upon the ground.

317. The instructor commands:

RAISE THE RIGHT CHEEK.

No. 1 embars under the notch nearest to him, perpendicularly to the cheek, and is assisted by No. 7. No. 5 embars in like manner under the rear notch, assisted by No. 9.

HEAVE.

318. No. 3 places a half block lengthwise under the cheek, its middle five inches in rear of the vertical diameter of the trunnions, and then a quarter block in the same direction, its middle under the front notch.

EASE AWAY.

319. The cheek is lowered upon the half block.

RAISE THE LEFT CHEEK—HEAVE—EASE AWAY.

320. No. 2, assisted by No. 8, embars under the front notch. No. 6, assisted by No. 10, embars under the rear notch. No. 4 places a half block and a quarter block in the same way as under the right cheek, and the bed is allowed to rest upon the two half blocks.

RAISE THE TRAIL.

321. The gunner places the block just in rear of the middle transom, and upon it the two wheel chocks to serve as fulcrums. Nos. 5 and 6, assisted by Nos. 9 and 10, embar upon these chocks, under the middle transom.

HEAVE.

322. No. 4, assisted by No. 3, places the long roller upon the half blocks under the cheeks, and chocks it.

EASE AWAY.

323. The bed is allowed to rest upon the quarter blocks and long roller.

TO REMOVE THE LONG ROLLER.

The long roller and blocks are removed in the inverse way.

LESSON XXII.

TO LIMBER.
TO UNLIMBER.
TO MOVE A PIECE, OR ITS CARRIAGE, TO THE FRONT OR REAR.
TO CROSS-LIFT A PIECE.

TO LIMBER.

324. The instructor commands:

LIMBER UP.

No. 2 inserts his handspike in the bore, and is assisted to bear down by No. 1. Nos. 3 and 4 chock the wheels front and rear. No. 4 then crosses his handspike under the stock, and is assisted to lift by Nos. 3, 5, 6; Nos. 5 and 6 next to the stock, facing to the rear, and Nos. 3 and 4 facing each other. The gunner, assisted by Nos. 7, 8, 9, and 10, bring up the limber.

HEAVE.

325. The trail is raised. Nos. 3 and 4, quitting the handspikes, seize the wheels of the limber and direct the pintle into the lunette. No. 3 gives the word FORWARD—BACK—RIGHT—LEFT, according as he wishes the limber to be moved, and when the pintle is in hooks the lashing chain.

TO UNLIMBER.

326. The instructor commands:

UNLIMBERED.

Nos. 3 and 4 chock the wheels. No. 3 unhooks the lashing chain. All apply themselves as in limbering.

HEAVE.

327. The trail is carefullly raised to disengage the pintle. Nos. 3 and 4 seize the limber wheels, and, after freeing the limber from the trail, assist Nos. 5 and 6 to lower the latter to the ground.

328. In limbering and unlimbering a howitzer, Nos. 1 and 2 insert their handspikes in the bore.

329. If the carriage is without its piece, Nos. 1 and 2 embar through the wheels and under the rear of the cheeks.

TO MOVE A PIECE, OR ITS CARRIAGE, TO THE FRONT OR REAR.

330. The instructor commands:

PIECE (OR CARRIAGE) TO THE FRONT (OR REAR)—HEAVE.

If the piece is unlimbered, Nos. 1, 2, 3, and 4 embar as in moving the piece to and from battery. Nos. 5 and 6 embar under the manœuvring bolts. By repeated efforts it is moved to the front or rear.

331. If the carriage, unlimbered, is without its piece, Nos. 1, 2, 3, and 4, or, when they are engaged, Nos. 7, 8, 9, and 10, apply themselves to the wheels by hand. Nos. 5 and 6 embar under the manœuvring bolts.

332. If the piece is limbered, Nos. 1, 2, 3, and 4 embar at the hind wheels. Nos. 5 and 6 embar at the fore wheels. Nos. 9 and 10 apply themselves by hand to the fore wheels. Nos. 7 and 8 go to the splinter-bar. The gunner directs the pole, and gives the command HEAVE at every effort.

333. If the carriage, limbered, is without its piece, all apply themselves by hand at the positions designated in No. 320

TO CROSS-LIFT A PIECE.

334. When it becomes necessary to move a carriage short distances to the right or left, the instructor commands:

CROSS-LIFT TO THE RIGHT, (OR LEFT.)

Nos. 2 and 4 embar perpendicularly under the left wheel. Nos. 1 and 3, crossing over, embar under the inside of the right wheel.

HEAVE.

335. All act together and throw the carriage to the right.

To move the carriage to the left, Nos. 2 and 4 cross over to the right side, and embar under the inside of the left wheel.

336. When the piece is on its carriage, short purchases should be taken.

LESSON XXIII.

A GUN BEING ON ITS CARRIAGE, TO PLACE A SHORT ROLLER UNDER THE REINFORCE.
A HOWITZER BEING ON ITS CARRIAGE, TO PLACE A SHORT ROLLER UNDER THE REINFORCE.
TO REMOVE THE SHORT ROLLER.
TO INSERT HANDSPIKES IN THE TRUNNION HOLES.
TO REMOVE THE HANDSPIKES.

---

337. The implements necessary are:

ONE SHORT ROLLER.
SIX WHEEL CHOCKS.
TWO ROLLER CHOCKS.

A GUN BEING ON ITS CARRIAGE, TO PLACE A SHORT ROLLER UNDER THE REINFORCE.

338. The piece is either limbered or unlimbered.

339. The instructor commands:

LOWER THE CHASE.

No. 2 inserts his handspike in the bore, and is assisted to bear down by No. 1. Nos. 3 and 4 chock the wheels front and rear; take off the cap squares; and then prepare to assist Nos. 1 and 2 by applying themselves to the handspike of No. 4, which is crossed upon the muzzle, both facing to the rear. Nos. 5 and 6 embar between the cheeks and reinforce, as near the trunnions as practicable. The gunner takes a short roller and a chock, and advances to the reinforce.

HEAVE.

340. The chase is lowered. Nos. 1 and 2 thrust the handspike further into the bore in proportion as the muzzle nears the ground, and then apply themselves to the handspike of No. 4. The gunner inserts the short roller perpendicularly to the stock, its ends equidistant from the cheeks, as far under the trunnions as it will go, and chocks it.

EASE AWAY.

341. The piece is carefully rested on the roller. The gunner takes out the elevating screw, and places it in rear of his post, resting it upright upon its handles.

TO YOUR POSTS.

342. All resume their posts, No. 2 leaving his handspike in the bore.

A HOWITZER BEING ON ITS CARRIAGE, TO PLACE A SHORT ROLLER UNDER THE REINFORCE.

Executed as prescribed for a gun in No. 326 and following. The roller rests under the reinforce at its junction with the recess. The gunner removes and returns the quoin.

TO REMOVE THE SHORT ROLLER.

343. The instructor commands:

LOWER THE CHASE.

Nos. 1, 2, 3, 4, 5, and 6 apply themselves as in No. 327. The gunner replaces the elevating screw.

HEAVE.

344. The chase is lowered sufficiently to enable the gunner to remove the roller.

EASE AWAY.

345. The base-ring is carefully rested on the elevating screw.

TO YOUR POSTS.

346. Nos. 3 and 4 unchock the wheels, and put on the cap-squares. The implements are replaced, and all resume their posts.

TO INSERT HANDSPIKES IN THE TRUNNION HOLES.

347. The instructor causes a short roller to be placed under the reinforce, as prescribed in No. 326 and following, and then commands:

RAISE THE CHASE.

No. 4 passes his handspike under that of No. 2. Nos. 5 and 6 stand ready near the trunnions to insert their handspikes.

HEAVE—EASE AWAY.

348. Nos. 1, 2, 3, and 4 raise the chaise. Nos. 5 and 6 run the butts of their handspikes under the trunnions, beveled sides to the front, the ends resting against the rimbases. The trunnions are allowed to rest upon the butts of the handspikes.

TO YOUR POSTS.

349. All resume their posts, Nos. 5 and 6 leaving their handspikes in the trunnion holes.

TO REMOVE THE HANDSPIKES.

350. The instructor commands:

RAISE THE CHASE—HEAVE—EASE AWAY.

Nos. 1, 2, 3, and 4 raise the chase to enable Nos. 5 and 6 to take out the handspikes, and then ease the trunnions into their holes.

The instructor then causes the short roller to be removed as in No. 343 and following.

LESSON XXIV.

TO SHIFT A GUN FROM THE TRUNNION HOLES TO ITS TRAVELLING BED.

TO SHIFT A GUN FROM ITS TRAVELLING BED TO THE TRUNNION HOLES.

TO SHIFT A HOWITZER FROM THE TRUNNION HOLES TO ITS TRAVELLING BED.

TO SHIFT A HOWITZER FROM ITS TRAVELLING BED TO THE TRUNNION HOLES.

TO CHANGE A LIMBER WHEN THE GUN OR HOWITZER IS ON ITS TRAVELLING BED.

TO CHANGE THE LIMBER OF A LOADED MORTAR WAGON.

(PLATES XXIV AND XXV.)

---

351. The implements necessary are:

ONE SHORT ROLLER.
FOUR BLOCKS.
ONE HALF BLOCK.
SIX WHEEL CHOCKS.
ONE TRACE-ROPE.

TO SHIFT A GUN FROM THE TRUNNION HOLES TO ITS TRAVELLING BED.

352. The instructor having caused the piece to be limbered, commands:

PLACE THE SHORT ROLLER UNDER THE REINFORCE.

Executed as in No. 338 and following.

ATTACH THE ROPE.

353. The gunner attaches the rope by its middle with a

double hitch to the knob of the cascable, and, passing its ends to Nos. 7, 8, 9, and 10, stands ready to haul down upon it, and guide the breech into the bolster. No. 3 sees that the lashing-chain is hooked. Nos. 4 and 6 cross their handspikes under that of No. 2, No. 6 next to the muzzle, and are assisted by Nos. 3 and 5 respectively.

SHIFT THE PIECE—HEAVE AND HAUL.

354. Nos. 1, 2, 3, 4, 5, and 6 lift smartly and push at the muzzle, and the piece is hauled until the trunnions are over their travelling position.

REMOVE THE SHORT ROLLER—RAISE THE CHASE.

355. No. 2 chocks his handspike above. Nos. 7 and 8 go to the assistance of Nos. 3 and 4, and Nos. 9 and 10 to the assistance of Nos. 5 and 6; all facing towards the muzzle. The gunner places himself under the chase at the head of the stock.

HEAVE—EASE AWAY.

356. The chief of detachment moves out the roller, which is stopped by the gunner on the head of the stock, and the chase is lowered upon it. The men at the handspikes take a new hold.

HEAVE—EASE AWAY.

357. The gunner takes out the roller, and the chase is lowered upon the stock.

TO YOUR POSTS.

358. The gunner takes off the rope. Nos. 3 and 4 put on the cap-squares and unchock the wheels. The implements are replaced, and all resume their posts.

TO SHIFT A GUN FROM ITS TRAVELLING BED TO THE TRUNNION HOLES.

359. The instructor commands:

PLACE THE SHORT ROLLER UNDER THE CHASE.

Nos. 3 and 4 chock the wheels front and rear. The short roller is inserted under the chase, and rolled back until it rests under the trunnions, by the means and commands prescribed for its removal in No. 355 and following. The gunner attaches the rope by the middle to the knob of the cascable, and passes its ends to Nos. 7, 8, 9, and 10. No. 4 crosses his handspike above that of No. 2.

SHIFT THE PIECE—HEAVE.

360. Nos. 1, 2, 3, and 4 bear down at the muzzle, and, as the piece rolls forward, guide the trunnions into their holes. The short roller is then removed as in No. 343 and following.

TO SHIFT A HOWITZER FROM THE TRUNNION HOLES TO ITS TRAVELLING BED.

TO SHIFT A HOWITZER FROM ITS TRAVELLING BED TO THE TRUNNION HOLES.

361. Executed as for the gun, except in removing and placing the short roller by the chase, which is done as follows:

Nos. 3 and 4 each hands a wheel chock to No. 2, who places one about eighteen inches in the bore under the butt end of his handspike, and the other in the muzzle above the handspike. No. 4 crosses his handspike under that of No. 2. Nos. 1, 2, 3, and 4 raise the chase, while the gunner removes or places the short roller.

In placing the short roller its vertical diameter should rest just in advance of the rimbases.

9

Remarks.—362. When the howitzer is transported on its travelling bed, a temporary bolster should be constructed to support the breech. The short roller resting on a quarter block lashed to the stock and supporting the knob of the cascable, may answer for this purpose.

363. If there is no place for the quoin under the stock, it may be lashed on the trail in front of the bolster; holes, or a groove, being made in its lower side to admit the nuts of the lunette bolts.

364. The short roller (of which one should always accompany every gun and howitzer) is suspended from the knob of the cascable by a cord passed through it.

365. The elevating screw is run in on the lower side of the stock, and held in its place by a lashing-strap.

366. The sponge and rammer are lashed upon the piece, their heads projecting beyond the base-ring. A convenient way of transporting them is by two iron collars, containing hooks, buckled upon the breech and chase.

367. The handspikes are placed against the cheeks, three on each side.

368. A trace-rope should accompany each piece of siege artillery. It will be found useful not only in shifting the piece, but in lashing, and in extricating the carriage and mortar wagon from difficulties.

369. To accustom the men to prepare a piece for travelling, the instructor may cause the implements to be placed as above indicated. To do this he will, before resuming posts in the manœuvre of shifting a piece to its travelling bed, command:

PUT ON THE IMPLEMENTS.

The gunner places the vent-cover, short roller, quoin, elevating screw, and water bucket; if it is necessary to lash the piece to its bed, he is assisted by Nos. 1, 2, 3, 4, 5, and 6. No. 2 puts in the tompion. Nos. 1 and 2 fasten on the sponge and rammer, and, assisted by Nos. 3 and 4, put on the handspikes.

370. To prepare the piece for action the instructor will, before shifting it to its trunnion-holes, command:

REMOVE THE IMPLEMENTS.

The same numbers that put up the implements remove them.

TO CHANGE A LIMBER WHEN THE GUN OR HOWITZER IS ON ITS TRAVELLING BED.

371. The instructor commands:

CHANGE THE LIMBER.

Nos. 3 and 4 chock the rear wheels front and rear, and build a scaffold of four blocks under and perpendicular to the stock, just in rear of the bolster. The gunner and Nos. 7, 8, 9, and 10 raise the trail by bearing down on the pole, so as to allow No. 4 to place a half block on top of the scaffold. The old limber is replaced by the new, and the trail raised as before to permit Nos. 3 and 4 to remove the half block and blocks.

TO CHANGE THE LIMBER OF A LOADED MORTAR-WAGON.

Executed as prescribed in No. 371.

372. In this case the leverage of the pole of the limber may be increased by No. 3 inserting a wheel chock, or the butt end of his handspike, between the stock and the rear of the fork of the limber.

ARTICLE III.

MANŒUVRES WITH THE HANDSPIKE.

LESSON XXV.

TO MOUNT A GUN UPON ITS CARRIAGE.
TO DISMOUNT THE GUN.
TO MOUNT A HOWITZER UPON ITS CARRIAGE.
TO DISMOUNT THE HOWITZER.

(PLATE XXVI.)

---

373. The implements necessary are:

ONE SHORT ROLLER.
TWO HALF ROLLERS.
FOURTEEN BLOCKS.
FOUR HALF BLOCKS.
SIX GUN CHOCKS.
SIX WHEEL CHOCKS.
TWO ROLLER CHOCKS.
TWO SKIDS.
ONE TRACE ROPE.

TO MOUNT A GUN UPON ITS CARRIAGE.

374. The piece is on two blocks, one under the junction of the chase with the reinforce, the other under the middle of the reinforce; the carriage, limbered, cap-squares removed, is in the prolongation of the axis of the piece, the head of its cheeks two yards from the knob of the cascable.

375. The instructor commands:

RAISE THE CHASE.

No. 2 inserts the butt of his handspike in the bore; chocks it above; and is assisted by No. 1. No. 6 crosses his handspike under that of No. 2, close to the muzzle, and is assisted by Nos. 5, 9, and 10. No. 8 crosses the handspike of No. 4 under that of No. 2, eighteen inches further to the front, and is assisted by No. 7. All face towards the muzzle. Nos. 3 and 4, assisted by the gunner and chief of detachment, place the skids parallel to the axis of the piece, their middle opposite to the trunnions, and their inner faces one inch outside of the face of the trunnions. No. 4 stands ready with a half roller.

HEAVE.

376. The chase is raised. No. 3 takes out the front block, and assists No. 4 to place the half roller under the junction of the chase with the reinforce, its ends resting equally upon the skids; they chock the piece on the half roller.

LOWER THE CHASE—HEAVE.

377. Nos. 6 and 8 cross their handspikes above the handspike in the bore, and the chase is borne down. No. 3 takes out the rear block, and assists No. 4 to place the half roller under the reinforce, about ten or twelve inches in rear of the trunnions; they chock the piece upon this half roller.

RAISE THE CHASE—HEAVE.

378. The chase is raised as before. The gunner and chief of detachment raise the front half roller, and Nos. 3 and 4 place each a half block under its ends upon the skids.

LOWER THE CHASE—HEAVE.

379. Executed as before. The gunner and chief of detachment raise the rear half roller, and Nos. 3 and 4 place each a

block under its ends upon the skids, end to end with the half blocks.

380. The operation of raising and lowering the chase is continued until the front scaffold consists on each side of one half block, three blocks, and one half block, and the rear scaffold of four blocks. The gunner and chief of detachment in raising the half rollers move them outwards, and the blocks are placed from the inside. On placing the last half blocks the front half roller is placed under the trunnions.

BACK THE CARRIAGE.

381. The gunner repairs to the pole. Nos. 5 and 6 apply themselves to the fore wheels. Nos. 7, 8, 9, and 10 apply themselves to the rear wheels. All exert themselves, and the carriage is run under the breech.

Nos. 1 and 2 maintain the piece on the front half roller; Nos. 3 and 4 remove the rear scaffold, and the carriage is run back carefully until the heads of the cheeks touch the remaining half roller. Nos. 3 and 4 chock the hind wheels front and rear. The gunner places the short roller on the stock under the breech, and attaches the rope to the knob of the cascable. Nos. 7, 8, 9, and 10 lay hold of the rope. Nos. 4 and 6 cross their handspikes under that of No. 2, that of No. 6 next the piece, and are assisted by Nos. 3 and 5 to lift and push at the muzzle. The chief of detachment removes the half roller, and the piece is drawn back to its trunnion holes.

The short roller is then removed as in No. 343, and following.

TO DISMOUNT THE GUN.

382. The instructor causes the short roller to be placed under the reinforce as in No. 338 and following, without removing the elevating screw. The gunner attaches the rope to the knob of the cascable, and passes its ends to Nos. 7 and 8, who take a turn with them around the manœuvring bolts.

PLACE AND FRONT SCAFFOLD.

383. Nos. 3 and 4 place the skids with their inner faces one inch outside of the cheeks, their outer ends opposite to the chase-ring, and upon each skid a half block, three blocks, and a half block, the inner ends of the blocks overlapping by two inches the heads of the cheeks.

DRAW OUT THE PIECE.

384. No. 6 crosses his handspike under that of No. 2, and is assisted by Nos. 5, 9, and 10. They raise the chase, and No. 4 places a half roller on the scaffold against the cheeks. The gunner moves the roller chock, so that when the roller touches it the trunnions will be over the half roller. Nos. 7 and 8 slack off carefully. By lifting at the muzzle the piece is allowed to run forward until its trunnions are over the half roller. Nos. 3 and 4 chock the piece. The gunner takes off the rope.

DRAW OUT THE CARRIAGE.

385. Nos. 1 and 2 steady the piece, while Nos. 3 and 4 unchock the wheels. The gunner and Nos. 5, 6, 7, 8, 9, and 10, draw out the carriage. Nos. 3 and 4 build up the rear scaffold of four blocks on each side, and place the other half roller on top of it, under the reinforce.

Then by alternately raising and lowering the chase at the command of the instructor, the scaffold is lowered, beginning with the half blocks, until the piece rests upon two blocks.

386. Before executing this manœuvre on the platform under the fire of the enemy the embrasure should be closed with sand bags.

TO MOUNT A HOWITZER UPON ITS CARRIAGE.

TO DISMOUNT THE HOWITZER.

Executed as for the gun.

LESSON XXVI.

TO MOUNT A HOWITZER AS A FIELD PIECE. TO DISMOUNT THE HOWITZER.

---

387. The implements necessary are:

FIVE BLOCKS.
TWO HALF BLOCKS.
SIX WHEEL CHOCKS.
ONE TRACE-ROPE.
TWO TRUNNION-LOOPS.

TO MOUNT A HOWITZER AS A FIELD PIECE.

388. The carriage, unlimbered, cap-squares removed, is placed in rear of the howitzer, in prolongation of the axis of the piece, its front two yards from the knob of the cascable.

389. The instructor having caused the howitzer to be raised upon its muzzle, as in No. 296 and following, commands:

BACK THE CARRIAGE—RAISE THE TRAIL.

The carriage is run up as in No. 381, until the front of the wheels are even with the trunnions. Nos. 3 and 4 chock the wheels front and rear. The gunner attaches one end of the rope to a manœuvring bolt.

Nos. 1 and 2, 9 and 10, 7 and 8, and 5 and 6 apply themselves by hand to the stock, in the order named, from the trail towards the wheels. The gunner, taking the handspike of No. 4, goes to the end of the trail, rests its small end upon the ground, and supports the trail on its butt. In proportion as the trail is raised he moves forward, keeping his handspike so as to support the stock at any moment, the butt of his handspike finally resting under the nut of the rear bolt of the elevating box. Nos. 5 and 6 remain with the gunner. Nos. 1, 2, 9, 10, 7, and 8 gradually withdraw from the stock; Nos. 1 and 2 to the assistance of Nos. 5 and 6, and Nos. 7, 8, 9, and 10 to the rope. Nos. 3 and 4 place the front chocks twelve inches further to the front, carefully run up the carriage, receiving the trunnions in the trunnion holes, put on the cap-squares and chock.

LOWER THE TRAIL.

390. No. 4 takes the handspike of No. 2, and, with No. 3, pushes against the stock in front. Nos. 1, 2, 5, 6, 7, 8, 9, and 10 haul upon the rope. The gunner retires to the end of the trail, and receives it upon the butt of his handspike. The men in succession carefully quit the rope, and apply themselves to the stock. No. 4, when the preponderance passes to the trail, inserts his handspike in the bore, and, assisted by No. 3, bears down. The gunner puts in the quoin.

TO DISMOUNT THE HOWITZER.

391. The instructor commands:

DISMOUNT THE HOWITZER.

Nos. 3 and 4 chock the wheels front and rear; take off the cap-squares; and place two blocks to receive the muzzle. The gunner attaches the rope to one of the manœuvring bolts, and then takes the handspike of No. 4 to support the trail.

RAISE THE TRAIL.

392. The trail is raised as in No. 389, and when a little above the horizontal the gunner supports it on his handspike. Nos. 1, 2, 9, 10, 7, 8, 5, and 6 successively repair to the rope; they hold on well, and ease the muzzle upon the blocks without a shock. The gunner, following up the movement, places the butt of his handspike under the rear nut of the elevating box. Nos. 1 and 2 go to the assistance of Nos. 3 and 4. Nos. 5

and 6 go to the stock and assist the gunner. Nos. 3 and 4 draw back to the rear chocks twelve inches; run the carriage carefully back that distance, and chock.

LOWER THE TRAIL.

393. All but Nos. 3 and 4 go to the stock, and assist the gunner to lower it. He gradually retires to the end of the trail, when he withdraws his handspike, and the trail is lowered to the ground.

LESSON XXVII.

TO MOUNT A SIEGE MORTAR UPON ITS BED.
TO DISMOUNT THE MORTAR.

---

394. The implements necessary are:

ONE TRACE-ROPE.
ONE HAMMER-WRENCH.

TO MOUNT A SIEGE MORTAR UPON ITS BED.

395. The mortar being placed upon its muzzle six inches in front of the bed, vent outwards, as in No. 307 and following, the instructor commands:

MOUNT THE MORTAR.

The gunner removes the bolts and cap-squares, and hands their parts to Nos. 1, 2, 3, and 4, who place them on the ground near the butts of their handspikes; makes a double hitch with the middle part of the rope around the mortar close to the muzzle-band, the tie to the front, and passes the ends up over the trunnions to the rear, to Nos. 5, 6, 7, 8, 9, and 10. Nos. 1 and 2 run their handspikes under the trunnions, and rest the butt ends, beveled sides up, upon the ground or platform.

HEAVE AND HAUL.

396. Nos. 1 and 2 acting at the trunnions, and Nos. 5, 6, 7, 8, 9, and 10 with a steady pull on the rope, cant the mortar against the front of the bolster. Nos. 1 and 2 shift the butts of their handspikes to the top of the bolster, inclining the small ends a little outwards. Nos. 3 and 4, facing to the front, insert their handspikes between the front of the cheeks and mortar, in order to press its muzzle outwards and upwards.

HEAVE AND HAUL.

397. All act steadily together; Nos. 1 and 2 lifting at the trunnions, and Nos. 3 and 4 at the muzzle. As soon as the muzzle is sufficiently elevated to permit it, No. 4 passes quickly to the front and inserts his handspike in the bore. The men continuing to haul upon the rope, the muzzle is raised and the trunnions descend to their places. Nos. 1 and 2 then insert their handspikes in the bore, and the gunner slips the rope from the muzzle to their small ends. The men at the rope haul upon it until the mortar is nearly vertical. Nos. 1, 2, 3, and 4 bring forward the bolts and cap-squares, and assist the gunner to place them. This done, the men ease away upon the rope, and allow the mortar to rest upon the bolster.

TO DISMOUNT THE MORTAR.

398. The instructor commands:

DISMOUNT THE MORTAR.

Nos. 1 and 2 place their handspikes in the bore. The gunner making a double hitch with the middle of the rope around their small ends, passes its ends to Nos. 5. 6, 7, 8, 9, and 10.

HEAVE AND HAUL.

399. The mortar is raised nearly vertical, and while maintained in this position by the rope, the gunner and Nos. 1, 2, 3, and 4 remove the bolts and cap-squares, as in No. 395.

Nos. 3 and 4, facing to the front, embar under the breech of the mortar in order to hold it in its vertical position. Nos. 1 and 2 take their handspikes from the bore. The gunner places the middle of the rope around the front part of the mortar close under the muzzle-band.

HEAVE AND HAUL.

400. A smart pull upon the rope, aided by a heave at the handspikes, pitches the mortar to the rear, where it alights upon the muzzle. The cap-squares are then replaced.

LESSON XXVIII.

TO MOUNT A SIEGE MORTAR UPON THE MORTAR-WAGON. TO DISMOUNT THE MORTAR.

(PLATES XXVII, XXVIII, AND XXIX.)

---

401. The implements necessary are:

TWO LONG ROLLERS.
ONE BLOCK.
TWO HALF BLOCKS.
TWO QUARTER BLOCKS.
SIX WHEEL CHOCKS.
FOUR ROLLER CHOCKS.
ONE TRACE-ROPE.
TWO WINDLASS HANDSPIKES, (attached to the wagon.)

TO MOUNT A SIEGE MORTAR UPON THE MORTAR-WAGON.

402. The mortar is upon its bed, which is upon the ground; the trail of the mortar-wagon, its stakes and bolster removed, is two yards in rear of the middle transom.

403. The instructor having caused a long roller to be placed under the bed, as in No. 316, and following, commands:

RUN UP THE WAGON—HEAVE.

Nos. 5 and 6 embar under the stock, and, assisted by Nos. 7, 8, 9, and 10, run up the wagon until the middle of the trail touches the middle of the long roller. Nos. 3 and 4 chock the wheels front and rear. No. 4. stands ready with a long roller.

RIG THE WINDLASS—HEAVE.

404. Nos. 1 and 2 go to the rear of the wagon and attach the middle of the rope to the windlass; they are assisted by

Nos. 7, 8, 9, and 10. The gunner attaches the rope to the rear manœuvring bolts. Nos. 5 and 6 embar under the front manœuvring bolts.

Nos. 1, 2, 7, and 8 heave upon the windlass, and Nos. 9 and 10 press against the rope with the handspikes of Nos. 1 and 2 to prevent its turns spreading too much upon the roller. Nos. 5 and 6 urge the mortar up until it is ascending the stock; they then place the butt ends of their handspikes upon the stock, beveled sides down, just below the lower roller, and follow up the movement. Nos. 3 and 4, aided by Nos. 5 and 6 with their handspikes, shift the rollers, and chock them whenever necessary.

When the rear ends of the cheeks have arrived upon the body of the wagon, the lower roller, on becoming disengaged, is taken away by No. 4, and the mortar is drawn up on one roller, until the rear ends of the cheeks touch the rear cross-bar plate; Nos. 9 and 10 holding their handspikes under the rear manœuvring bolts in order to ease the bed when it cants to the rear. Nos. 3 and 4 chock the roller front and rear. Nos. 1 and 2 chock the windlass by allowing the handspike in the upper mortice to rest against the mortar.

Limber up.

405. Executed as in No. 324 and following; Nos. 1, 2, 7, and 8 bearing down upon the handspikes of Nos. 1 and 2, inserted between the windlass and the rear cross-bar, being careful to diminish their efforts in proportion as the stock is raised.

Stow the mortar.

406. Nos. 1 and 2 cast off the rope from the windlass. Nos. 7 and 8 take it to the front, being assisted to haul upon it by Nos. 9 and 10. Nos. 1 and 2 embar under the rear manœuvring bolts. Nos. 3 and 4 take the chocks from the roller. Nos. 5 and 6 stand ready with their handspikes to ease the bed when it cants to the front.

HEAVE AND HAUL.

407. The mortar is drawn forward until it cants. Nos. 3 and 4 give each a half block and wheel chock to the gunner, who places them as fulcrums on the rear of the wagon. Nos. 1, 2, 7, and 8 by repeated purchases lower the bed upon the wagon.

408. If the mortar is to travel, the bed is firmly chocked. The blocks, rollers, handspikes, &c., are stowed on the wagon, and well lashed to their places.

409. *Remarks.*—Should the mortar take a diagonal direction upon the stock, it can be gradually righted by giving a counter diagonal direction to one of the rollers.

When the lower roller reaches the nuts of the lunette plate, it is relieved by shifting the upper roller. Nos. 3 and 4 are assisted in this operation by Nos. 5 and 6, who embar under the rear of the cheeks.

TO DISMOUNT THE MORTAR.

410. The instructor commands:

PLACE A LONG ROLLER—HEAVE.

Nos. 3 and 4 furnish the gunner with two half blocks and two wheel chocks, which he adjusts as fulcrums on the rear of the wagon; they then chock the wheels front and rear, and stand ready to place a long roller brought up by No. 4.

Nos. 1, 2, 7, and 8 raise the bed, and the roller is run under it until its vertical diameter is in a line with the vertical diameter of the trunnions.

RIG THE WINDLASS—HEAVE.

411. Nos. 1 and 2, assisted by Nos. 7, 8, 9, and 10, wind the rope upon the roller of the windlass, and the gunner attaches its ends by an anchor-knot to the rear manœuvring bolts.

The mortar is drawn to the rear until the cheeks touch the rear cross-bar plate. Nos. 7 and 8 embar with the handspikes of Nos. 1 and 2 under the rear manœuvring bolts to ease the bed when it cants to the rear. Nos. 3 and 4 chock the roller front and rear. Nos. 1 and 2 secure the windlass by allowing the handspike of the upper mortice to rest against the mortar.

UNLIMBER.

412. Executed as in No. 326 and following. The stock is carefully raised to free it from the pintle, and then lowered without a shock to the ground. Nos. 1 and 2 insert their handspikes between the windlass and the rear of the wagon, and are assisted by Nos. 7 and 8 to bear down upon them. Nos. 3 and 4 place the half blocks and quarter blocks at the end of the stock to receive the lower roller, and then unchock the roller.

EASE AWAY.

413. Nos. 1 and 2 allow the rope to unwind. Nos. 5 and 6 place their handspikes as in mounting the mortar. Nos. 3 and 4 shift the rollers until the mortar finally rests on one roller upon the half blocks.

BACK THE WAGON.

414. Nos. 3 and 4 unchock the wheels. Nos. 1 and 2 and the gunner take off the rope. The wagon is run back as in No. 403.

The long roller is then removed as in LESSON XXI. The gunner replaces the bolster.

LESSON XXIX.

TO MOUNT A GUN UPON THE MORTAR-WAGON.
TO DISMOUNT THE GUN.
TO MOUNT A HOWITZER UPON THE MORTAR-WAGON.
TO DISMOUNT THE HOWITZER.

(PLATES XXX AND XXXI.)

---

415. The implements necessary are:

TWO LONG ROLLERS.
ONE SHORT ROLLER.
ONE HALF ROLLER.
TEN BLOCKS.
THREE HALF BLOCKS.
FOUR GUN CHOCKS.
SIX WHEEL CHOCKS.
FOUR ROLLER CHOCKS.
TWO SKIDS.
ONE TRACE-ROPE.
TWO WINDLASS HANDSPIKES, (attached to the wagon.)

TO MOUNT A GUN UPON THE MORTAR-WAGON.

416. The piece is on two blocks, one under the front of the trunnions, the other about a foot in rear of the rimbases; the wagon, unlimbered, its stakes removed, is in the prolongation of the axis of the piece, its trail on the ground about two yards from the knob of the cascable.

417. The instructor commands:

RAISE THE CHASE—HEAVE.

No. 2 inserts the butt of his handspike in the bore, and is assisted by No. 1. No. 6 crosses his handspike under that of

No. 2, near the muzzle, and is assisted by Nos. 5, 9, and 10. No. 8 crosses the handspike of No. 4 under that of No. 2, eighteen inches from the muzzle, and is assisted by No. 7. Nos. 3 and 4 place the skids parallel to the axis of the piece, the middle opposite to the trunnions.

The chase is raised. No. 3 removes the front block, and assists No. 4 to place a long roller under the reinforce, just in front of the trunnions; they chock it front and rear.

LOWER THE CHASE—HEAVE.

418. The men at the handspikes bear down the chase. No. 3 removes the rear block, and assists No. 4 to place the long roller under the reinforce, about five inches in rear of the trunnions; they chock it in rear.

RAISE THE CHASE—HEAVE.

419. The men at the handspikes raise the chase. No. 4 removes the front roller, and the muzzle is lowered to the ground.

RUN UP THE WAGON—HEAVE.

420. The wagon is run forward, as in No. 403; the stock under the breech rests upon a long roller placed by Nos. 4 and 3 on the stock in rear of the lunette-plate bolts. Nos. 3 and 4 chock the wheels front and rear.

RIG THE WINDLASS—HEAVE.

421. Nos. 1 and 2 go to the rear of the wagon and attach the middle of the rope to the windlass. The gunner passes its ends over and under the trunnions, the standing part innermost, and ties them by a right-knot on the top of the piece; he then forms a loop of the ends of the rope, inserting in it the handspike of No. 4, in order to steady the piece, and places the short roller on the ground under the chase.

Nos. 1, 2, 7, and 8 heave upon the windlass, and Nos. 9 and 10 press against the ropes with the handspikes of Nos. 1

and 2 to prevent its turns spreading too much upon the roller Nos. 3 and 4 attend to the long roller. Nos. 5 and 6 follow the upper roller with the butts of their handspikes ready to chock it.

The lower roller, on becoming disengaged, is removed by No. 4. When the breech is drawn against the breech hurter, the windlass is secured by allowing the handspike in the upper mortice to rest against the knob of the cascable. Nos. 3 and 4 chock the roller front and rear.

RAISE THE STOCK ON FOUR BLOCKS AND A HALF BLOCK—HEAVE.

422. Nos. 3 and 4, assisted by Nos. 5 and 6, remove the skids, and form a scaffold of a block and a half block on each side in front of the muzzle, their inner ends even with the stock, and place upon it a half roller to serve as a fulcrum. Nos. 1 and 2 embar upon this half roller under the swell of the muzzle, inclining the small ends of their handspikes outwards, and are assisted by Nos. 7 and 9, and 8 and 10, respectively, Nos. 7 and 8 on the outside of the handspikes. Nos. 5 and 6 bear down upon the end of the stock with the butts of their handspikes.

The muzzle is raised. Nos. 3 and 4 remove the long roller. Nos. 5 and 6 embar under the trail perpendicularly to the stock, in order to assist the men at the muzzle. Nos. 3 and 4 place a scaffold of two blocks and a half block under and perpendicular to the stock, near the front cross-piece.

The men at the handspikes then take another purchase under the end of the stock, assisted, as before, by Nos. 5 and 6, while Nos. 3 and 4 move forward the rear scaffold until it rests just behind the manœuvring staples.

By gradually raising the front scaffold, and repeating the purchases, the stock is raised until the rear scaffold consists of four blocks and a half block.

RUN UP THE LIMBER.

423. Nos. 3 and 4 remove the front scaffold. The gunner and Nos. 7, 8, 9, and 10 back the limber and raise the pole.

Nos. 3 and 4 guide the pintle into the lunette. No. 6 inserts the butt of his handspike between the fork and the stock in rear of the pintle. Nos. 7, 8, 9, and 10 bear down the pole. Nos. 3 and 4 remove the rear scaffold. No. 3 hooks the lashing chain.

To your posts.

424. Nos. 1 and 2 and the gunner cast off the rope. Nos. 3 and 4 unchock the wheels, and put in the stakes. The implements are replaced, and all resume their posts.

TO DISMOUNT THE GUN.

425. The instructor commands:

Rig the windlass.

Nos. 3 and 4 remove the stakes. Nos. 1 and 2 attach the rope by its middle to the windlass, and take as many turns (about five) around the roller as will allow the piece to descend. The gunner passes the ends of the rope over and under the trunnions, and ties them by a right-knot on top of the piece, the standing part of the rope being innermost; he then forms a loop of the ends of the rope to receive a handspike for steadying the piece. No. 1 secures the windlass by inserting a handspike in the upper mortice, and allowing it to rest against the knob of the cascable.

Unlimber.

426. No. 3 unhooks the lashing chain. Nos. 3 and 4 chock the wheels front and rear, and place a scaffold of four blocks under the stock close in rear of the manœuvring staples. The gunner and Nos. 7, 8, 9, and 10 go to the pole and raise it sufficiently to enable No. 6 to insert the butt of his handspike between the fork and the stock in rear of the pintle. The pole is then borne down, and No. 4 places a half block on top of the scaffold, when the pole is raised and the limber drawn out.

Nos. 3 and 4 form a scaffold of three blocks and a half block on each side parallel to the axis of the piece in front of the muzzle, and place the half roller on top of it. Nos. 1 and 2, assisted by Nos. 7, 8, 9, and 10, embar upon the half roller under the end of the stock, and raise it. No. 4 removes the half block from the rear scaffold, and, assisted by No. 3, moves forward the scaffold under the bolster.

By gradually lowering the front scaffold, and repeating the purchases, the trail is lowered until it rests upon one block. The men at the handspikes then embar under the swell of the muzzle. No. 4 removes the block, and, assisted by No. 3, places a long roller under the reinforce just in front of the trunnions.

PLACE THE SKIDS.

427. Nos. 3 and 4 remove the front scaffold, and place the skids, one on each side of the stock and parallel to its direction, their inner ends opposite to the bolster.

EASE AWAY.

428. Nos. 1 and 2, assisted by Nos. 7 and 8, allow the piece to descend, and Nos. 3 and 4 receive the chase on a long roller at a point about two feet in rear of the chase-ring. The piece is lowered until it rests upon this roller on the skids. Nos. 4 and 3 place the half roller under the reinforce about a foot in rear of the trunnions.

BACK THE WAGON.

429. Nos. 3 and 4 unchock the wheels. Nos. 1 and 2 and the gunner cast off the rope, and the wagon is run back as in No. 403. By alternately raising and lowering the chase, the piece is placed upon two blocks.

TO YOUR POSTS.

430. The stakes are put in, the implements replaced, and all resume their posts.

TO MOUNT A HOWITZER UPON THE MORTAR-WAGON.

Executed as for the gun.

431. *To limber.* Pass two handspikes across and under the trail, to which apply eight men, two at each end of each handspike. Raise the trail and limber the wagon.

432. *To remove the long roller.* Embar with two handspikes under the muzzle, each on a fulcrum formed with one half block and a wheel chock. Raise the piece, and run the roller close to the muzzle. Take a second purchase on the wheel chocks as fulcrums. Raise the muzzle, withdraw the roller, and lower the piece to its place on the wagon.

TO DISMOUNT THE HOWITZER.

Executed as for the gun.

To unlimber and *to place the long roller* are executed in the reverse manner to that prescribed in Nos. 431 and 432.

433. *Remark.*—The gun can be placed upon the mortar-wagon without using the windlass, in the following manner:

The wagon, unlimbered, its stakes removed, is in the prolongation of the axis of the piece, its trail on the ground about two yards from the knob of the cascable.

Raise the gun as in No. 374 and following, until it is on a scaffold of one half block, three blocks, and a half block on each skid, and the half roller under the trunnions. Maintain the piece on this half roller, and run the wagon up until the side rails nearly touch the scaffold.

Raise the stock of the wagon on a scaffold of four blocks placed crosswise under it just in rear of the staples. Bear down on the muzzle and place a long roller on the wagon just in rear of the front cross-bar plate. Raise the muzzle and remove the half roller and the half blocks from its scaffold, and place a second long roller under the chase at its junction with the reinforce. Attach the rope to the knob of the cascable, and run the gun back to its place on the wagon.

The rollers are then removed, and the wagon limbered, as prescribed in No. 422 and following.

LESSON XXX.

TO SHIFT A GUN FROM ONE CARRIAGE TO ANOTHER.
TO SHIFT A HOWITZER FROM ONE CARRIAGE TO ANOTHER.

(PLATE XXXII.)

---

434. The implements necessary are:

THREE SHORT ROLLERS.
SIX WHEEL CHOCKS.
SIX ROLLER CHOCKS.
ONE SHIFTING-PLANK.
ONE TRACE-ROPE.

TO SHIFT A GUN FROM ONE CARRIAGE TO ANOTHER.

435. The piece is unlimbered; the spare carriage, limbered—cap-squares taken off and elevating screw removed—is placed accurately in prolongation of the former, two yards from its trail.

436. The instructor having caused handspikes to be inserted in the trunnion holes, as in No. 347 and following, commands:

BACK THE CARRIAGE.

Nos. 7, 8, 9, and 10 apply themselves to the hind wheels of the spare carriage, and Nos. 5 and 6 apply themselves to the fore wheels. The gunner directs the pole, and the carriage is backed, wheel against wheel, to the unlimbered carriage. Nos. 3 and 4 transfer the rear chocks from the unlimbered carriage to the front of the hind wheels of the limbered carriage.

PLACE THE PLANK AND ROLLERS, AND ATTACH THE ROPE—HEAVE AND HAUL.

437. The gunner places himself on the inside of the wheels between the two carriages, and lowers the roller on the stock until it is in a position to support the plank, when he chocks it; runs the plank, which is handed him by No. 6, under the chase as far as it will go, beveled side down; places a roller on the plank under the reinforce, as far forward as possible, Nos. 1, 2, 3, and 4 depressing the muzzle for that purpose; attaches the rope to the knob of the cascable, and passes its ends to Nos. 5, 6, 7, 8, 9, and 10; places a third roller at the end of the plank on the stock of the spare carriage, with a roller chock in front of it, near the screw box; and then applies himself to the rope.

Nos. 1, 2, 3, and 4 raise the chase, and the piece is drawn back until its trunnions are over the chin bolts of the spare carriage; they then depress the muzzle sufficiently to enable the gunner to return the third roller to the end of the plank. Nos. 7. and 8 take two turns with the rope around the manœuvring bolts.

DRAW OUT THE CARRIAGE.

438. Nos. 3 and 4 unchock the wheels of the unlimbered carriage, and, assisted by Nos. 1 and 2, slightly raise the chase to enable the gunner to remove the roller which is under it. Nos. 9 and 10 and 5 and 6 move the carriage forward about six inches, when the chase is lowered, the swell of the muzzle resting on the stock. Nos. 9 and 10, assisted by Nos. 3 and 4, draw the carriage slowly out, its trail two yards from the muzzle, the gunner at the same time removing the plank.

SLACK OFF.

439. Nos. 7 and 8 slack off equally and carefully upon the rope, and ease the trunnions into their holes. The short roller is then removed from under the reinforce as in No. 343 and following.

TO SHIFT A HOWITZER FROM ONE CARRIAGE TO ANOTHER.

Executed as for the gun.

440. *Remark.*—A piece may be shifted from one carriage to another by placing it as prescribed in No. 383 and following, and then substituting the new carriage for the old.

LESSON XXXI.

TO SHIFT A GUN FROM THE MORTAR-WAGON TO ITS CARRIAGE.

TO SHIFT A GUN FROM ITS CARRIAGE TO THE MORTAR-WAGON.

TO SHIFT A HOWITZER FROM THE MORTAR-WAGON TO ITS CARRIAGE.

TO SHIFT A HOWITZER FROM ITS CARRIAGE TO THE MORTAR-WAGON.

---

441. The implements necessary are:

TWO LONG ROLLERS.
ONE SHORT ROLLER.
ONE HALF BLOCK.
SIX WHEEL CHOCKS.
SIX ROLLER CHOCKS.
ONE TRACE-ROPE.

TO SHIFT A GUN FROM THE MORTAR-WAGON TO ITS CARRIAGE.

442. The carriage and wagon are both limbered, and the head of the cheeks of the carriage placed two yards from the windlass.

443. The instructor commands:

PLACE THE LONG ROLLERS UNDER THE CHASE AND REIN-FORCE—HEAVE.

The gunner places a half block and a wheel chock on the end of the stock of the mortar-wagon, or on the fork of the limber, to serve as a fulcrum. Nos. 1 and 2 embar with the handspike of the latter under the muzzle and raise the chase, Nos. 4 and 3 at the same time placing a long roller under the trunnions and chocking it front and rear. Nos. 1 and 2 bear down the muzzle, and Nos. 4 and 3 place a second long roller under the middle of the reinforce. The gunner attaches the rope to the knob of the cascable, and passes it to Nos. 7, 8, 9, and 10.

BACK THE CARRIAGE.

444. The carriage is backed, wheel against wheel with the wagon, as in No. 424, and Nos. 3 and 4 chock the wheels in contact in front. The gunner places the short roller on the head of the stock to receive the breech. Nos. 3 and 4 unchock the long roller under the trunnions. The others repair to the rope.

The piece is drawn back until the trunnions are over the chin bolts. Nos. 7 and 8 take two turns of the rope around the manœuvring bolts. Nos. 5 and 6 embar between the chase and cheeks in order to relieve the wagon from the weight of the muzzle.

DRAW OUT THE WAGON.

445. Nos. 3 and 4 transfer the chocks from the wheels of the mortar wagon to the wheels of the piece, and the wagon is drawn out two yards to its front, as in No. 438.

SLACK OFF.

446. Nos. 1, 2, 3, and 4 lower the muzzle, and Nos. 7 and 8 slack off the rope equally and carefully, allowing the trunnions to descend into their holes.

The short roller is then removed, as in No. 343 and following.

TO SHIFT A GUN FROM ITS CARRIAGE TO THE MORTAR-WAGON.

447. The carriage and wagon are limbered, and the rear of the wagon is placed two yards from the muzzle.

448. The instructor causes the short roller to be placed under the reinforce, as in No. 338 and following, and directs the gunner to attach the rope to the knob of the cascable.

Nos. 1, 2, 3, 4, 5, and 6 lift and push at the muzzle, and the piece is drawn back until the trunnions are over the chin bolts, when Nos. 7 and 8 take two turns of the rope around the manœuvring bolts.

BACK THE WAGON—HEAVE AND HAUL.

449. Nos. 5 and 6 embar between the chase and cheeks in order to raise the muzzle, and the wagon is backed wheel against wheel with the carriage. Nos. 3 and 4 chock its hind wheels in front; place a long roller on the rear part of the wagon under the chase; chock it in front; and stand ready to insert the other long roller. The gunner takes off the rope and attaches it to the muzzle. Nos. 3 and 4 unchock the long roller, and place the chocks near the front cross-piece of the wagon. The piece is drawn forward until the breech is slightly in advance of the breech hurter.

REMOVE THE LONG ROLLERS.

450. The gunner takes off the rope, and adjusts a fulcrum at the end of the stock of the wagon. Nos. 1 and 2, by bearing down the muzzle, enable Nos. 3 and 4 to remove one of the long rollers, leaving the other under the trunnions; they then embar under the muzzle, and lower it into the bolster. Nos. 4 and 3 run out the remaining roller by the front.

DRAW OUT THE CARRIAGE.

Executed as in No. 438.

TO SHIFT A HOWITZER FROM THE MORTAR-WAGON TO ITS CARRIAGE.

TO SHIFT A HOWITZER FROM ITS CARRIAGE TO THE MORTAR-WAGON.

Both executed as for the gun. When the wagon and carriage are brought together, their hind wheels overlap each other so as to bring the head of the stock as near as possible to the rear of the wagon.

LESSON XXXII.

TO CHANGE OR TO GREASE A WHEEL.
TO DISMOUNT A CARRIAGE AND ITS LIMBER.
TO REMOUNT THE CARRIAGE AND ITS LIMBER.
TO DISMOUNT THE MORTAR-WAGON.
TO REMOUNT THE MORTAR-WAGON.

(PLATE XXXIII.)

---

451. The implements necessary are:

SIX BLOCKS.
TWO HALF BLOCKS.
SIX WHEEL CHOCKS.

TO CHANGE OR TO GREASE A WHEEL.

452. The piece may be either limbered or unlimbered. The spare wheel lying upon the ground, near the wheel to be changed.

453. The instructor commands:

CHANGE THE RIGHT HIND WHEEL.

The pole is moved to the left, and No. 3 chocks the left hind wheel front and rear. The gunner being furnished by Nos. 3 and 4 each with one block, one half block, and a wheel chock, lays the half blocks on the ground, end to end, under the right of the axle-body, perpendicularly to the direction of the axletree; places a block upright upon each of the half blocks, and upon the upright blocks wheel chocks to serve as fulcrums. Nos. 2 and 6, assisted by Nos. 1 and 5 respectively, embar upon these fulcrums under the axletree.

HEAVE.

454. The wheel is raised from the ground. Nos. 3 and 4, facing each other, apply themselves to it, lift it off and roll it out of the way; raise the spare wheel, apply themselves to it in the same manner, and lift it on.

455. *Remarks.* When the piece is unlimbered, a wheel may be changed by using the trail as a lever, in the following manner:

To change the right wheel. No. 4 chocks the left wheel front and rear. No. 3 removes the linch pin and washer. The trail is raised as in limbering, and the gunner places a prop about thirty inches in length under the right cheek, close in rear of the axletree.

By bearing down the trail the right wheel is raised from the ground, when it may be changed or greased by Nos. 3 and 4.

456. In travelling the wheels should be greased at least once in two days.

TO DISMOUNT A CARRIAGE AND ITS LIMBER.

457. The carriage is without its piece, and unlimbered, and the rear of the limber placed two yards from the trail.

458. The instructor commands:

DISMOUNT THE CARRIAGE AND ITS LIMBER.

Nos. 3 and 4 chock the wheels front and rear, furnish the gunner each with a block, remove the linch pins and washers, and, assisted by Nos. 5 and 6, place each a scaffold of two blocks under and perpendicular to the axletree, midway between its middle and the wheels.

RAISE THE TRAIL.

459. Nos. 1 and 2 embar through the wheels under the cheeks. Nos. 7, 8, 9, and 10 apply themselves by hand to the stock. The trail is raised.

The gunner lays one block upon the ground lengthwise under the stock, places the other block upright upon it, and upon the upright block a wheel chock perpendicularly to the direction of the stock, and twenty inches in rear of the axletree. In order to steady the carriage, Nos. 1 and 2, facing to the rear, embar under the axletree and against the cheeks, the butts of their handspikes on the ground.

LOWER THE TRAIL, AND TAKE OFF THE WHEELS.

460. The trail being borne down, the wheels are raised free from the ground. Nos. 3 and 5 and 4 and 6 apply themselves to the wheels.

HEAVE.

461. Acting together, they lift them both off at the same time, and let them fall outwards upon the ground.

RAISE THE TRAIL.

462. The trail is raised until the axletree rests upon the scaffolds which are under it. The gunner then lays two blocks, one on top of the other, under and perpendicular to the stock at the rear ends of the cheeks, and places the wheel chock on them.

LOWER THE TRAIL.

463. As the trail is lowered Nos. 3 and 4 remove the blocks from under the axletree.

RAISE THE TRAIL.

464. Nos. 1 and 2 ease the head of the cheeks upon the ground, and the gunner removes his two blocks.

LOWER THE TRAIL.

465. The trail is lowered to the ground, and Nos. 3 and 4 replace the linch pins and washers.

To the limber.

466. Nos. 3 and 4 remove the linch pins and washers from the limber wheels. Nos. 1 and 2 run their handspikes between the sweep-bar and axletree, and rest the butt ends upon the splinter-bar; they are assisted to lift by Nos. 7 and 8. Nos. 3 and 5 and 4 and 6 apply themselves to the wheels.

Heave.

467. Nos. 1, 2, 7, and 8 lift the limber, and at the same time Nos. 3 and 5 and 4 and 6 lift off the wheels and allow them to fall outwards to the ground. The limber is lowered, and Nos. 3 and 4 replace the linch pin and washers.

To your posts.

468. All resume their posts at the stock of the carriage, and replace the implements.

TO REMOUNT THE CARRIAGE AND ITS LIMBER.

469. The instructor commands:

Mount the carriage and limber.

Nos. 3 and 4 each furnish the gunner with a block, remove the linch pins and washers, and place chocks nearly in the position which they will occupy when the wheels are on. Nos. 1 and 2 stand ready to steady the carriage by embarring under the front of the axletree. Nos. 9, 10, 7, 8, 5, and 6 apply themselves by hand to the stock.

Raise the trail.

470. The trail is raised, and the gunner forms a scaffold of his two blocks under and perpendicular to the stock at the ends of the cheeks, and places a chock upon it. Nos. 3 and 4 each take a block and repair to the front of the axletree.

LOWER THE TRAIL.

171. The trail is borne down. Nos. 5 and 6 each give a block to Nos. 3 and 4, respectively, and Nos. 3 and 4 form two scaffolds of blocks under the axletree.

RAISE THE TRAIL.

472. Nos. 5 and 6 assist to raise the trail. The gunner shifts his two blocks, lays one upon the ground, sets the other upright upon it, and upon the upright block places the chock twenty inches in rear of the axletree.

LOWER THE TRAIL AND PUT ON THE WHEELS.

473. The trail is borne down. Nos. 3 and 5 and 4 and 6 raise the wheels and bring them near the ends of the axletree.

HEAVE.

474. The wheels are put on at the same moment. Nos. 3 and 4 tighten the chocks, and replace the linch pins and washers.

LOWER THE TRAIL.

475. Nos. 1 and 2 embar through the wheels under the cheeks. The gunner removes his blocks, and the trail is lowered to the ground.

TO THE LIMBER.

476. Nos. 1 and 2 insert their handspikes as in dismounting the limber, and are assisted to lift by Nos. 7 and 8. Nos. 3 and 4 remove the linch pins and washers, and assisted by Nos. 5 and 6, raise the wheels.

HEAVE.

477. All act together and the limber is raised, and the wheels put on at the same time. No. 3 and 4 replace the linch pins and washers.

TO DISMOUNT THE MORTAR-WAGON.

478. The instructor commands:

DISMOUNT THE WAGON.

Nos. 1 and 2 run their handspikes under the windlass and over the axletree, and are assisted to lift by Nos. 7, 8, 9, and 10. Nos. 3 and 5 and 4 and 6 apply themselves to the wheels.

HEAVE.

479. All act together and the wheels are lifted off and allowed to fall outwards, when the body of the wagon is lowered to the ground.

TO REMOUNT THE MORTAR-WAGON.

The wagon is mounted in the inverse way to that prescribed for dismounting it.

480. *Remark.*—A carriage may be dismounted or mounted by a single lift in the following manner:

The gunner lays a block under and perpendicular to the stock, just in rear of the axletree. Nos. 1 and 2 pass their handspikes under the axletree, to Nos. 5 and 6, and are assisted by Nos. 7 and 8 and 9 and 10. Nos. 3 and 4, assisted by the chief of detachment and gunner, take off or put on the wheels.

LESSON XXXIII.

TO LOWER A BARBETTE CARRIAGE FROM ITS CHASSIS, THE PIECE BEING MOUNTED.
TO REMOUNT THE BARBETTE CARRIAGE UPON ITS CHASSIS.
TO GREASE THE ROLLERS OF A BARBETTE CARRIAGE, THE PIECE BEING MOUNTED.
TO GREASE THE FORKS OF THE TRAVERSE WHEELS.

(PLATE XXXIV.)

---

481. The implements necessary are:

THREE BLOCKS.
TWO HALF BLOCKS.
FOUR WHEEL CHOCKS.
TWO PLANKS, 15 feet long, beveled at the ends.
ONE FIELD LIMBER, ammunition box removed.

TO LOWER A BARBETTE CARRIAGE FROM ITS CHASSIS, THE PIECE BEING MOUNTED.

482. The piece is in battery, and the limber placed accurately in the prolongation of its axis, about six yards to the rear.

483. The instructor commands:

RAISE THE TRAIL.

Nos. 3 and 4 chock the rollers, and place each a wheel chock upon the rails near the manœuvring staples to serve as fulcrums. Nos. 5 and 6 embar upon these chocks under the staples. No. 2 inserts his handspike in the bore, and is assisted to bear down by No. 1. No. 4 stands ready with a block.

HEAVE.

484. As the trail is raised, Nos. 4 and 3 place the block on the tongue under and perpendicular to the transom and axle-tie.

REMOVE THE TRAVERSE WHEELS.

485. The gunner takes out the prop, and then applies himself to the end of the tongue to lift. No. 2 passes his handspike through the manœuvring loop, and is assisted by Nos. 1, 7, and 8. No. 6 crosses his handspike under the tongue near the rear transom, and is assisted by Nos. 5, 9, and 10. All face to the front. Nos. 3 and 4 stand ready to remove the traverse wheels.

HEAVE.

486. The rear of the chassis is raised. Nos. 3 and 4 remove the wheels, and the chassis is gently lowered upon the traverse circle.

PLACE THE PLANKS.

487. Nos. 3 and 4, assisted by Nos. 5 and 6, form a scaffold of a block and a half block on each side of the carriage under and perpendicular to the chassis, about four inches in rear of the middle transom, and then place the planks resting on them, their inner edges against the rails of the chassis, and their front ends about four inches in front of the middle transom, beveled sides up.

BACK THE LIMBER.

488. The gunner and Nos. 7, 8, 9, and 10 back the limber up the planks; raise the pole to engage the pintle in the lunette, and then bear down upon the pole in order to raise the trail. No. 4 removes the block from under the trail. No. 3 keys the pintle.

RUN DOWN THE PIECE.

489. Nos. 3 and 4 unchock the wheels. All apply themselves by hand, as in No. 332, and run the piece carefully down the planks to the terreplein.

TO REMOUNT THE BARBETTE CARRIAGE UPON ITS CHASSIS.

490. The rear of the chassis rests upon the traverse circle, and the piece, limbered, is placed accurately in the prolongation of the tongue, about six yards to the rear.

491. The instructor commands:

PLACE THE PLANKS.

Nos. 3 and 4, assisted by Nos. 5 and 6, place the planks as prescribed in No. 487.

BACK THE PIECE.

492. Nos. 1 and 2 embar through the wheels near the tire, under the front manœuvring bolts. Nos. 3 and 4 embar in a similar way over the rear manœuvring bolts. Nos. 5 and 6 embar under the rear of the carriage wheels. Nos. 7 and 8 and 9 and 10 apply themselves by hand to the limber wheels. The gunner directs the pole.

HEAVE.

493. The piece is backed up the planks into battery. Nos. 3 and 4 chock the wheels.

RAISE THE TRAIL—DRAW OUT THE LIMBER.

494. The gunner and Nos. 7, 8, 9 and 10 bear down the pole, while Nos. 4 and 3 place a block under and perpendicular to the transom and the axle-tie. The pole is then raised to disengage the pintle from the lunette, and the limber and planks are removed.

REPLACE THE TRAVERSE WHEELS.

495. Nos. 3 and 4 stand ready with the traverse wheels. The men apply themselves to the rear of the chassis, as prescribed in No. 485.

HEAVE.

496. As the chassis is raised, Nos. 3 and 4 put in the wheels. The gunner replaces the prop.

The block under the transom and axle-tie is removed by the means prescribed for placing it in No. 483 and following.

497. *Remark.*—The iron parts of carriages which are not lacquered should always be kept well greased.

TO GREASE THE ROLLERS OF A BARBETTE CARRIAGE, THE PIECE BEING MOUNTED.

498. The piece is run from battery, as in No. 102. Nos. 3 and 4 remove the wheels; place two half blocks lengthwise on the rail of the chassis, one in front and the other in rear of the roller to be greased, and upon them two wheel chocks to serve as fulcrums. Nos. 1 and 2 embar on these fulcrums under the front and rear manœuvring bolts, and, assisted by Nos. 3 and 4, raise the roller from the rail. The gunner moves out the roller about six inches; greases the spindle, and pushes the roller back. Nos. 1 and 2 unbar. Nos. 3 and 4 put on the wheels.

TO GREASE THE FORKS OF THE TRAVERSE WHEELS.

499. Raise the rear of the chassis, as prescribed in No. 485, and remove the nuts of the fork bolts with a wrench.

LESSON XXXIV.

TO PLACE THE CHASSIS FOR A 24-PDR. HOWITZER CARRIAGE FOR A FLANK CASEMATE IN POSITION.
TO MOUNT THE HOWITZER.
TO MOUNT THE CARRIAGE UPON ITS CHASSIS.
TO DISMOUNT THE HOWITZER CARRIAGE FROM ITS CHASSIS, THE PIECE BEING MOUNTED.
TO DISMOUNT THE HOWITZER.

---

500. The implements necessary are:

ONE HALF ROLLER.
FOUR BLOCKS.
TWO HALF BLOCKS.
FOUR GUN CHOCKS.
TWO SKIDS.
ONE HAMMER-WRENCH.

TO PLACE THE CHASSIS FOR A 24-PDR. HOWITZER CARRIAGE FOR A FLANK CASEMATE IN POSITION.

501. Two handspikes are passed across and under the chassis, one in rear of the traverse fork, the other two feet from the pintle hole, and four men, one at each end of these handspikes, lift the chassis and carry it to its place. The men at the rear handspike raise that end of the chassis. The gunner with the wrench takes off the three nuts which attach the fork and removes it, when the trail is lowered to the ground.

TO MOUNT THE HOWITZER.

502. The skids are laid in rear and in prolongation of the chassis, their outer edges in line with those of the chassis.

The piece is rolled upon these skids, its muzzle even with their front ends. A handspike is run into the bore, to which four men apply themselves, and the muzzle is raised; the half roller is then laid across the skids under the junction of the chase and reinforce. By alternately bearing down and raising the muzzle the piece is raised upon the half roller, on one block, and one half block, laid across the skids; the half roller being placed three or four inches in front of the junction of the chase and reinforce.

The cap-squares are removed, and the front of the carriage placed on the skids as near the gun as convenient, the trail resting on the ground. Nos. 1 and 2 bear down on the handspike in the bore. No. 6 passes his handspike under the cascable, and is assisted to lift by No. 5. The gunner and Nos. 3 and 4 run up the carriage until the trunnion holes are nearly under the trunnions. Nos. 3 and 4 put on the cap-squares. All then run the carriage forward until the head of the cheeks touch the hurter bolts.

TO MOUNT THE CARRIAGE UPON ITS CHÂSSIS.

503. The gunner bears down on the roller-handspike. Nos. 1 and 2, assisted by No. 5, lift at the handspike in the bore and raise the front of the carriage. The others push the carriage forward until the rollers in the head of the cheeks pass over the counter-hurters, and the guide on the front transom enters into the guide space.

The gunner bears down on the roller-handspike. No. 2 lays down the handspike, and all push the carriage forward; No. 6 with a handspike at the trail assisting to pass it over the counter-hurters, and guiding the flange of the roller into the guide space. (To pass it more conveniently over the counter-hurters, two pieces of scantling, each about three feet long, four by three inches, the ends beveled on opposite sides, with a mortice on the lower side to receive the counter-hurter, may be laid on the rear of the rails. The carriage will roll on these over the counter-hurters.)

No. 6 then passes his handspike across the breech of the piece under the knob of the cascable. Nos. 5 and 6 place themselves at each end of this handspike. Nos. 3 and 4 take hold of the handles. Nos. 1 and 2 seize the rings on each side of the cheeks. The gunner bears down on the roller-handspike. All act together and run the piece up the chassis into battery.

Nos. 1, 2, 5, and 6 apply themselves to a handspike placed across and under the rear end of the chassis, which they raise and hold up, while the gunner, assisted by Nos. 3 and 4, replace the fork and nuts, and put in the pintle.

As these carriages are sent to the forts with the traverse wheels removed for the convenience of transportation, the chassis may be put in position, and the piece mounted, before they are put on.

TO DISMOUNT THE HOWITZER CARRIAGE FROM ITS CHASSIS, THE PIECE BEING MOUNTED.

504. The pintle is removed, and the carriage run into battery. A handspike is passed under the rear end of the chassis, which is raised, and the fork removed as prescribed in No. 501; when the trail is lowered to the ground, and the skids placed in prolongation of the chassis. The gun carriage is then run back until the ends of the cheeks touch the counter-hurters.

The gunner bears down on the roller-handspike to raise the trail as much as possible, and, assisted by Nos. 3 and 4, who place the beveled ends of their handspikes under the outer edges of the trail, passes it over the counter-hurters on to the skids.

When the front rollers touch the counter-hurters, No. 2 puts his handspike in the bore. Nos. 1 and 2, assisted by No. 5, raise the muzzle. Nos. 3 and 4 lift at the rings and push back the carriage until the front rollers rest on the skids. The carriage is then run back on the skids until the muzzle is over their front ends.

TO DISMOUNT THE HOWITZER.

505. No. 2 inserts his handspike in the bore, chocks it below, and bears down on the muzzle. No. 4 lays the round part of his handspike on the cheeks under the breech. Nos. 1 and 2, assisted by No. 5, raise the chase, and the others push the piece forward as far as it can go. Nos. 3 and 4

lay a block and a half block across the skids, touching the head of the cheeks. Nos. 1 and 2 lift at the muzzle, and No. 4 places the half roller on the top; the piece is rested on this half roller.

Nos. 1 and 2 bear down on the handspike in the bore. Nos. 5 and 6 lift on that of No. 6, passed across and under the cascable. The gunner and Nos. 3 and 4 back the carriage until its head rests on the rear end of the skids, and the trail upon the ground. Nos. 3 and 4 place a block and a half block across the skids under the breech.

The muzzle is raised and the half block removed from under the half roller. The muzzle is lowered and the half block removed from under the breech. The muzzle is again raised and the block removed from under the half roller, which is now placed under the trunnions. The muzzle is borne down and the block removed from under the breech, it being replaced by a half block.

The piece may now be slewed in any direction, rolled upon blocks, or placed in any required position.

ARTICLE IV.

MANŒUVRES WITH MACHINES.

(PLATES XXXV, XXXVI, XXXVII, XXXVIII, AND XXXIX.)

---

506. The MACHINES usually employed in the mechanical manœuvres are:

THE LIFTING JACK.
THE GIN.
THE SLING CART.
THE CASEMATE TRUCK.

These, with the implements used in the mechanical manœuvres for siege pieces, enable the detachment to manage the heaviest pieces of artillery in all cases in which the service ordinarily presents.

507. Dimensions, weights, and strength of ropes used in the mechanical manœuvres.

Dimensions, weights, and strength of ropes.

Designation.	Girth.	Length.	Weight.				Strength.	Remarks.
			Of one fathom.		Of the whole rope.			
	Inches.	*Feet.*	*Lbs.*	*oz.*	*Lbs.*	*oz.*	*Lbs.*	
Gin fall (field and siege)	4¼	75	5	4	67	8	8,064	
Gin fall (garrison and casemate) ...	5	120	6	8½	130	0	11,200	
Gin sling	6	26	10	6	44	9	16,128	An eye at one end served with leather.
Drag rope	4	28	4	10	21	8	5,378	
Double prolonge	3¼	78	3	1	31	0	4,760	A loop 18 inches long at one end.
Single prolonge	3¼	48	3	1	24	8	4,760	
Trace-rope	2¼	30	1	6½	7	0½	2,268	
Lashing-line	1¾	10		10½	1	1	1,371	
Marline	......	100	....			11	....	

The prolonges above described are those used in the mechanical manœuvres; they should be designated by their length in order to distinguish them from those used in field service.

The *size* of a rope is designated by its circumference in inches; its *length* is usually expressed in fathoms.

The utmost *strength* of good hemp rope is sixty-four hundred pounds to the square inch. The weight which it will bear before breaking is expressed in tons by one-fifth of the square of the circumference in inches. In practice a rope should not be subjected to more than one-half this strain. It stretches from one-seventh to one-fifth; and its diameter is diminished from one-seventh to one-fourth before breaking. A difference of quality in the hemp may produce a difference of one-fourth in the strength of ropes of the same size.

The strength of Manilla rope is less than that of hemp rope.

The above table is calculated for hemp rope.

The weight of Manilla rope is to that of hemp as 811 is to 1,000.

THE LIFTING JACK.

(PLATE XXXV.)

---

508. This is a small but powerful geared screw, worked by two men turning its handle, which is chiefly useful where the space to work in is confined, or where the manœuvring detachment is reduced to a small number.

The manœuvres with this machine are necessarily slow; but for a single lift it is very convenient, and can be advantageously applied in many instances. It is found highly serviceable in extricating pieces from difficulties during their transportation; and hence, one or more of them should accompany every battery of siege artillery.

509. As the foot of the lifting jack cannot raise a weight sufficiently high for its head to get under it, a piece of scantling called the *lifting block* is used to lay on the foot. In applying the foot of the jack to any weight, this block may be laid *flat, on its edges, or upright.* If used on the head of the jack, it should be laid *flat,* or *on its edge.* If it is desired to lift a greater height blocks should be placed under the bed.

510. All the manœuvres described may be performed by seven men—one gunner and six other cannoneers.

The gunner adjusts the jack, and places the lifting block.

Nos. 1 and 2 carry and work the jack.

Nos. 3 and 4 chock and unchock the gun, wheels, &c., and place and remove the blocks and half rollers.

Nos. 5 and 6 assist to bear down the muzzle; alternate with Nos. 1 and 2 in working the jack; and aid Nos. 3 and 4 to place and remove the blocks and half rollers.

MANŒUVRES WITH THE LIFTING JACK.

LESSON XXXV.

A PIECE LYING ON THE GROUND TO PLACE BLOCKS UNDER THE CHASE AND REINFORCE.
TO REMOVE THE BLOCKS.

511. The implements necessary are:

TWO BLOCKS.
SIX GUN CHOCKS.
ONE LIFTING BLOCK.

A PIECE LYING ON THE GROUND TO PLACE BLOCKS UNDER THE CHASE AND REINFORCE.

512. Pass the small end of a handspike into the bore, allowing about eight inches of the butt end to project, under which place the foot of the jack. Raise the piece, and put a block under the chase as far back as possible.

Apply the foot of the jack under the swell of the muzzle, and move the block to the rear of the trunnions, so that the muzzle will preponderate as the screw is lowered; place a block under the breech; raise the muzzle again, and bring forward the front block to the desired position.

TO REMOVE THE BLOCKS.

513. Apply the jack as before. Move the front block in rear of the trunnions, lower the muzzle, and remove the breech block; raise the muzzle with the jack, and bring the front block towards the neck; insert a handspike in the bore, as before, and apply the foot of the jack under it; raise the

muzzle and remove the front block, letting the gun rest on the ground.

514. *Remark.*—The blocks might be placed and removed, by first raising one end of the piece and then the other; but this would require the lifting jack to be moved.

LESSON XXXVI.

TO SHIFT A PIECE FROM THE TRUNNION HOLES TO ITS TRAVELLING BED.
TO SHIFT A PIECE FROM ITS TRAVELLING BED TO THE TRUNNION HOLES.

---

515. The implements necessary are:

TWO SHORT ROLLERS.
TWO HALF BLOCKS.
FOUR WHEEL CHOCKS.
TWO ROLLER CHOCKS.
ONE TRACE-ROPE.

TO SHIFT A PIECE FROM THE TRUNNION HOLES TO ITS TRAVELLING BED.

516. Chock the wheels of the carriage, and remove the cap-squares; bear down on the muzzle, and remove the elevating screw, placing at the same time a half block against the box of the elevating screw.

517. Apply the jack under the swell of the muzzle and raise the chase, placing a half block on the head of the stock; then by a second lift with the jack place the rollers on the stock, one just in rear of the trunnions, the other under the reinforce; chock the latter roller towards the muzzle, and remove the half blocks from the stock.

518. Attach the rope to the knob of the cascable, and haul upon it so as to bring the breech over the bolster; chock the rear roller towards the muzzle.

519. Apply the head of the jack under the swell of the muzzle and raise it, the breech resting on the bolster; remove

the rollers; lower the piece to its travelling position; untie the rope; replace the cap-squares; and unchock the wheels.

TO SHIFT A PIECE FROM ITS TRAVELLING BED TO THE TRUNNION HOLES.

520. Chock the wheels and remove the cap-squares.

521. Apply the jack under the muzzle and raise the chase, placing two rollers under the piece, one just in rear of the elevating screw-box, the other midway between this and the trunnion holes; chock the former towards the muzzle, and hold the latter in place until the piece bears upon it.

522. Attach the rope to the neck of the gun, and unchock the breech roller; haul upon the rope until the trunnions are over the chin bolts; place a chock upon the stock at such distance from the breech-roller as to allow the trunnions to come over their position, and untie the rope.

523. Apply the head of the jack under the swell, inclining it towards the muzzle, and raise the chase so as to allow the trunnions to pass over the chin bolts; push the piece forward until the trunnions are over the holes; chock the front roller; bear down on the muzzle and remove the breech roller; and lay a half block on the stock in rear of and against the box of the elevating screw.

524. Apply the jack under the muzzle and raise the chase to remove the chase roller; allow the piece to descend into the trunnion holes by lowering the jack.

525. Bear down on the muzzle and remove the half block from the stock; replace the elevating screw and cap-squares, and unchock the wheels.

LESSON XXXVII.

TO MOUNT A SIEGE GUN.
TO DISMOUNT THE GUN.
TO MOUNT AN 8-INCH SIEGE HOWITZER.
TO DISMOUNT THE HOWITZER.
TO CHANGE, TO GREASE, OR TO RAISE A WHEEL.

---

526. The implements necessary are:

TWO HALF ROLLERS.
SIXTEEN BLOCKS.
SIX HALF BLOCKS.
FOUR WHEEL CHOCKS.
TWO SKIDS.

TO MOUNT A SIEGE GUN.

527. The piece is lying upon two blocks, one under the base-ring, the other under the trunnions; and the carriage, unlimbered, is on a line with and in front of the piece, the trail about two yards from the muzzle.

528. Lay the skids parallel to the axis of the piece and two inches outside of the trunnions, their ends on a line with the knob of the cascable.

529. Insert the small end of a handspike, beveled side up, in the bore; apply the jack under it and raise the muzzle, placing a half roller under the trunnions. Lower the muzzle by bearing down upon the handspike in the bore, and place a half roller under the reinforce, near the base-ring.

530. Continue the manœuvre by alternately raising the muzzle with the jack, applying it as may be found most con-

venient, and lowering it by means of the handspike in the bore, as follows:

Raise the muzzle, and apply the foot of the jack under the swell of the muzzle, the lifting block laid on edge.	Place a half block under each end of the front half roller.
Lower the muzzle..........	Place a block under each end of the rear half roller.
Raise the muzzle, the lifting block laid flat upon the foot of the jack.	Place a half block.
Raise the muzzle, the lifting block placed upright.	Replace the half block by a block.
Lower the muzzle............	Place a block.
Raise the muzzle, the lifting block upright.	Place a half block.
Raise the muzzle, the head of the jack under the end of the handspike in the bore.	Replace the half block by a block.
Lower the muzzle............	Place a half block.
Raise the muzzle, the lifting block on edge upon the head of the jack.	Place a half block.
Lower the muzzle..........	Replace the half block by a block.
Raise the muzzle, the head of the jack under the swell of the muzzle, and the lifting block on edge...........	Replace the half block by a block.
Lower the muzzle............	Place a block.

Raise the muzzle, the jack and lifting block as before.	Place a half block
Raise the muzzle; place two half blocks under the bed of the jack, and apply the head under the swell of the muzzle.	Replace the half block by a block.

531. The gun now rests upon two scaffolds; the half roller of the rear scaffold, which is four blocks high, nearly under the base ring; that of the front scaffold, of four blocks and a half block, under the trunnions.

532. Back the carriage, the trail passing between the scaffolds, until the rear of the cheeks touch the front half roller, and the muzzle projects beyond the head of the cheeks. Bear down on the handspike in the muzzle and place a half block under each end of the half roller on the rear scaffold.

533. Apply the head of the jack under the swell of the muzzle; and raise it sufficiently high to allow the chin bolts to pass under the trunnions; remove the front scaffold, and back the carriage until the trunnions are over the trunnion holes.

534. Lower the jack and let the trunnions descend upon the ends of two handspikes inserted in the trunnion holes; bear down on the muzzle and remove the half block from under the half roller.

535. Apply the jack under the muzzle and raise it sufficiently to withdraw the handspikes from the trunnion holes, then lower the trunnions to their places.

536. Remove the blocks and skids; replace the cap-squares, and unchock the wheels.

TO DISMOUNT THE GUN.

537. The carriage is unlimbered.

538. Chock the wheels; remove the cap-squares; lay the skids parallel to the axis of the piece, two inches outside of the trunnions, the rear ends on a line with the knob of the cascable; and place on each skid a scaffold of four blocks and a half block, the middle of each a little in front of the base-ring.

Insert the small end of a handspike in the bore; lower the muzzle by bearing down on this handspike, and place a half roller on the blocks.

539. Raise the muzzle with the jack so as to allow the chin bolts to pass under the trunnions; unchock the wheels, and run the carriage forward until the rear ends of the cheeks are eight inches in front of the trunnions; chock the wheels.

540. Place upon each skid a scaffold of four blocks and a half block, the middle opposite to the trunnions; lay a half roller on the blocks; lower the muzzle so as to allow the gun to rest upon the scaffold; and run out the carriage until the trail is two yards from the muzzle.

541. Continue the manœuvre by alternately raising and lowering the muzzle, as in mounting the piece, (diminishing the scaffold each time by a half block, by replacing each block as it is removed by a half block,) until the piece is lowered upon two blocks.

542. *Remark.*—When the piece is on its platform, by placing the rear ends of the skids even with the rear of the platform, and the rear scaffold as far back as possible, with the front half roller on the front end of its supporting blocks, the carriage can be run to battery, and the trail made to clear the blocks.

TO MOUNT AN 8-INCH SIEGE HOWITZER.

543. The piece is lying upon two blocks, one under the base-ring, the other under the trunnions; and the carriage, unlimbered, is on a line with and in front of the piece, the trail about two yards from the muzzle.

544. Lay the skids parallel to the axis of the piece sufficiently far apart to clear the cheeks of the carriage, and with their rear ends projecting one foot beyond the knob of the cascable.

545. Raise the piece by the method already prescribed for the gun, on two scaffolds of four blocks and a half roller.

546. Move the front scaffold under the trunnions. Bear down the muzzle and move the rear scaffold under the neck of the cascable, increasing its height at the same time by one block.

547. Back the carriage until the travelling bolts touch the front half roller; insert the small ends of two handspikes in the bore with a chock over them to keep them steady and even, and place the jack under their projecting ends.

548. Lay the lifting block on the head of the jack, which is raised on a block, and run up the screw until the piece is raised from the front half roller; take away the front scaffold; back the carriage until the trunnions are over their holes, and lower the screw until the trunnions settle in them; remove the rear scaffold, and put on the cap-squares.

TO DISMOUNT THE HOWITZER.

549. The carriage is unlimbered.

550. Chock the wheels; remove the cap-squares, and lay the skids parallel to the axis of the piece, far enough apart to clear the cheeks, the rear ends projecting one foot beyond the knob of the cascable.

551. Bear down the muzzle so as to raise the breech sufficiently high to place under it a scaffold of five blocks and a half roller, and rest the neck of the cascable on the half roller

552. Insert two handspikes in the bore, as prescribed in No. 547, and place the jack, supported on a block to give it

sufficient height, under their ends. Raise the piece until the trunnions clear the chin bolts; unchock the wheels; back the carriage as close to the jack as possible, and chock the wheels.

553. Place a scaffold of four blocks and the half roller under the trunnions, or as nearly so as the travelling bolts will permit, the front ends of the blocks opposite to the trunnions; lower the piece until it rests on the half roller; remove the jack and run out the carriage.

Lower the piece to the ground as prescribed for the gun.

554. *Remark.*—This manœuvre can be performed on the rectangle of the platform, as prescribed for the gun, (No. 542.)

TO CHANGE, TO GREASE, OR TO RAISE A WHEEL.

555. Apply the jack under the head of one of the cheeks, or at the end of the axletree.

THE GIN.

556. There are three kinds of gins used in service, the *Field and Siege*, the *Garrison* and the *Casemate*. The last two differ from each other only in height; the first differs from the others in construction and size.

Either of them may be used as *shears* for garnishing with their guns such works as are without ramps.

THE FIELD AND SIEGE GUN.

(PLATE XXXV.)

557. When the gin is put together and raised, that part included between the legs and pry-pole is called the inside; the outside being the part without the legs; the right corresponding to the right hand of a man standing at the middle and outside of the windlass, facing towards it; the left corresponding to his left hand.

558. The detachment is composed of the same number of men, and told off in the same manner, as prescribed in No. 250. It having been marched to the gin, the instructor teaches the men its nomenclature, and explains the names and uses of the implements.

559. The odd numbers are placed on the right, and the even numbers on the left side of the gin.

560. The gunner, or the chief of detachment, carries the head of the gin, (when put together;) passes the fall around the pulleys at the head of the gin; secures the loose end of the fall to the sling; hooks the single block to it; and superintends the tying of all knots.

No. 1 carries the foot of the right leg; works the right handspike; and assists in passing the fall over the pulleys, in slinging the piece, and in moving the carriage.

No. 2 carries the foot of the left leg, works the left handspike, and assists in passing the fall over the pulleys, in slinging the piece, and in moving the carriage.

No. 3 puts the braces in the mortices of the right leg, works the inside handspike on the right, keys and unkeys the right cap-square, and assists in moving the carriage.

No. 4 puts the braces in the mortices of the left leg, works the inside handspike on the left, keys and unkeys the left cap-square, and assists in moving the carriage.

No. 5 carries the top of the right leg, places the handspikes of Nos. 1 and 3 in the mortices, and assists in placing the sheaves and in moving the carriage.

No. 6 carries the top of the left leg, places the handspikes of Nos. 2 and 4 in the mortices, and assists in placing the sheaves and in moving the carriage.

Nos. 7 and 8 wrap the running end of the fall around the windlass, hold on or ease off, and assist in carrying sheaves and handspikes, in moving the carriage, &c.

Nos. 9 and 10 assist in carrying implements, in moving the carriage, &c.

MANŒUVRES WITH THE FIELD AND SIEGE GIN.

LESSON XXXVIII.

TO PUT THE GIN TOGETHER.
TO REEVE THE FALL.
TO CARRY THE GIN WHEN PUT TOGETHER.
TO RAISE THE GIN.
TO MOVE THE GIN WHEN RAISED.
TO LOWER THE GIN.

---

561. The implements necessary are:

FIVE HANDSPIKES.

ONE FALL.

ONE SLING.

ONE LASHING LINE.

ONE HAMMER-WRENCH.

THREE PIECES OF PLANK, with a small hole in each to receive the points of the gin.

TO PUT THE GIN TOGETHER.

562. The different parts of the gin having been brought to the place designated, the instructor commands:

PUT THE GIN TOGETHER.

Nos. 1 and 2 bring up the windlass. Nos. 3 and 5 bring the right leg, and lay it with its outside underneath, in its proper position with reference to the windlass. Nos. 4 and 6 bring up the left leg, and place it in a corresponding position. Nos. 7 and 8 bring the sheaves, bolts, and fall, and place them near the head of the gin. Nos. 9 and 10 bring up the braces and pry-pole, and assist Nos. 3 and 4 in putting the braces into the mortices of the left leg, and then into those of the right. Nos. 1 and 2 put in the windlass. Nos. 5 and 6 bring the tops of the legs together and bolt them, when they put in the sheaves and pry-pole. The gunner pins the braces.

TO REEVE THE FALL.

563. The gin being put together, and still lying upon the ground, the instructor commands:

REEVE THE FALL.

Nos. 5 and 6 raise the pry-pole until it clears the pulleys. The gunner receiving from Nos. 1 and 2 one end of the fall, passes it through the left sheave from below, and hands it back to them. They pass it through the sheave of the single pulley, (hooked for convenience on the middle brace,) and return it to the gunner, who passes it through the right sheave from below, and gives it to No. 1, by whom it is secured by wrapping it around the middle brace.

564. If the gin has been raised, the instructor gives the same command, when the gunner, mounting upon the upper brace, receives from Nos. 1 and 2 one end of the fall, which he passes over the left sheave from without to within. The fall is then reeved in the manner prescribed.

TO CARRY THE GIN WHEN PUT TOGETHER.

565. The gin is lying upon the ground, its outside downwards.

566. The instructor commands:

CARRY THE GIN.

The gunner applies himself at the head. Nos. 5 and 6 apply themselves at the ends of the upper braces. Nos. 3 and

4 apply themselves at the ends of the middle braces. Nos. 1 and 2 apply themselves at the ends of the lower braces.

567. The instructor, having indicated the direction, commands:

MARCH.

The men lift the gin together, and march off, keeping step.

568. The handspikes, fall, and sling may be carried either on the gin or by the remaining men.

TO RAISE THE GIN.

569. The instructor commands:

RAISE THE GIN.

The gunner applies himself at the head of the gin. Nos. 1, 2, 3, and 4 apply themselves near the upper brace. Nos. 5 and 6 each place a foot against the lower ends of the legs to steady them.

HEAVE.

570. The gin is raised. Nos. 5 and 6 take hold of the pry-pole as soon as there is no longer any danger of the legs slipping, and by pulling down upon it, assist in raising the gin.

TO MOVE THE GIN WHEN RAISED.

571. The instructor wishing to move the gin a short distance, commands:

MOVE THE GIN.

Nos. 1 and 2 place each a handspike under the windlass from without, retaining the small ends. Nos. 3 and 4 seize the butt ends. Nos. 5 and 6 apply themselves at the handle of the pry-pole.

MARCH.

572. The gin is lifted with care, and placed in the desired position.

TO LOWER THE GIN

573. The gin is lowered in a similar manner to that prescribed for raising it. Nos. 5 and 6 raise the pry-pole and assist in easing the gin to the ground, the outside downwards.

LESSON XXXIX.

TO MOUNT A GUN.
TO DISMOUNT A GUN.
TO MOUNT A HOWITZER.
TO DISMOUNT A HOWITZER.
TO SLING A MORTAR MOUNTED ON ITS BED.
TO SLING A MORTAR WITHOUT ITS BED.

---

574. The implements necessary are:

FIVE HANDSPIKES.
ONE FALL.
ONE SLING.
ONE LASHING LINE.
ONE HAMMER-WRENCH.
THREE PIECES OF PLANK, with a small hole in each to receive the points of the gin.

TO MOUNT A GUN.

It is immaterial upon which side of the piece the legs of the gin are placed, but for uniformity they are generally placed on the right.

575. The gin being placed with its pulleys directly over the trunnions, and the foot of the pry-pole thirteen feet from the lower brace, the instructor commands:

MOUNT THE PIECE.

No. 1 puts a handspike in the bore. No. 2 passes the eye or loop end of the sling around the knob of the cascable. No. 1 passes the other end under the handspike in the bore and hands it to No. 2, who draws it through the loop and fastens it either by a knot or with the lashing-rope. The gunner hooks the single pulley to the sling just in rear of the trunnions, and fastens the loose end of the fall to the sling near the same place. Nos. 1 and 2 then go to their places at the windlass. The gunner applies himself to the handspike in the bore to steady the piece. Nos. 7 and 8 pass the running end of the fall from the outside under the windlass, and take three turns with it from right to left around the left of the windlass; they then step back three paces, holding on by the running end or slack, No. 7 being nearest the windlass.

HEAVE.

576. Nos. 1 and 2, or 3 and 4, according to the position of the windlass, place their handspikes in the upper mortices, and bear down until the ends of their handspikes are near the ground, the other two handspikes being inserted in the then upper mortices. No. 1 gives the command HEAVE, at which the first two handspikes are withdrawn and tossed to the inside of the gin, the small ends resting on the lower brace and against the legs. Nos. 1, 2, 3, and 4 bear down on the handspikes. Nos. 5 and 6 in the mean time put the disengaged handspikes in the upper mortices. The operation is thus continued until the piece is raised to the required height; No. 1 always giving the command HEAVE, and Nos. 5 and 6 placing the disengaged handspikes in the upper mortices.

SECURE THE WINDLASS.

577. The men at the handspikes secure the windlass by allowing the handspikes in the upper mortices to bear against the middle brace and legs.

RUN UP THE CARRIAGE.

578. All the men, except Nos. 7 and 8, bring up the carriage as in No. 369, until the trunnion holes are directly under the trunnions.

SLACK OFF.

579. Nos. 7 and 8 slack off the fall slowly; the gunner steadies the piece by means of the handspike in the bore; and the piece is lowered into its proper position. Nos. 3 and 4 put on the cap-squares, and key them.

580. *Remark.*—If, from any circumstance, it is not convenient to sling the piece in the manner prescribed, it may be slung with short piece of rope passed around each trunnion, and the ends fastened together on the top of the piece; or, the trunnion-rings may be put on.

Hook the pulley to this sling or to the trunnion-rings; bear down with one or two men on the handspike in the bore to balance the piece, and when it is raised sufficiently high run the carriage under it, and place a piece of handspike in the trunnion holes, and a block on the stock (or on the rear transom in a casemate carriage) to receive the breech. Lower the gun, the trunnions directly over the trunnion holes, until the lower surface of the gun bears on the piece of handspike. Remove the sling from the trunnions, and run the carriage, with the gun on it, back until the head of the cheeks are in rear of a perpendicular let fall from the head of the gin. Pass the sling around the chase; hook the pulley to it; and work the gin until the weight no longer bears on the piece of handspike in the trunnion holes; remove this piece, and lower the trunnions to their places; bear down on the muzzle, and remove the block from under the breech.

TO DISMOUNT A GUN.

581. The gin is placed in the same position with reference to the piece as prescribed for mounting it.

582. The instructor commands:

DISMOUNT THE PIECE.

The piece is slung, the cap-squares taken off, and the running end of the fall passed around the windlass in the same manner and by the same men as prescribed for mounting it.

The commands HEAVE, SECURE THE WINDLASS, RUN OUT THE CARRIAGE, and SLACK OFF, are then given and executed in the manner already prescribed.

583. *Remark.*—If the ground is not firm, pieces of plank prepared for this purpose must be placed under the legs and the pry-pole before raising the piece.

TO MOUNT A HOWITZER.
TO DISMOUNT A HOWITZER.

A howitzer is slung, mounted, and dismounted in the manner already prescribed for the gun.

TO SLING A MORTAR MOUNTED ON ITS BED.

584. The sling* is passed under the front notches, then crossed over the top of the mortar and passed under the rear notches. The single pulley is hooked to the sling where it crosses the top of the mortar. The mortar is raised or lowered by the gin in the manner prescribed for the gun.

TO SLING A MORTAR WITHOUT ITS BED.

585. The sling is passed around the trunnions.

TO SHIFT THE FALL.

586. As the turns gain once the diameter of the fall at each revolution of the windlass, they will, when the weight has been raised a considerable height, come against the opposite leg; the instructor then commands:

HALT—SHIFT THE FALL.

The windlass is secured as in No. 577. Nos. 7 and 8 hold

---

* Made of 4½-inch white rope, 24 feet long, with the ends spliced together.

on to the slack. The numbers at the handspikes on the side towards which the turns on the windlass have gained, overhaul a sufficient length of the end of the fall and make a double hitch with it around the leg below the lower crossbar, passing the end inside of the windlass and braces to the chief of detachment, who mounts on the windlass, and makes with it a rolling hitch on the standing part of the fall, near the upper brace, when he descends.

EASE AWAY.

587. No. 7 slacks off until the weight bears on the end of the fall.

SHIFT THE FALL.

588. Nos. 7 and 8 ease the slack. The men at the handspikes shift the turns on the windlass to its opposite end. Nos. 7 and 8 tighten them and hold on.

The men work on the windlass until the weight bears on the fall, when the windlass is secured. The chief of detachment unties the rolling hitch, and the manœuvre is resumed.

589. *Remarks.*—Six men (including the chief of detachment) are sufficient for mounting or dismounting any siege piece by the siege gin; but for the purpose of instruction, this gin being more easily handled than the casemate and garrison gins, the same number of men have been prescribed as are necessary for them.

In this case Nos. 1, 2, 3, and 4 work the handspikes; No. 5 holds on to the running end of the fall, and the chief of detachment steadies the piece.

GARRISON AND CASEMATE GINS.

(PLATE XXXVI.)

590. The garrison and casemate gins differ from the siege gin in having two braces of iron instead of the three wooden crossbars or braces, and in having the pry-pole inserted between the legs, which are kept together by the clevis bolt. The upper pulley (generally treble) is hooked to the clevis.

591. The gin is put together on the ground, and raised by moving up the legs and pry-pole towards each other. The pry-pole has cleats nailed to it, to enable a man to mount to the head of the gin to hook on the pulley and to reeve the fall.

592. The gin is lowered by gradually drawing out the legs and pry-pole until the men can get near enough towards the head to support it; it is then lowered upon the piece or on the ground, as the case may be.

Ratchet windlass.

593. A ratchet windlass is now applied to gins, and the handspike is inserted in a box to which a pawl is attached. This pawl catches in the notches of the ratchet when the handspike is borne down, and slides over them as it is raised. Another pawl is hung from the legs, which catches in the opposite notches of the ratchet, and prevents the windlass from turning backwards.

As the handspikes are kept in such a position that the men can apply themselves with advantage, one man is enabled with this windlass to raise double the weight he could with one of the old pattern.

THE USE OF THE GIN AS SHEARS.

594. By removing the pry-pole the legs of the gin may be used as shears.

When the garrison or casemate gin is to be thus used, a block of wood of the same dimensions as the head of the pry-pole, with a hole in it large enough to receive the clevis bolt, must be inserted in place of the pry-pole.

595. The detachment is composed of the same number of men and told off in the same manner as in No. 250. The posts of the men are:

Nos. 1, 2, 3, and 4 at the handspikes.
Nos. 5 and 6 at the guys.
Nos. 7 and 8 at the slack of the fall.
Nos. 9 and 10 at the counter guy.

MANŒUVRES WITH THE GIN AS SHEARS.

LESSON XL.

TO RAISE A PIECE OVER THE CREST OF A PARAPET OR EDGE OF A WALL.
TO LOWER A PIECE OVER THE CREST OF A PARAPET OR EDGE OF A WALL INTO THE DITCH.
TO RAISE A PIECE AND PASS IT THROUGH A CASEMATE EMBRASURE OR ANY SIMILAR OPENING.
TO PASS A PIECE THROUGH A CASEMATE EMBRASURE OR ANY SIMILAR OPENING AND LOWER IT INTO THE DITCH.

---

596. The implements necessary are:

FIVE HANDSPIKES.
ONE FALL. Or more, if the height requires it.
ONE TRUNNION-SLING. Strong rope, the ends knotted or spliced together.
ONE DOUBLE PROLONGE. For the counter guy.
THREE SINGLE PROLONGES. Two for guys to the gin, and one for steadying the gun.
ONE TRACE ROPE.
TWO LASHING LINES.
ONE SINGLE PULLEY AND FALL. Extra.
THREE MAULS.
SIX STAKES. 5½ feet long, their heads banded with iron.
ONE COLLAR. For the head of the gin.

TO RAISE A PIECE OVER THE CREST OF A PARAPET OR EDGE OF A WALL.

597. The lower brace is removed. A piece of plank two and a half to three inches thick, with holes to receive the

points, is placed under the gin. If the ground is not sufficiently firm, this may be placed upon two other pieces laid perpendicularly to it, and under the holes made to receive the points.

598. The gin is lying on the ground, its outside downwards, the feet towards the ditch, and the head raised on a block placed under the right leg.

The implements are placed two yards from the head of the gin, the handspikes laid parallel to the braces.

599. The instructor commands:

EQUIP THE GIN.

The chief of detachment moves five paces from the head of the gin and places himself in the prolongation of its axis, when he marks a point for a stake at four paces to the right, and another at four paces to the left of his position. No. 5 places a stake at the first, and No. 6 one at the second point. Nos. 7 and 8 take each a maul and assist Nos. 5 and 6 to drive these stakes, giving them a considerable inclination from the gin; they then drive two others, inclined as the first, two paces beyond them, in the direction the guys will take when the gin is raised. (In practice these distances cannot be observed; but the guys should be given as nearly this inclination as possible, and advantage taken of any permanent objects to attach them to.)

No. 9, directed by the chief of detachment, places himself in prolongation of the axis of the gin, facing towards it, and about fifteen paces from the foot of the wall, and there places a stake; assisted by No. 10 he drives this stake, inclining it from the gin, and then drives a second stake, inclined as the first, two paces beyond it.

The chief of detachment and Nos. 1 and 2 reeve the fall, &c., as prescribed in No. 563; attach the single prolonges to the collar, and pass their ends to Nos. 5 and 6, who stretch them in the direction of their stakes; attach the double prolonge to the opposite side of the collar; pass the end (into the ditch) to Nos. 9 and 10; and then place the collar on the head of the gin so as to allow each guy to take its proper direction.

RAISE THE GIN.

600. The chief of detachment and Nos. 1, 2, 3, 4, 7, and 8 raise the gin—Nos. 5 and 6 slacking up their guys, and Nos. 9 and 10 assisting, by hauling on the counter guy—and place it about two paces from the crest. Nos. 5 and 6 take each a turn of his guy around the first stakes, and slack or tighten it as directed by the chief of detachment.

The gin being raised until its head is slightly inclined towards the ditch, the guys are fastened to the second stakes by a double hitch, and the counter guy is attached to its stakes in a similar manner.

SLING THE PIECE.

601. Nos. 9 and 10 pass the trunnion-sling over the trunnions. Nos. 1 and 2 overhaul the fall, and lower the pulley into the ditch. Nos. 9 and 10 pass the hook of the pulley through the bight of the sling, and attach a single prolonge to the sling to serve as a guy to guide or steady the gun while being raised.

RAISE THE PIECE.

This is done as prescribed in No. 563.

602. *To tighten the knots and stretch the ropes*, the instructor will cause the weight to be partly raised and then lowered; and without altering the ropes he will have the feet of the gin moved forward to within twenty-five inches of the crest of the parapet or edge of the wall.

603. The inclination of the gin, measured from the middle of the line joining the feet to a perpendicular let fall from its head, should not exceed twenty-five inches; the heavier the weight the greater the necessity for not allowing this inclination to be exceeded.

604. When the gin is placed in its new position, work the windlass and raise the piece; Nos. 5 and 6 observing their stakes and giving notice if anything becomes deranged. After the weight bears fairly upon the stakes, Nos. 5 and 6 may be employed in other duties if required.

605. When the trunnions are about one foot above the crest, the instructor commands:

HALT—BRING IN THE PIECE.

The men cease heaving at the windlass, and secure it by letting the upper handspikes bear on the legs.

The chief of detachment mounts on the second brace; receives from No. 4 a single pulley, which he hooks to the third brace near the left leg, the point of the hook turned from the ditch; doubles (with the casemate or garrison gin) the end of a rope which he attaches by a timber hitch to the left leg (when the muzzle is turned towards the left, and *vice versa*) as high up as he can conveniently reach while standing on the second brace, and passes the hook of the single pulley through the bight; and receives from No. 2 the end of a fall, which he passes through the pulley. No. 4 overhauls the end of the fall towards the ditch, and attaches it to the neck of the piece by a timber hitch on the top of the gun.

The muzzle is supposed to be towards the left leg; if it is reversed, the duties here prescribed for the even numbers will then be performed by the odd numbers.

The chief of detachment descends and takes a handspike. No. 3 attaches a lashing rope to the knob of the cascable by a double hitch, and passes the end under the windlass between the legs. Nos. 3 and 4 haul on this rope.

Nos. 1 and 2 and the chief of detachment with their handspikes, and Nos. 3 and 4 at the rope, pass the piece between the legs in a direction perpendicular to the windlass, assisted in this, if necessary, by Nos. 5, 6, 7, and 8; in which case the slack of the fall, held by Nos. 7 and 8, must be made fast. Nos. 5 and 6 lay planks on each side of the piece at a suitable distance to receive rollers. The chief of detachment places a roller near the base-ring and chocks it on both sides. Nos.

1 and 2 haul on the fall attached to the neck, and raise the muzzle a little higher than the breech, keeping it tight, and then take three turns with it around the windlass and hold on to the slack.

LOWER THE PIECE—EASE AWAY.

606. Nos. 7 and 8 ease the slack of their fall until the chase is lower than the breech, and the weight is transferred to the fall attached to the neck.

HALT.

607. Nos. 3 and 4 unhook the pulley at the trunnions, and hang it on the second brace. Nos. 5 and 6 steady the piece with the rope at the cascable. Nos. 7 and 8 remove the fall from the windlass, and then hold on by the slack of the fall, now held by Nos. 1 and 2.

RAISE THE PIECE.

608. The chief of detachment unchocks the roller with a handspike.

The windlass is worked, and the chief of detachment, as soon as he can, places a second roller in front of the trunnions, and the piece is rolled back on the level on which the gin stands.

TO LOWER A PIECE OVER THE CREST OF A PARAPET OR EDGE OF A WALL INTO THE DITCH.

609. The piece is passed under the windlass of the gin on the rollers, the muzzle towards the ditch, and is pushed forward until the trunnions are nearly over the crest, when the gin is equipped, and the piece slung as prescribed in No. 601.

610. The windlass is worked, and, when the trunnions are about a foot above the crest, the instructor commands:

HALT—PASS THE PIECE.

The men cease heaving, and leave the handspikes in the upper mortices bearing against the legs. The chief of detachment takes a handspike. No. 3 attaches a rope to the knob of the cascable, passes it under the windlass between the legs, and carries it to the right of the gin. Nos. 3 and 4 haul on this rope. The chief of detachment and Nos. 1 and 2 with their handspikes, and Nos. 3 and 4 at the rope, assisted, if necessary, by the spare men, pass the piece between the legs and place it parallel to the windlass, the breech to the right. No. 3 unties the rope from the cascable, fastens a prolonge to the trunnion-sling, and throws the end to the men in the ditch.

LOWER THE PIECE—EASE AWAY.

611. Nos. 7 and 8 slack off the fall slowly, and the piece is allowed to descend into the ditch.

TO RAISE A PIECE AND PASS IT THROUGH A CASEMATE EMBRASURE OR ANY SIMILAR OPENING.

612. The additional implements necessary are:

FOUR HANDSPIKES. TWO ROLLERS.	In the casemate.
ONE GUN SLING.	(Or a piece of fall, about three times the length of the gun.) In the ditch.

Besides the usual detachment for working the gin, four additional men are required, who, with the chief of detachment, are stationed at the embrasure to receive the gun.

613. The piece is in the ditch, the breech to the wall.

The gin is equipped, as before, on the edge of the parapet, over the embrasure through which the piece is to pass.

614. The men in the ditch attach each end of the sling to the neck by a timber hitch, the bight of which, laid on top of the gun, should reach nearly to the vent; the hook of the

pulley attached to the fall of the gin is passed into this bight; the middle of a prolonge is made fast to the cascable by a double hitch, and the ends passed over the sling beyond the hook of the pulley; these ends are then passed under the reinforce, brought up on top, drawn tight, and tied in a right knot.

Several turns are taken around the piece and over the sling with a lashing line a little in rear of the trunnions, and the ends fastened on top with a right knot. (These knots may be made with a bow, or a tool handle may be inserted in them, so that they can be easily untied.) A prolonge is fastened around the trunnions to serve as a guy to steady the piece while raising it.

The gin is worked as previously prescribed, and the piece raised breech foremost.

615. When the trunnions are as high as the sole of the embrasure, the instructor commands:

HALT—BRING IN THE PIECE.

The chief of detachment places a roller on the sole to receive the breech of the piece, chocks it towards the ditch, and then unties the knot of the prolonge which is around the breech. The assistants haul on the end of this rope.

RAISE THE PIECE.

616. The gin is worked and the piece raised, the assistants allowing the prolonge to slip out gradually. When the prolonge no longer bears on the sling, the chief of detachment uncrosses its ends and returns them to the assistants, who, pulling on them, draw the piece in on the roller.

The chief of detachment then unties the lashing rope. The assistants receive and hold on the ends, allowing them to slip out gradually, while the gin is worked and the piece raised and drawn in. The chief of detachment places a second roller under the piece. The assistants haul on the lashing rope, and the piece is brought into the embrasure.

TO PASS A PIECE THROUGH A CASEMATE EMBRASURE, OR ANY SIMILAR OPENING, AND LOWER IT INTO THE DITCH.

For the additional implements and men required see No. 612.

617. The chief of detachment fastens to the knob of the cascable the middle of a prolonge, intended to bind the sling to the piece as prescribed in No. 614; attaches the sling to the neck of the piece as prescribed in No. 614, the bight reaching a little in rear of the trunnions, so as to allow the muzzle to preponderate; and attaches to the cascable another rope which is used to steady the piece when running it out of the embrasure.

The carriage is run from battery and chocked firmly in its position. The assistants take a turn with each end of the prolonge attached to the cascable, around the rollers, or the naves of the wheels, or around a post, or any other suitable fixture.

The piece is moved forward on rollers by handspikes, until the trunnions are near the edge of the embrasure; the hook of the pulley from the gin is then passed into the bight of the sling, which is lashed to the piece as prescribed in No. 614.

The piece being steadied with the rope at the cascable, is pushed forward until the trunnions are over the edge of the embrasure and the muzzle inclines downwards.

RAISE THE PIECE.

618. The gin is worked until the weight bears on the fall, when the instructor commands:

HALT.

The assistants remove their rope from the cascable, fasten it around the trunnions, and throw the end to the men in the ditch.

LOWER THE PIECE—EASE AWAY.

619. The piece is allowed to descend gradually into the ditch, where the men place two blocks to receive it, one under the muzzle, the other under the breech.

THE SLING CART.

(PLATES XXXVII AND XXXVIII.)

620. The sling cart is used for moving pieces of artillery short distances. It is a lever on wheels, and may be used simply as such.

There are two kinds: one for the heaviest calibres, which, being limbered with a siege limber, may be drawn by horses; and the other, called the *hand sling cart*, designed for moving siege pieces in the trenches.

621. The siege limber may also, in case of necessity, be used as a sling cart.

622. The detachment, including the chief of detachment, is composed of five men, except for slinging the 10-inch columbiad, which requires five men additional.

MANŒUVRES WITH THE SLING CART.

LESSON XLI.

TO SLING A SIEGE GUN, HOWITZER, OR MORTAR.
TO LOWER A SIEGE GUN, HOWITZER, OR MORTAR TO THE GROUND.
TO SLING A SEA-COAST HOWITZER OR COLUMBIAD.
TO SLING A 10-INCH COLUMBIAD.
TO SLING A SIEGE MORTAR MOUNTED ON ITS BED.
TO SLING A SEA-COAST MORTAR.
TO TRANSPORT A SIEGE PIECE SHORT DISTANCES BY A LIMBER.
TO RAISE A PIECE UPON ONE OR MORE BLOCKS BY A LIMBER.
TO SLING A PIECE ON TWO LIMBERS SO THAT IT MAY BE TRANSPORTED WITH HORSES.

623. The implements necessary are:

TWO BLOCKS.
FOUR WHEEL CHOCKS
ONE SLING-CHAIN of 36 links, with a short hook at each end.
ONE TWO AND ONE-HALF INCH ROPE, 45 feet long.
ONE SLING-CHAIN, additional, for a siege mortar mounted on its bed.

TO SLING A SIEGE GUN, HOWITZER, OR MORTAR.

624. The instructor commands:

BACK THE CART OVER THE PIECE.

Nos. 1 and 2 go to the end of the pole. Nos. 3 and 4 and the chief of detachment apply themselves at the wheels. The cart is then backed over the piece, the pole being in the direction of the breech, and the axle directly over the trunnions. Nos. 3 and 4 chock the wheels.

SLING THE PIECE.

625. No. 1 fastens the middle of the prolonge to the end of the pole. Nos. 3 and 4 carry one end of the prolonge to the rear of the cart. Nos. 1 and 2 raise the pole by hand, Nos. 3 and 4 at the same time applying themselves at the prolonge.

When the pole thus raised is nearly vertical, Nos. 1 and 2 seize the other end of the prolonge to steady the pole. The chief of detachment lays the middle of the sling-chain over the piece in rear of the trunnions, carries each end around the trunnions from the rear to the front, and hooks them around the axle hooks, being careful to take up all the slack. Nos. 1 and 2, assisted, if necessary, by Nos. 3 and 4, haul upon the prolonge until the end of the pole can be reached by hand, when they seize and bear it to the ground. The chief of detachment hooks the cascable chain around the knob of the cascable in such a manner that the piece will swing level when the pole is horizontal. Nos. 1 and 2 raise the pole until it rests on the pole-prop.

The piece is thus raised about eight inches from the ground.

626. For transportation it should be ordinarily raised higher; which can readily be done by blocking up the piece and raising it again in the manner above prescribed.

TO LOWER A SIEGE GUN, HOWITZER, OR MORTAR TO THE GROUND.

627. The piece is lowered to the ground by the same means, but in an inverse manner to that just prescribed.

Nos. 1 and 2 bear the end of the pole to the ground. The chief of detachment unhooks the cascable chain. Nos. 1 and 2 allow the pole to rise gently until it is nearly vertical. If the piece does not then rest upon the ground, it is blocked up and unslung; when, by repeating the manœuvre, it may be lowered to the ground.

After the piece has been unslung, Nos. 3 and 4 ease the pole down carefully by means of the prolonge until Nos. 1 and 2 can reach it with their hands; the latter then assist them in easing it down.

TO SLING A SEA-COAST HOWITZER OR COLUMBIAD.
TO SLING A 10-INCH COLUMBIAD.

Executed as prescribed for a siege piece in No. 624 and following.

TO SLING A SIEGE MORTAR MOUNTED ON ITS BED.

The instructor gives the same commands and the duties are performed by the same numbers as prescribed for a siege piece in No. 624 and following.

628. The sling cart is backed over the mortar, the pole being in the direction of the breech, and the axle directly over the trunnions.

If the bed is resting on the ground, it may be slung by first raising the pole nearly vertical, passing the sling chain around the front manœuvring bolts, hooking it over the axle hooks, and hauling upon the prolonge.

It is then blocked up, and the sling taken off the bolts and passed under the bed just in front of the cap-square bolts; this brings the sling a little in front of the centre of gravity of the mortar and bed.

The pole being now horizontal, Nos. 1 and 2 bear down upon it until the end rests upon the ground. Nos. 3 and 4 remove the blocks. The chief of detachment passes the other sling chain around the rear manœuvring bolts and over the pole, and then hooks it in such a manner that the bed will be level, when Nos. 1 and 2 raise the pole until it rests on the pole-prop.

The bed is thus raised about eight inches from the ground.

If necessary, it may be blocked up, and raised higher by a similar manœuvre.

629. The breech should always slightly preponderate, in order to prevent the pole from flying up.

TO SLING A SEA-COAST MORTAR.

630. Sea-coast mortars and their beds must be slung separately.

631. The mortar is raised by passing the sling chain through the clevis, over the axle, and hooking it around the pole at its junction with the axle, the pole having been previously raised for this purpose.

The bed is raised and slung in a similar manner to that already prescribed for the siege mortar on its bed.

TO TRANSPORT A SIEGE PIECE SHORT DISTANCES BY A LIMBER.

632. The piece is raised upon two blocks, one under the breech, the other under the muzzle, when a chain is passed around the piece just in front of the reinforce, or about six inches in front of the trunnions.

The limber, its pole being in the direction of the breech, is run over the piece until the pintle is over the chain, when the pole is slightly raised, and the chain passed over the pintle and fastened. The pole is borne to the ground, the front block removed, and a rope fastened over the pole and around the knob of the cascable. The pole is then raised, and the rear block removed.

633. If the chain is passed around the piece any nearer to the trunnions than prescribed, the pole will have too great a tendency to fly up.

TO RAISE A PIECE UPON ONE OR MORE BLOCKS BY A LIMBER.

634. The trunnion-loops, or an ordinary chain, is passed over the knob of the cascable and over the pintle, and made fast while the pole is raised. The piece is then raised by bearing down the pole.

635. The wheels should not be chocked, as they will soon find their proper bearing.

TO SLING A PIECE ON TWO LIMBERS SO THAT IT MAY BE TRANSPORTED WITH HORSES.

636. The pole of one of the limbers is removed, a block is placed under the trunnions, and the limber run forward, with its fork over the piece, the pintle over the knob of the cascable.

The muzzle is raised, and the front block removed. The muzzle is borne down, and the pintle fastened to the knob of the cascable with the chain or lashing rope. The fork is borne down to the piece and lashed to it around the reinforce.

The other limber is backed over the neck of the piece, when the pole is raised and the neck attached to the limber by taking two turns with a prolonge around the pintle, and two turns over the fork in front of the axletree, so that the weight will balance the pole, the end of the prolonge being fastened with a jamming hitch. The piece is then raised by bearing down the pole.

THE CASEMATE TRUCK.

(PLATE XXXVIII.)

637. This machine is intended for moving sea-coast pieces and their carriages in the galleries of casemate batteries.

638. The detachment is composed of the same number of men, and told off in the same manner as prescribed in No. 250.

MANŒUVRES WITH THE CASEMATE TRUCK.

LESSON XLII.

TO PLACE A CASEMATE CHASSIS ON THE TRUCK.
TO LOWER THE CHASSIS TO THE GROUND.
TO REMOVE THE CHASSIS FROM THE CASEMATE.
TO PLACE A GUN CARRIAGE ON THE TRUCK.
TO LOWER THE GUN CARRIAGE TO THE GROUND.
TO SHIFT THE GUN CARRIAGE FROM THE TRUCK TO ITS CHASSIS.
TO SHIFT THE GUN CARRIAGE FROM ITS CHASSIS TO THE TRUCK.

639. The implements necessary are:

ONE LONG ROLLER.
TWO BLOCKS.
TWO HALF BLOCKS.
FOUR BRICOLES.

TO PLACE A CASEMATE CHASSIS ON THE TRUCK.

640. The chassis is on the ground, the truck near it, with its front wheel and tongue removed.

641. Two handspikes are passed across and under the front part of the tongue of the chassis. Eight men, two at each end of each handspike, raise the end of the chassis. Nos. 9 and 10 and the chief of detachment run the truck under the chassis near the men, and turn it so that its axis may be in the same vertical plane with that of the chassis, the end of the truck from which the wheel has been removed being on the ground towards the rear of the chassis.

642. The men at the handspikes lift, and the truck is run to the rear, until the centre of the wheels are four and one-half to five feet from the centre of the rear transom, and the chassis is balanced on the truck. Nos. 1 and 2 support and direct the front of the chassis, and the gunner and Nos. 9 and 10 its rear. Nos. 3, 4, 7, and 8 take bricoles and hook into the rings. Nos. 5 and 6 carry a handspike on each side opposite to the wheels, to work at the bolts when it is necessary to overcome any obstacle.

All move the chassis to its embrasure, the tongue near the tongue hole.

TO LOWER THE CHASSIS TO THE GROUND.

643. Two blocks are placed lengthwise under each rail, and a half block crosswise on the top of them, near the middle of the chassis and near the truck. The rear of the chassis is raised. Nos. 1 and 2 bear down on the front of the tongue. The gunner and Nos. 8 and 9 take out the truck, and lower the chassis on the blocks.

644. The men move to the front of the chassis and raise it. Nos. 9 and 10 remove the blocks. The gunner places a long roller under the front transom. If the pavement is uneven, the long roller should be placed on two boards.

645. The men move to the rear of the chassis. Nos. 1 and 2 embar with their handspikes under the rear transom to raise the rear traverse wheels from the pavement. All push the chassis forward. The gunner sees that the tongue goes fairly into its opening.

646. If the roller runs out before the chassis is placed, the gunner calls the handspike men to the front transom, raises it, and replaces the roller. When the traverse wheels are on their circle he puts in the pintle.

TO REMOVE THE CHASSIS FROM THE CASEMATE.

647. The pintle is taken out. With two handspikes passed under the front transom, the front of the chassis is raised, and

the long roller placed under the rails. The rear of the chassis is raised; the tongue run out of the tongue hole; and the chassis placed upon the truck as prescribed in No. 641 and following.

648. *Remark.*—To prevent injury to the pavement, planks should be laid under the wheels of the truck.

TO PLACE A GUN CARRIAGE ON THE TRUCK.

649. The gun carriage is on the ground standing on the head of its cheeks; the truck near it, with its front wheel and tongue removed.

650. The truck is run up, the end on the ground under the guides, and its wheels chocked; the trail of the carriage is lowered upon it. The trail is borne down and the head of the carriage raised sufficiently high for the gunner and assistants to replace the truck wheels and tongue. Nos. 1 and 2 apply themselves at the tongue. The others apply themselves as prescribed in No. 642. The carriage is then moved on the truck to its place.

TO LOWER THE GUN CARRIAGE TO THE GROUND.

651. The front wheel of the truck is removed, and its front transom rested on the ground. The carriage is then raised on the head of its cheeks.

TO SHIFT THE GUN CARRIAGE FROM THE TRUCK TO ITS CHASSIS.

652. The front of the truck is placed at right angles, or nearly so, to the chassis, and as near to the front transom as possible. The front wheel is removed, and the front transom of the truck rested on the rail of the chassis, when the wheels are chocked.

The carriage is turned up on the head of its cheeks, as near the front transom of the chassis as it can be placed, and slewed until its axis is in a line with that of the chassis. The trail is then lowered to its place.

TO SHIFT THE GUN CARRIAGE FROM ITS CHASSIS TO THE TRUCK.

653. The gun carriage is turned up on the head of its cheeks, and slewed so as to have the guides turned towards the truck, which is placed as prescribed in No. 652. The trail is then lowered upon the truck; the wheel replaced, and the carriage moved off.

LESSON XLIII.

TO PLACE A HEAVY GUN ON THE TRUCK.

TO REMOVE A HEAVY GUN FROM THE TRUCK AND PLACE IT ON TWO BLOCKS.

TO PLACE A HEAVY GUN ON THE TRUCK BY A GIN.

---

654. The implements necessary are:

ONE LIFTING JACK.
TWO HALF ROLLERS.
EIGHT BLOCKS.
FOUR HALF BLOCKS.
FOUR GUN CHOCKS.
FOUR WHEEL CHOCKS.
TWO SKIDS.

TO PLACE A HEAVY GUN ON THE TRUCK.

655. The gun is on two blocks.

656. The skids are laid as prescribed in No. 528; then by means of handspikes, or the lifting jack, the gun is raised on a half roller under the trunnions, the half roller resting on one block on each skid. The muzzle is borne down and two blocks placed on the ground lengthwise side by side, their middle under the base-ring, and two others crosswise upon them, thus forming a scaffold of three blocks high for the base-ring to rest on.

The muzzle is raised with the lifting jack; the truck, with the wheel and tongue out, passed under the gun, the front of the truck (which now rests on the ground) under the breech. the trunnions of the gun nearly over the middle transom, and between it and the wheels of the truck. The wheels are then chocked, the gun lowered upon the truck, and the jack removed.

The muzzle is borne down—the gun pressing on the rear

transom of the truck will raise the front part under the breech—the wheel and tongue inserted, and the gun moved to its place.

TO REMOVE A HEAVY GUN FROM THE TRUCK AND PLACE IT ON TWO BLOCKS.

657. The muzzle is borne down and the truck wheel and tongue removed. The blocks are placed under the breech as for mounting; the muzzle raised with the jack; and the truck removed. The skids, blocks, and half roller are placed, and the piece lowered on two blocks.—(See No. 656.)

658. In mounting guns in a casemate gallery, the carriage furthest from the door of entrance is to be placed first, and its gun put in position, before the next gun and carriage is brought in.

TO PLACE A HEAVY GUN ON THE TRUCK BY A GIN.

659. The gun is raised by means of the gin, and the truck run under it. The gun is then lowered to its place; the trunnions just over the front of the middle transom.

LESSON XLIV.

TO MOUNT A GUN.
TO DISMOUNT A GUN.

---

660. The implements necessary are the same as prescribed in No. 639, with the addition of a casemate gin.

TO MOUNT A GUN.

661. The carriage is traversed to one side; and the gun—on blocks, or on the truck cart—is near the middle of the casemate, the muzzle towards the embrasure. The gin is over the gun and carriage; the latter on the side of the pry-pole.

662. The gun is slung in the usual manner. The gin is worked until the gun is raised sufficiently high, when the chassis is traversed under it, and the gun carriage so placed that the trunnion holes come exactly under the trunnions. The gun is then lowered to its place, the sling removed, and the gin carried to the next casemate.

663. To prevent the pavement from being injured by the points, a truck wheel, or a piece of three-inch plank with holes to receive them, is placed under each foot.

TO DISMOUNT A GUN.

Executed in the inverse manner to that prescribed for mounting in No. 661. The gun is placed on the truck, or on blocks.

LESSON XLV.

TO REMOVE OR TO GREASE THE TRUCK WHEELS WHEN THE GUN IS MOUNTED.

---

664. The implements necessary are:

ONE MANŒUVRING HANDSPIKE. Siege.
ONE WHEEL CHOCK. Siege.

665. The gun carriage is run from battery. Nos. 3 and 4 remove the linch pins. Nos. 1 and 2 place the chock on the rail close to the front of the axletree, and embar with the handspike, on the chock as a fulcrum, under the understrap of the side of the carriage to be raised.

Nos. 3 and 4 remove the truck wheel. The gunner greases it as well as the spindle. Nos. 3 and 4 replace the wheel.

666. *Remarks.*—The traverse wheels cannot be greased when the gun is mounted.

667. When necessary the piece should be dismounted, the gun carriage removed, and the chassis withdrawn and turned over; the caps of the journal boxes taken off, and the axles greased and replaced.

668. The truck and traverse wheels should be greased before mounting with hog's lard, or a mixture of fish-oil and tallow.

669. Carriages that have been standing some time should be greased before being used.

670. A wrench should be provided for each battery, and the nuts always tightened before the carriage is used.

PART III.

MISCELLANEOUS.

ARTICLE I.

TO EMBARK AND DISEMBARK ARTILLERY AND ORDNANCE STORES.

671. When artillery and its stores are to be shipped for an expedition, prepare first a list of all the articles, stating their number, individual weight, and the total weight of each kind.

672. In estimating the weights, allow double for that of bulky articles which occupy much space without weighing much.

673. Divide the total quantity to be transported among the vessels, and make statements in duplicate of the articles on board each vessel, one of which lists should go with the vessel, and the other remain with the officer shipping the stores.

674. The articles must be divided among the vessels according to the circumstances of the case; but as a general rule place in each vessel everything necessary for the service required at the moment of disembarkation, so that there will be no inconvenience should other vessels be delayed.

675. If a siege is to be undertaken, place in each vessel with each piece of artillery its implements, ammunition, and the carriages necessary to transport the whole or a part; the platforms, tools, instruments, and materials for constructing batteries; skids, rollers, scantling, and plank.

676. If a particular calibre of gun is necessary for any operation, do not place all of one kind in one vessel, to avoid being entirely deprived of them by an accident to it.

677. Dismount the carriages, wagons, and limbers by taking off the wheels and boxes, and, if absolutely necessary, the axletrees. Place in the boxes the linch pins, washers, &c., with the tools required for putting the carriage together again. Number each carriage, and mark each detached article with the number of the carriage to which it belongs.

678. The fixed ammunition must be carefully packed in its prescribed boxes. The cartridge bags, fuzes for shells, and their ammunition, either in substantial boxes with rope handles or in barrels. Powder in barrels, in a magazine constructed in a vessel to hold it.

679. Sponges, rammers, worms, and ladles should be united in bundles. Other implements, intrenching tools, levels, rules, &c., in bundles or boxes. Implements in bundles and boxes of complete sets, as far as practicable.

680. Small arms should be in their prescribed boxes.

681. The contents of each box, barrel, or bundle should be marked distinctly upon it. The boxes should be made small for the convenience of handling, and have rope handles to lift them by.

682. The position of the different articles in each vessel should be noted in a column in the list on board.

683. Place the heaviest articles below, beginning with the shot and shells, (empty,) then the guns, platforms, carriages, wagons, limbers, ammunition boxes, &c. Boxes of small arms and ammunition in the dryest and least exposed part of the vessel. The skids, scantling, and boards may be in the more exposed parts, or in the run.

Articles required to be disembarked first should be put in last, or so placed that they can be readily got at.

If the disembarkation is to be performed in front of the enemy, some of the field pieces should be so placed that they can be disembarked immediately, with their carriages, implements, and ammunition; also the tools and materials for throwing up temporary intrenchments on landing.

684. When there are several vessels laden with artillery and stores for an expedition, each vessel should have on each quarter, and on a signal at masthead, a number that can be easily distinguished at a distance. The same number should be entered on a list of supplies shipped in each vessel. The commander can then know exactly what resources he has with him. Some vessels, distinguished by particular signal, should be laden solely with such powder and ammunition as may not be required for the immediate service of the pieces.

685. If it is necessary to reship, or leave any articles on board the vessels, care should be taken to note them on the list.

686. Boats of proper capacity must be provided for the disembarkation, according to the circumstances in each case.

687. It may be necessary to establish temporary wharves on tressels, and to erect shears, cranes, or derricks.

688. On a smooth sandy beach, heavy pieces, &c., may be landed by rolling them overboard as soon as the boats ground, and hauling them up with sling carts.

ARTICLE II.

TABLES OF DIMENSIONS AND WEIGHTS OF GUNS, CARRIAGES, SHOT, SHELLS, MACHINES, AND IMPLEMENTS; OF CHARGES FOR SHELLS; OF RANGES FOR HEAVY ORDNANCE, ETC.

689. *Principal dimensions and weights of guns.*

	IRON.				
	Sea-coast.		Siege and garrison.		
	42	32	24	18	12
	In.	*In.*	*In.*	*In.*	*In.*
Diameter of the bore	7	6.4	5.82	5.3	4.62
True windage	.16	.15	.14	.13	.10
Length of the bore	110	107.6	108	109	103.4
Length of the bore in diameters	15.71	16.78	18.56	20.56	22.38
Length from rear of base-ring to face of muzzle	117	114	114	114	108
Whole length of the piece	129	125.2	124	123.25	116
Semi-diameter of the base-ring	12.2	11.2	10.7	9.875	8.7
Semi-diameter of the swell of the muzzle	8.4	7.7	7.793	6.935	5.932
Distance between these semi-diameters	115	112	111	111.6	105.8
Natural angle of sight			1° 30′	1° 30′	1° 30′
Distance from rear of base-ring to rear of trunnions	43.2	42.2	43	43.5	42
Diameter of the base-ring	24.4	22.4	21.4	19.75	17.4
Distance between the rimbases	22	20.7	18	16.8	14.8
Diameter of the trunnions	7	6.4	5.82	5.3	4.62
Length of the trunnions	6.5	6	5	4.75	4.5
Distance from axis trunnions to face of muzzle	70.3	68.6	68.09	67.85	63.69
Weight ....pounds	8,465	7,200	5,790	4,913	3,590
Preponderance ....pounds	440	466	225	200	200

690. *Principal dimensions and weights of columbiads and howitzers.*

	IRON.					
	Columbiads.		Howitzers.			
			Sea-coast.		Siege and garrison.	
	10-in.	8-in.	10-in.	8-in.	8-in.	24-pdr.
	In.	*In.*	*In.*	*In.*	*In.*	*In.*
Diameter of the bore	10	8	10	8	8	5.82
True windage	.12	.12	.12	.13	.13	.14
Length of bore, exclusive of chamber	99	100	96	85.5	38.5	53.25
Length of bore, exclusive of chamber, in diameters	9.9	12.5	9.6	10.68	4.81	9.15
Diameter of the chamber	8	6.4	7	6.4	4.62	4.62
Length of the chamber	12	11	9.5	7.5	8	4.75
Length from rear of base-ring to face of muzzle	120	119	112	98	52	62
Whole length of the piece	126	124	124.25	109	61.5	69
Semi-diameter of base-ring	16	13	13.25	11.10	9.125	6.9
Semi-diameter of swell of muzzle	10.75	8.5	10.125	8.25	8.225	5.85
Distance between these semi-diameters	117.5	117	109.5	96	51.5	61.8
Natural angle of sight	1° 21′	1° 23′			1°	1°
Distance from rear of base-ring to rear of trunnions	41.5	41.5	41	37.4	24	24.69
Diameter of base-ring	32	26	26.5	22.2	18.25	13.8
Distance between the rimbases	31	25	25	20.7	18	12.8
Length of the trunnions	9	6.5	7.5	6	5	3.25
Diameter of the trunnions	10	8	8	6.4	5.82	4.62
Distance from axis of trunnions to face of muzzle	73.5	73.5	67	57.4	25.09	35
Weight ... pounds	15,400	9,210	9,500	5,740	2,614	1,476
Preponderance ... pounds	470	350	450	380	460	70

691. *Principal dimensions and weights of mortars.*

	IRON.			
	Heavy.		Light.	
	13-in.	10-in.	10-in.	8-in.
	In.	*In.*	*In.*	*In.*
Diameter of the bore	13	10	10	8
True windage	.13	.13	.13	.12
Length of the bore, exclusive of the chamber	26	25	15	12
Length of the bore, exclusive of the chamber, in diameters	2	2.5	1.5	1.5
Superior diameter of the chamber (at the bottom of the shell)	9.5	7.15	7.6	6.08
Inferior diameter of the chamber	7.25	5.64	5	4
Length of the chamber	13	10	5	4
Whole length of the mortar	53	46	28	22.5
Distance from face of muzzle to front of trunnions	41	37	20	16.5
Distance between the rimbases	36	27.5	20.5	16.25
Length of the trunnions	8.5	6.5	5	4
Diameter of the trunnions	12	9	8	6
	Lbs.	*Lbs.*	*Lbs.*	*Lbs.*
Weight	11,500	5,775	1,852	930

692. *Dimensions and weights of shot.*

	13-in.	12-in.	10-in.	8-in.	42	32	24	18	12
	In.	*In.*	*In.*	*In.*	*In.*	*In.*	*In.*	*In.*	*In.*
Diameter	12.87	11.87	9.87	7.88	6.84	6.25	5.68	5.17	4.52
	Lbs.	*Lbs.*	*Lbs.*	*Lbs.*	*Lbs.*	*Lbs.*	*Lbs.*	*Lbs.*	*Lbs.*
Weight	294	231	128	65	42.7	32.6	24.4	18.5	12.3

693. *Dimensions and weights of shells.*

	Columbiads and sea-coast howitzers.		Mortars.			Guns and howitzers.				
	10-in.	8-in.	13-in.	10-in.	8-in.	42	32	24	18	12
	In.	*In.*	*In.*	*In.*	*In.*	*In.*	*In.*	*In.*	*In.*	*In.*
Diameter	9.87	7.88	12.87	9.87	7.88	6.84	6.25	5.68	5.17	4.52
Thickness of sides and bottom. True	2	1.5	2.1	1.6	1.25	1.2	1	.9	.9	.7
Thickness of sides and bottom. Greatest	2.1	1.58	2.25	1.7	1.33	1.25	1.05	.95	.94	.74
Thickness of sides and bottom. Least	1.9	1.42	1.95	1.5	1.17	1.15	.95	.85	.86	.66
Thickness of fuse hole	3	2.25	2.1	1.6	1.25	1.8	1.35	1.35	1.35	1.05
Diameter of fuze hole. Exterior	1.45	1.338	1.8	1.75	1.3	1	.9	.9	.9	.9
Diameter of fuze hole. Interior	1	1	1.483	1.51	1.113	.73	.698	.698	.698	.743
Distance between ears	6	5	7	6	5	......	......	......	......	......
	Lbs.	*Lbs.*	*Lbs.*	*Lbs.*	*Lbs.*	*Lbs.*	*Lbs.*	*Lbs.*	*Lbs.*	*Lbs.*
Weight	101	50.5	197	87.5	44.5	31	22.5	17	13.4	8.4

NOTE.—The 8-inch mortar shell is used for the siege howitzer.

694. *Dimensions and weights of spherical case shot.*

		8-in.	42	32	24	18
		In.	*In.*	*In.*	*In.*	*In.*
Diameter		7.38	6.84	6.25	5.68	5.17
Thickness of metal at the sides.	True	.7	.65	.60	.55	.5
	Greatest	.725	.675	.625	.575	.525
	Least	.675	.625	.575	.525	.475
Thickness of metal at fuze hole		1.6	1.5	1.5	1.1	1.1
Radius of reinforce at fuze hole		3	2.75	2.5	2.3	2.1
Diameter of fuze hole	Exterior	1.2	1.2	1.2	.9	.9
	Interior	.96	.975	.975	.735	.735
		Lbs.	*Lbs.*	*Lbs.*	*Lbs.*	*Lbs.*
Mean weight		30	20.32	16	11.86	8.7

The thickness of metal at the fuze hole is supposed to be measured in the axis of the fuze hole between the spherical surfaces of the shell and the reinforce. The fuze holes of shells and spherical case shot taper .15 inch to 1 inch.

695. *Weights of carcasses.*

	13-in.	10-in.	8-in.	42	32	24	18	12
	Lbs.	*Lbs.*	*Lbs.*	*Lbs.*	*Lbs.*	*Lbs.*	*Lbs.*	*Lbs.*
Mean weight	194	86	43	30	21.60	16	12.5	8

Carcasses are shells having three additional holes of the same dimensions as the fuze hole, pierced at equal distances apart in the upper hemisphere of the shell, with their exterior openings touching the great circle which is perpendicular to the axis of the fuze hole.

696. *Dimensions and weights of grape shot.*

	8-in.	42	32	24	18	12
	In.	*In.*	*In.*	*In.*	*In.*	*In.*
Diameter of large gauge	3.60	3.17	2.90	2.64	2.40	2.06
Diameter of small gauge	3.54	3.13	2.86	2.60	2.36	2.02
	Lbs.	*Lbs.*	*Lbs.*	*Lbs.*	*Lbs.*	*Lbs.*
Mean weight	6.1	4.2	3.15	2.4	1.8	1.14

697. *Dimensions and weights of canister shot.*

	24-pounder.	32-pounder.	24-pounder and 8-in. siege howitzer.	18-pounder.	12-pounder and 32-pounder howitzer.
	In.	*In.*	*In.*	*In.*	*In.*
Diameter of large gauge	2.26	2.06	1.87	1.70	1.49
Diameter of small gauge	2.22	2.02	1.84	1.67	1.46
	Lbs.	*Lbs.*	*Lbs.*	*Lbs.*	*Lbs.*
Mean weight	1.5	1.14	.86	.64	.43

698. *Dimensions and weights of grenades.*

Six-pounder spherical case shot may be used for hand grenades, and shells of any calibre for rampart grenades.

699. *Dimensions and weights of canisters.*

	SIEGE AND GARRISON GUNS.					8-INCH HOWITZERS.	
	42	32	24	18	12	Siege.	Sea-coast.
	In.	*In.*	*In.*	*In.*	*In.*	*In.*	*In.*
Height of finished canister......	8.7	8.1	7.35	6.8	6	12.03	12.35
Number of tiers of shot..........	4	4	4	4	4	4	4
Number of shot in each of the three lower tiers	7	7	7	7	7	12	12
Number of shot in fourth tier....	6	6	6	6	6	12	12
Whole number of shot...........	27	27	27	27	27	48	48
	Lbs.	*Lbs.*	*Lbs.*	*Lbs.*	*Lbs.*	*Lbs.*	*Lbs.*
Weight of finished canister	48	37	29	23	15	53.5	54.5

700. *Dimensions and weights of a stand of grape.*

	8-in.	42	32	24	18	12
	In.	*In.*	*In.*	*In.*	*In.*	*In.*
Height of stand between the outsides of the plates.....	9.85	8.75	8.2	7.5	6.8	5.8
	Lbs.	*Lbs.*	*Lbs.*	*Lbs.*	*Lbs.*	*Lbs.*
Weight of stand complete...	74.5	51.25	39.75	30.61	22.15	14.84

A stand of grape consists of nine shot, put together by means of two cast-iron plates, two rings, and one pin and nut.

701. *Principal dimensions of siege gun carriages and limbers.*

	12 pdr. gun.	18-pdr. gun.	24-pdr. gun and 8-inch howitzer.
	In.	*In.*	*In.*
Height of axis of trunnions above the ground	52.2	52.6	53
Vertical field of fire. Above the horizontal line. Gun	13°	12°	12°
Vertical field of fire. Above the horizontal line. Howitzer	......	......	15°
Vertical field of fire. Below the horizontal line. Gun	4°	4°	4°
Vertical field of fire. Below the horizontal line. Howitzer	......	......	10°
Distance between the points of contact of the wheels and trail with the ground line	100	101	101
Distance from the front of the wheels to the end of the trail, the piece being in battery	141	142	142
Distance of the muzzle of the piece in battery from the front of the wheels. Gun, in front of wheels	30.74	35.35	35.34
Distance of the muzzle of the piece in battery from the front of the wheels. Howitzer, in rear of wheels	......	......	7.66
Length of gun carriage, without wheels	130	133	133.6
Length of limber, without wheels	176.65	176.65	176.65
Length of limber, without wheels or pole	59.8	59.8	59.8
Length of limber, with wheels and pole	184.9	184.9	184.9
Length of the carriage limbered up	278.9	280.9	280.9
Whole length of the axletree	81.8	81.8	81.8
Track of the wheels	60	60	60
Height of the wheels	60	60	60
Disk of finished wheels	2	2	2

702. *Principal weights of siege gun carriages and limbers.*

	12-pounder gun.	18-pounder gun.	24-pounder gun and 8-inch howitzer.
	Lbs.	*Lbs.*	*Lbs.*
Gun carriage, without wheels	1,440	1,542	1,714
Limber, without wheels	585	585	585
One wheel	404	404	404
Gun carriage complete, without implements	2,248	2,350	2,522
Limber complete	1,393	1,393	1,393
Gun carriage and limber, without implements	3,641	3,743	3,915

703. *Dimensions and weights of mortar beds.*

	Siege.		Coehorn.	Eprouvette.
	8-in.	10-in.		
	In.	*In.*	*In.*	*In.*
Length	42	51.8	31	22
Exterior width, including manœuvring bolts	34	40	15	22
	Lbs.	*Lbs.*	*Lbs.*	*Lbs.*
Weight	920	1,830	132	280

704. *Principal dimensions and weights of barbette carriages.*

Dimensions.	12-pounder gun.	18-pounder gun.	24-pounder gun.	32-pounder gun and 8-inch howitzer.	42-pounder gun.
	In.	*In.*	*In.*	*In.*	*In.*
Height of axis of trunnions in battery above the traverse circle.	71.76	71.76	73.45	75.77	77.47
Vertical field of fire. Above the horizontal line	11°	11°	11°	11°	11°
Vertical field of fire. Below the horizontal line	5°	5°	5°	5°	5°
Length of gun carriage from front of wheels to rear of lunette.	89.5	89.5	90.75	90.75	92.05
Whole length of the chassis	184.06	184.06	183.38	182.86	182.71
Horizontal distance from centre of pintle to front end of rails	9.5	9.5	9.5	9.5	9.5
Horizontal distance from centre of pintle to centre of traverse wheels	120.33	120.33	120.33	120.33	120.33
Horizontal distance from centre of pintle to the face of the piece in battery. Gun	59	63.15	63.29	63.70	65.30
Horizontal distance from centre of pintle to the face of the piece in battery. Howitzer	....	....	....	52.5	....
Weights.	*Lbs.*	*Lbs.*	*Lbs.*	*Lbs.*	*Lbs.*
One gun carriage roller	135	135	135	146	146
One gun carriage wheel	308	308	308	308	308
One traverse wheel and fork	97	97	97	97	97
One pintle, (new pattern)	17	17	17	17	17
Gun carriage complete, without implements	1,666	1,686	1,959	2,213	2,308
Chassis complete, without pintle	1,294	1,294	1,614	2,030	2,194

705. *Principal dimensions and weights of casemate carriages.*

Dimensions.	24-pdr. gun.	32-pdr. gun.	42-pdr. gun.	8-in. columbiad.	24-pdr. howitzer.
	In.	*In.*	*In.*	*In.*	*In.*
Height of axis of trunnions in battery above the traverse circle.	48.75	49.95	50.65	50.65	48.25
Vertical field of fire. { Above the horizontal line	9°	8°	8°	8°	....
Vertical field of fire. { Below the horizontal line	4°	4°	4°	4°	....
Length of gun carriage from front of cheeks to rear of trail roller	67.35	67.35	67.35	67.20	48.25
Whole length of chassis (including 3 inches for the tongue fork)	189.15	189.15	189.15	189.15	151
Width of chassis between outside of rails	40	44.50	46.76	49.16	22
Horizontal distance from centre of pintle to rear end of chassis.	235	235	235	235	144
Weights.	*Lbs.*	*Lbs.*	*Lbs.*	*Lbs.*	*Lbs.*
Gun carriage, without truck wheels	908	1,064	1,120	1,128	....
One gun carriage truck wheel	223	223	223	223	....
Chassis, without traverse wheels	2,120	2,430	2,575	2,600	....
One rear traverse wheel	99	99	99	99	....
One front traverse wheel	30	30	30	30	....
One pintle	92	92	92	92	50
Carriage complete, without implements	1,354	1,510	1,566	1,574	620
Chassis complete, without pintle	2,378	2,688	2,833	2,858	660

706. *Weight of lifting jack.*

	Length.	Width.	Thickness.	Weight.
	In.	*In.*	*In.*	*Lbs.*
Lifting jack	......	......	......	160
Lifting block for lifting jack	12	5.5	3.5	4.5

707. *Dimensions and weights of gins.*

Dimensions.	Field and siege.	Garrison.	Casemate.
	In.	*In.*	*In.*
Length of legs	175.5	256.5	172.5
WEIGHTS.			
	Lbs.	*Lbs.*	*Lbs.*
Of pry-pole	55	224	175
Of gin without blocks	455	823	642
Of pulley blocks, Single	37	....	....
Of pulley blocks, Double	....	65	65
Of pulley blocks, Treble	....	84	84

708. *Dimensions and weight of the sling cart.*

DIMENSIONS.	Large.	Hand.
	In.	*In.*
Length from rear of wheels to front end of pole.	242.4	160.75
Length of axletree	92	75.50
Height of wheels	96	72
Distance between the wheels on the ground	58.75	60.4
WEIGHTS.		
	Lbs.	*Lbs.*
One wheel	701	....
Whole weight, (without sling-chains)	2,282	1,115
Trunnion-chain and rings	23	....
Sling-chain	84	....

709. *Dimensions and weight of the mortar-wagon.*

DIMENSIONS.	Inches.
Length	143.6
Whole length when limbered up	287.85
WEIGHTS.	
	Lbs.
Carriage body without wheels	984
One wheel	404
Limber without wheels	585
Carriage and limber complete, (without implements)	3,185

710. *Lengths and weights of finished implements.*

KIND.	Length.	WEIGHT.			
		Sponge.	Rammer.	Ladle.	Worm.
	In.	*Lbs.*	*Lbs.*	*Lbs.*	*Lbs.*
42-pounder sea-coast gun	128	10.25	9.75	13.75	7.5
32-pounder sea-coast gun	128	10	8.4	13.15	7.5
24-pounder siege and garrison gun	128	9.65	8.15	12.4	7.5
18-pounder siege and garrison gun	128	8.7	8	10.	7.5
12 pounder siege and garrison gun	128	7.8	7.35	7.8	7.5
10-inch columbiad, Sponge for bore	118	12			
10-inch columbiad, Sponge for chamber	128	11			
10-inch columbiad, Rammer	128		9.75		
8-inch columbiad, Sponge for bore	118	10.25			
8-inch columbiad, Sponge for chamber	128	10			
8-inch columbiad, Rammer	128		8.4		
10-inch sea-coast howitzer	56	10.25	9.75		
8 inch sea-coast howitzer	80	8.5	7		
8-inch siege howitzer	56	3.7			
24-pounder casemate howitzer	80	5			
13-inch and 10-inch heavy mortars	44	3.2			
10 inch light and 8-inch and stone mortars	34	2			
24-pounder coehorn mortar	18	.8			

711. *Weights of implements.*

Kind.	Lbs.	Kind.	Lbs.
Trail handspike	7.25	Gunner's quadrant (wood)	.84
Manœuvring handspike	8.25	Gunner's level	.6
Long manœuvring handspike	12	Maul	10
Truck handspike	18.5	Quoin, (for siege mortars)	7
Roller handspike	7	Chock	1.4
Pass box	7	Plummet	1
Budge barrel	15.5	Scraper	2.3
Gunner's havresack	1.86	Gunner's sleeve	.25
Pointing wire	.08	Basket	4
Gunner's gimlet	.08	Tarpaulins, Large	54
Vent punch	.08	Tarpaulins, Smalll	9
Finger stall	.003	Mortar tompions, 8-in.	5
Breech sight	.65	Mortar tompions, 10-in.	7
Vent cover	.45	Broom, (corn)	1.25
Lanyard, (for friction primers)	.1	Shell hooks	2
Fuze setter	2.66	Funnel	.32
Fuze mallet	2.75	Powder measures, 4 oz	.3
Fuze saw	.75	Powder measures, 8 oz	.5
Fuze rasp	.75	Powder measures, 1 lb	.75
Fuze auger	.3	Powder measures, 3 lbs	1.6
Fuze gimlet	.1	Tar bucket	7
Shell-plug saw	.31	Watering bucket (leather)	8
Fuze-plug reamer	.3	Shovel	4.75
Fuze extractor	3.53	Pickaxe	6.5
Gunner's pincers	.85	Felling axe	6
Gunner's calipers	.5	Handbill	2
		Drag rope	16.5
		Men's harness	23

712. *Dimensions of cartridge bags.*

	GUNS.					COLUMBIADS.		HOWITZERS.		
									Sea-coast.	
	42-pdr.	32-pdr.	24-pdr.	18-pdr.	12-pdr.	10-inch.	8-inch.	8-in. siege.	10-in.	8-in.
	In.	*In.*	*In.*	*In.*	*In.*	*In.*	*In.*	*In.*	*In.*	*In.*
Diameter of cartridge	6	5.5	5	4.6	4.2	7.5	6	4.2	7.5	6
Length of one pound of powder in a cartridge	.98	1.16	1.45	1.75	2	.63	.98	2	.83	.98
Whole length of bag cut	18	18	18	17	14	24	20	14	18	15
Length of cartridge filled	11	10.5	9	7	6.5	14	12.5	9	11	9
	Lbs.	*Lbs.*	*Lbs.*	*Lbs.*	*Lbs.*	*Lbs.*	*Lbs.*	*Lbs.*	*Lbs.*	*Lbs.*
Usual charge of powder	10.5	8	6	4.5	3	18	10	4	12	8

Cartridge bags for siege and garrison service are usually made of woollen stuff.

713. *Manner of strapping shells.*

Sabots for shells for heavy guns, howitzers, and columbiads are made of plank.

The shells are placed in the sabot, and the straps put on in such a manner that the fuze hole may fall in one of the angles between two straps, and that the axis of the fuze hole may stand at an angle of 45° with that of the sabot. The eyes of the shell should not be covered by the straps. The straps are fastened at each end with two nails in the side, and two in the bottom of the sabot. In loading the piece care must be taken to place the fuze hole in the upper part of the bore.

714. *Charges for shells for mortars.*

CHARGE.	13-in.		10-in.		8-in.	
	Lbs	*oz.*	*Lbs.*	*oz.*	*Lbs.*	*oz.*
To fill the shell	11	0	5	0	2	9
To burst the shell	6	0	2	0	1	0
To blow out the fuze	0	6	0	5	0	4
For ordinary service, Of cannon powder	7	0	3	0	1	12
For ordinary service, Of incendiary match or other composition	0	8	0	6	0	6

715. *Charges for shells for columbiads and heavy guns.*

CHARGE.	COLUMBIADS.		GUNS.				
	10-in.	8-in.	42	32	24	18	12
	Lbs. oz	*Lbs. oz*	*Lbs. oz*	*Lbs. oz*	*Lbs. oz*	*Lbs. oz*	*Lbs. oz*
To fill the shell......	3 4	1 12	1 8	1 5	1 0	0 11	0 8
To burst the shell ...	1 6	1 0	0 12	0 11	0 8	0 7	0 5
To blow out the fuze plug............	0 10	0 8	0 6	0 2	0 2	0 1½	0 1
For ordinary service.	3 0	1 8	1 4	1 0	0 12	0 10	0 7

The fuzes for these shells are made with paper cases, and are inserted at the time of loading the piece. The fuze plugs are made of wood, or of brass, driven or screwed into the fuze hole; they are covered with a cap of peculiar construction which contains the priming of the fuze. The size of the plug is indicated by that of the fuze hole in the shell. The bursting charge is poured into the shell through the hole in the fuze plug.

716. *The number of balls in a pile.*

In the following table of the number of balls in a pile, the second line shows the number in a triangular pile, the base of which is the corresponding number in the first line. The other numbers show the contents of square and oblong piles; the length and width of the base being in the upper line and in the left-hand column respectively.

	2	3	4	5	6	7	8	9	10	11	12	13	14	15	16	17	18	19	20
Tri.	4	10	20	35	56	84	120	165	220	286	364	455	560	680	816	969	1140	1330	1540
2	5																		
3	8	14																	
4	11	20	30																
5	14	26	40	55															
6	17	32	50	70	91														
7	20	38	60	85	112	140													
8	23	44	70	100	133	168	204												
9	26	50	80	115	154	196	240	285											
10	29	56	90	130	175	224	276	330	385										
11	32	62	100	145	196	252	312	375	440	506									
12	35	68	110	160	217	280	348	420	495	572	650								
13	38	74	120	175	238	308	384	465	550	638	728	819							
14	41	80	130	190	259	336	420	510	605	704	806	910	1015						
15	44	86	140	205	280	364	456	555	660	770	884	1001	1120	1240					
16	47	92	150	220	301	392	492	600	715	836	962	1092	1225	1360	1496				
17	50	98	160	235	322	420	528	645	770	902	1040	1183	1330	1480	1632	1785			
18	53	104	170	250	343	448	564	690	825	968	1118	1274	1435	1600	1768	1938	2109		
19	56	110	180	265	364	476	600	735	880	1034	1196	1365	1540	1720	1904	2091	2280	2470	
20	59	116	190	280	385	504	636	780	935	1100	1274	1456	1645	1845	2040	2244	2451	2660	2870

717. *Ranges of heavy ordnance.*

The *range* of a gun or howitzer in this table is the first graze of the ball on the horizontal plane on which the carriage stands.

Kind of ordnance.	Powder.	Ball.	Elevation.	Range.	Remarks.
	Lbs.		° ′	*Yds.*	
18-PDR. SIEGE AND GARRISON GUN.	4.5	Shot.	1 0	641	
	4.5	do.	2 0	950	
	4.5	do.	3 0	1,256	
On barbette carriage.	4.5	do.	4 0	1,450	
	4.5	do.	5 0	1,592	
24-PDR. SIEGE AND GARRISON GUN.	6	Shot.	0 0	412	
	6	do.	1 0	842	
	6	do.	1 30	953	
On siege carriage.	6	do.	2 0	1,147	
	6	do.	3 0	1,417	
	6	do.	4 0	1,666	
	6	do.	5 0	1,901	
	8	do.	1 0	883	
	8	do.	2 0	1,170	
	8	do.	3 0	1,454	
	8	do.	4 0	1,639	
	8	do.	5 0	1,834	
32-PDR. SEA-COAST GUN.	6	Shot.	1 45	900	
	8	do.	1 0	713	
	8	do.	1 30	800	
On barbette carriage.	8	do.	1 35	900	
	8	do.	2 0	1,100	
	8	do.	3 0	1,433	
	8	do.	4 0	1,684	
	8	do.	5 0	1,922	
	10.67	do.	1 0	780	
	10.67	do.	2 0	1,155	
	10.67	do.	3 0	1,517	

Ranges of heavy ordnance.

Kind of ordnance.	Powder.	Ball.	Elevation.		Range.	Remarks.
	Lbs.		°	′	*Yds.*	
42-PDR. SEA-COAST GUN.	10.5	Shot.	1	0	775	
	10.5	do.	2	0	1,010	
	10.5	do.	3	0	1,300	
On barbette carriage.	10.5	do.	4	0	1,600	
	10.5	do.	5	0	1,955	
	14	do.	1	0	770	
	14	do.	2	0	1,128	
	14	do.	3	0	1,380	
	14	do.	4	0	1,687	
	14	do.	5	0	1,915	
		Shell.				
10-INCH SEA-COAST HOWITZER.	12	90 lbs.	1	0	580	
	12	do.	2	0	891	Time 3 sec.
	12	do.	3	0	1,185	Time 4 sec.
On barbette carriage.	12	do.	3	30	1,300	
	12	do.	4	0	1,426	Time 5.25 sec.
	12	do.	5	0	1,650	Time 6 sec.
		Shot.				
8-INCH COLUMBIAD.	10	65 lbs.	1	0	919	Axis of gun 16 feet above the water.
	10	do.	2	0	1,116	
On barbette carriage.	10	do.	3	0	1,402	
	10	do.	4	0	1,608	
	10	do.	5	0	1,813	
	10	do.	6	0	2,010	
	10	do.	8	0	2,397	Shot ceased to ricochet on water.
	10	do.	10	0	2,834	
	10	do.	15	0	3,583	
	10	do.	20	0	4,322	
	10	do.	25	0	4,875	
	10	do.	27	0	4,481	
	15	do.	27	30	4,812	

Ranges of heavy ordnance.

Kind of ordnance.	Powder.	Ball.	Elevation.		Range.	Remarks.
	Lbs.	Shell.	°	′	*Yds.*	
8-INCH COLUMBIAD —Continued.	10	50 lbs.	1	0	919	
	10	do.	2	0	1,209	
	10	do.	3	0	1,409	
	10	do.	4	0	1,697	
	10	do.	5	0	1,813	
	10	do.	6	0	1,985	
	10	do.	8	0	2,203	
	10	do.	10	0	2,657	
	10	do.	15	0	3,556	
	10	do.	20	0	3,716	
	10	do.	25	0	4,387	
	10	do.	27	0	4,171	
	15	do.	27	30	4,468	
		Shot.				
10-INCH COLUMBIAD	18	128 lbs.	0	0	394	Axis of gun 16 feet above the water.
	18	do.	1	0	752	
On barbette carriage.	18	do.	2	0	1,002	
	18	do.	3	0	1,230	
	18	do.	4	0	1,570	
	18	do.	5	0	1,814	
	18	do.	6	0	2,037	Shot ceased to ricochet on water.
	18	do.	8	0	2,519	
	18	do.	10	0	2,777	
	18	do.	15	0	3,525	
	18	do.	20	0	4,020	
	18	do.	25	0	4,304	
	18	do.	30	0	4,761	
	18	do.	35	0	5,433	
	20	do.	39	15	5,654	
		Shell.				
	12	100 lbs.	1	0	800	
	12	do.	2	0	1,012	
	12	do.	3	0	1,184	
	21	do.	4	0	1,443	

Ranges of heavy ordnance.

Kind of ordnance.	Powder.	Ball.	Elevation.		Range.	Remarks.
	Lbs.	Shell.	°	'	*Yds.*	
10-IN. COLUMBIAD—Continued.	12	100 lbs.	5	0	1,604	
	18	do.	0	0	448	
	18	do.	1	0	747	
	18	do.	2	0	1,100	
	18	do.	3	0	1,239	
	18	do.	4	0	1,611	
	18	do.	5	0	1,865	
	18	do.	6	0	2,209	
	18	do.	8	0	2,489	
	18	do.	10	0	2,848	
	18	do.	15	0	3,200	
	18	do.	20	0	3,885	
	18	do.	25	0	4,150	
	18	do.	30	0	4,651	
	18	do.	35	0	4,828	Time 35 sec.
		Shell.				
12-IN. COLUMBIAD.	20	172 lbs.	10	0	2,770	Time 11 sec.
	20	do.	15	0	3,731	Time 16 sec.
	20	do.	22	0	4,280	Time 20 sec.
	20	do.	25	0	4,718	Time 26 sec.
	20	do.	30	0	5,004	
	20	do.	35	0	5,339	Time 32 sec.
	20	do.	37	0	5,266	Time 31 sec.
	20	do.	39	0	5,064	
	25	do.	10	0	2,881	Time 11.5 sec.
	25	do.	15	0	3,542	Time 15 sec.
	25	do.	30	0	5,102	
	25	do.	35	0	5,409	Time 32 sec.
	25	do.	37	0	5,373	Time 32 sec.
	25	do.	39	0	5,506	Time 36 sec.
	25	180 lbs.	35	0	5,644	
	25	do.	39	0	5,615	
	28	do.	35	0	5,671	
	28	do.	39	0	5,761	3⅛ miles. Time 36 sec.

Ranges of heavy ordnance.

Kind of ordnance.	Powder.	Ball.	Elevation. °	Elevation. ′	Range.	Remarks.
	Lbs.	Shell.	°	′	*Yds.*	
13-INCH SEA-COAST MORTAR.	20	200 lbs.	45	0	4,325	
12-INCH SEA-COAST MORTAR.	20	Shell. 200 lbs.	45	0	4,625	Experimental.
10-INCH SEA-COAST MORTAR.	10	98 lbs.	45	0	4,250	Time 36 sec.
8 INCH SIEGE HOWITZER.	4	Shell 45 lbs.	0	0	251	Time $\frac{3}{8}$ sec.
	4	do.	1	0	435	Time $1\frac{1}{8}$ sec.
	4	do.	2	0	618	Time 2 sec.
On siege carriage.	4	do.	3	0	720	Time 3 sec.
	4	do.	4	0	992	Time 4 sec.
	4	do.	5	0	1,150	Time 5 sec.
	4	do.	12	30	2,280	
8-INCH SEA-COAST MORTAR.	4	Shell. 45 lbs.	1	0	405	
	4	do.	2	0	652	
	4	do.	3	0	875	
On barbette carriage	4	do.	4	0	1,110	
	4	do.	5	0	1,300	
	6	do.	1	0	572	
	6	do.	2	0	828	
	6	do.	3	0	947	
	6	do.	4	0	1,168	
	6	do.	5	0	1,463	
	8	do.	1	0	646	
	8	do.	2	0	909	
	8	do.	3	0	1,190	
	8	do.	4	0	1,532	
	8	do.	5	0	1,800	

Ranges of heavy ordnance.

Kind of ordnance.	Powder.	Ball.	Elevation.		Range.	Remarks.
	Lbs.	Shell.	°	′	*Yds.*	
10-INCH SIEGE MORTAR.	1	90 lbs.	45	0	300	Time 6.5 sec.
	1.5	do.	45	0	700	Time 12 sec.
	2	do.	45	0	1,000	Time 14 sec.
	2.5	do.	45	0	1,300	Time 16 sec.
	3	do.	45	0	1,600	Time 18 sec.
	3.5	do.	45	0	1,800	Time 19 sec.
	4	do.	45	0	2,100	Time 21 sec.
		Shell.				
8-INCH SIEGE MORTAR.	0.8	45 lbs.	45	0	209	Time 6.75 sec.
	0.12	do.	45	0	376	Time 9 sec.
	1.0	do.	45	0	650	Time 11.5 sec.
	1.4	do.	45	0	943	Time 14 sec.
	1.8	do.	45	0	1,318	Time 16.5 sec.
	1.12	do.	45	0	1,522	Time 18.5 sec.
	2.0	do.	45	0	1,837	Time 20.5 sec.

Table of approximate ranges, &c., for rifled guns in use in the armies of the United States in 1861–'62.

PARROTT'S SYSTEM.

Kind of gun.	Kind of projectile. *Pounds.*	Charge, pounds.	Elevation, degrees.	Time of flight, seconds.	Range, yards.	Drift to the right, yards.	Remarks.
200-pounder	Shell 155	16	5.	6.12	2,000	....	Length of bore, 136 inches; diameter of bore, 8 inches; weight, 16,000 pounds.
Do	Shell 200	16	5.30	6.06	2,100	....	
100-pounder	Shell 100	10	3.15	4.42	1,450	....	Length of bore, 130 inches; diameter of bore, 6.4 inches; weight of gun, 9,650 pounds. Bursting charge, (long shell,) 4½ pounds. Bursting charge, (short shell,) 3½ pounds. With reduced charges and high elevations, the 100 pounder may be used as a mortar.
Do	Shell 100	8	3.37	4.70	1,450	....	
Do	Shot 99¼	10	5.	....	2,247	4.	
Do	Shell 82	10	6.	9.	2,600	....	
Do	Shot or shell 100	10	10.	12.62	3,665	7.5	
Do	Shot 84	10	10.	....	3,873	30.	
Do	Shot 100	10	12.	16.50	4,300	....	
Do	Shot 100	10	13.	17.	4,500	....	
Do	Shot or shell 100	10	15.	17.58	4,914	41.54	
Do	Shot or shell 84	10	15.	18.81	5,215	40.42	
Do	Shot or shell 100	10	20.	22.54	5,942	72.04	
Do	Shot 82	10	20.	23.	6,244	105.21	
Do	Shot or shell 100	10	25.	28.58	6,798	78.33	
Do	Shot 82	10	25.	28.70	7,150	92.	
Do	Shot or shell 82	10	30.	32.49	7,929	153.	
Do	Shot or shell 82	10	35.	36.95	8,428	200.	
Do	Round shot 32	10	15.	15.87	3,416	26.	
30-pounder	Shell 29	3¼	3.30	4.5	1,506	....	Length of bore, 120 inches; diameter of bore, 4.20 inches; weight of gun, 4,250 pounds.
Do	Shell 29	3¼	5.16	6.82	2,200	....	

Table of approximate ranges, &c.—Continued.

PARROTT'S SYSTEM—Continued.

Kind of gun.	Kind of projectile.	Charge, pounds.	Elevation, degrees.	Time of flight, seconds.	Range, yards.	Drift to the right, yards.	Remarks.
	Pounds.						
30-pounder	Shell 29	3¼	10.	12.19	3,642	....	
Do	Shell 29	3¼	15.	17.68	4,874	....	
20-pounder	Case-shot 19½	2	0.	.75	230	....	Length of bore, 79 inches; diameter of bore, 3.67; weight of gun, 1,800 pounds.
Do	Case-shot 19½	2	1.	1.75	560	....	
Do	Case-shot 19½	2	2.	3.00	950	....	
Do	Case-shot 19½	2	3.37	4.75	1,500	....	
Do	Case-shot 19½	2	3.30	4.50	1,500	....	
Do	Shell 18¾	2	5.	....	2,200	....	
Do	Shell 18¾	2	6.	7.	2,200	....	
Do	Shell 18¾	2	10.	11.82	3,300	....	
Do	Shell 18¾	2	15.	17.20	4,500	....	
10-pounder	....	1	0.	0.	260	....	Length of bore, 70 inches; diameter of bore, 2.9 inches; weight of gun, 900 pounds.
Do	....	1	1.	1.	600	....	
Do	....	1	2.	2.	900	....	
Do	....	1	2.30	3.	1,100	....	
Do	....	1	3.	3.25	1,300	....	
Do	....	1	3.30	4.	1,500	....	
Do	....	1	4.	4.30	1,600	....	
Do	....	1	4.30	5.45	1,700	....	
Do	....	1	5.	6.25	1,950	....	

Table of approximate ranges, &c.—Continued.

PARROTT'S SYSTEM—Continued.

Kind of gun.	Kind of projectile.	Charge, pounds.	Elevation, degrees.	Time of flight, seconds.	Range, yards.	Drift to the right, yards.	Remarks.
	Pounds.						
10-pounder	....	1	5. 30	7.	2, 150	....	
Do.	....	1	6.	7. 30	2, 300	....	
Do.	....	1	7.	8. 30	2, 600	....	
Do.	....	1	10.	10. 30	3, 000	....	
Do.	....	1	12.	13.	3, 600	....	
Do.	....	1	15.	16.	4, 200	....	
Do.	....	1	20.	20.	5, 000	....	
Do.	....	1	25.	23. 30	5, 600	....	
Do.	....	1	30.	27. 30	5, 900	....	
Do.	....	1	35.	31. 30	6, 200	....	

JAMES'S SYSTEM.

Kind of gun.	Kind of projectile.	Charge, pounds.	Elevation, degrees.	Time of flight, seconds.	Range, yards.	Drift to the right, yards.	Remarks.
	Pounds.						
Old 42-pounder	Shot 81½	8	5.	....	2, 221	....	Length of bore, 110 inches; diameter of bore, 7 inches; weight of gun, 8,465 pounds.
Do.	Shot 81½	8	7.	....	2, 702	....	
Do.	Shot 81½	8	10.	....	3, 454	....	
Do.	Shot 81½	8	15.	....	4, 347	....	

Table of approximate ranges, &c.—Continued.

ARMSTRONG'S SYSTEM.

Kind of gun.	Kind of projectile.	Charge, pounds	Elevation, degrees.	Time of flight, seconds.	Range, yards.	Drift to the right, yards.	Remarks.
	Pounds.						
30-pounder	Shot 29	3⅝	10.	....	3, 705	....	
Do	Shot 29	3⅝	15.	....	4, 776	....	
Do	Shot 29	3⅝	20.	....	6, 069	....	
Do	Shot 29	3⅝	25.	....	6, 770	....	
Do	Shot 29	3⅝	30.	....	7, 384	....	
Do	Shot 29	3⅝	35.	....	8, 860	....	

UNITED STATES ORDNANCE SYSTEM.

Kind of gun.	Kind of projectile.	Charge, pounds	Elevation, degrees.	Time of flight, seconds.	Range, yards.	Drift to the right, yards.	Remarks.
	Pounds.						
4½-inch	Shot 33	3¼	0.	1. 25	670	....	Length of bore, 120 inches; diameter of bore, 4.30 inches; weight of gun, 3,450 pounds.
Do	....	....	1.	2. 25	750	....	
Do	....	....	2.	3. 25	1, 210	....	
Do	....	....	3.	4. 25	1, 400	....	
Do	Shot 33	3¼	4.	5. 50	1, 676	....	The *shot* (33 pounds) here named is what is known as *Dyer's* projectile. It is uncertain, strips badly, and is in nearly all respects inferior to Shenkl's projectiles, which, besides being more certain, give about 10 per cent. increased range.
Do	Shot 33	3¼	5.	6.	2, 078	....	
Do	Shot 33	3¼	6.	7. 25	2, 236	....	
Do	Shell, (Shenkl's per'n)	3¼	6. 50	8.	2, 600	....	
Do	Shot 33	3¼	7.	8. 50	2, 560	....	
Do	Shot 33	3¼	8.	9. 50	2, 600	....	
Do	Shell, (Shenkl's per'n)	3¼	8. 50	10.	3, 000	....	

Table of approximate ranges, &c.—Continued.

UNITED STATES ORDNANCE SYSTEM—Continued.

Kind of gun.	Kind of projectile.	Charge, pounds.	Elevation, degrees.	Time of flight, seconds.	Range, yards.	Drift to the right, yards.	Remarks.
	Pounds.						
3-inch		1	0.	1.5	380		Length of bore, 65 inches; diameter of bore, 3 inches; weight of gun, 820 pounds.
Do		1	1.	2.	645		
Do		1	2.	3.3	1,010		
Do		1	3.	4.3	1,310		
Do		1	4.	5.	1,525		
Do		1	5.	6.5	1,835		
Do		1	6.	7.8	2,100		
Do		1	7.	8.5	2,325		
Do		1	8.	10.	2,400		
Do		1	9.	11.	2,970		
Do		1	10.	11.5	2,910		
Do		1	11.	12.5	3,110		
Do		1	12.	13.25	3,270		
Do		1	13.	14.75	3,410		
Do		1	14.	15.5	3,710		
Do		1	15.	16.	3,820		
Do.		1	16.	17.	4,180		

I.—The wind blowing *across* the plane of fire has a very great effect upon the *direction* of the projectile; and it diminishes the *range* very much when blowing *against* the projectile in the direction of its flight. Allowance must always be made to counteract these effects.

II.—The best rule for time of flight is one second for 300 yards, (for 3,000 yards and under.)

HINTS ON THE SIGHTS ATTACHED TO PARROT'S RIFLE GUNS.

III.—The idea is to keep the small eye-hole in the sliding piece of the *brass*, or back-sight, always in the same parallel to the bore as the top of the *iron* sight on the rimbase, *except such a lateral movement of the eye-piece* as we may desire to give in order to allow for drift, wind, &c. When the eye-piece is so placed that the nut is just even with the stem on which it moves, the line of sight is parallel to the bore. By screwing in or out the eye-piece and its nut, you can vary the line of sight to *right* or *left* within certain limits. The use of the nut is only to *jam* or keep fast the eye-piece in its place. When the eye-piece has four arms, each with a sight-hole, the object is to divide the lateral movement more closely, as it is then only necessary to turn the eye-piece ¼ around to bring another sight-hole to the top, where it must, of course, always be when the gun is sighted. The graduation in degrees, &c., depends on the distance between sights in each gun.

When the *top* of the collar of the sliding-piece is at any particular division marked on the brass column, and the line from the sight-hole to the top of rimbase sight is horizontal, the axis of the gun will be elevated to the degree marked by said division. The use of the sights to give a particular elevation to the gun, of course, pre-supposes some horizon, such as the surface of water; but having once got an object and fixed the sights to it, they will serve to bring back the gun to the same point.

IV.

1,760 yards is	1	mile.	4,400 yards is	2½	miles.
2,640 yards is	1½	"	5,280 yards is	3	"
3,520 yards is	2	"	6,160 yards is	3½	"

NOTE.—The tables, &c., on pages 248, 249, 250, and 251 were furnished by Brigadier General W. F. Barry, Inspector of Artillery, United States army.

PLATE 1.

24 pdr. Siege Gun.

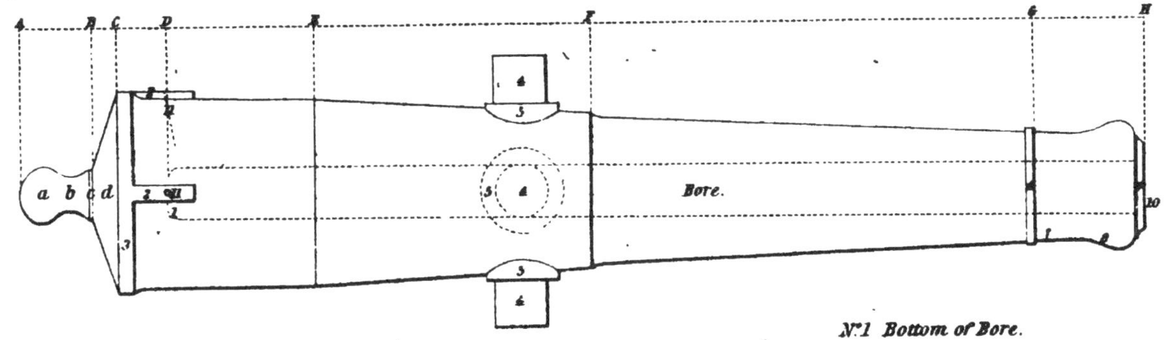

A C. Cascable. { a Knob. b Neck. c Fillet. d Base of Breech. }

B C. Base of Breech.
C D. Breech.
D E. First Reinforce.
E F. Second Reinforce.
F G. Chase.

N°. 1 Bottom of Bore.
" 2 Lock piece.
" 3 Base ring.
" 4 Trunnions.
" 5 Rimbases.
" 6 Chase ring.
" 7 Neck.
" 8 Swell of Muzzle.
" 9 Lip and Fillet.
" 10 Face.
" 11 Vent.

Scale 1/3.

Lt. B. H. Rush 2d Art. Delt. D. McClelland Sc. Washn. D.C.

PLATE 2.

24 pdr. gun on a Siege Carriage.

No. 1 Pintle hole.
" 2 Manœuvring bolt.
" 3 Wheel guard plate.
" 4 Elevating Screw box.
" 5 Elevating Screw.
" 6 Travelling trunnion bolt.
" 7 Firing trunnion bed.
" 8 Cap square.
" 9 Chin bolt.
" 10 Key bolt.
" 11 Cap square Chain.
" 12 Key Chain and key.
" 13 One axle-tree (iron)
" 14 One axle-body (wood)
" 15 Under strap.
" 16 Trunnion plate.
" 17 Lock chain hook.

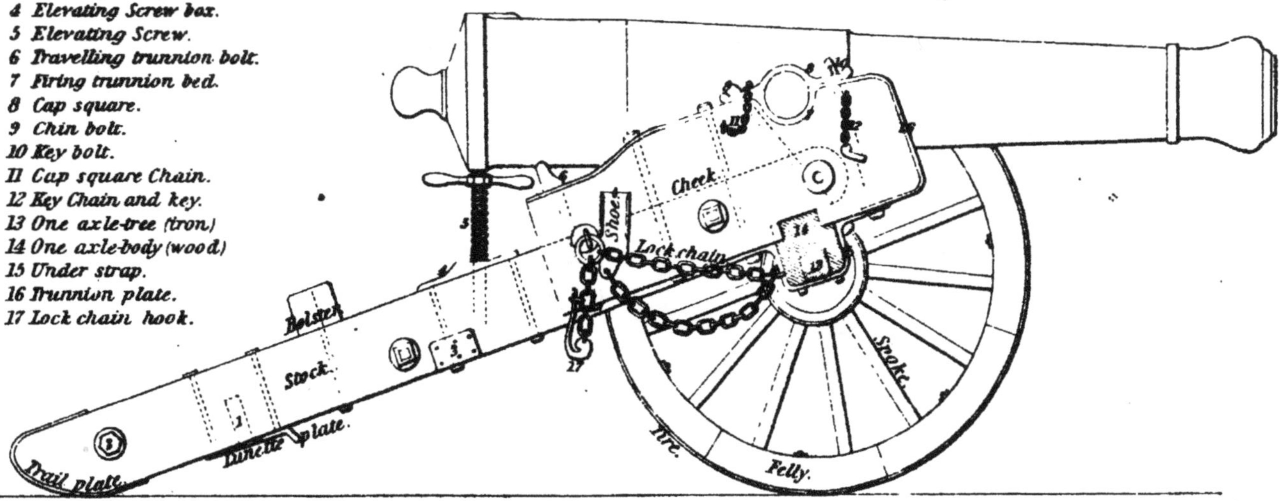

Scale 1/30.

Lt. R.H. Rush, 2d Art. Delt.

D. McClelland Sc.

24 pdr. gun on a Siege Carriage.

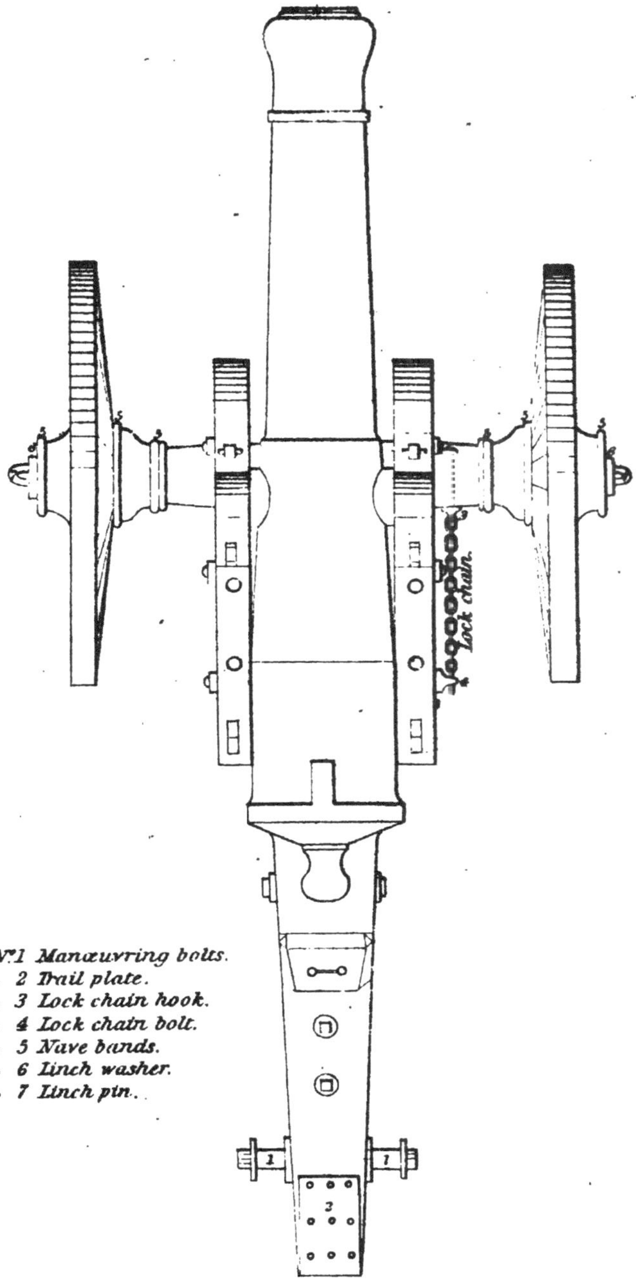

Nº 1 Manœuvring bolts.
" 2 Trail plate.
" 3 Lock chain hook.
" 4 Lock chain bolt.
" 5 Nave bands.
" 6 Linch washer.
" 7 Linch pin.

Lt. R.H. Rush 2d Art. Delt. D. McClelland Sc.

PLATE 4.

24 pdr. gun on a Siege Carriage,
in travelling position.

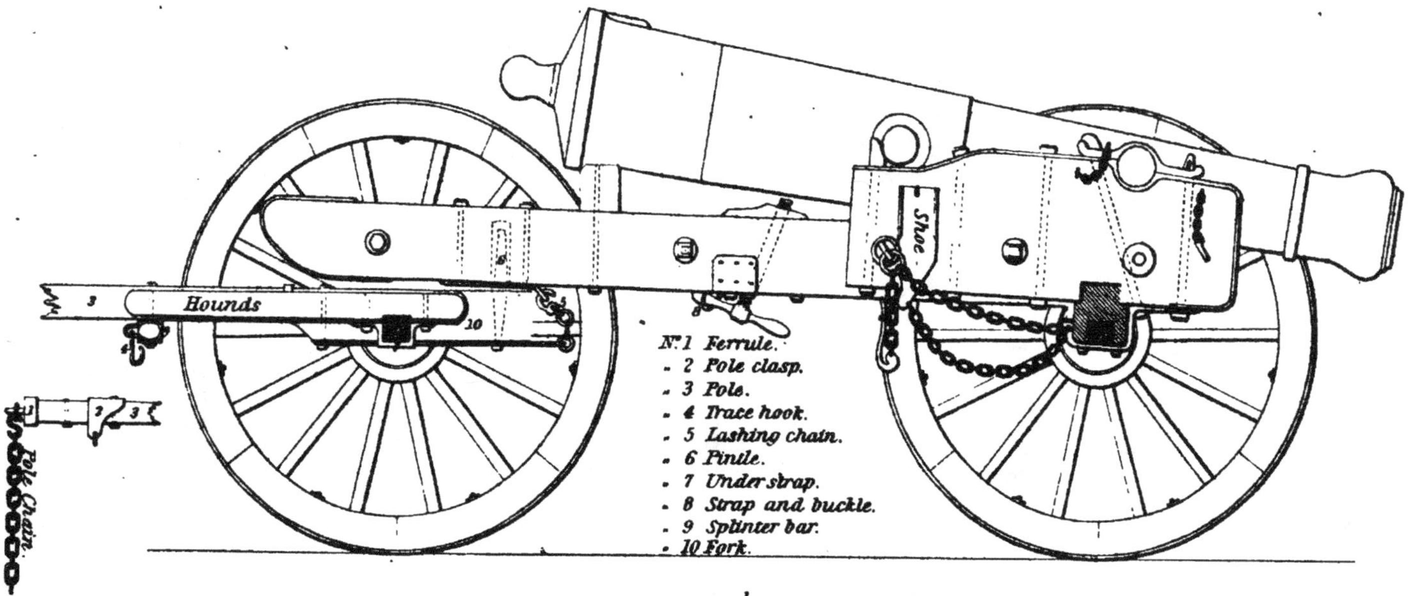

N.º 1 Ferrule.
„ 2 Pole clasp.
„ 3 Pole.
„ 4 Trace hook.
„ 5 Lashing chain.
„ 6 Pintle.
„ 7 Under strap.
„ 8 Strap and buckle.
„ 9 Splinter bar.
„ 10 Fork.

Scale $\frac{1}{30}$.

Lt. R. H. Rush. 2.d Art. Delt. D. M.c Clelland Sc.

PLATE 5.

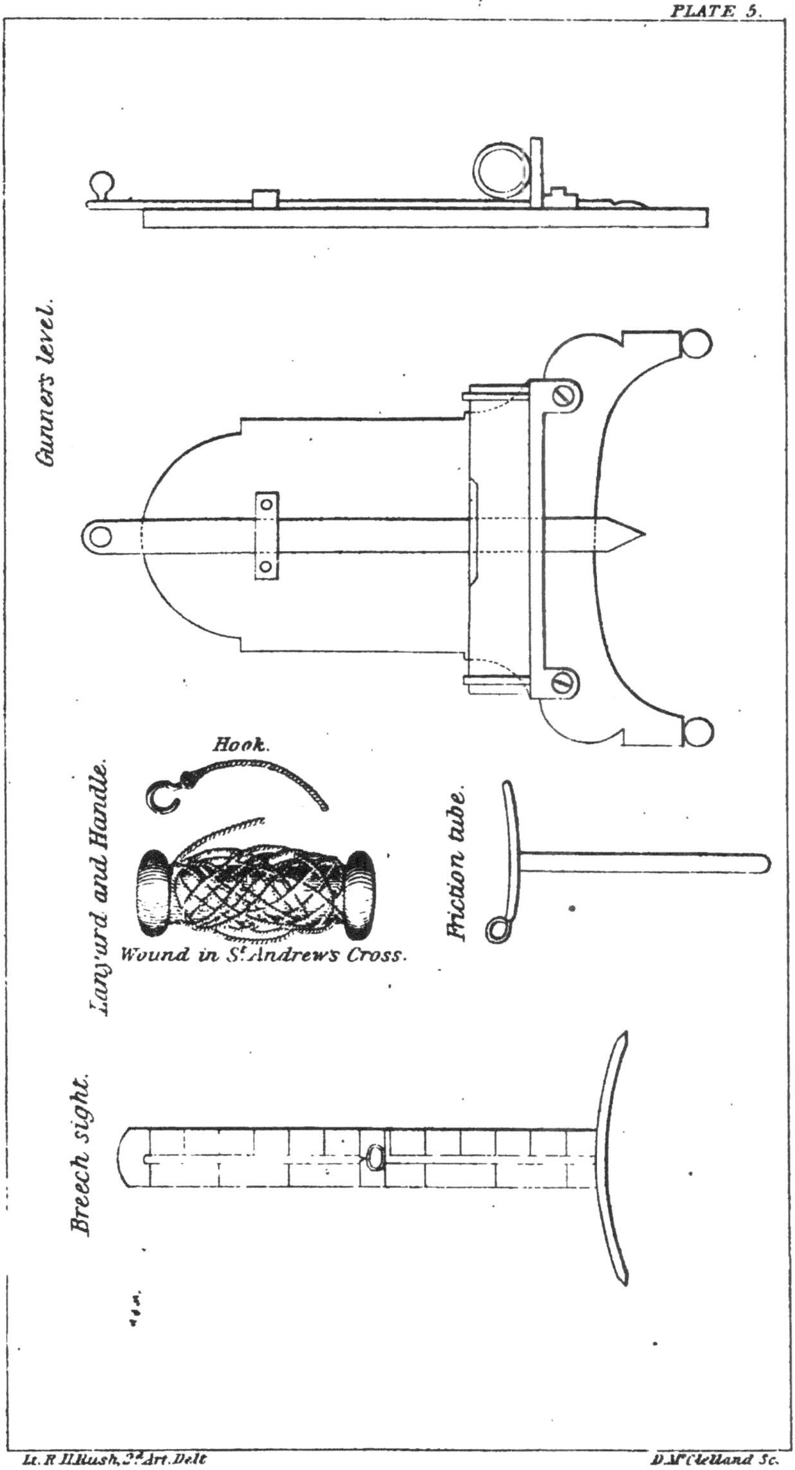

Lt. R. H. Rush, 3d Art. Delt

D. McClelland Sc.

PLATE 6.

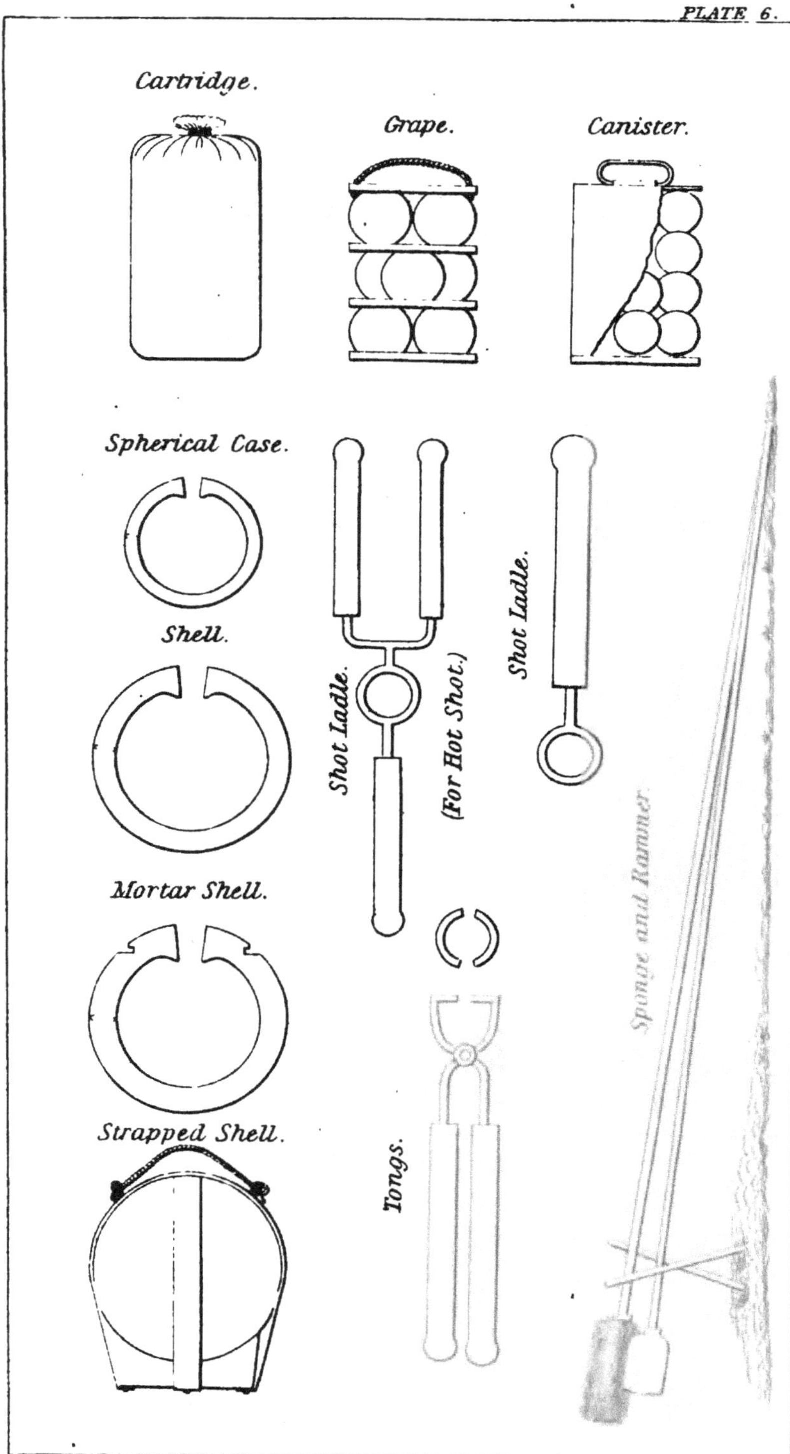

Lt. E.H. Rush, 3d Art. Delt.

D. McClelland Sc.

PLATE 7.

Quoin.

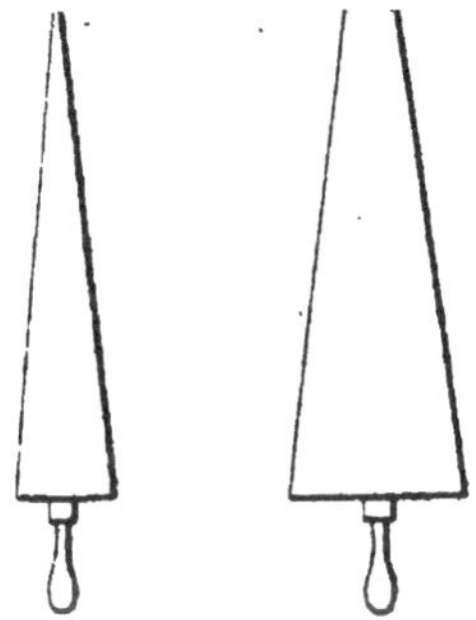

8 inch Siege Howitzer.

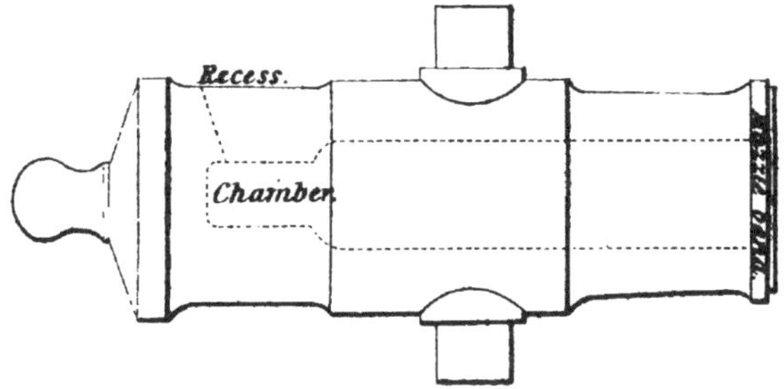

Loading Tongs.

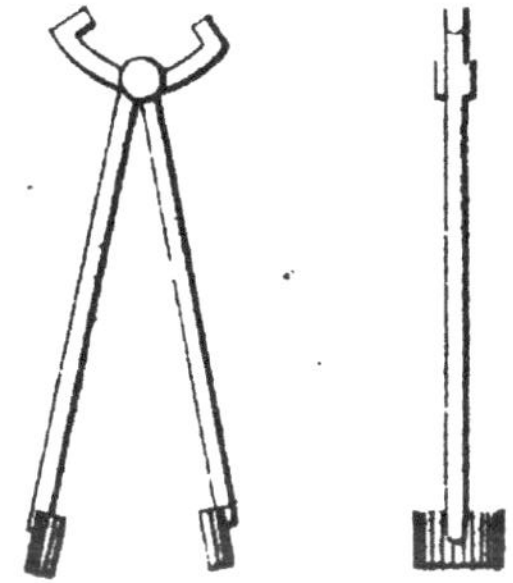

For nomenclature see Plate 1st.

Lt. R. H. Rush, 2d Art. Delt.

D. McClelland Sc.

PLATE 8.

8 inch Siege Mortar.

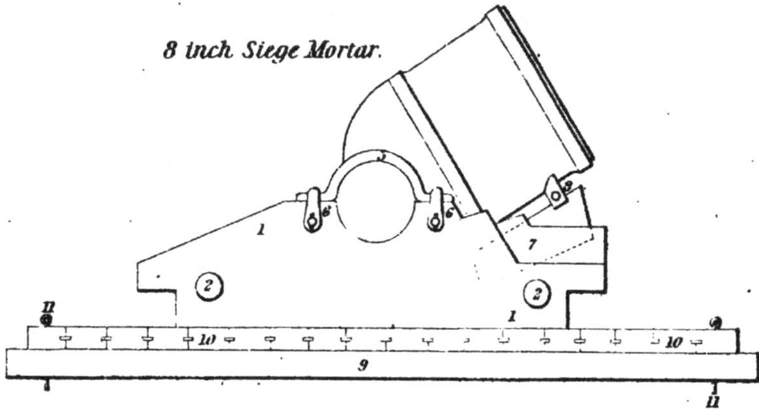

8 inch Mortar bed.

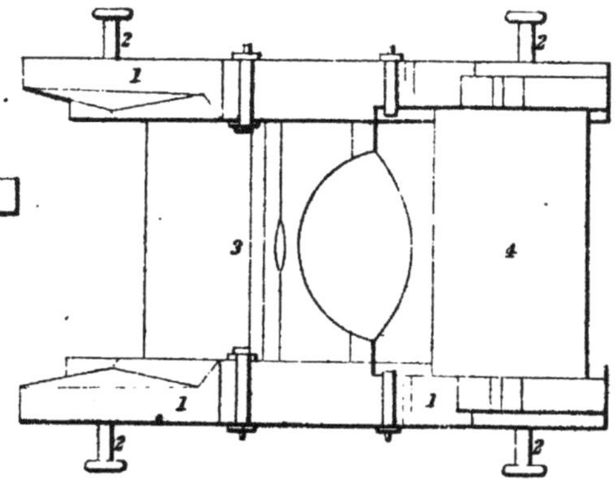

N°1 Cheeks.
„ 2 Manœuvring bolts.
„ 3 Middle transom.
„ 4 Front transom.
„ 5 Cap square.
„ 6 Cap square straps.
„ 7 Bolster.
„ 8 Quoin.
Platform. { „ 9 Sleeper. „ 10 Deck plank. „ 11 Eye bolts.

Lt. R. H. Rush, 2d Art. Delt.

D. McClelland Sc.

Mortars.

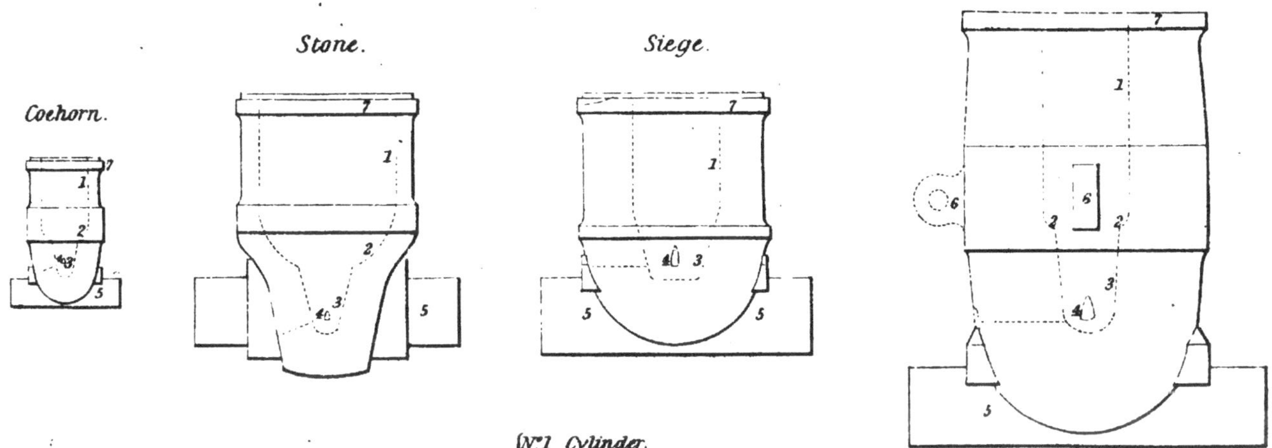

Bore. { Nº 1 Cylinder.
" 2 Spherical surface.
" 3 Chamber. }
" 4 Vent.
" 5 Trunnions.
" 6 Ear.
" 7 Muzzle band.

Lt. R. H. Rush. 2ᵈ Art. Delt.

D. McClelland Sc.

PLATE 10.

32 pdr. Sea Coast gun.

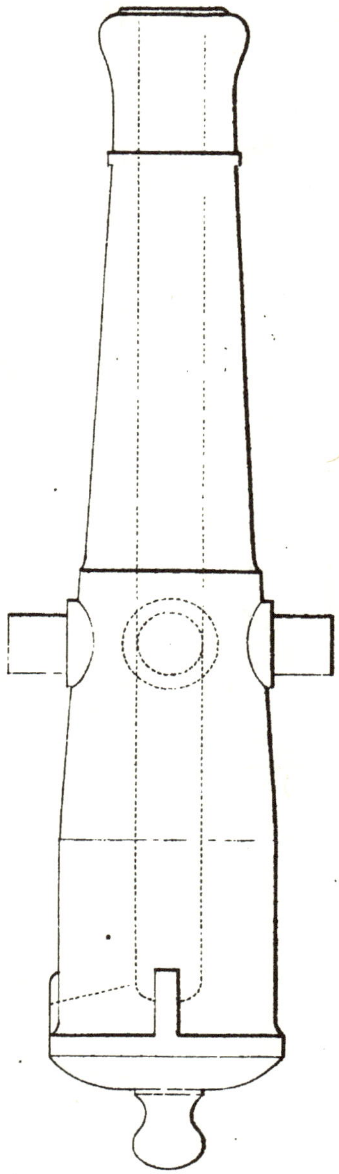

For nomenclature see Plate 1st.

Lt. R. H. Rush, 2d Art. Delt.

D. McClelland Sc.

24 pdr. Gun mounted on a Barbette Carriage.

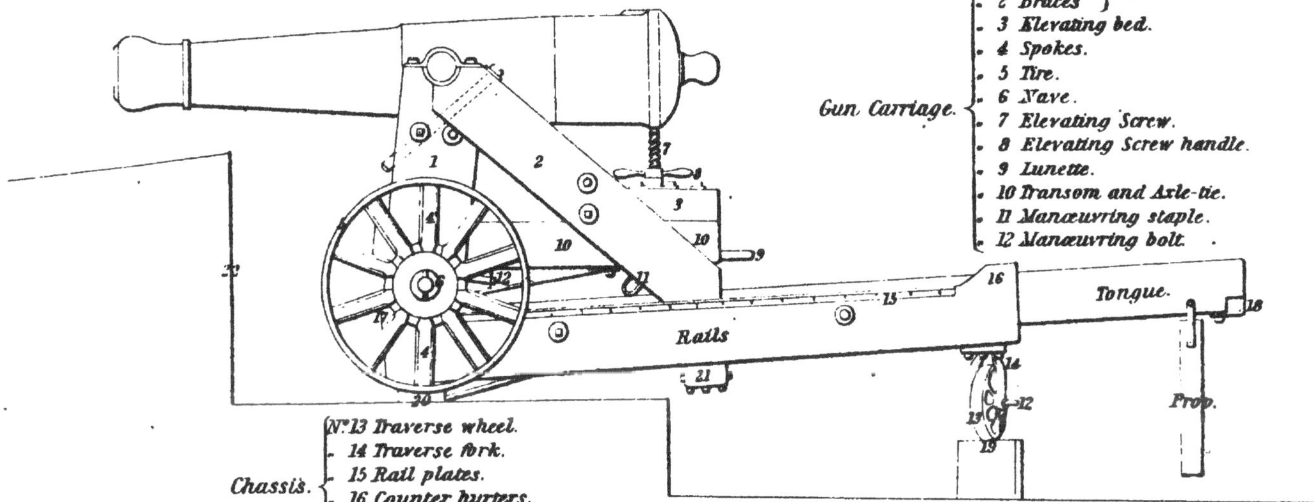

Gun Carriage.

- No. 1 Uprights } Cheeks.
- 2 Braces }
- 3 Elevating bed.
- 4 Spokes.
- 5 Tire.
- 6 Nave.
- 7 Elevating Screw.
- 8 Elevating Screw handle.
- 9 Lunette.
- 10 Transom and Axle-tie.
- 11 Manœuvring staple.
- 12 Manœuvring bolt.

Chassis.

- No. 13 Traverse wheel.
- 14 Traverse fork.
- 15 Rail plates.
- 16 Counter hurters.
- 17 Hurters.
- 18 Manœuvring loop.
- 19 Traverse circle.
- 20 Pintle block.
- 21 Middle transom.
- 22 Parapet.

Lt. R. H. Rush, 2d Art. Delt.

D. McClelland Sc.

PLATE 12.

32 pdr Gun mounted on a Barbette Carriage.

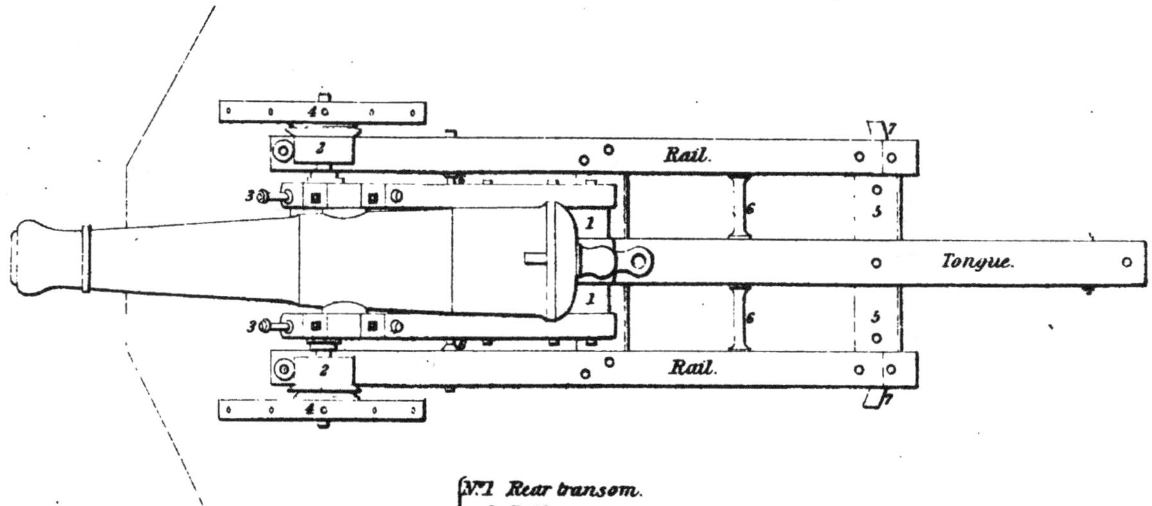

Gun Carriage. — No. 1 Rear transom. — 2 Rollers. — 3 Manœuvring bolts. — 4 Wheels.

Chassis. — 5 Rear transom. — 6 Pipes. — 7 Traverse wheels.

Lt. R. H. Rush, 2d Art. Delt.

D. McClelland Sc.

Sea Coast Howitzer.

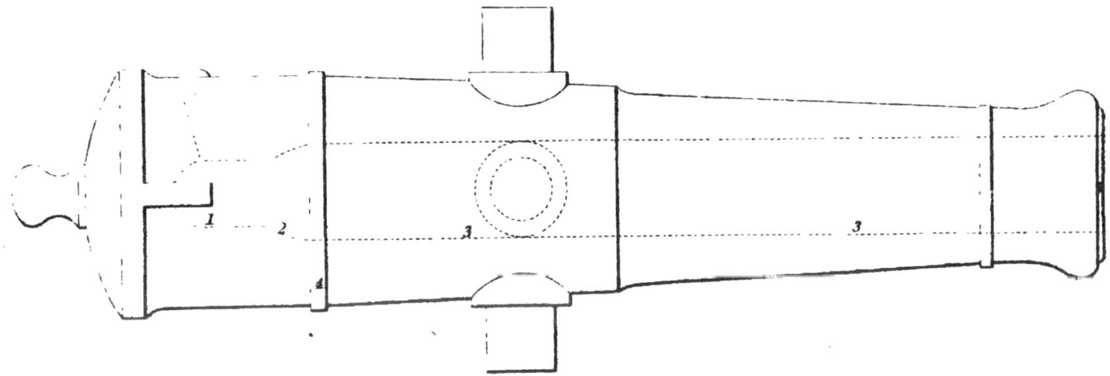

Bore { N°1 Chamber
" 2 Conical surface.
" 3 Cylinder.

" 4 Reinforce band.
" 5 Lip.

For remaining nomenclature see Plate 1st.

Lt. R. H. Rush, 2d Art. Delt

D. McClelland Sc

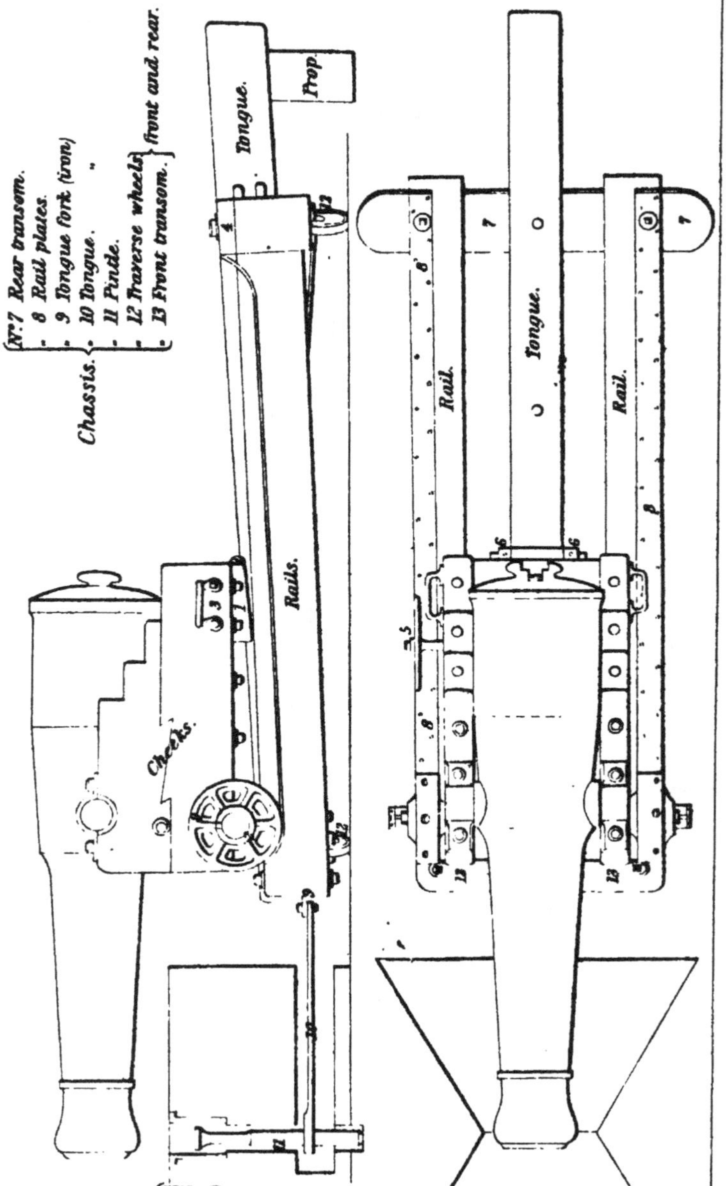

8 inch Columbiad on a Casemate Carriage.

Gun Carriage. { N°1 Rear transom and Slide.
" 2 Truck wheels.
" 3 Trail handles.
" 4 Counter hurters.
" 5 Elevating Screw handle.
" 6 Eccentrics and Roller.

Front Transom. between the head of cheeks.
Guides. between the cheeks against front transom.

Lt. R. H. Rush, 2ᵈ Art. Delt. D. M'Clelland Sc.

24 pdr. Howitzer on a Flank Casemate Carriage.

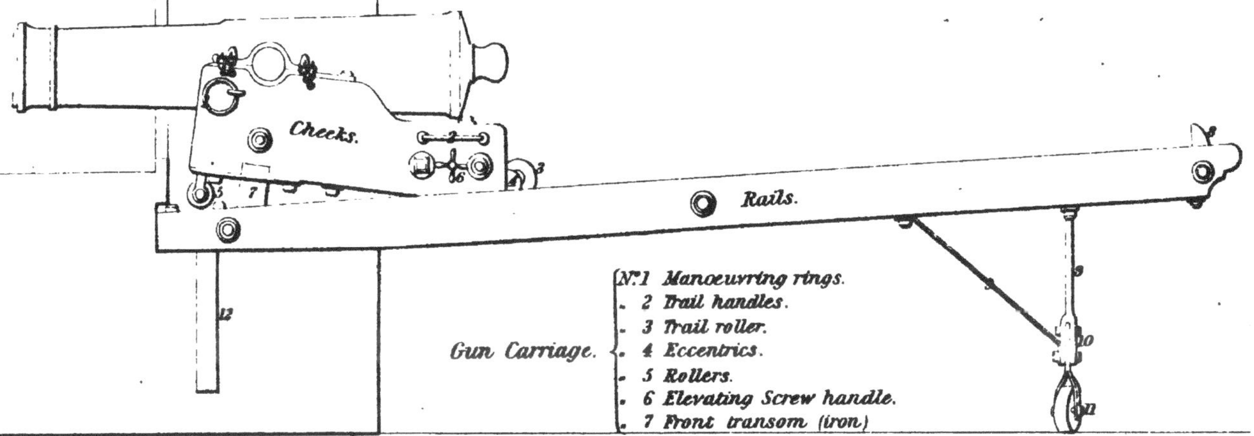

Gun Carriage.

- N.º 1 Manoeuvring rings.
- " 2 Trail handles.
- " 3 Trail roller.
- " 4 Eccentrics.
- " 5 Rollers.
- " 6 Elevating Screw handle.
- " 7 Front transom (iron)

Chassis.

- " 8 Counter hurters.
- " 9 Prop and Brace.
- " 10 Fork.
- " 11 Traverse wheel.
- " 12 Pintle.

Lt. R.H. Rush. 2d Art. Delt. — D. McClelland Sc.

24 pdr. Howitzer on a Flank Casemate Carriage.

Fig. 1.

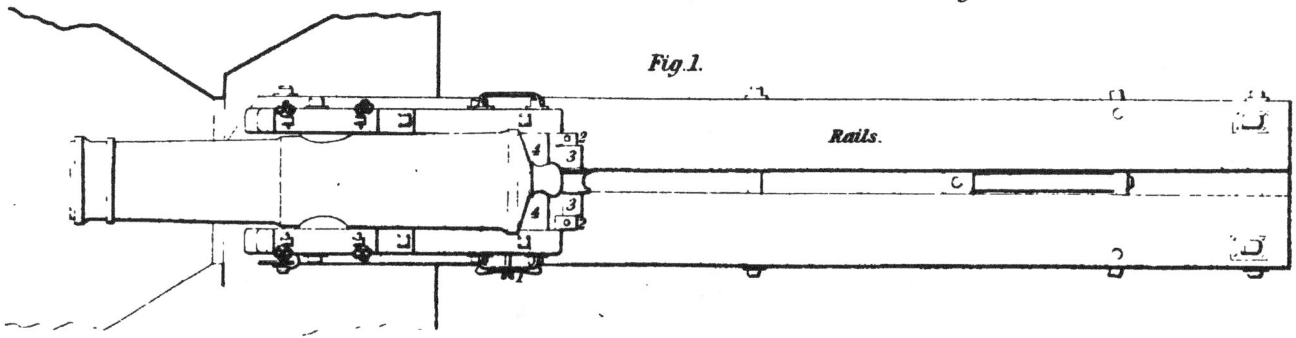

24 pdr. Howitzer.

Fig. 2.

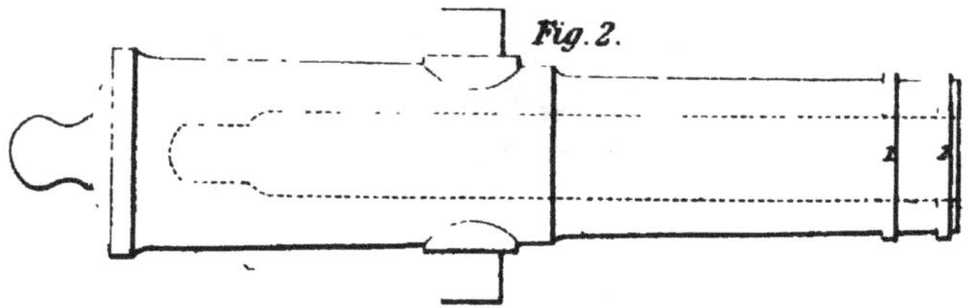

Fig. 1.

Gun Carriage. { No. 1 Elevating Screw handle.
" 2 Eccentrics.
" 3 Trail Roller.
" 4 Rear transom (iron) }

Fig. 2.

No. 1 Chase ring.
" 2 Muzzle band.

For nomenclature see Plate 7.

Lt. R.H. Rush, 2d Art. Delt.

D. McClelland Sc.

8 inch Columbiad.

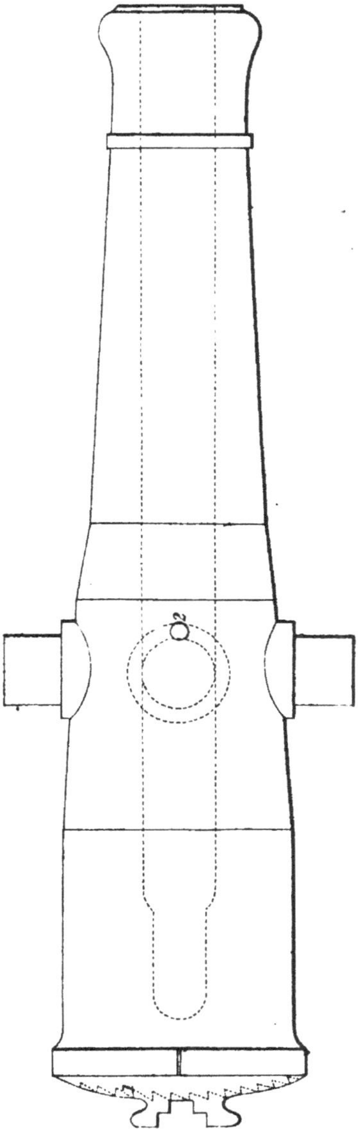

No. 1 Ratchets.
" 2 Middle sight.

For nomenclature see Plate 9.

Lt. R. H. Rush, 2d Art. Delt. D. McClelland Sc.

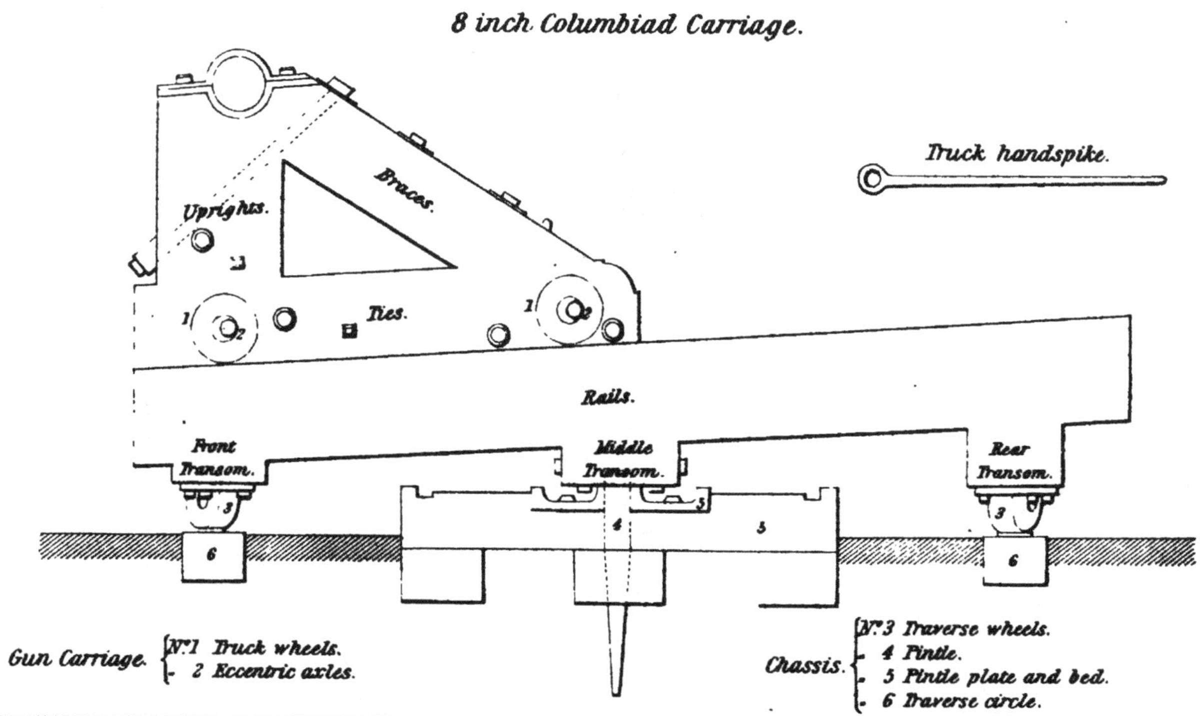

Lt. R. H. Rush, 2d Art. Delt.

D. McClelland Sc.

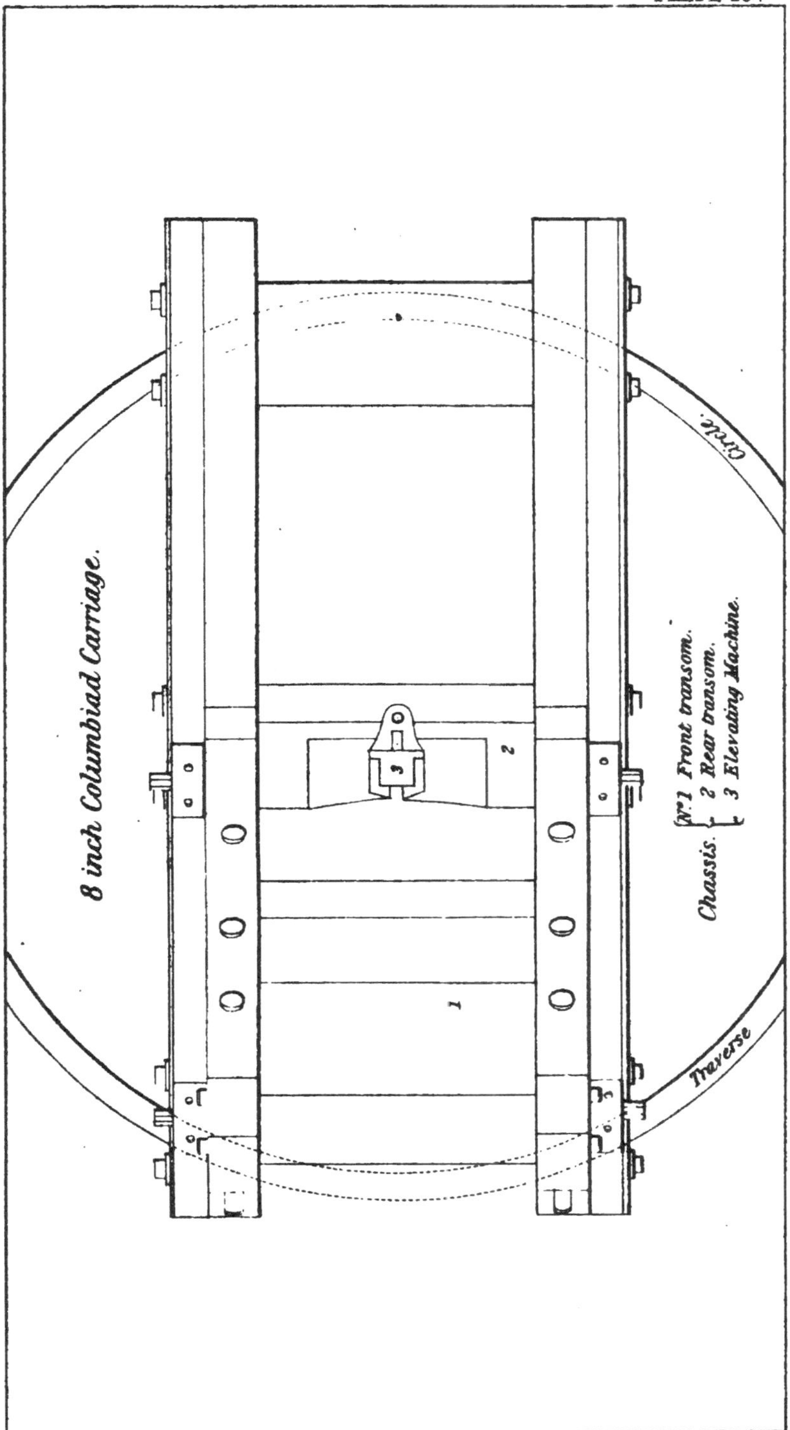

Lt. R. H. Rush. 2d Art. Delt. D. McClelland Sc.

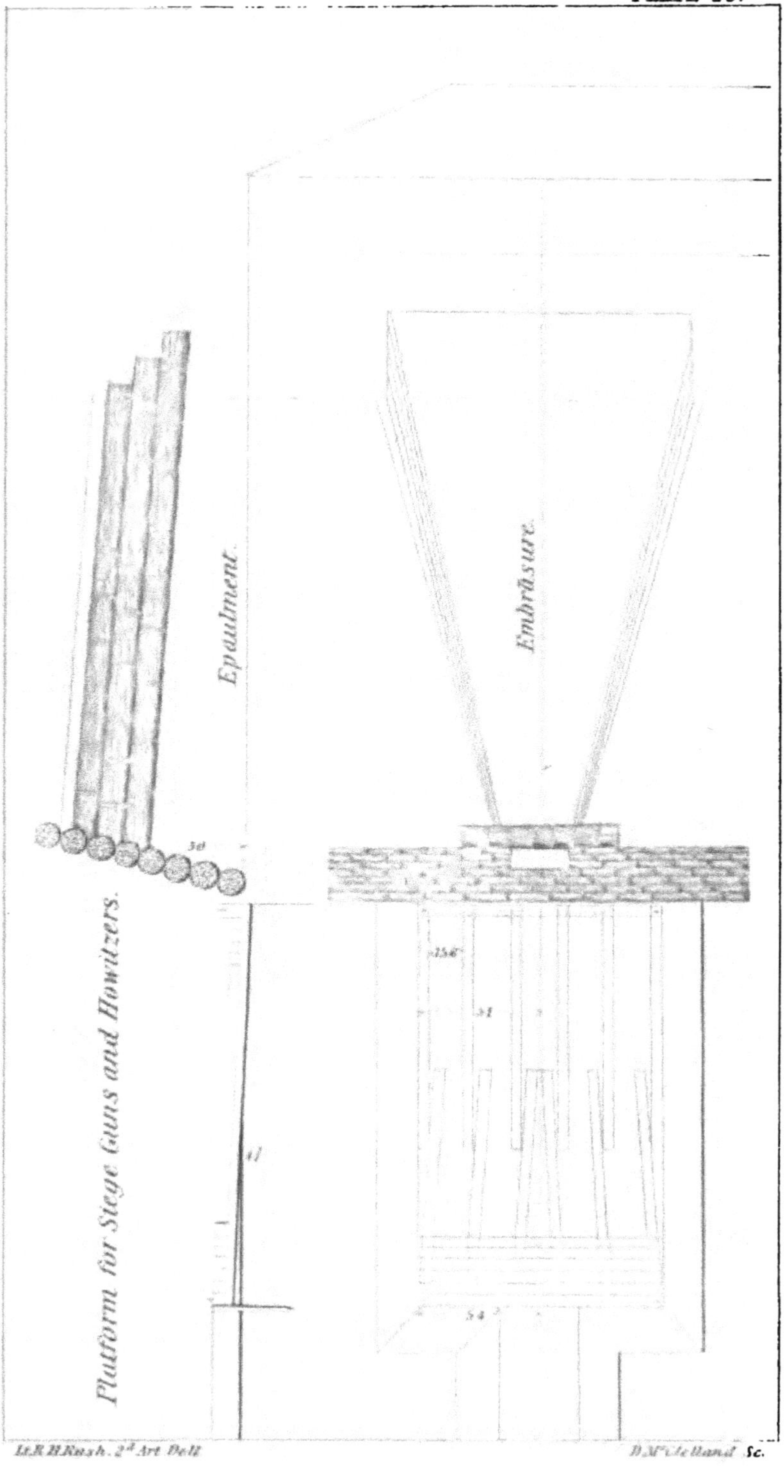

Lt. R. H. Rush. 2d Art. Delt. D. McClelland Sc.

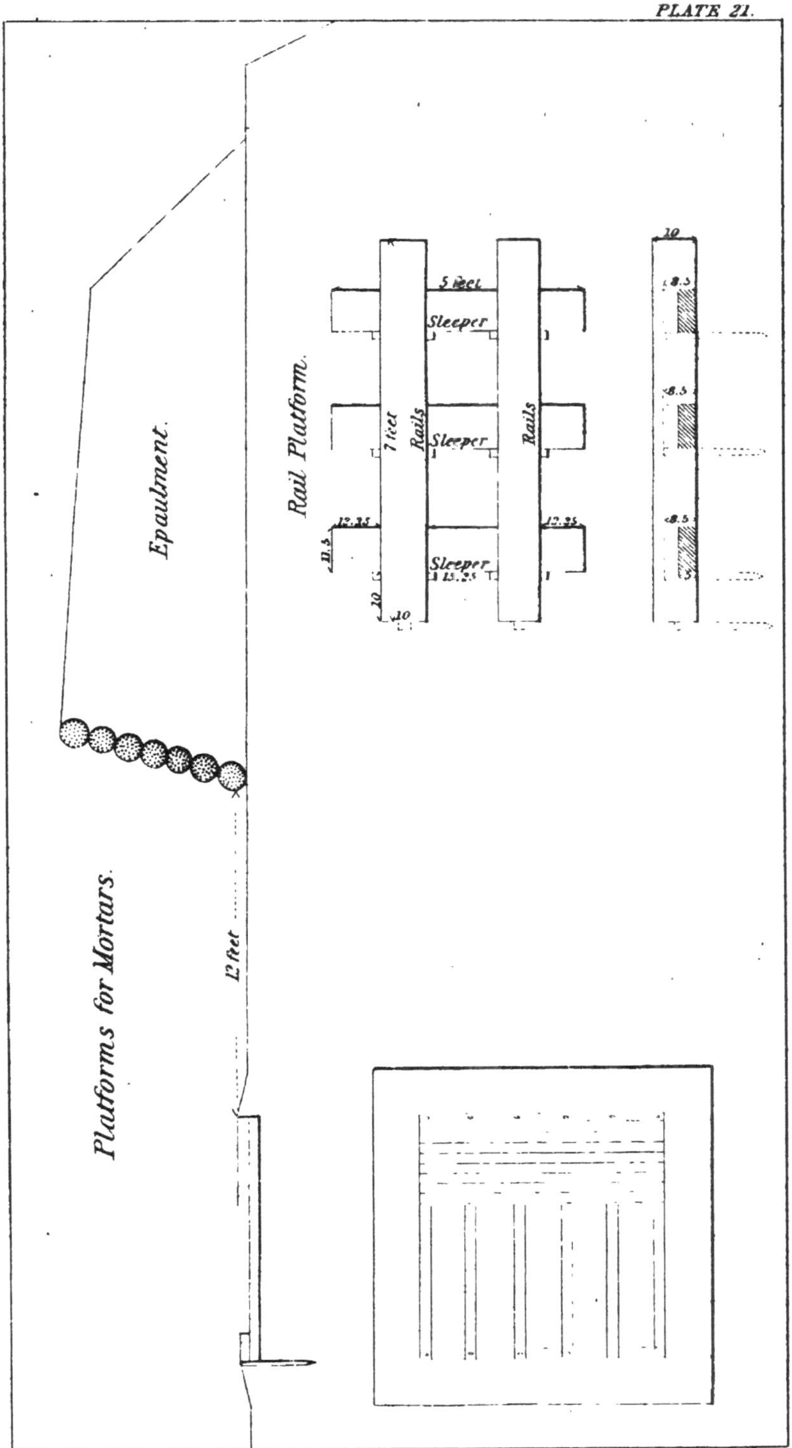

Lt. R H. Rush, 2d Art. Delt.   D. McClelland Sc.

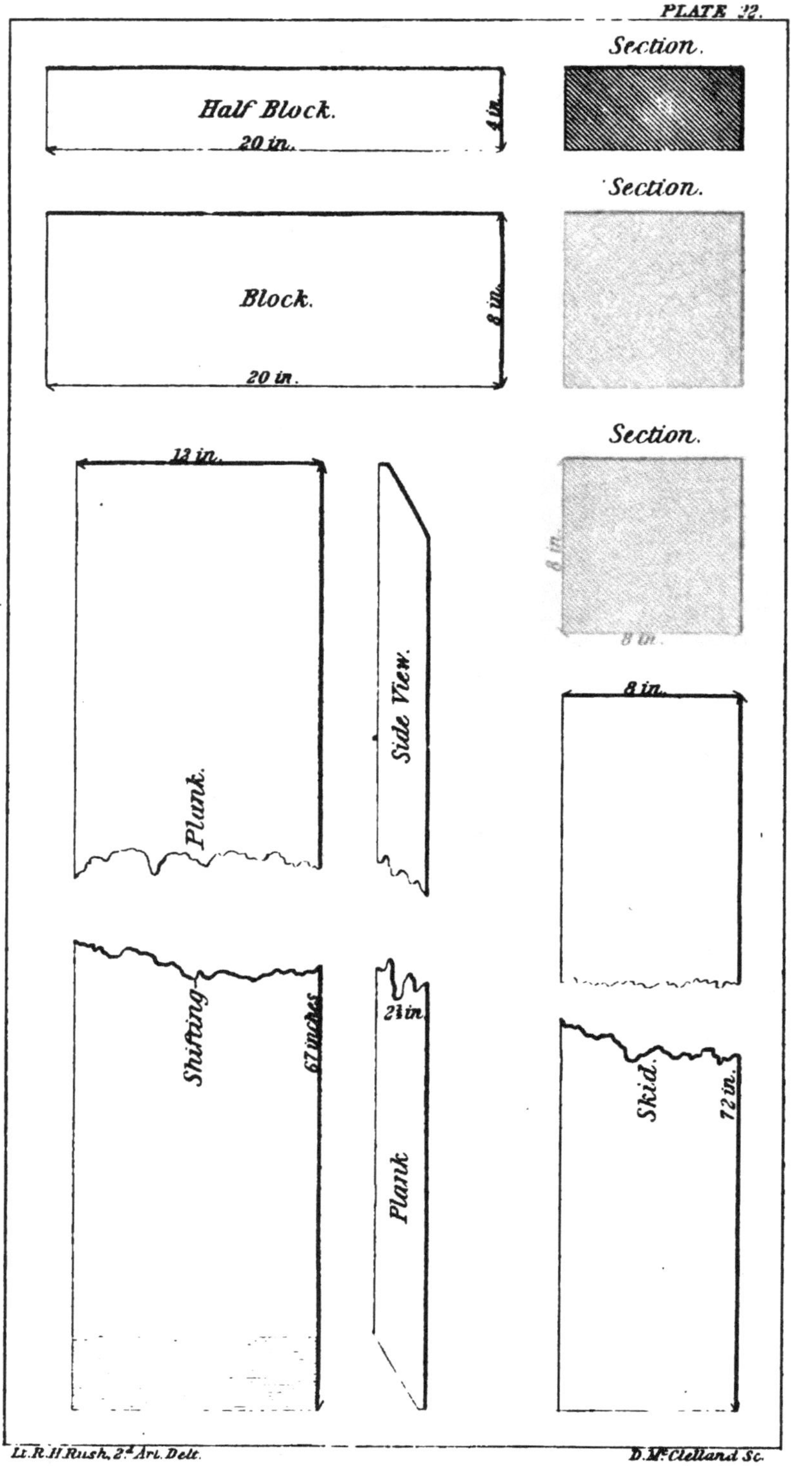

Lt. R. H. Rush, 2d Art. Delt. D. McClelland Sc.

PLATE 23.

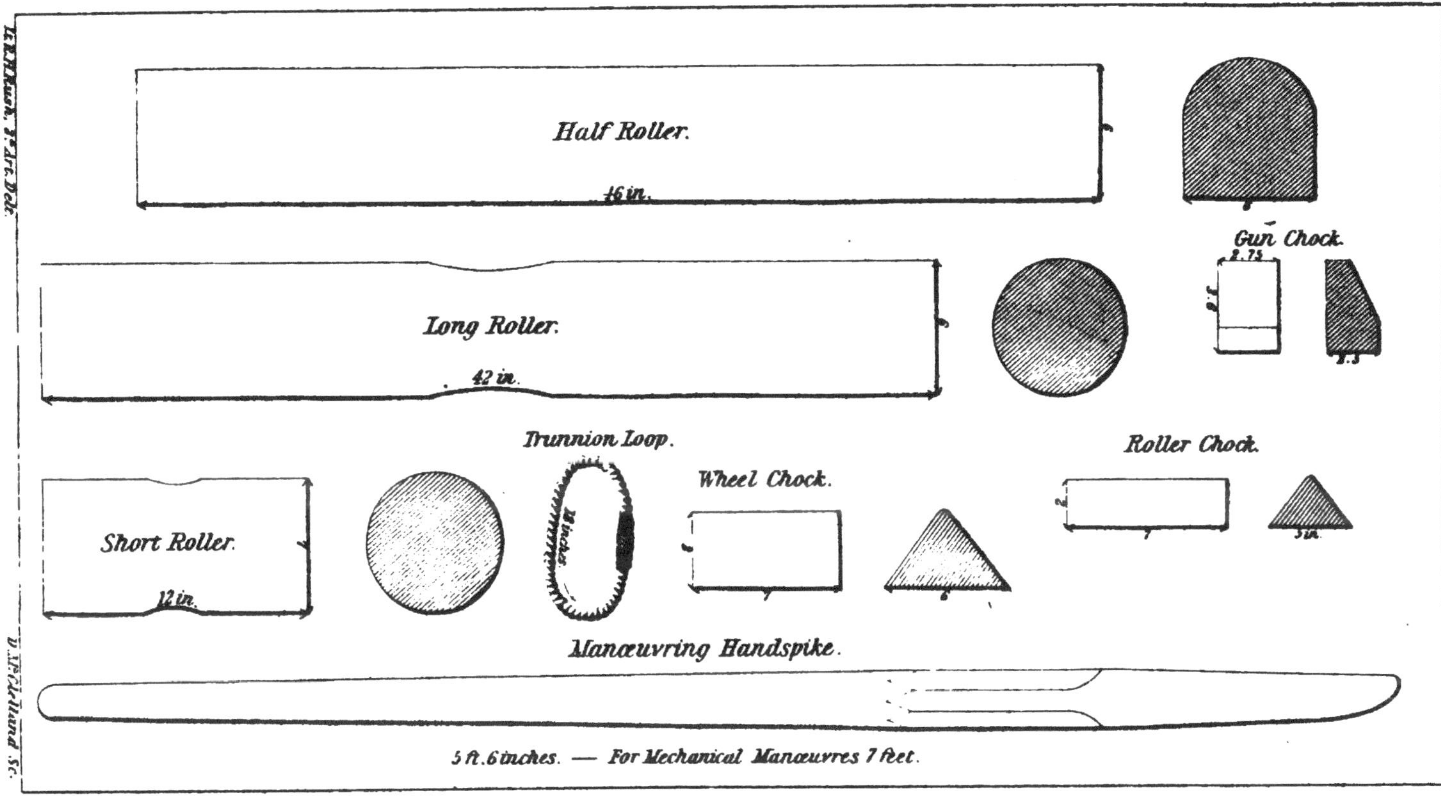

Lt. E. H. Rush, 3d Art. Delt.

D. McClelland Sc.

To shift a piece from the Trunnion holes to its Travelling bed.

Fig. 1.

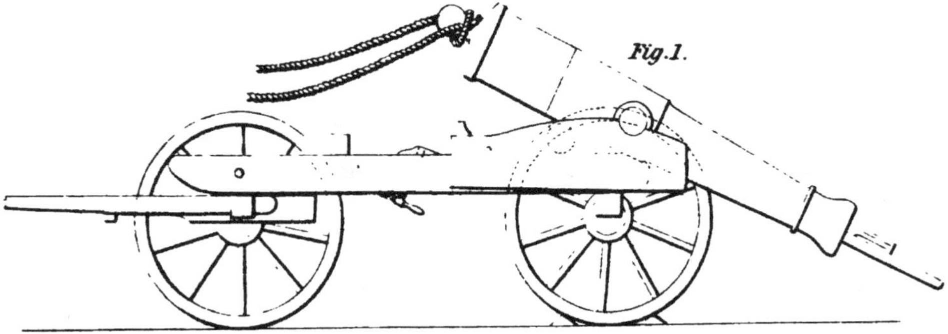

Fig. 2.

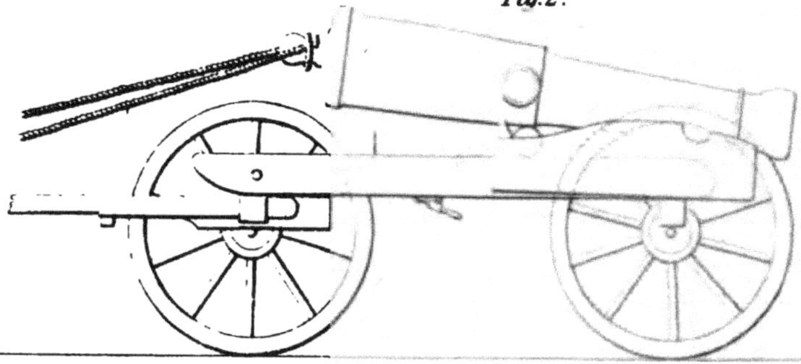

Lt. R. H. Rush, 2d Art. Delt.

D. McClelland Sc.

PLATE 25.

To change a Limber when the piece is on its Travelling bed.

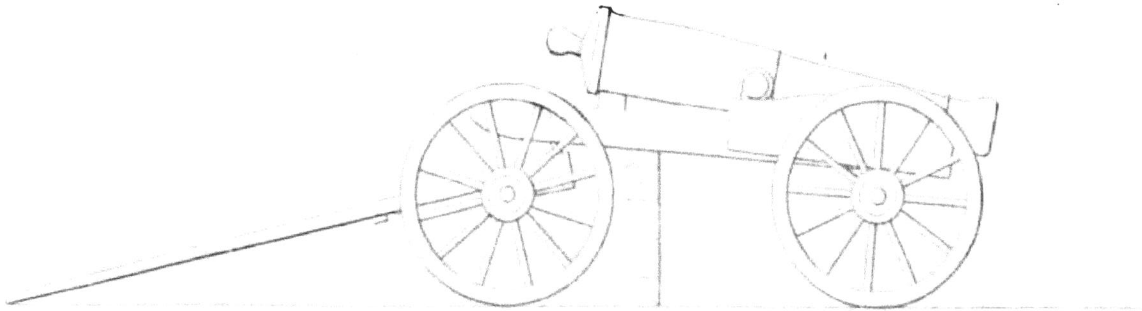

To change a Limber when the piece is on the Mortar Wagon.

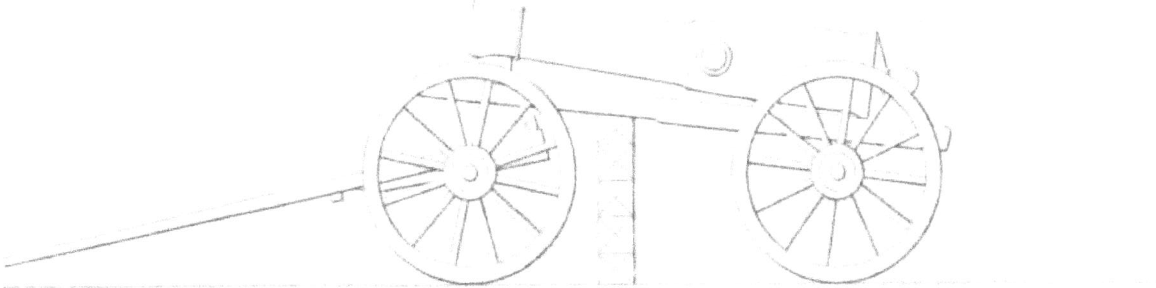

Lt. R. H. Rush. 2d Art. Delt.

P. McClelland Sc.

To mount a Gun upon its Carriage.

Fig. 1.

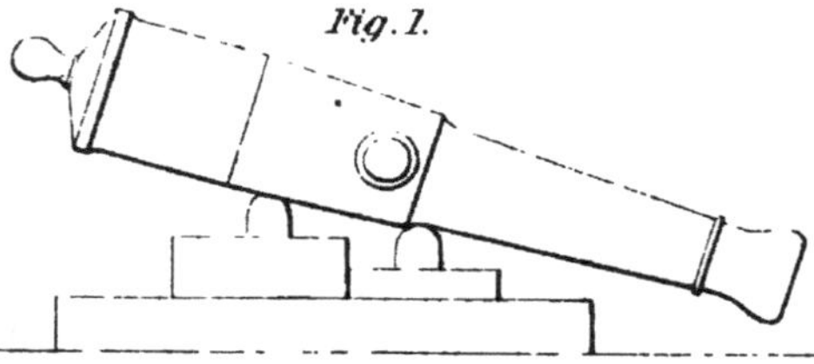

Fig. 2.

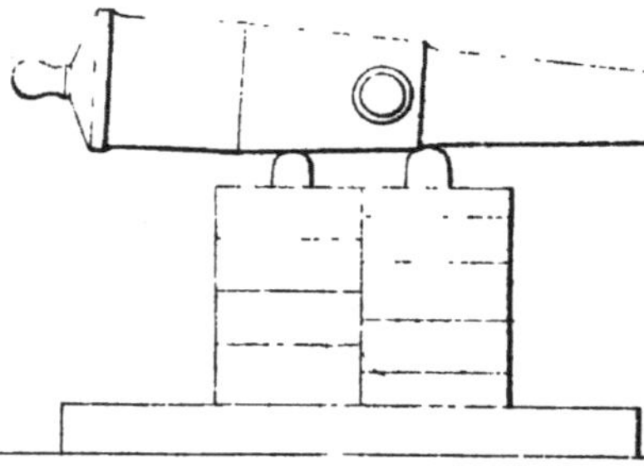

Fig. 3.

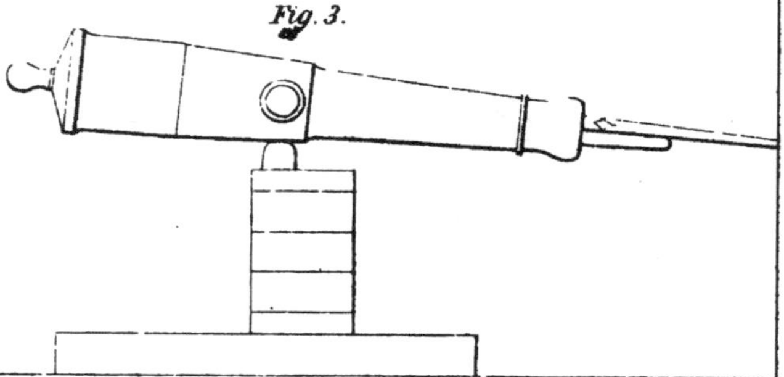

Fig. 4.

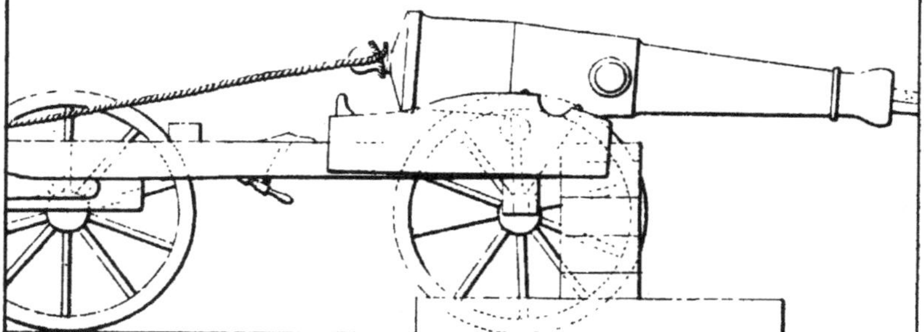

Lt. R. H. Rush, 2d Art. Delt. D. McClelland Sc.

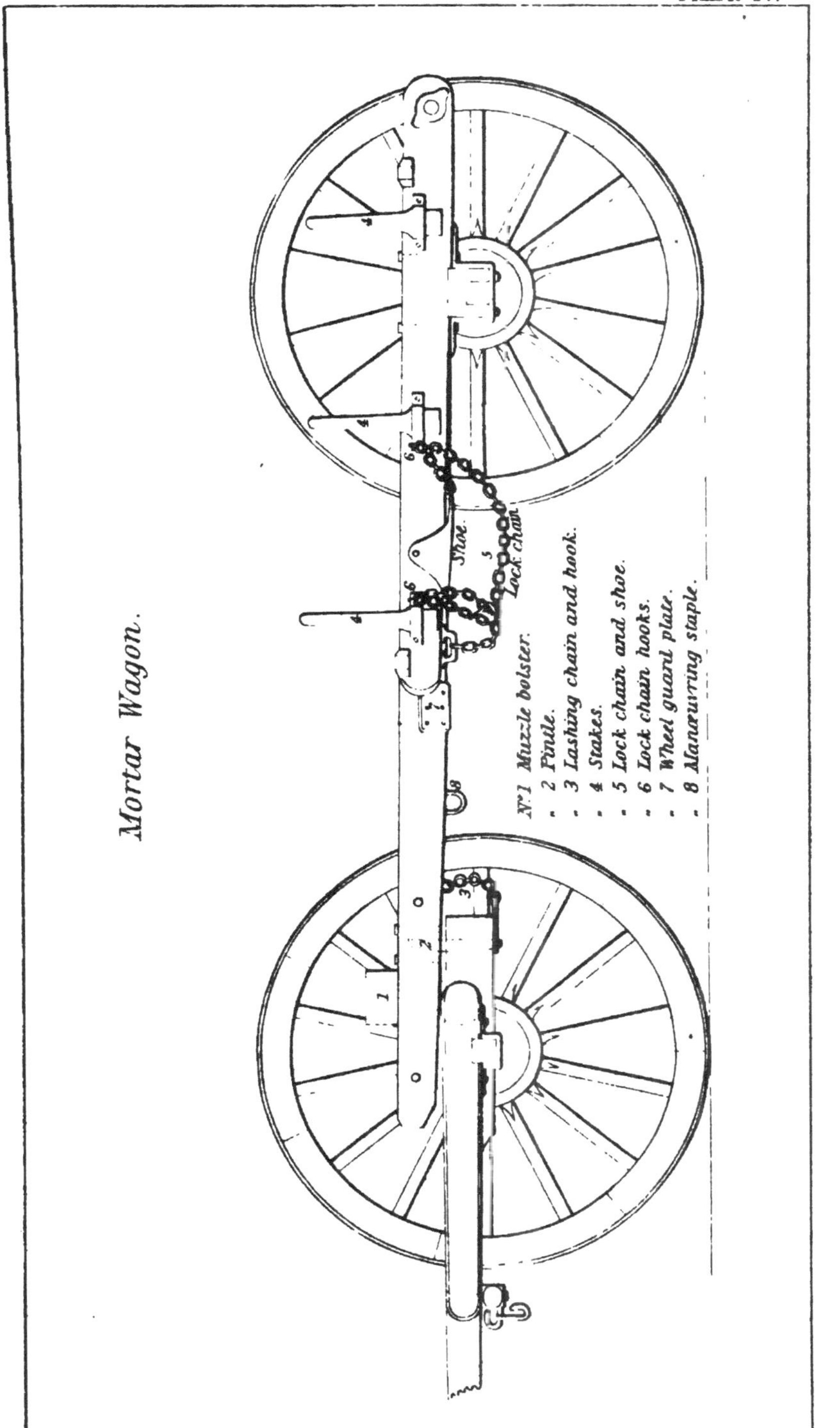

Lt R. H. Rush. 2d Art. Delt. D. McClelland Sc.

Mortar Wagon.

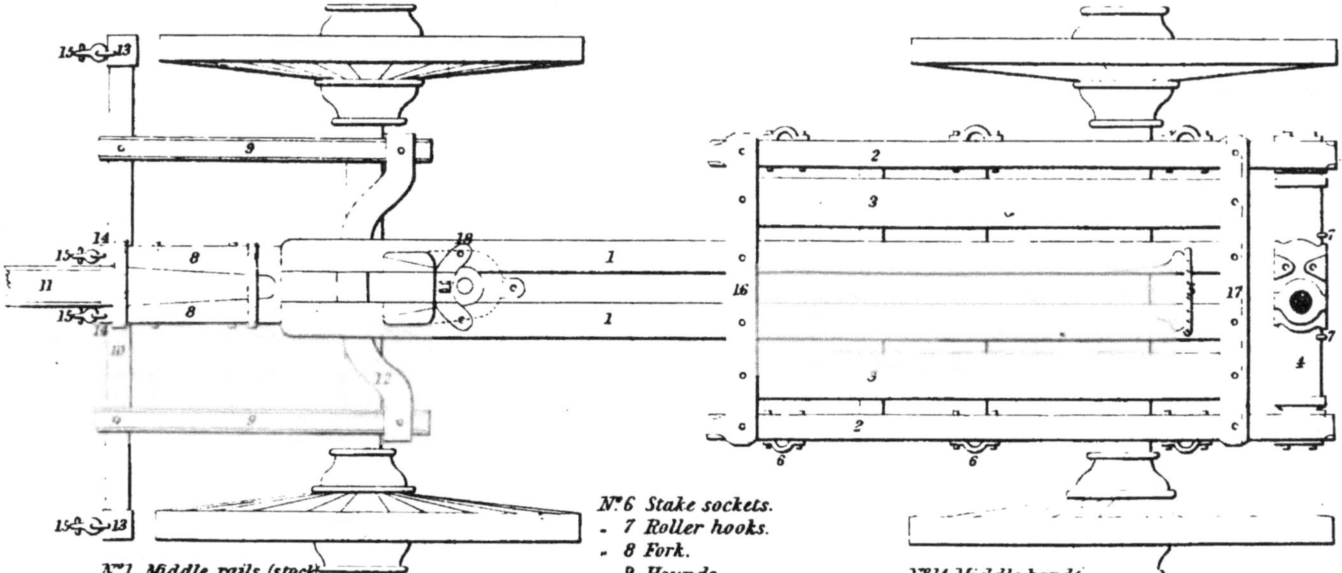

N°. 1 Middle rails (stock)	N°. 6 Stake sockets.	N°. 14 Middle bands.
" 2 Side rails.	" 7 Roller hooks.	" 15 Trace hooks.
" 3 Bottom planks.	" 8 Fork.	" 16 Front cross bar plate.
" 4 Windlass.	" 9 Hounds.	" 17 Rear cross bar plate.
" 5 Breech hurter.	" 10 Splinter bar.	" 18 Pintle bridle and nuts.
	" 11 Pole.	
	" 12 Sweep bar.	
	" 13 End bands.	

Lt. R. H. Rush. 2d. Art. Delt.

D. McClelland Sc.

To mount a Siege Mortar upon the Mortar Wagon.

Fig. 1.

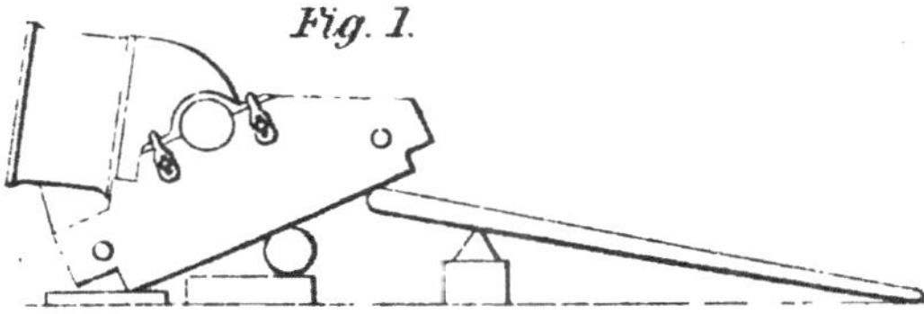

Fig. 2.

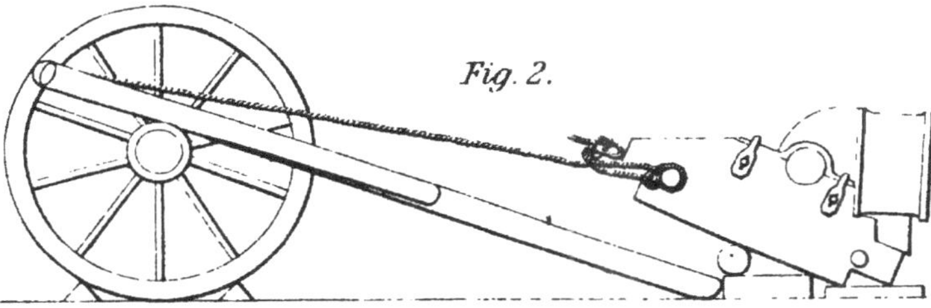

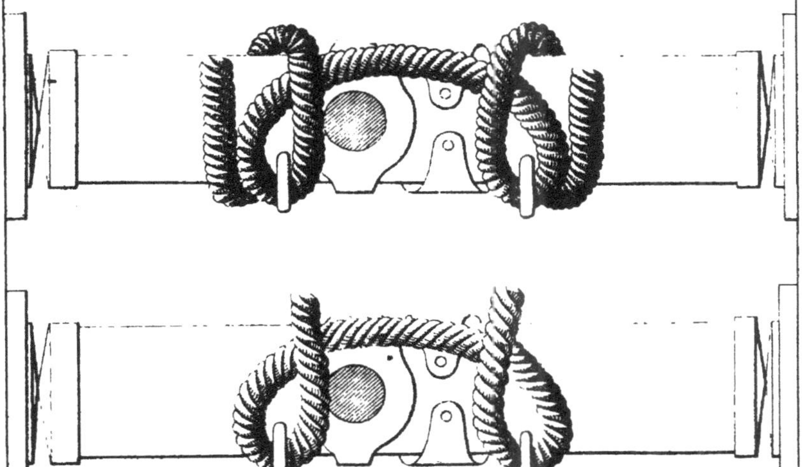

Knot for Manœuvring bolt.

Lt. R. H. Rush. 2d Art. Delt.   D. McClelland Sc.

To mount a Gun on a Mortar Wagon.

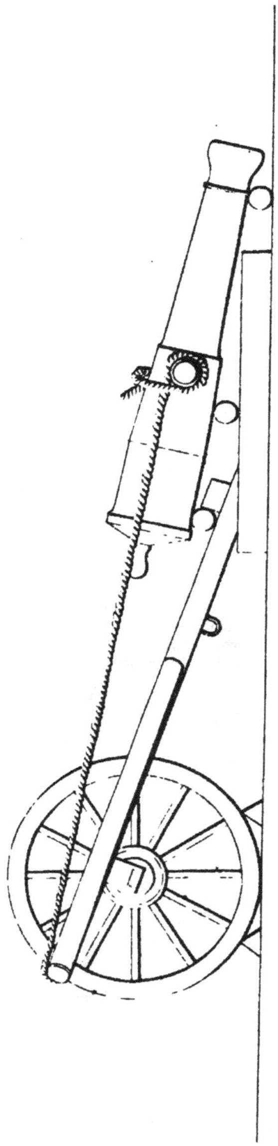

Lt R. H. Rush, 2d Art. Delt.

D. McClelland Sc.

PLATE 31.

To mount a Gun on a Mortar Wagon without using the Windlass.

Fig. 1.

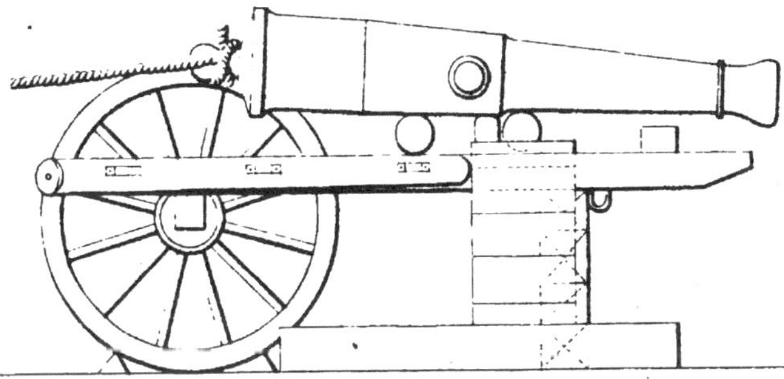

Fig. 2.

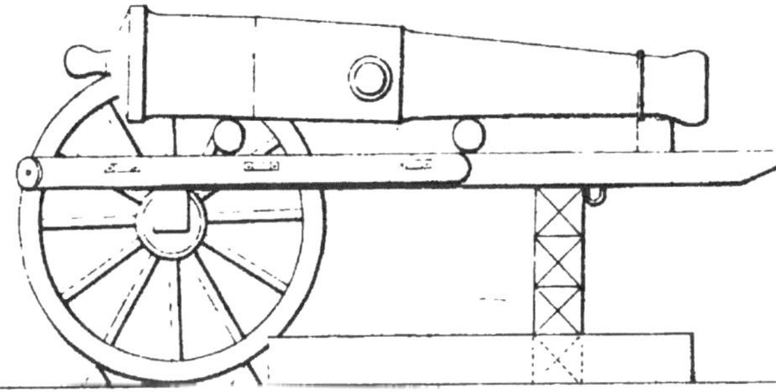

Lt. R. H. Rush. 2d Art. Delt.

D. McClelland Sc.

PLATE 32.

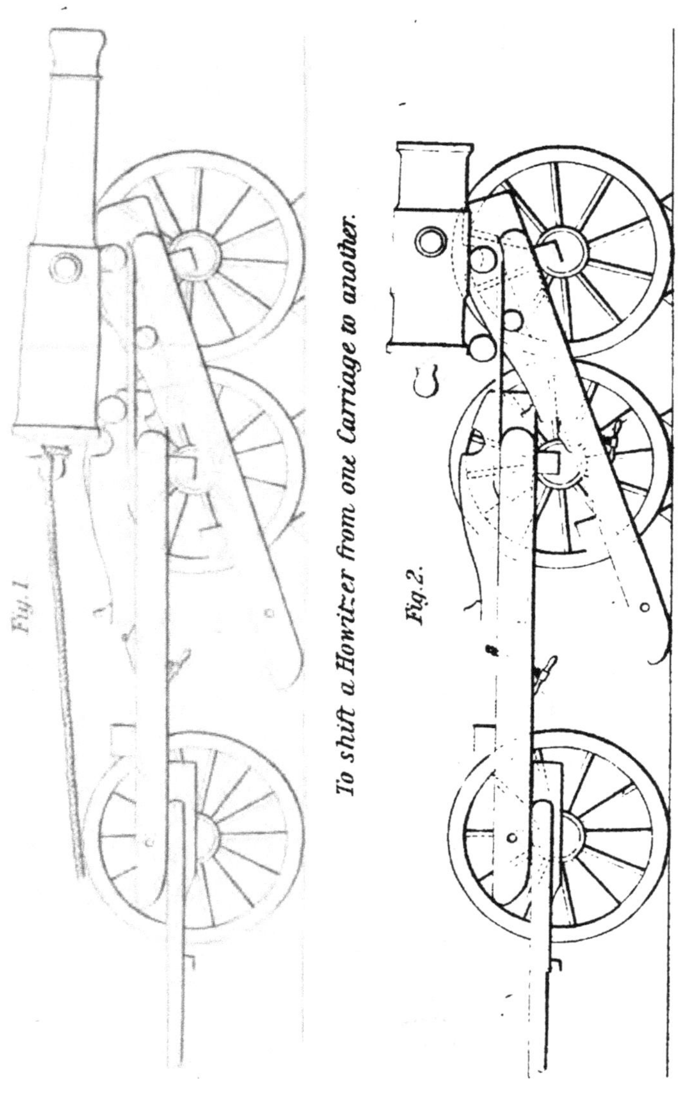

To shift a Gun from one Carriage to another.

Fig. 1

To shift a Howitzer from one Carriage to another.

Fig. 2.

Lt. R. H. Rush. 2d Art. Delt. D. McClelland Sc.

To change a Wheel.

Fig. 1.

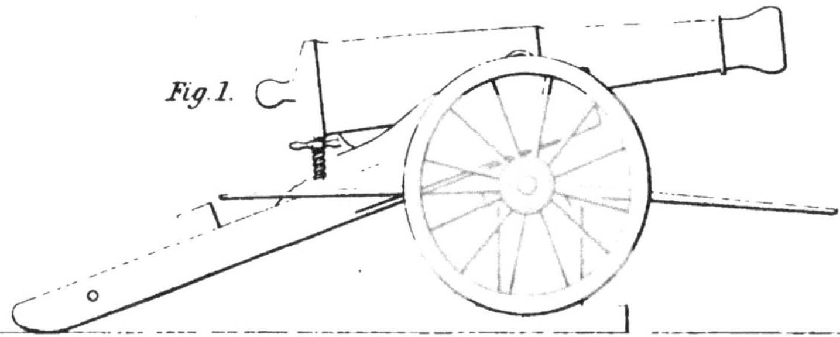

Fig. 2.

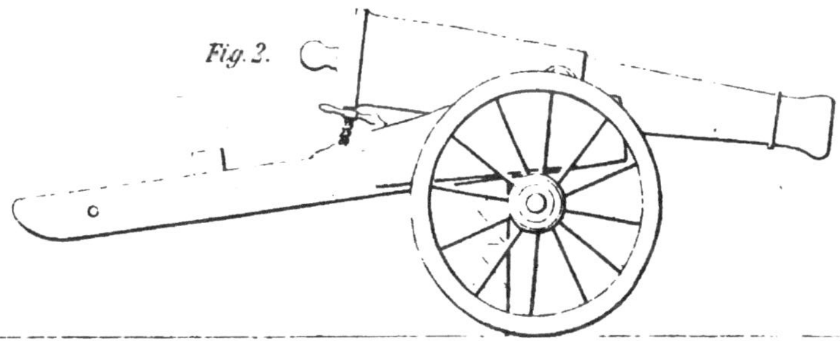

Lt. R.H.Rush. 2d Art. Delt.

D. McClelland Sc.

To lower a Barbette Carriage from its Chassis,
the piece being mounted.

Lt. R. H. Rush, 2d Art. Delt.

D. McClelland Sc.

PLATE 35.

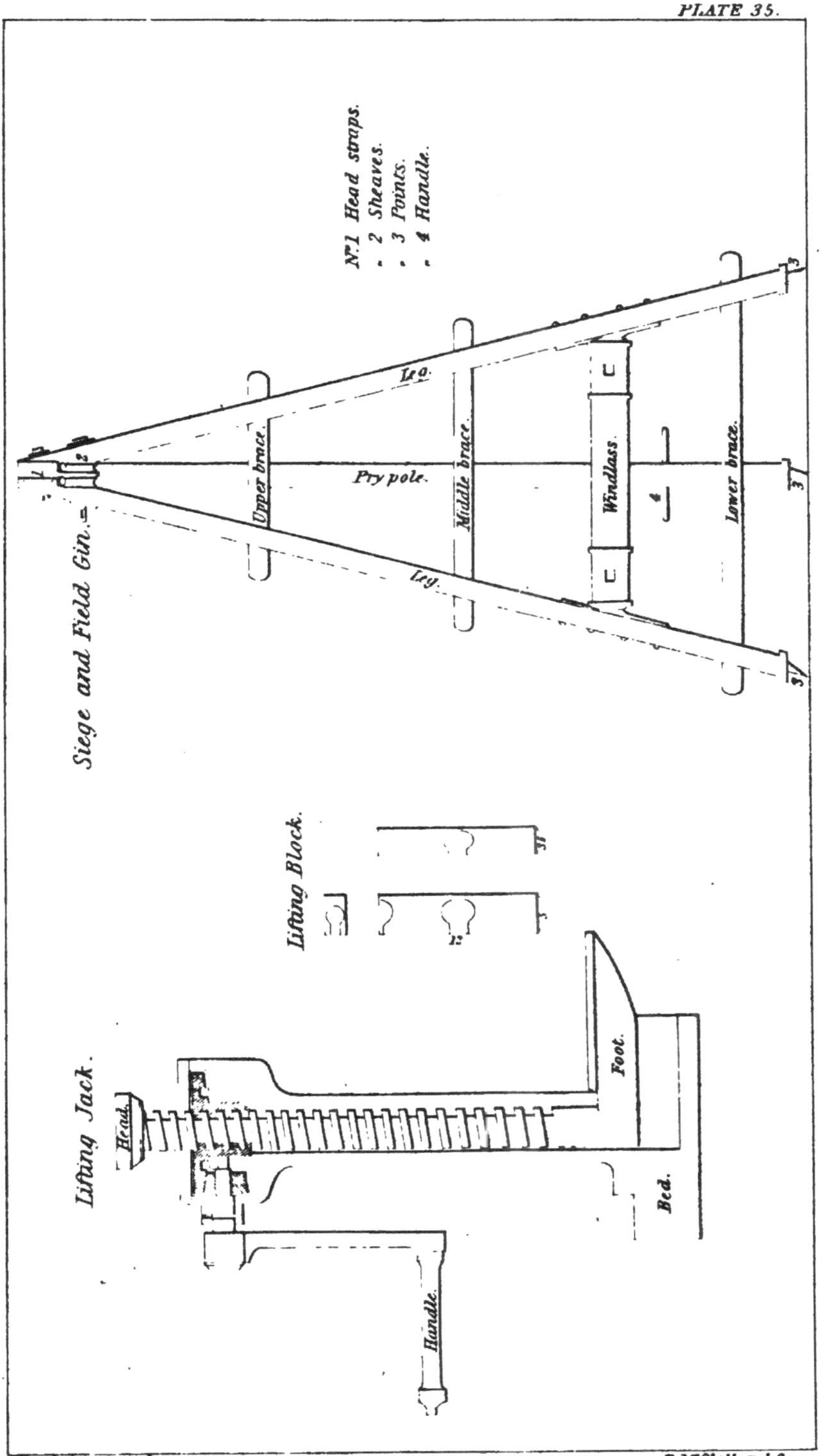

Lt. R. H. Rush. 2d Art. Delt. D. McClelland Sc.

Garrison Gin.

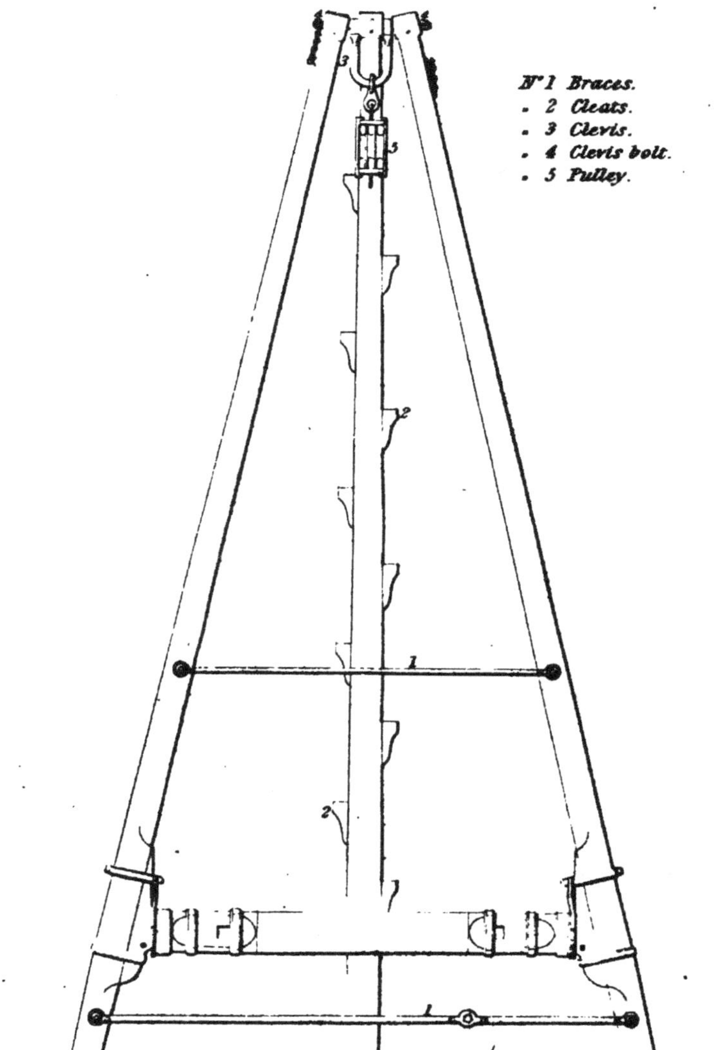

Lt. R. H. Rush. 3d Art. Delt.

D. McClelland Sc.

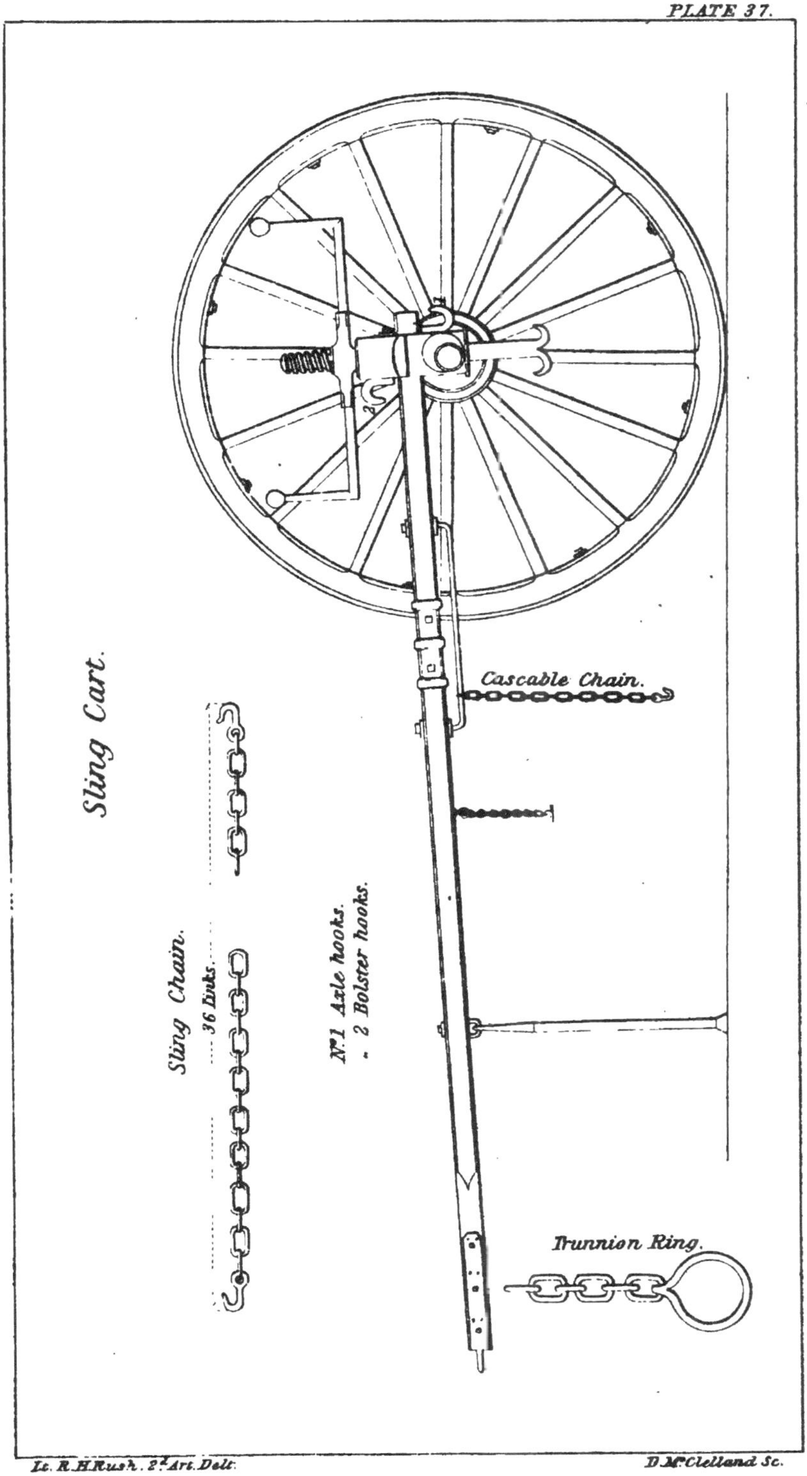

Lt. R. H. Rush. 2d. Art. Delt. D. McClelland Sc.

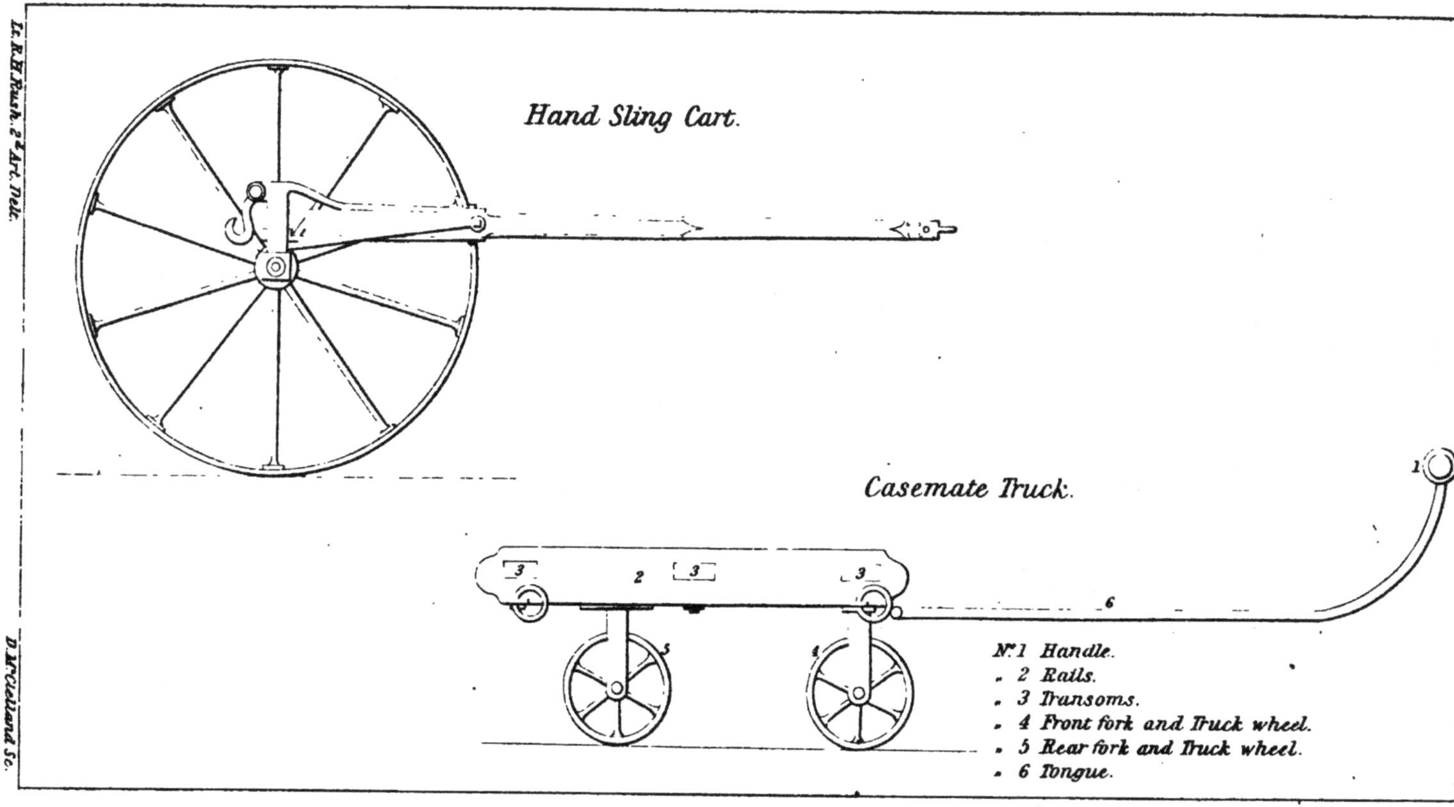

Lt. R.H. Rush. 2d Art. Delt.

D. McClelland Sc.

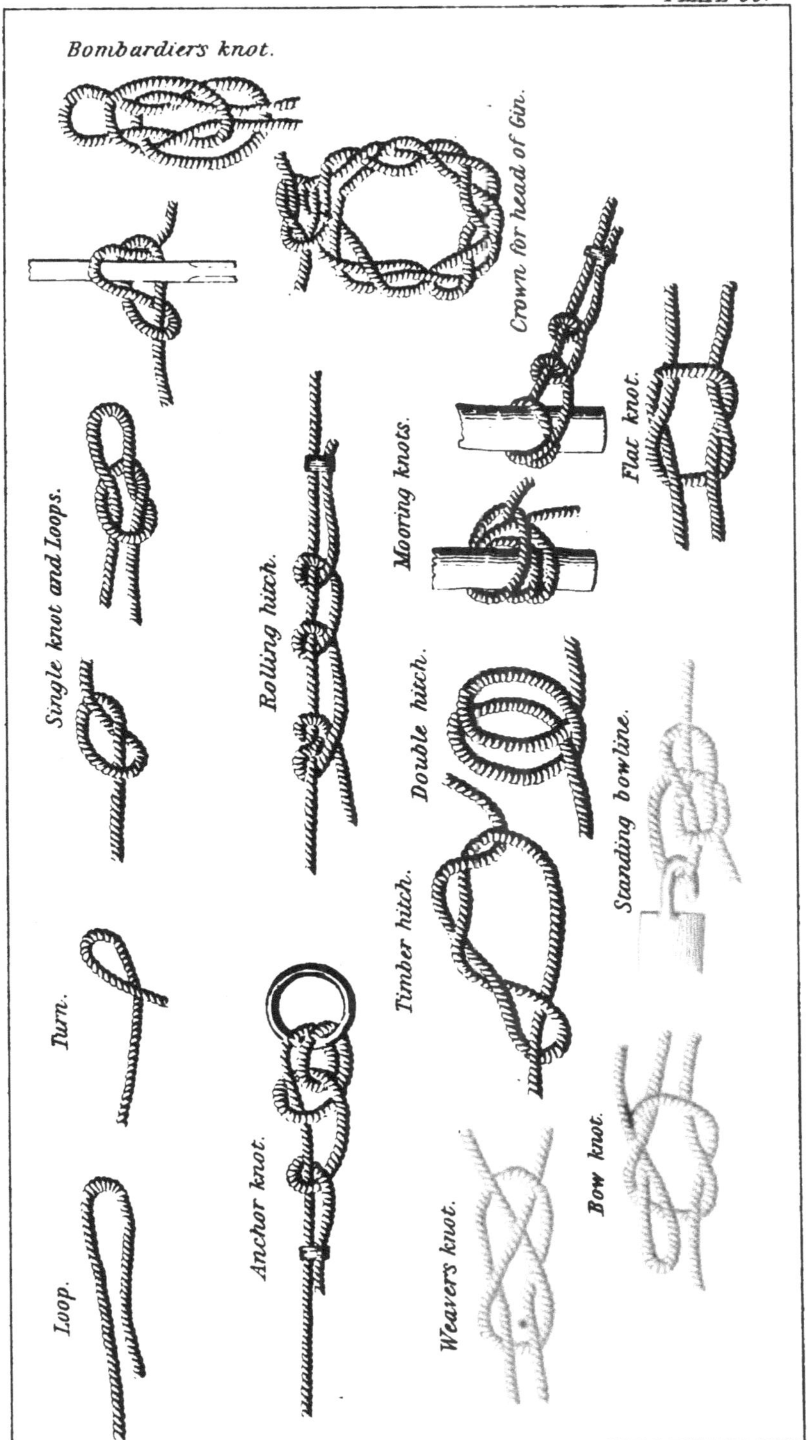

Lt. R. H. Rush. 2d Art. Delt. D. McClelland Sc.

CPSIA information can be obtained
at www.ICGtesting.com
Printed in the USA
LVHW110812120522
718525LV00003B/67

9 783375 000912